By William Bernhardt
Published by the Ballantine Publishing Group:

PRIMARY JUSTICE
BLIND JUSTICE
DEADLY JUSTICE
PERFECT JUSTICE
CRUEL JUSTICE
NAKED JUSTICE
EXTREME JUSTICE
DARK JUSTICE
SILENT JUSTICE
MURDER ONE

DOUBLE JEOPARDY
THE MIDNIGHT BEFORE CHRISTMAS
THE CODE OF BUDDYHOOD
LEGAL BRIEFS

MURDER ONE

William Bernhardt

BALLANTINE BOOKS • NEW YORK

This book contains an excerpt from the forthcoming [hard cover] edition of *Final Round* by William Bernhardt. This excerpt has been set for this edition only and may not reflect the final content of the forthcoming edition.

A Ballantine Book
Published by The Ballantine Publishing Group

Copyright © 2001 by William Bernhardt

www.ballantinebooks.com

Library of Congress Cataloging-in-Publication Data is available upon request.

ISBN 0-345-42815-3

Manufactured in the United States of America

First Mass Market Edition: December 2001

10 9 8 7 6 5 4 3 2 1

For Clint and April

O love, they die in yon rich sky,
They faint on hill or field or river:
Our echoes roll from soul to soul,
And grow for ever and for ever.

—Alfred Lord Tennyson
(from *The Princess*)

Prologue

*   *

Prologue

*   *

"Sergeant Callery, would you please describe the condition of the body when you found it?"

Callery swallowed hard before answering. "Are you sure you want me to?"

This would be the focal point, Ben Kincaid realized, for the entire trial—all that came before and all that followed. Every murder trial had one—an indelible moment in which sympathies were polarized and the full gravity of the crime struck the jury like a ball peen hammer to the head. Even though he knew there was not a soul in the courtroom who did not already know the answer to this question in gruesome and graphic detail, this would be the moment when everything changed, and not for the better.

"I'm sure," Assistant District Attorney Nick Dexter said. He obviously didn't mind the delay. A little suspense preceding the big moment could only increase the jury's attention level. "Please tell us what you saw."

Sergeant Callery licked his lips. His eyes drifted toward the floor. His hesitation was not just for dramatic effect. He was not anxious to proceed.

And Ben didn't blame him. Describing a crime scene was always difficult. But when it was a cop talking about the murder of another cop—one he knew personally and had worked with on many occasions—it bordered on the unbearable.

"When I arrived, I discovered that Sergeant McNaughton's body had been stripped of clothing. He was chained naked to

3

the base of the main fountain in Bartlett Square—right in the center of the downtown plaza. He'd been hog-tied; his arms and legs were pulled back to such an extent that some of his bones were actually broken. He'd been stabbed repeatedly, twenty or thirty times. A word had been smeared across his chest—written in his own blood."

"And what was the word?"

"It was hard to tell at first, given the condition of the body. But when we finally got him down and put him on a stretcher, it looked to me like it said 'faithless.' "

"Was there anything else . . . noteworthy about the body?"

The witness nodded. The spectators in the courtroom gallery collectively held their breath. They knew what was coming.

"His penis had been severed. Cut off—and stuck in his mouth."

To Ben, it was an almost surreal moment, as if they were all actors in a play. After all, everyone knew what questions would be asked, as well as what answers would be given. There were no surprises; they were just going through their prescribed motions. And yet, the singular horror of the crime had an impact that left no one in the courtroom unmoved.

This case had been high drama from the outset. Everyone knew about this ghastly crime. How could they not? The body had been on display for almost an hour before the police managed to get it down. Workers going downtown that cold Thursday morning couldn't help but see the macabre, almost sacrificial tableau.

The location had been well chosen. Downtown Tulsa was a place where people worked, but almost no one went there for any other reason. From the time the workday ended until sunup, it was virtually deserted. Even the police rarely patrolled; the inner downtown streets were inaccessible by car and there was simply no justification for mounted patrols at that time of night, when no one was present. And so the killer was able to create a grisly spectacle that had been etched into the city's collective consciousness during the seven months since the crime occurred.

"Why are they spending so much time describing the body?" a voice beside Ben whispered. "How is that relevant to who committed the crime?"

The question came from the defendant—Ben's client, Keri Dalcanton. She was a petite woman, barely five foot two. She had rich platinum blond hair and skin the color of milk. She was wearing no makeup today—on Ben's advice. She was a natural beauty, with perhaps the most perfectly proportioned body Ben had observed in his entire life. And he'd had a lot of time to observe it, during the months they'd spent preparing for this trial.

Even in the courtroom, Ben was struck by how Keri exuded youth and energy. But that was not surprising. She was only nineteen.

"It isn't relevant," Ben whispered back. "But Dexter knows the gory details will appall most jurors and make them more inclined to convict. That's why we're spending so much time here."

"But it isn't fair," Keri said, her eyes wide and troubled. "I didn't do those things. I couldn't—"

"I know." Ben patted her hand sympathetically. He wanted to take care of his client, but at the moment it was more important that he pay attention to the testimony. If Dexter thought Ben wasn't listening, all kinds of objectionable questions would follow.

Dexter continued. "Did you check the body for vital signs?"

"Of course. When I first arrived. But it wasn't necessary. He was dead. As anyone could see at a glance." A tremor passed through Callery's shoulders. "No one could have lived in that condition."

"Why did it take so long to free the body?"

"We weren't allowed to alter the position of the body until the forensic teams had been out to make a video record and to search for trace evidence. Even after that was done—Sergeant

McNaughton's body had been double-chained to the fountain and the lock was buried. We couldn't get him loose. We eventually had to bring out a team of welders. Even then, progress was slow."

"And during this entire time, the decedent's naked mutilated body was on public display?"

"There wasn't much we could do. We couldn't cover the body and work at the same time. And there's no way to block off Bartlett Square."

"Were you and your men finally able to get the body free?"

"Eventually. Even then, though"—his head fell—"nothing happened the way it should. His right arm had been pulled back to such an extreme degree that when we released the chains—it snapped off. And the second we moved McNaughton's body, his—member—spilled out onto the ground." The man's jaw was tight, even as he spoke. "It would've been horrible, even if I hadn't known Sergeant McNaughton so well and trained under him. I've been on the force six years, but this was the worst, most horrible . . . goddamnedest thing I've seen in my career. Or ever will see."

Ben knew Judge Hart didn't like swearing in her courtroom, but he had a hunch she would excuse it this time.

The media representatives in the gallery—and there were a lot of them—were furiously taking notes. The McNaughton murder had dominated the papers and the airwaves for at least a month after the crime occurred, and the onset of the trial had refueled the obsessive coverage. Ben had never had so many microphones shoved in his face against his will; he'd never seen so many people insist that he had some sort of constitutional duty to give them an interview. His office manager, Jones, had even found a reporter hiding in the office broom closet, just hoping he might overhear some tasty tidbit of information. His legal assistant, Christina McCall, had the office swept for listening devices. A blockade of reporters awaited them every time they left the office; another greeted them as soon as they arrived at the courthouse. It was like living under siege.

Dexter was asking routine predicate questions to get his exhibits admitted. It was an obvious preliminary to passing the witness.

"*Psst*. Planning to cross?"

Ben glanced over his shoulder. It was Christina. For years, she'd been indispensable to him as a legal assistant. And now she was on the verge of graduating from law school.

"I don't see much point," he whispered back to her. "Nothing he said was in dispute."

Christina nodded. "But I'm not sure this business with the body was handled properly. I think the police bungled it six ways to Sunday."

"Granted. But why? Because they were so traumatized by the hideous death of their colleague, a fact we don't particularly want to emphasize. And what difference does it make? None of the evidence found at the crime scene directly incriminates Keri."

"You may be right. But I still think any cross is better than none. Whether he actually says it or not, Dexter is implying that Keri is responsible for these atrocities. We shouldn't take that lying down."

Ben frowned. He didn't want to cross, but he had learned to trust Christina's instincts. "Got any suggestions?"

She considered a moment. "I'd go with physical strength."

"It's a plan."

Dexter had returned to his table. Judge Sarah Hart, a sturdy woman in her midfifties, was addressing defense counsel.

"Mr. Kincaid, do you wish to cross?"

"Of course." Ben rose and strode to the podium. "Sergeant Callery, it sounds as if you and your men had a fair amount of trouble cutting that body free. Right?"

The change in Callery's demeanor and body language when Ben became his inquisitor was unmistakable. He drew back in his chair, receding from the microphone. "It took a while, yeah."

"Sounds to me like it was hard and required a great deal of strength."

"I suppose."

"And if it was hard to get the body down, it must've been even more difficult to get the body up." He paused, letting the wheels turn in the jurors' minds. "The individual who chained Sergeant McNaughton up there must've been one seriously strong person, wouldn't you agree?"

Callery had obviously been expecting this. "Not necessarily, no. The killer could've—"

Ben didn't give him a chance to recite whatever explanation he and Dexter had cooked up ahead of time. "How much did Sergeant McNaughton's body weigh?"

"I couldn't say exactly."

"You must have some idea."

"It would just be a guess."

"You were there, weren't you, officer?"

"Ye-ess . . ."

"You were, I assume, paying some degree of attention when your men were cutting the body loose?"

Callery tucked in his chin. "Yes—"

"So how much did McNaughton's body weigh?"

Callery frowned. "I'd guess about two ten, two twenty pounds."

"Two hundred and twenty pounds. And of course, he was dead, right?"

"I think everyone in the courtroom is aware of that fact, counsel."

Just like a game of cat and mouse, Ben marveled, not for the first time. Two diametrically opposed archenemies pretending to be civil. "Would it be fair to say that it's harder to move a dead body than a live one?"

Callery nodded. "Much."

"So we're talking about two hundred and twenty pounds of pure deadweight, right?"

"About that, yeah."

"But someone somehow managed to carry the body to Bartlett Square—without the use of a car—to elevate it, hog-tie it, and wrap it around the central fountain."

"That's about the size of it."

"Sergeant Callery, you were pretty good at estimating your deceased colleague's weight. Would you care to guess what my client, Ms. Dalcanton, weighs?"

He grinned faintly. "I would never be so indelicate."

"Then I'll tell you. A hundred and three pounds. Wearing shoes." He paused. "So you're saying that these feats of tremendous strength, which frankly I doubt you and I could manage working together, were accomplished by this tiny woman? How?"

A bad question, as it turned out. "We believe she drove the body there. We found faint traces of tire tracks on Fifth, parallel to the fountain. Someone drove onto the pedestrian walkway beside Bartlett Square. We believe she wrapped the chains around the body's hands and feet while it was still in the car, then dragged him to the fountain. As the coroner can confirm, the body had any number of scrapes and abrasions that could be the result of being dragged over the pavement in this manner. Once she had the chain around the fountain, we believe she was able to improvise a rudimentary pulley system to haul the body up."

Ben silently cursed himself. This was a classic case of asking one question too many. "It still sounds to me as if it would require a good deal of strength."

"Maybe. But if I've learned anything in my years on the force, it's that size is no indicator of strength. Sometimes the most potent medicine comes in small bottles."

"That's quaint, officer, but are you seriously suggesting—"

"Besides," Callery said, rushing his words in edgewise, "whoever said Keri Dalcanton wasn't strong?" A small smile played on his lips. "I hear she gets lots of exercise. All that high-octane dancing must build up some stamina."

There was an audible response from the gallery. Callery was referring to the fact that Ben's client worked—at least until she became a permanent resident of the Tulsa County Jail seven months ago—at a "gentleman's club" at Thirty-first and Lewis. In other words, she was a stripper. Another dramatic—and damning—fact that everyone in the courtroom already knew *all* too well. The press wouldn't let them forget. No article overlooked the salacious side of the story. The headlines began STRIPPER SUSPECTED and continued with SEX CLUB SIREN SEIZED.

"Sergeant Callery, it took three men to lower McNaughton's body to the ground. Are you seriously suggesting—"

"Hey, I saw that picture in the paper. You know, the one with her in nothing but a bright red G-string thingie? Looked to me like she had lots of muscles."

"Your honor, I object!" Ben knew what Callery was talking about, though. The day Keri Dalcanton was arrested, a morning paper, in an unaccountable lapse of taste, had run a picture of her taken on the job. Something a reporter swiped from a backstage bulletin board, apparently. Tasseled pasties on her ample breasts; bright red G-string on her rock-'n'-roll hips. The paper apologized the next day, explaining that it was the only photo of Ms. Dalcanton they could locate, as she had covered her face when arrested. One of the lamest excuses for tabloid coverage by purportedly "legitimate" journalists Ben had heard yet.

Ben approached the bench. "Your honor, I object to any discussion or sly references to my client's former occupation."

Judge Hart lowered her eyeglasses and gave Ben the no-nonsense look he knew all too well. "On what grounds?"

"It will work extreme prejudice against Ms. Dalcanton."

"Probably. But she should have thought of that before she took the job. Overruled."

"But your honor—"

"I've ruled, Mr. Kincaid."

"Then I'll object on a different basis."

She arched an eyebrow. "And that would be . . . ?"

"I object because . . . because the photo in question has not been admitted into evidence."

"Do you want it to be?"

"Hmm. Good point."

Ben returned to the defense table knowing that his cross had been a bust. He hadn't put a dent in the prosecution's case, and given what few arrows he had in his quiver, he was unlikely to do so at any time in the future. He could see the determination in the eyes of the prosecution and police officers, and he could see the revulsion in the eyes of the jury. Even Judge Hart, normally a sympathetic, fair judge, was cutting him no slack. This time, the stakes were too high. The crime was too appalling, and too well known.

He had to face facts. Barring some kind of miracle, Keri Dalcanton was going to be convicted.

The media mob was no less aggressive when Ben and Christina returned after the lunch break. Even though Keri was not with them, the press pushed, shoved, and thrust themselves into Ben's path, trying to bait him into delivering a tasty sound bite for the evening news.

"Assistant D.A. Dexter says the prosecution has a slam-dunk case. Care to comment?"

Ben refused to play. "Sorry, I won't talk about an ongoing trial. The judge doesn't like it—and neither do I."

After that, the questions flew past in an unrestrained flurry.

"How can you possibly refute the mountain of evidence the prosecution has against your client?"

"Is it true Keri Dalcanton's diaphragm was found in the victim's mouth?"

"Can you confirm the rumor that McNaughton's widow has hired a hitman to take out your client?"

A woman Ben recognized as one of the evening newscasters grabbed his arm. "Are you aware that polls show over eighty percent of all Tulsa citizens believe your client is guilty? How can you continue to defend her under these circumstances?"

Ben stopped. This was one he couldn't let pass. "You know," he said, trying not to look into the minicams, "there's a reason why our founding fathers instituted the jury system. It's so the accused could be tried based on evidence, rather than based on public opinion. Because public opinion can be so easily manipulated—especially by people like you." He gazed out into the throng. "But you can't respect the way the system is supposed to work. You want to convict people before the trial has started. You want to hang them based on rumors and polls and the suspicions of a populace that gets its information from your slanted ratings-hungry broadcasts. Everything you do disrupts what should be a simple process and makes it more complicated. Can't you see what a gigantic disservice you're doing?"

Ben's lecture did not appear to have much impact. "What can you tell us about your client's alleged sexual perversities?" someone shouted. "Is it true the chains were a regular part of their satanic lovemaking rituals?"

Ben shook his head. It was hopeless.

"When you look in the mirror, do you see a monster staring back at you?"

Ben stopped again. This was a question he hadn't heard before. "Only when I've been up all night watching *Xena* reruns."

"How amusing. I guess this is all one big joke to you. A fun way to bring home a big bucket of cash. You sicken me."

Ben turned toward the raven-haired woman positioned before the courtroom doors. She was in her midforties, although she looked younger. She was tall and still quite attractive, her beauty marred somewhat at present by her red puffy face. She had been crying—judging by appearances, for days.

Ben knew who she was, although he wished he didn't. She was Andrea McNaughton. The victim's wife. Widow, now.

"Mrs. McNaughton," Ben started, "I know this must be hard for you—"

"Don't patronize me." She raised her hand and slapped him hard across the face. "I don't have to take that from you."

Ben pressed his hand against his stinging cheek. Behind her, he saw the news cameramen jockeying for position. It seemed they were going to get something special for the six o'clock news after all. "Mrs. McNaughton, I understand your feelings. But please try to understand that I have a duty—a duty to provide a zealous defense for my client."

"Don't try to justify your poisonous existence to me!"

Ben sighed. "Mrs. McNaughton, perhaps it would be best if you didn't attend the trial—"

"Oh, you'd like that, wouldn't you? You'd like me to give your conscience a break. Well, I'm not going to do it, do you hear me? I won't let up for a moment. I'll be in that courtroom every day. Every time you try to humiliate a witness, I'll be looking over your shoulder. Every time you pull one of your flashy courtroom tricks, I'll be watching. I'll be in your dreams—and your nightmares. I'll never let you rest."

And a good day to you, too, Ben thought. He stepped around her and walked quietly into the courtroom.

It got easier with time, in a way. And in a way, not. Certainly he was used to the media's efforts to encapsulate the truth in tidy melodramatic snippets, their inclination to focus on the most exploitative details. Certainly he was used to the popular denigration of defense lawyers and the all-too-easy right-wing refusal to acknowledge the importance of their work. And certainly he was used to the tumult and outrage of those close to the deceased, who inevitably assuage their grief, and possibly their guilt, by latching their hatred onto whoever the police first suspect.

It did get easier to handle. But it didn't make him like it.

The prosecution's first witness that afternoon was Detective Sergeant Arlen Matthews, the Tulsa P.D. detective who led the team that conducted the initial search of Keri Dalcanton's apartment.

"After I got the warrant from Judge Bolen," Matthews

explained, "I took two uniformed officers and drove to Ms. Dalcanton's apartment just off Seventy-first Street."

"Was the suspect at home?" Assistant D.A. Dexter asked.

"Yes, she was."

"Did she admit you into her apartment?"

"She didn't want to. But I had a warrant. She didn't have any choice."

"So what did you do, once you were inside the apartment?"

"We split up." Matthews was a short, compact man with a direct, no-frills demeanor. His hair was close-cropped and he had a square, slightly protruding jaw. "It was a small apartment—just a central living area, a kitchenette, and a bedroom. We each took a room."

"What was Ms. Dalcanton doing while you and your men conducted the search?"

Matthews drew in his breath. "Throwing a hissy fit, if you know what I mean."

Ben made a note on his legal pad. *Hissy fit*—was that a Tulsa P.D. term of art?

"She was screaming, calling us names, getting in the way. She scratched one of my men with her fingernails."

"That was an accident," Keri muttered under her breath.

"She was wild-eyed and red-faced—she'd lost it," Matthews continued. "She was crazy-actin'. I thought she must have some kind of mental problem—either that or she was very worried about what we might find."

Ben jumped to his feet. "Objection."

Judge Hart nodded. "Sustained. The witness will restrict his testimony to what he saw and heard—without speculating."

"She was like a banshee," Matthews continued, utterly unrepentant. "She jumped on me, piggyback style, trying to pull me back. She pounded me with her fists, on my chest, and the sides of my head. If that isn't crazy, I don't know what is."

"It wasn't like that," Keri murmured quietly. "They were tearing my home apart. Breaking everything in sight. They knew about me and Joe and they hated me. They were intentionally trying to humiliate me."

Ben nodded. He understood her side of the story. But he also understood the impact this testimony was having on the jurors—every one of whom was currently staring at Keri.

"Were you able to proceed with your search?" Dexter asked, continuing the examination.

"With some difficulty, yeah. At one point, she threw herself in front of me, trying to stop me from looking under her bed."

"Were you able to look under the bed?"

"Oh yeah. That's where we found the proof."

"The proof?" Dexter took a step closer to the witness stand. "What was that?"

"The suit. This black leather bondage getup. Dog collar and everything. Soaked in blood. We believe it's what the victim was wearing when he was killed."

"And this was found under Ms. Dalcanton's bed?"

"You got it."

"Did you find anything else noteworthy in the apartment?"

"Yeah. We found chains that matched those used to strap the victim to the fountain in Bartlett Square."

"Anything else?"

"Yes. We found Joe McNaughton's badge and wallet, also under her bed."

"I see." Dexter turned toward the jury. Ben knew this was going to be one of those improper—and unstoppable—summations in the form of a question. "So you found blood-stained clothes, the victim's wallet, his badge, and matching chains—all in Ms. Dalcanton's possession."

"We did, yes."

"Did Ms. Dalcanton have any explanation for these discoveries?"

"Eventually. At first, she claimed she didn't know anything, didn't know who Joe McNaughton was, he'd never been to her place. So forth. But after we showed her everything we'd found, she began to crack. Started to confess. We read her rights, and she waived counsel. In writing. She started crying, wailing. Kind of fell apart at the seams. Then we began to hear some truth."

"Objection," Ben said again.

Judge Hart nodded. "Again I will remind the witness that he is to give an account of what he saw and heard, without attempting to characterize it."

"Sure," Matthews grunted.

"The jury is instructed to disregard the witness's last remark." Hart peered sternly toward the witness box. "I do not want to have to give you this reminder again, Detective."

"Got it."

Dexter resumed his questioning. "How long did you interrogate Ms. Dalcanton?"

"At that time? About an hour."

"Did you make a record of the conversation?"

"Yeah, we taped it. And I took notes."

"Do you have those notes here with you today?"

"I do."

"Feel free to consult them as necessary to refresh your recollection."

"Sure." Matthews reached into his back pocket and pulled out a small notepad. "Thanks."

"Please tell the jury what Ms. Dalcanton told you on this occasion."

He nodded. "Like I said, after we showed her everything we had, she changed her story. Admitted that she'd been having an affair with Joe McNaughton. Apparently she met him at this strip joint on Thirty-first where she works. He'd gone in with some of the boys after work one night and . . . one thing led to another. He was married, of course, but as you can see, Ms. Dalcanton is a seriously attractive kid, and being a stripper, she knew how to do things that . . . well, I don't think she left Joe much of a chance."

This time, Judge Hart didn't wait for an objection. "Is that what she said, Sergeant?"

Matthews peered up. "Not in so many words, but I—"

"Seen and heard, Sergeant. That's all we want to hear about. What you've seen and heard."

"Yeah, okay."

Judge Hart raised her gavel and pointed. "I mean it. One more slip and I will excuse you from the courtroom."

"All right. I'll be careful. Uh, sorry, ma'am."

Ben was less than overwhelmed by Matthews's display of repentance. But before he could blink twice, the prosecution had marched ahead.

"Did Ms. Dalcanton have any explanation for the presence of the victim's badge and wallet?"

"Not really. She said that after they first met, he started coming over to her apartment a lot. To hear her tell it, she became like some kind of sex addict. She just couldn't get enough of him, and of course, he didn't mind too much. Toward the end, he was coming over two, sometimes three times a day."

"And would they have sexual intercourse during these visits?"

"Oh yeah. That was pretty much all they'd do. Lots and lots of sex."

"Did she provide any explanation for the chains and the blood-soaked garments?"

"Sort of. Said they used that stuff in their . . . um, sexual activities."

"Excuse me?"

"They liked kinky sex. Kinky and rough."

The buzz in the gallery was discernible—part dismay, part tittering.

Dexter frowned. "Very rough indeed. Judging from the quantity of blood on the leather suit. Did she provide any details regarding their . . . activities?"

"Your honor!" Ben said, jumping to his feet. "Relevance?"

Judge Hart nodded. "I think we've all got the general idea, Mr. Dexter. Let's move on."

"As you wish." He glanced down at his notes. "I suppose

she claimed he left the badge and wallet during one of their trysts?"

"She did. But there's a problem with that."

"Oh?" Dexter said, cocking an eyebrow. Ben loved the way he could appear surprised during testimony that had no doubt been rehearsed repeatedly. "What's the problem?"

"She claimed he wasn't at her apartment that night—the night of the murder. But several officers—including me— saw Joe at work earlier that day. And he had his badge. He couldn't have lost it until that night after he left work. And just before he was killed."

Dexter nodded thoughtfully. "Had there been any . . . alteration in the relationship? Prior to Sergeant McNaughton's death?"

"Yeah. Joe McNaughton broke up with her just before he was killed."

Ben knew this would be the time when the prosecution would try to establish motive. The next few minutes were not likely to be pleasant ones for the defense. Especially since the prosecution's ultimate source was Keri's own admissions.

"What happened?"

"According to the defendant, Joe's wife got wind of what was going on and she read him the riot act. Told him in no uncertain terms she would divorce him and clean him out if he didn't break it off."

"Despite the fact that Joe McNaughton worked as a police officer, it was well known that he was quite wealthy, wasn't he?"

"Very wealthy. Trust fund from his grandparents."

"So McNaughton tried to break off his relationship with Keri Dalcanton."

"That's what she told us. He didn't want to. He was stuck on her but good. But under the circumstances, he felt he had no choice."

"How did Ms. Dalcanton take this news?"

Matthews thought before answering. Ben had a pretty good idea why. If he said what he wanted to say, the judge would shut him down—and possibly strike his entire testimony. He had to be more subtle.

Matthews leaned back in his chair, a grim expression set on his face. "I think the subsequent events speak for themselves."

Dexter nodded. "Indeed. So do I." He glanced up at the judge. "No more questions."

Ben jumped to his feet, not waiting for an invitation from the judge. He wanted to appear eager and ready to go, as if he had many important points to make that would leave the prosecution's case in tatters.

The truth was rather less promising. He'd listened to the audiotape of Keri talking to Matthews. He had twisted and stretched it a bit, but on all the critical points, he had accurately characterized what she said.

"Sergeant Matthews," Ben began, "you told the jury about the clothes and the chains and the wallet. Where did you find the murder weapon?"

Matthews was nonplussed. "We didn't find the murder weapon."

It was Ben's turn to feign surprise. "Excuse me? You didn't find the murder weapon?"

"You know perfectly well we didn't."

"Why?"

Matthews shrugged. "Knives are small and light and fungible. They can't be tracked or traced or registered. They're easy to hide. Or to dispose of."

"So she got rid of the knife but kept the bloodstained suit?"

"I dunno. Maybe she hid it somewhere."

"Sergeant Matthews, you've been on the force eighteen years. Wouldn't you say the murder weapon is a critical piece of evidence in any murder prosecution?"

"I'd say it would be nice to have. But it isn't required. We've got an airtight case against your client. The evidence is overwhelming."

Not really proper testimony, but Ben supposed he had asked

for it. "Another thing I didn't hear you mention was Keri Dalcanton's confession, although you used the word 'confession' repeatedly. When did she admit she killed McNaughton?"

Matthews did his best to appear bored and unfazed by the defense tactics. "She never confessed to the killing. As you know."

"Never confessed? But according to you, she had broken down completely and was finally telling the truth. You called it a confession. How could she possibly omit that one detail?"

"She'd broken down, but she hadn't totally lost her mind. She wasn't suicidal, if you know what I mean. Don't be fooled by the stripper thing—she's a very smart lady."

"Did it ever occur to you, Detective, that the reason she didn't confess might be that she didn't do it?"

"To be honest, yes. But how do you explain the clothes, the blood, the chains? No, she's the one. It couldn't possibly be anyone else."

Ben heard an anguished sobbing behind him in the gallery. Even though he knew he shouldn't look, he couldn't resist.

It was Andrea McNaughton, the widow. Apparently this testimony had been too much for her. She was bent forward, her head pressed against her hands.

Ben returned his attention to the witness. "But she never admitted committing the murder, did she?"

"No."

"In fact, she denied it."

"That's what she said, yes."

"But you arrested her anyway."

Matthews allowed himself a smile. "If we never arrested people who denied committing the crime, we'd never arrest anyone."

Good point, Ben thought. Just wish he hadn't made it during my cross-ex. "How did you establish probable cause for the warrant?"

"Same way I always do. I told Judge Bolen everything we

knew. About the relationship between Joe and the defendant. The fact that they'd been seen together and were believed to be intimate. That there was believed to have been a breakup that could give rise to a motive for murder. That we thought her car had been used to transport the body."

"What was the scope of the warrant?"

Matthews sighed wearily. "The first warrant only gave us the right to search the defendant's car. I realized that wasn't good enough, so I went back and got a second warrant that allowed us to enter and search her apartment. I presented both warrants to the defendant at the appropriate time. We did everything strictly by the book. I'm telling you, counsel—you're barking up the wrong tree."

Wouldn't be the first time, either. "Was Judge Bolen satisfied that you had established probable cause?"

"Evidently. He issued the warrants."

"Then why didn't he give you the right to search her apartment the first time?"

"It was just an oversight. What does it matter? Like I said, he issued the second warrant in due time."

For some reason, Ben wasn't ready to let this go. "It still seems odd—two warrants for one search."

"There's nothing odd about it." Matthews was beginning to get testy. He grabbed the evidence notebook from the rail before him. "The first time, Judge Bolen gave us a warrant to search her car. See?" He held the warrant up and waved it before Ben's face. "I didn't even realize when I got it that it was limited to the car, but as soon as I noticed, I went back and got another warrant. See?" He held up the second one. "We had both warrants at Ms. Dalcanton's apartment before we discovered any of the evidence. Got it?"

Yeah, he got it. Ben took both warrants and held them in his hands. He had seen them many times before. He had read and reread every line, looking for any possible omission or transgression, any failing he could use to suppress the warrants and thus invalidate the search and exclude all evidence collected pursuant thereto. Unfortunately, there was nothing there. They complied with proper form in every respect. They had a clear description, the name of the defendant, a basis for investigation, the judge's signature . . .

Wait a minute. Ben peered at the signature at the bottom of each form. Although he had stared at these warrants a million times during the past few months, he didn't know that he had ever held both of them side by side before. And only by holding them side by side could he notice that not only were both warrants signed . . .

The signatures were identical.

Ben placed one warrant over the other and held them up to the light. Those signatures weren't just similar. They were *identical*.

Judge Hart peered at Ben strangely. "Is there a problem, counsel?"

"No, ma'am. Or—actually, yes. Yes, there is." He laid the two warrants on the bench before the judge. "These warrants haven't been signed."

Matthews leaned out of the witness chair. "What are you talking about? The signatures are right there in the corner."

"A signature is there, yes. But it wasn't signed. It's been stamped. Either stamped or photocopied." Ben showed the judge that the signatures were identical, then he shifted his gaze to the witness. "What do you do, Matthews? Carry a big stack of these around in the patrol car with you?"

Matthews rose to his feet. "I don't know what you're talking about."

Ben pushed the warrants closer to the judge. "I'll bet Matthews got presigned—or prestamped—forms and filled them out himself."

Assistant D.A. Dexter rushed to the bench. "Your honor! I must object—"

Ben cut him off. "Judge, I request permission to voir dire the witness about these warrants."

Judge Hart nodded. "Under the circumstances, I'll have to grant that."

Ben walked right up into Matthews's face. "What really happened when you saw Judge Bolen? Or did you even bother to go?"

Matthews's face flushed with anger. "I've told you already, I went to the judge's chambers."

"And what did you do?"

"I established probable cause! Like I'm supposed to!"

Ben's voice hit top volume. "Then why didn't the judge sign the warrants?"

Matthews took several quick short breaths, puffing his ruddy cheeks. "If you must know, I went to see the judge, according to procedure. But the judge was busy with his misdemeanor docket and couldn't see me right away. He's the only judge in the courthouse that time of night. I thought if we waited your client would have time to dispose of the evidence. So I asked the judge's clerk for an emergency warrant. Two of them, eventually. And he gave them to me."

"By emergency warrant, you mean a presigned warrant."

"I didn't have time to wait for anything else!" Sweat was trickling down the sides of Matthews's face. "But the point is, I saw the judge. I got a warrant. I did everything I'm supposed to do."

"Wrong," Ben shot back. "You're required by the Constitution of the United States to appear before a judge or magistrate and to establish probable cause for a warrant. It's the process that's important, not the product. If every judge handed out warrants without hearing the facts, the constitutional prohibitions against unlawful search and seizure would become meaningless." Ben whirled around to face the judge. "Your honor, I move that these warrants be suppressed. And I move that all the evidence collected pursuant to these warrants, including my client's verbal testimony, be excluded!"

Dexter leaned forward, horrified. "But your honor! That would wipe out our entire case!"

"Fine," Ben said. "Then I additionally move that the charges against my client be dismissed."

The response from the gallery was audible. It was like a tremendous sucking of air, a suspended moment of collective disbelief. Ben could hear Andrea McNaughton's sob-wracked voice carrying through the courtroom. "No," she was saying, loud enough for everyone to hear. "Please, God, no."

Ben tried to focus everyone's attention on the issue at hand. "Your honor, you know the Fourth Amendment did not contemplate that warrants would be distributed in this cavalier manner."

Judge Hart didn't bother disagreeing. "I won't for one moment condone what the police department—and one of my colleagues on the bench—have done here. But I'm not willing to eviscerate the prosecution's case on a capital crime—"

"There's case law!" Ben turned in time to see Christina running forward, carrying a laptop computer she kept in the courtroom with a Pacific Reporter CD-ROM. "I remembered reading it in class. It's directly on point."

"I can't believe it," Dexter said. "I've never heard of any such case."

"Well, there it is," Christina said. "Read it and weep."

Dexter's face became tight and tense. "Who is she, anyway?"

"My legal assistant," Ben answered.

"A legal assistant?" He turned toward the bench. "Your honor! She can't be heard by the court! She isn't even a lawyer!"

"And she knows the case law better than you do. Rather embarrassing, isn't it?" Judge Hart peered at the flickering blue screen. "*State versus Gabardino,* 1985. Yes." Her eyes quickly scanned the report. "I remember it, too. And it is directly on point. Bottom line, if the police don't properly establish probable cause, then any warrant issued isn't worth the paper it's printed on. Damn." She readjusted her glasses. "I'm sorry, Mr. Prosecutor. I hate this. But I have no choice. If there was any way I could cure the violation without invalidating the evidence, I would. But it just isn't possible. The warrants are hereby suppressed. Any evidence obtained pursuant to them is inadmissible."

The buzz in the gallery intensified. Even though the lawyers were at the bench, everyone could hear what was happening—and no one could believe it.

"No!" Dexter shouted. "That puts my whole case in the toilet!"

"I'm afraid I must agree with that evaluation," the judge said. "What you've got left wouldn't've gotten you past the preliminary hearing. You're dismissed, Mr. Dexter." She pounded her gavel. "The defendant is free to go."

"Nooo!" The cry rose from the back of the courtroom, a long keening wail. "Please, no!" Ben didn't bother looking to see who it was. He already knew.

"And let me say one thing more," Judge Hart added, glaring down harshly at Sergeant Matthews. "I don't want to get home and hear or read about how police do their best but those crazy liberal judges put criminals back on the street. I didn't want to do this. But you left me absolutely no choice. When you give your press conference this afternoon, make one thing perfectly clear. You have no one to blame for this result but yourself!" Hart grabbed her gavel and slammed it down. "This court is in recess. Good-bye and good riddance!" She rose abruptly and hurried to the back door leading to her private chambers.

The courtroom dissolved into pandemonium. Everyone was talking at once, except those few still so shocked they couldn't speak. Several reporters dashed toward the back door, eager to be the first to phone in this titanic surprise turn of events.

"Goddamn you, Kincaid," Dexter said, grabbing him by the arm. "How can you live with yourself?"

"Get your filthy paws off me," Ben said, shaking him loose. "Unless I'm very much mistaken, you knew exactly how those warrants were obtained. For all I know this 'emergency warrant' crap has been going on for years. But did you come clean about it? No. You kept your mouth shut so you could hang onto your illegally obtained evidence. You're just as much to blame as Matthews."

Dexter tried to reply, but Ben didn't hang around to listen. He returned to the defense table—where his client was waiting.

Her expression was dazed and barely comprehending. "She said . . . the case is dismissed?"

"She did."

"Does that mean it's over?"

"It does." Ben smiled. "You're free, Keri. Free to go."

"But—can they try me again? Drum up some new evidence?"

Ben shook his head. "Not after a dismissal for cause at trial by the judge. Double jeopardy attaches." He laid his hand on her shoulder. "It's over, Keri. For good."

Wordlessly, Keri flung her arms around Ben's neck. "Oh, my God. I can't believe it." She hugged him tightly. A moment later, Ben felt a drop of moisture that told him she was crying. "Thank you. Thank you so much."

Over her shoulder, Ben saw the television reporters going into action through the open courtroom doors. The female anchorwoman was apparently delivering a live bulletin. "And so, in this stunning turn of events that some are already calling the greatest miscarriage of justice in the history of the state of Oklahoma . . ."

Ben winced. It was starting. And it would only get worse.

"Mr. Kincaid!" another reporter shouted. "You've always had a reputation for high morals and integrity—until now. Care to comment?"

No, he did not. Ben steered Keri toward the back door. Given the circumstances, he felt certain Judge Hart would permit them to escape through her chambers.

He stepped around the defense table—and saw Andrea McNaughton making her way toward them. Her arms were outstretched; her fingers were curled like claws.

Ben held up his hands. "Mrs. McNaughton, please. I know you must be terribly—"

He didn't get a chance to finish. She pivoted suddenly and hurled herself, not at him, but at Keri. She knocked Keri to the floor, making her head thud harshly against the tile, then sat astride her, pounding her head and chest with her fists. "You bitch!" Andrea cried. "You filthy murderous bitch!"

"Bailiff!" Ben shouted. He ran behind Andrea and tried to pull her off Keri. No use. Andrea's blows continued to rain down on Keri, pummeling her chest with one hand, while she tried to pull Keri's hair out with the other. A fist landed square in the center of Keri's face. Keri screamed in pain; blood spurted everywhere. Only when the bailiff arrived were they finally able to pry Andrea away.

The bailiff pulled Andrea's arms behind her back and snapped cuffs over her wrists. "Consider yourself in custody."

Ben held up his hands. "Brent, she's upset, for obvious reasons. I don't think we want to press charges—"

"Like hell we don't!" Keri pushed herself up off the floor, her face smeared with blood. "I want her to pay for what she did!"

"Filthy whoring bitch!" Andrea shouted, spitting in Keri's face.

Keri wiped it away, furious. "Don't blame me for what happened. If you'd been giving Joe what he needed, he wouldn't've had to come to me!"

Andrea strained against the cuffs, craning her neck forward. "I'll get you! I *will* get you!"

"Get her out of here!" Ben urged. The bailiff dutifully hauled Andrea toward the back. "Keri—!"

Too late. She was gone. But she couldn't have gone far. Ben knew there would be a fleet of reporters wanting to interview her, and now, for the first time in months, she would be free to talk. Which she probably would. No matter how carefully lawyers counseled their clients, few were able to resist the siren call of fifteen seconds on TV. And after all she had been through, Keri probably had a lot she wanted to say.

And at this point, Ben didn't much care. He didn't want to worry about this case; he didn't even want to think about it.

All he wanted was to get home, get a shower, feed his cat, play the piano, and think about anything—anything at all—other than this miserable affair. He knew this case would never win him any praise or benefit. The only thing he could be grateful for was that it was over. That's how he tried to comfort himself, as he snuck out of the courtroom. It was finally over.

He couldn't know, then, how wrong he was. It wasn't over. The nightmare was only beginning. And it would get far worse than Ben had ever dreamed possible.

ONE

* *

The Blue Squeeze

* 1 *

"So what're we gonna do about it?"

Barry Dodds didn't want to encourage him. "We're gonna play cards, Arlen—that's what we're gonna do. So play already."

A toothpick darting out from between his teeth, Arlen Matthews tossed out a few chips. "Seems to me this isn't something we should take lying down. Seems to me we ought to do something about it."

Mark Callery called. "Do something? Like what?"

Dodds pressed his hand against Callery's arm. They were about the same age, but Dodds was a captain, and he knew that because of his senior rank, Callery, unlike Matthews, respected his opinion. "Don't encourage him."

"I just wanted to know."

"And I'm saying, don't ask."

"What's the matter with you, Barry?" Matthews asked. "Don't we still have freedom of speech in this country? Let the boy talk."

"No good can come of this discussion." Dodds was a short man with the beer belly that almost seemed like a mandatory stage in almost every police officer's career. "You boys would be better off if you just forgot about it."

"Is that right?" Matthews obviously didn't agree. He addressed himself to the fourth member of the group. "What do you think, Frank?"

Frank didn't respond immediately. He was an extremely

31

large man; down at headquarters, they called him The Hulk. Given his enormous size, his colleagues imagined that it took longer for thoughts to make the trip from his brain to his mouth, sort of like the larger dinosaurs. "Can't say, really."

"That's what I like about you, Frank. You always know exactly where you stand." Matthews obviously wasn't satisfied. "I tell you what I think. I think this was a travesty of justice and I think we ought to do something about it."

"Hasn't this mess caused you enough trouble already?" Dodds was the youngest of the four and the most senior in rank, a fact which he knew caused some trouble, even if it was never directly mentioned. "The courts have spoken. You can't take the law into your own hands. That's not how the system works."

Matthews was not pleased. "Don't lecture me on the system, college boy."

Dodds grimaced. In truth, many of the police officers, and all of the younger ones, had college degrees. But because he had a graduate degree in criminology, because he had been promoted rapidly and he spoke the Queen's English, to Matthews he was always the "college boy."

"I think we should just let it alone."

"You'd feel different if it had been you up there on the witness stand." Matthews threw down his cards—which was no great loss since he was holding a pair of twos. "You'd feel different if that attorney had made you look like a lyin' jackass."

Dodds, the last player still holding his cards, scooped in the pot. "He was just doing his job."

Matthews jumped up on his feet. "Just doing his job? Just doing his job?"

"I didn't say I liked it, okay?" Dodds had been trying to calm Matthews down all night, and frankly, he was getting sick of it. "I just said there's no point in acting like it was some big surprise. You know what's gonna happen when you take the stand. The defense attorney's going to try to make you look like one of the Three Stooges. There's nothing new about it."

"This is different."

"It isn't."

"Like hell. This time it was one of our own. It was Joe. My partner. And if you had any loyalty to Joe—"

"Don't you dare lecture me about Joe." Dodds had had it, all he could take. "Joe and I went to school together, all right? I've known him longer than any of you. I would've died for him, understand? *Died* for him!" He stood up to Matthews and jabbed him in the chest. "So don't you lecture me about loyalty. Don't you dare!"

The room fell quiet. Matthews and Dodds glared at one another, like two jungle beasts waiting to see who would make the first move. No one did.

Eventually, Frank cleared his throat. "So are we gonna play cards here?"

Matthews kept his eyes trained on Dodds. "I'm sick of cards."

"But it was my turn to deal."

"There ain't gonna be any more cards, got it?" Matthews pounded the table. "It's sick. Our buddy is dead, the lyin' whore that killed him is running free, and we're sitting here like a bunch of pansy-assed queers playing cards!"

Callery's voice was quiet, and his eyes were trained on the table. "You know, Arlen, you weren't the only one who was up on the witness stand. I testified, too. I went first. You think I enjoyed it? I didn't. I didn't like that lawyer prying into every little thing. I didn't like him insinuating that we botched the investigation. But it's over now. We have to move on."

Matthews looked away. "It's different for you."

"It isn't, Arlen."

"It is. Goddamn it, can't you see? It *is*." To his companions' shock and horror, Matthews's small eyes began to well up. "It wasn't your fault, okay? I was the one who screwed up. I was the one who used Judge Bolen's crappy warrants. It's my fault that murdering bitch is still walking the streets."

Dodds gently placed his hand on his colleague's shoulder. "Give yourself a break, Arlen. You couldn't've known."

"I should've known, damn it. It's my job to know. I let Joe down. He was my partner. And I let him down." Tears began to stream down his face.

Even though it was obviously the last thing on earth he wanted to do, Frank broke his silence. "Arlen . . . it's none of my business, but . . . I think maybe you should get some help. Maybe some counseling. Central Division's got that woman who comes in twice a week—"

Matthews's face swelled up with rage. "I don't want counseling, you idiot! I want the fucking little cunt who killed Joe!"

Another silence followed, this one even longer than the one before. No one knew what to say next.

"It's this simple," Matthews said, his chest heaving. "Are you Joe's friend, or not? 'Cause there's no way any friend of Joe's would let what happened happen and just walk away without doing anything about it." He leaned across the table. "So what about it, Frank? Are you Joe's friend?"

Frank took his usual eternity to reply. "You know I am, Arlen."

"What about you, Mark?"

Callery frowned. "Joe was my first supervisor, my first day on the job. He taught me practically everything I know."

"I'll take that as a yes." He turned toward Dodds. "And what about you? You claim Joe was your oldest friend. You claim you'd of died for him. Was that just talk? Or does it actually mean something?"

Dodds glared back at him, not answering.

It was Callery who broke the silence. "What did you have in mind, Arlen?"

"We're cops, aren't we?"

"Ye-es . . ."

"We're supposed to catch the bad guys, right?"

"Yes, but—"

"So I say that's what we do."

"But, Arlen, the case is over. Double jeopardy has—"

"There are ways around that."

Dodds stared at Matthews, stunned. "Arlen, stop right there. I don't know what you're thinking, but whatever it is—"

"What's the matter? Haven't got the guts for it, college boy?"

Dodds fell silent, biting back his own anger.

"I want that cheap piece of ass that killed our friend. And I want that cheap lying whore of a lawyer who got her off and made us look like fools."

"We all do," Callery replied. "But how are you gonna do it? There's no way."

"There is a way." Calmly, almost in control of himself now, Matthews fell back into his chair. "I've got three words for you, boys: The Blue Squeeze."

* 2 *

Ben stood beside the reception table sampling Dean Belsky's canapés. There were a wide variety of them, but they all seemed to involve cucumbers. Ben hated cucumbers. Actually, it wasn't so much that he hated them as it was that he didn't understand their purpose. After all, they didn't taste like anything. They weren't especially good for you. They didn't quell your appetite. What was the point? And yet, there they were, as far as the eye could see, rows and rows of sliced, diced, warm and wilty cucumbers. All in all, it was about the most unappetizing display of appetizers he'd seen in his life.

"Paula, look! *Cucumbers!*" Jones, Ben's office manager, surged past him and bellied up to the table; his girlfriend,

Paula, trailed in his wake. He slid his plate under half a dozen of the nearest selections. "I was starving." He glanced at Ben. "Aren't you having any?"

"I'd rather eat air. Actually, it's about the same."

"Nonsense. Cucumbers are great. So cool, so refreshing." He took a bite into one of them. The expression on his face rapidly changed. "Unless, of course, they've been out on the table a wee bit too long. When did this reception start?"

"Beats me. Seems like forever."

"Ah, don't be such a party pooper. This is a big day." Jones turned his attention to Paula. "Want some, sugar pie?"

"No thanks. I'll just savor the inside lining of my mouth."

Ben smiled. "A woman after my own heart." Paula was the head research librarian for the Tulsa City-County system. She and Jones had met on the Internet more than a year ago and been inseparable ever since. "Better watch out, Jones. I may steal her away from you."

"As if you stood a chance." He sniffed. "We're soul mates." He clasped her hand. "And hopefully we always will be."

"And I hope we always will be," she corrected. " 'Hopefully' is an adverb meaning full of hope."

"That's my cute little librarian gal. You'll always be my sweet thing, won't you, punkin?"

"You know it, huggy bear."

They rubbed noses.

Ben didn't know whether to be enchanted or repulsed. "All right, you two, calm down. We're in a public place, remember?"

Jones pulled away from Paula's face. "I remember, Boss. But it's easy to forget when you're around my hot little love bug."

"Uh-huh. So when are you going to make an honest woman of her?"

A touch of frost settled amongst their little group.

Paula laughed, a bit too heartily, trying to smooth over the awkwardness. "Bad question, Ben. Jones is still in his twenty-first century sensitive male mode."

"And that means?"

She winked and mouthed the words: "Can't commit."

"Anybody seen Christina?" Jones asked. "We're here for her, after all."

"Haven't seen her," Ben answered. "Probably searching for a robe short enough to fit. Haven't seen Loving, either."

"That's odd. He said he would be—" Jones stopped. "Wait—oh, my God! There he is."

"What's the big—" Ben swiveled around.

"Hey ya, Skipper," Loving said, with typical exuberance. "Am I late?"

"No, no," Ben said, trying not to laugh. "You're fine. A good fifteen minutes till the ceremony starts." He turned away, unable to suppress his mirth.

"What?" Loving said. "What is it? Did I do somethin'?"

"No. N-not at all," Jones stammered out. He was doing a considerably less capable job of containing himself. "You certainly look . . . dapper this morning."

"What is it? My clothes?" Loving, Ben's investigator, was about the size of a bear and built like a brick wall. But this morning, that admirable girth was encased in an ill-fitting tuxedo. With morning coat. "You told me this was a dress-up thing."

"Yes," Jones said. He was full-out laughing now. "Yes, I did . . ."

"And I wanted Christina to know how important I think this is. Wanted to treat her special day with respect." He hooked a thumb under his lapel. "When she sees this, she'll know how much I care about her."

"That," Ben said, "or she'll think you just came from a royal wedding."

"What a bunch of boobs," Paula said. She took Loving's arm and sidled up next to him. "I think you look dashing."

"Really?" Loving beamed. "I wasn't sure, you know?" He lowered his voice a notch. "I haven't actually worn this thing since high school."

"Ah. That would explain the fit."

"Ben!"

He twisted his neck in the direction of the voice and saw a familiar red-haired figure blazing a trail through the reception crowd. She was wearing a black gown and had a mortarboard tucked under her arm.

"Ben!" she said, bubbling. "You came! I'm so happy!"

"Well, of course I came," he said, standing there awkwardly. "I couldn't miss seeing my, um, you know, one's legal assistant graduating from law school."

Paula patted his arm. "Nice job, Ben. Very clinical." She gave Christina a hug. "We're so proud of you, Christina. All of us."

"Are you staying for the ceremony?"

Ben opened his mouth, but whatever he was planning to say, he never got the chance. "Of course we are," Paula said quickly. "All of us."

"That's wonderful!" Christina had always been on the exuberant side, but this morning, she was positively effervescent. "Can you believe I'm finally graduating?" She spun around, and the brick wall wearing a tuxedo caught her eye. "Loving, look at you! You look *extraordinaire*!"

Loving tugged on his bow tie. "Me? Nah . . ."

"You do! Very scrummy! If you wear that thing much longer, you're going to have to beat the girls off with a stick."

"Shucks. I wasn't tryin' to look good. I just wanted you to know what a big deal we think today is. And how proud we are of you."

She leaned forward and kissed him on the cheek. "You're very sweet." She turned back toward Ben. "Don't you think my gown has a certain je ne sais quoi? Don't you like it?"

"Better than most of your wardrobe."

"Wanna see what I have on under it?"

"No." Ben gave her a long look. "You do have something on under it, don't you?"

"Of course." She lifted the hem of the gown and gave him a

fast flash of a pink poodle skirt lined with black fake fur, white socks, and saddle oxfords.

"You know," Ben said, "once you're a lawyer, you won't be able to dress so . . . eccentrically."

"Which is why I dressed up today. I have the whole rest of my life to be boring." She saw that the other graduates were beginning to file out the rear. "I have to go get in line now." She paused, this time looking at Ben. "See you after the ceremony?"

"Wouldn't miss it."

And then she was gone, like a strawberry-blond poltergeist, three shakes and a cloud of dust.

It was well past time someone reinvented the graduation ceremony model, Ben mused, as he sat on one of the front rows of the First Baptist Church sanctuary, bored to tears. There were too many people crammed into too little space, none of them smiling. Even the graduates looked as if they might drop off at any moment. After "a few opening remarks" from the dean, it was time for the musical entertainment, which was neither.

And then, of course, the dreaded commencement address, delivered by a distinguished state senator. Why were these things so often delivered by politicians? Ben supposed it was because they were always ready to give a speech and didn't require an honorarium. This address went on for more than half an hour, and it seemed to Ben to have a lot more to do with getting the speaker reelected than offering words of wisdom to the graduates. As a part-time adjunct professor, Ben had tried to suggest a few innovative alterations to the dean—like skipping the whole ceremony. But for some strange reason, his proposal hadn't garnered much support.

At long last, it was time to award the diplomas.

"Here it is!" Loving said excitedly, jabbing Ben in the ribs. "It's almost time."

"Almost time? They're still in the A's. Christina is an M."

"She'll be up before ya know it," Loving said, and he was almost right, because Ben managed to take a little eyes-open nap, a trick he had taught himself during Western Oklahoma motion dockets. By the time he knew what was going on again, they were finishing up the L's.

"Steven Edward Lytton, PLA Vice President," the announcer said, and somewhere behind him, Ben heard a booming chorus of shouts and cheers.

"What boobs," Ben muttered, under his breath.

"They're not boobs," Loving said. "They're family. They're proud of him. It's what families do."

"Loving . . . you aren't planning . . ."

But there was no time. "Christina Ingrid McCall, National Moot Court, Law Review, Order of the Coif."

In the blink of an eye, Jones, Paula, and Loving were on their feet, whooping and hollering at the top of their lungs.

Ben wondered if the dean was watching. "Why are you doing this?" he growled under his breath.

"Don't you get it?" Loving hissed between hoots. "We're her family."

He was right, of course. Ben pushed to his feet and pounded his hands together. He even whooped a little.

After the ceremony, the group gathered at the office at Two Warren Place for a postceremony celebration. Jones had ordered champagne, chilled and ready when they arrived. Paula had made brownies and Loving picked up some exquisite bacon cheeseburgers from Goldie's.

"A toast," Jones said, hoisting his glass in the air.

"Another one?" Ben asked. By his count, they'd already had about three bottles of toasts, and they were all starting to wobble a bit.

Jones ignored him. "To our own Christina," he said. "She's been the world's best legal assistant for years. Now she'll be the world's best lawyer!" He hiccuped. "Excluding the Boss, of course."

"Of course," Ben said. Boy, she'd been a lawyer for what, an hour and a half? And already he was an afterthought.

"I think she should give a speech," Loving said. With his bow tie unstrung and dangling from his neck, he looked like a cross between a lounge singer and his bouncer. "Speech! Speech!"

Christina flushed, either with champagne or embarrassment. "I am not giving a speech."

"Hey, if you're gonna be a lawyer, you're gonna have to give some speeches."

"All the more reason not to give one now."

"Well then I will," Ben said. He raised his glass. "A short one, anyway. I've been delighted to work with you for some time now, Christina, but I've never been prouder of you than I am today."

Christina's eyes sparkled.

"Congratulations, kiddo—you're a lawyer now."

She shook her head. "No, not yet. I have to be tested by fire. In the courtroom."

"You'll get your chance."

"Hey, is this a private party, or can anyone guzzle your champagne?" Major Mike Morelli, Tulsa P.D.'s chief homicide detective, strolled into the office wearing his trademark trenchcoat. "Way to go, slugger." He gave Christina a hug.

"Thanks, Mike."

"You bet. Just don't get too many major criminals off the hook right away, okay? My job's hard enough as it is." He leaned over next to Ben. "Can I talk to you for a minute?"

Ben sat up. "Sure. You mean—?" He jerked a thumb.

Mike nodded. "Don't want to disturb the revelry."

Together, they made their way to Ben's interior office. He'd been at this location for more than a year now, but it was still as barren as the day he moved in—the result of a combination of tight finances and lack of interest. He had a desk and two chairs, a file cabinet, a framed diploma, and that was about it.

They each took one of the available seats. "So what's up?"

"Just wanted to warn you, Ben—I'm going to be gone for a little while."

"Gone? Why?"

"Got an undercover assignment. And I don't know how long it will take. So you'll have to find someone else to watch *Xena* with you and pretend that we admire it for its sophisticated scripts."

"Nothing dangerous, I hope."

Mike shrugged. "Who knows? Did you read about the murder last night?"

Ben nodded. A corpse found in a swing at LaFortune Park. Hard to overlook.

"We think we've got a line on the killer. Which took some doing, since we can't even ID the victim. It's a faint trail, but worth chasing. And will probably take a while. So I wanted to give you the heads-up."

"Thanks, I appreciate that," Ben said, but he sensed there was more to this than he'd gotten so far.

"You might also mention it to Julia. If you happen to see her. I mean, I don't know, she probably doesn't care. But still. I wouldn't want her to worry."

"Of course," Ben said, even though he knew there was no chance that his younger sister, Mike's ex-wife, would be inquiring after him.

"Who knows, she may finally realize she needs help with that kid of hers. Heard anything about Joey?"

Ben shook his head, and for about the millionth time wondered—Did Mike know? Was this just a game, or was he really oblivious to the fact that Joey was his son? Granted, Julia had never acknowledged the paternity to Mike or anyone else, but it was obvious to Ben every time he looked at the kid. Was it possible that Mike missed it?

"Something else, Ben." Mike squirmed, shifting his weight from one side of the chair to the other. Ben could tell he was more uncomfortable now than he had been talking about Julia. "About the Dalcanton case."

Ben waved his hand. "It's over, Mike. The court's ruled."

"It may be over for you, Ben, but for a lot of other people I know, it isn't. And never will be. Until someone pays the price for killing Joe McNaughton."

"I can't lose sleep over what some rednecks are stewing about."

"I'm not talking about rednecks here, Ben. Or country bumpkins or militia freaks. I'm talking about cops. Good cops."

"Mike, every time I win a case, I make some cop angry. That's just part of the job. I'm used to it."

"This is different, Ben. Way different. Joe McNaughton was a police officer. Moreover—he was well loved, very popular with the rank and file. And the way he died"—Mike shuddered—"in public, and gruesome in the extreme—that really knocked some of the boys for a loop. Probably didn't help that he was killed by some cheap South Side stripper, either."

Ben sat up. "Mike, she was never convicted. And I don't think—"

"Yeah, yeah. But I can tell you this—there's not a guy on the force who isn't absolutely convinced that she's guilty. No one's happy about the way the trial turned out. And a lot of them just aren't willing to let it go."

"So what are you saying? You think Keri is in danger?"

"Maybe. But mainly I'm worried about you."

"Me? I'm just the lawyer."

" 'Just the lawyer' is not a phrase I hear much at headquarters. Son-of-a-bitch lawyer, yes. Low-life ambulance-chasing scumbag mother—"

Ben held up his hands. "I get the picture."

"I wouldn't worry so much if I was going to be around. But I'm not. So watch your back, okay, kemo sabe?"

"Okay." Ben pushed himself out of his chair. "When are you leaving?"

"Immediately." He followed Ben back to the conference

room where the rest of the group was still celebrating. "Well, as soon as I finish that last bottle of champagne."

Two hours later, Mike was gone, but the rest of them were still partying. The exuberance of the evening had not diminished with the last of the bubbly. In fact, if anything, Ben thought the rampant merriment had increased.

They were unwrapping presents now. Loving gave Christina a briefcase embossed with her initials, and Jones and Paula gave her a flowering plant for her new interior office. Christina was obviously pleased and touched.

"What about you, Skipper?" Loving asked, his voice loud and celebratory.

"I bet the Boss has something great for her," Jones said. "I think he's kind of soft on her, just between you and I."

"Between you and *me*, dear," Paula said. "So what's your present, Ben?"

Ben coughed uncomfortably. "Uh . . . yeah. Present. Right."

Loving looked aghast—and Christina looked shattered.

"Don't tell me," Loving said.

"Boss, you didn't—"

"No, no, I have something. Really." Ben scrambled awkwardly behind a desk. "I just wasn't expecting to present it so . . . publicly."

Loving winked at Christina. "Must be somethin' intimate."

Christina rolled her eyes. "From Ben? Yeah, right."

"Well, it's about time he gave her something intimate," Jones said. "How long has she been—" Loving jabbed him in the ribs, knocking the wind out of him.

"Here it is." Ben dragged out a large oversize package, long and thin like a poster, only somewhat thicker and more solid. It was wrapped in red and green paper—Christmas leftovers, obviously.

Christina's eyes brightened immediately. "You did get me something!" She wrapped her arms around his neck and pressed her cheek against his. "You old softie, you."

"Is she talking about the Boss?" Jones asked. Loving shushed him.

Christina tore into the package without hesitation. Barely a second passed before the interior was revealed, black and green and wobbly.

Christina's eyes crinkled. "Is it . . . a desk blotter?"

Jones looked up toward heaven. "He got her a desk blotter."

Loving pursed his lips. "Very intimate."

Paula nodded. "Sexy, even."

Ben appeared perplexed. "What? I just thought, she's going to have a new office, and she's going to want it to look all lawyerlike, so she needs a desk blotter."

"It's nice," Christina said, keeping her voice even. "I really like it."

Ben noted that the other three were glaring at him. "What's your problem?"

But there was no time to explain. Before anyone could even attempt it, they heard a harsh pounding at the outer doors. "Open up!"

Paula jumped. "Who the hell is that?"

The pounding continued. Christina moved closer to Ben. "Someone you forgot to invite to the party?"

Ben started toward the front doors, but before he could get there, they burst open.

The voice returned, this time amplified by the unmistakable sound of an electronic bullhorn. *"Police! Nobody moves!"*

* 3 *

In a matter of seconds, the ambience in Ben's office switched from a tipsy gala to a surreal nightmare, a cop show out of Kafka. Uniformed officers surged through the door like storm troopers, weapons out, wearing heavy flak gear.

A piercing white light swept across the room, blinding them. It seemed to be coming from outside the bay windows. Ben went to take a look, but the sound of the churning blades tipped him off before he got there. It was Police One—the Tulsa P.D. chopper.

Down below, he spotted dark shadowy figures hustling around the building. He'd been around cops enough to know what it was—the SOT team (what the rest of the world called a SWAT team) in their BDUs, their Remington 7005s at the ready, forming a tactical perimeter.

"What in the name of—" Ben eyed the seven officers now in his office, two plainclothes, five uniforms. He recognized at least one of them. He couldn't remember the name, but he knew the man had been a witness in the Dalcanton case.

Ben stepped forward. "What's going on here?"

The plainclothes cop pushed Ben back. "I'm Detective Sergeant Matthews. We're going to search the premises. Don't get in the way. If you don't cooperate, I'll have you physically restrained."

"You want to search? That's it? What's with the big dog-and-pony show outside?"

Matthews moved so close Ben could smell his breath.

46

"When we're dealing with cop killers, we don't take any chances."

"Cop killers?" Christina said. "What are you babbling about? There's no one here but staff."

"We know." He motioned to his officers to spread out through the office. "Like I said, we're going to search. Don't worry, shyster. We've got a warrant."

"From who? Judge Bolen?"

"No." Matthews lowered his voice. "From your personal pet. Judge Hart."

Ben felt a cold chill at the base of his spine. This was no mistake. They knew who he was. And they knew what they were doing here.

"I want to see the warrant."

Matthews dropped it in his hands. Ben scanned it as quickly as possible. Unfortunately, everything appeared to be in order—even the signature. He touched a wet finger to it, and the ink smeared.

"What's the basis for this?" Ben asked. "How did you make probable cause?"

"I'm not required to brief you on my case," Matthews said. "And I don't plan to."

The two words that resonated most in Ben's brain were "my case." "What are you looking for?"

"I don't have to answer that question, either."

"If you'll give me a clue, maybe I can—"

"Just stay out of our way, Kincaid."

"I'm telling you—"

Matthews shoved Ben back, hard. His teeth clenched together and his lips curled. "Listen to me, you goddamn piece of filth. I don't know if you're a murderer or just someone who gets his jollies helping murderers. That's for someone else to decide. But I can tell you this. I don't like cop killers and I don't like people who help cop killers. They should be executed on sight, far as I'm concerned. And if you get in my way, that just might happen."

Ben stared back at him coldly. "You're making a mistake."

"See those weapons my men are holding? Those are Smith and Wesson forty-caliber semiautomatic handguns loaded with Federal hollow points. Fast, accurate, and deadly. The two in the rear are carrying Remington 870 twelve-gauges loaded with double-ought buckshot. If my men should be forced to use their weapons in pursuit of a cop killer's accomplice, they'd never be prosecuted. More likely they'd become national heroes. So stay the hell out of our way."

Ben stepped aside.

"Spread out," Matthews instructed his team. "Everybody take a room."

"Stick with them," Ben said, instructing his own team, Christina and Loving, Jones and Paula. "Each of you take one of the officers. Don't get in their way, but don't let them out of your sight." Something about the expression on Matthews's face gave him the feeling he couldn't be too careful. He didn't know what they were looking for, but whatever it was, he wanted to make sure it didn't come out of a police officer's back pocket.

Ben started after them, but Matthews grabbed him and shoved him sideways. Ben tumbled into a desk.

"My apologies," Matthews said. "Didn't see you there." He moved closer to Ben and lowered his voice. "No courtroom tricks are gonna get you out of this, asshole."

If there were any doubts in Ben's mind about what was happening before, there were none after that. Ben pulled himself together and followed one of the uniforms into the nearest office. The others did the same.

Ben watched as an officer ripped open the drawers in Jones's desk and dumped the contents on the floor.

"Is it the McNaughton case? Is that what this is about?"

The officer grunted and continued tearing apart the office.

"Is that necessary?" Ben growled.

The officer did not look up. "Get in my way, I'll cuff you. Which I would enjoy."

Ben buttoned his lip and kept an eye on the man's hands.

Outside, the other officers searched with the same ham-handed technique. Entire file cabinets were dumped out on the floor. Desk drawers were emptied; even the trash was spilled. Desktops were cleared—phones, laptops, and all. Ben hadn't expected them to worry about keeping things tidy, but he'd been on searches before with Mike and he knew this wasn't how it was usually done. It almost seemed as if the object was not so much to find something as to create the biggest upheaval possible.

A high-pitched shriek brought him out of his reverie. "Christina!"

Abandoning his post, Ben raced into her office, where she'd been watching one of the uniforms destroy everything in sight. When Ben arrived, the officer had Christina's arms pinned behind her back and was snapping handcuffs on her.

"What the hell's going on here?" Ben shouted. He was mad now, damn it. If they wanted to run some petty harassment vendetta against him, fine. But manhandling Christina was something else again.

"We warned you what would happen if you tried to interfere." He pushed Christina into the corner.

"He was trying to go through the files in my laptop," Christina said. "They need a special specific warrant to do that. *State versus Cresswell.*"

"She's right," Ben said. "Screw with her computer and you may invalidate this whole dubious search."

That seemed to slow the young officer. He backed away from the laptop, his teeth gritted.

"Now uncuff her and stop abusing your authority. You should be ashamed of yourself."

That was more that the young man could take. "I should be ashamed of myself? Coming from you, that's pretty ironic. At least I haven't put any murderers back on the street."

"Neither have I. I just point out to the judge when the police screw up their cases."

The kid uncuffed Christina, then stormed out of the office, leaving it looking as if an earthquake had struck.

"Ben, what's going on here?" Christina asked, rubbing her sore wrists.

"I don't know."

They were both riveted by the sound of bellowing from the next office over. "Found it!"

Ben and Christina both raced into Ben's office. Matthews was there; Paula was huddled off to the side.

He was holding a knife. A butcher-sized knife. Caked with blood.

"What is that?" Christina asked. Her voice trembled.

"Unless I miss my guess," Matthews said, "this is the knife that was used to kill Joe McNaughton."

"Where the hell did it come from?" Ben asked.

Matthews smiled thinly. "From your office, Kincaid."

"No way. You planted it."

"I didn't. I found it in the bottom drawer of your file cabinet, under some papers. Right where you left it."

"You're lying through your teeth!"

"I'm sorry, Ben, but—he isn't." It was Paula. Her eyes were lowered and her voice was slow and . . . confused. "I was watching him the whole time he searched. And I was especially watching his hands. He didn't plant it. Not just now, anyway."

"But that—"

Matthews motioned to one of the officers in the hallway. "Put this man under arrest."

The uniform whipped out his cuffs, yanked Ben's arms back roughly, and snapped the metal restraints around his wrists.

"Is this your idea of justice?" Ben asked. "Arresting the defense attorney?"

Matthews smirked. "Justice is never simple."

"This is an outrage. I've never seen that knife before in my life!"

"Yeah. That's what they all say." Matthews removed a card from his shirt pocket. "You have the right to remain silent. If you waive that right, anything you say can and will be used against you . . ."

"Cut the crap. What's this all about?"

Matthews stopped. His eyes locked with Ben's. "What's this about? It's about seeing a murderer brought to justice. Maybe two of them." He leaned into Ben's face. "How much did you do, Kincaid? Did you help with the murder, or just the cover-up? Were you fucking her all along, or just after she was arrested?"

"You miserable son of a bitch. I never—"

Christina pushed between them. "He's not answering any questions."

"Get out of my way, lady," Matthews barked.

Christina grabbed the man by the collar. "I'm not a lady, jerkface. I'm his attorney. And if I say he's not answering any questions, he's not answering any questions. Got it?"

Matthews shook her off, rubbing his neck. His teeth were clenched tight enough to pop a filling. "Frank, take this scumbag downtown." The other plainclothes officer pulled Ben toward the door, yanking him by the cuffs.

"Find Mike," Ben called. "As soon as possible."

"I'll be right there, Ben," Christina shouted behind them. "Don't say anything. As soon as you've been processed, we'll talk."

Matthews couldn't bear to leave without a parting shot. He leaned into Christina's ear and spoke in a low tone. "When we're done with your scum-sucking boss, lady, he'll be lucky if he remembers *how* to talk."

MONDAY ONE

Teal, that's what showed, too. Matthew Reynolds had a
front-row seat to this, yet you are standing at the urinal trying to squeeze out a few more drops of piss next to the
governor. Will

* 4 *

The officers shoved Ben down the stairs of Two Warren Place
and outside, using as much force as possible. Ben was paraded
through a phalanx of at least twenty SOT officers. A searchlight
beamed down from the chopper overhead, practically blinding
Ben and insuring that there was no one in a half-mile radius who
couldn't see him. They led him to the back of the Armored Per-
sonnel Carrier and shoved him inside.

Fifteen minutes later they arrived at the police headquarters building downtown and dragged him up to the fourth
floor. He waited while the four officers accompanying him
checked their weapons in a locker. As Ben well knew, no one
was allowed to take weapons onto the fourth floor—not even
cops. They wanted to eliminate all possibility of an arrestee
grabbing a weapon and making an escape. The cops traded
their guns for keys, which they placed in their holsters, a sign
that they had stored their weapons. Then they dragged Ben
inside the county jail.

Because the holding cell belonged to the county, Ben was
patted down by sheriff's deputies. They were none too gentle
about it, and didn't avoid any place where a weapon of any
kind could conceivably be hidden.

"Is this a frisking," Ben asked, "or are you giving me a
physical?"

The officer to his left "accidentally" cuffed him on the jaw
with his elbow.

They dragged him inside the cell block. "Stand on those

footsteps, asshole," the jailer said, pointing to a set of yellow prints painted on the floor. Ben complied. "Lean forward." The jailer searched him again, just as thoroughly, if not more so.

When he was done, the jailer barked, "Take off your clothes."

Ben squirmed. "On our first date?"

The jailer kicked him in the back of his knees. "Take off your goddamn clothes."

When Ben was naked, and the officers had let him stand around exposed long enough to humiliate him, they tossed him a pair of the orange coveralls that were standard attire for all inmates. Then they dragged him to a small cell.

Ben noticed that the cells on either side both had someone inside. One if not both of them were probably plants, he realized. He would have to be careful with what he said.

The jailer removed his cuffs. Just as Ben began to stretch his aching arms, the jailer twisted his right arm around and pinned it behind his back. He shoved Ben forward till his face was pressed against the hard bars of the cell.

"I hope you're enjoying this," Ben grunted, though he could barely move his mouth. " 'Cause I'm going to be out of here before the second shift arrives."

"I don't think so, creep," the jailer whispered. "We have special rules for lawyers who help cop killers. The wheels just don't seem to turn as quickly."

"All I did was my job," Ben said. "Why are you doing this?"

The other man's voice hissed in his ear. "Joe McNaughton was my best friend. He and his wife are my kids' godparents."

Ben closed his eyes. So what you're saying is, this stay isn't going to be quite as nice as a night at the Ramada Inn.

Without warning, the jailer whirled him around and pounded him in the gut, hard. Ben doubled over. The jailer followed up with another blow, then another. Ben fell to his knees.

"I'm hitting you in the stomach because I don't want to

leave a mark. If you tell anyone about this, I'll say you had to be restrained while attempting escape. And every man on the force will back me up. No one will speak up for the creep who helped kill Joe McNaughton. But you'll get some extra time for attempted escape."

He opened the cell door and kicked Ben inside. Ben crashed against the opposite wall of the tiny cell, banging his head against the concrete.

"Get used to being treated like this," the jailer growled, as he locked the cell door behind Ben. "It ain't gonna get any better. And you're gonna be here a good long time."

* 5 *

Kirk Dalcanton couldn't decide which he thought more feeble: the spindly rotted staircase or the decrepit old man leading him up it.

"Last tenants I had in here, they didn't give a damn about anyone or anything except themselves." The elderly man could only manage one step every thirty seconds or so, which made the ascent even more painfully slow, not to mention hazardous. "And maybe not even themselves. Tore the place apart. Left in the dead of night and never paid me a dime. You're not going to do that, are you, son?"

"No. No, I mean, I wouldn't. I'll pay in advance, if you want."

"That'd be all right, sure. Not that I don't trust you. But you know how it is."

Kirk wrenched a wad of cash out of his pocket. For once, he

was flush, at least by his standards. He grabbed about a hundred bucks and shoved it into the pocket of the old man's ratty cardigan. For a dump like this, that ought to last him a month.

"I appreciate that, son, I do. Gets harder and harder to get good people, if you know what I mean. Quality folk. Not like it was in the old days. Back during the oil boom, even before. Then I had a list of people as long as your arm wanting to get in here. I couldn't rent space fast enough. People wanted to be near downtown, where the action was. Wasn't considered a bad neighborhood back then. Nowadays, all the yuppies and high-flyers run south and everyone else follows them and pretty soon I don't have anyone I can rent to except crack heads and pimps and people who disappear in the dead of night and don't pay their rent."

Kirk batted his eyelashes, trying not to fall asleep halfway up the stairs. You're bo-*ring*! old man, he wanted to shout at the top of his lungs. But he decided to restrain himself. At least until he signed the lease.

"Here we go," the landlord said, as he crossed the threshold at the top of the stairs. "Only one room up here, and that's yours." He opened the door and flung out his arm, like he was presenting some breathtaking view. What he was actually displaying was a dump. Possibly the worst, most horrible-looking dive Kirk had ever seen in his life.

Kirk stepped inside and took a quick inventory, trying to keep his face from revealing the disgust and revulsion he felt. Exposed wooden planks that passed for a floor, many of them broken or even missing. Bare white walls, with off-color blotches that showed where filthy words had been whitewashed out. There was an exposed sink with a cracked mirror overhead, a toilet in a tiny dark closet. That was what passed for the bathroom.

He saw a chair but no table. Where was a man supposed to eat? There was a bed; he supposed he should be grateful for small mercies. But if there had ever been springs in that mattress, he couldn't tell it now, and the tattered bedspread had a smell that made him gag. This was far worse than the place where he'd stayed with his sister, and he'd thought that was a real rat's nest at the time. He'd seen better places than this in the worst parts of Stroud—and that was after the tornado hit.

"I'll take it," Kirk said.

"Well, wonderful," the old man said. "I'm pleased. Truly pleased. I have a good feeling about this."

You wouldn't, you stupid old man, Kirk thought, if you had any idea what I've been up to lately. Or what I'm likely to be doing in the future. But of course, you don't know anything about that. You just see a chance to get your bony little fingers on a quick hundred bucks. That's what you have a good feeling about.

"What's this place like when it gets chilly out?" Kirk asked. This was more than just an academic question. A serious cold snap was expected any day now.

"Well, it's cold, naturally. What would you expect?"

"Does the central heating—"

The landlord started shuffling toward the door. "My recommendation would be that you get one of those space heaters. Maybe a bottle of cheap wine. Snuggle up to them when night falls. Keep you good and warm." The man turned slightly and actually winked. "And it'll be a hell of a lot cheaper than a woman, right? Although, on this street, not by much."

Sleazy old goat, Kirk thought bitterly. What did he mean by that? What was he suggesting? Why would he want that kind of woman? Or was he implying that he wouldn't want any kind of woman? Was that it?

All of a sudden, Kirk hated the man. He flashed on that book they'd made him read in high school—*Crime and Punishment*, right? Took damn near forever for Kirk to finish that one. Boring book, but the guy in it had the right idea. If this landlord didn't disappear soon, he was going to end up dead, too.

"If I need anything, who should I call?" Kirk asked.

The old man shrugged his spindly shoulders. "God?" He flashed a withered smile, then closed the door behind him.

Wiseass, Kirk thought, as the old man thankfully disappeared from his sight. First the comment about women, then the smart remark about God. Did the decrepit creep have any idea what had happened? Did he know that God had stopped answering Kirk's prayers?

He threw his backpack onto the floor, causing a crash that threatened to break through the floorboards. He collapsed on the stone-hard bed, suddenly exhausted. He didn't know when it had happened, exactly. He'd been praying all his life, ever since he first learned how back in that one-room white-boarded Baptist church in Stroud. And God had always answered in prayers. Not in words, like some weird Oral Roberts-like message from beyond. But Kirk had always had the sense that someone was listening, that even if he didn't always get everything he wanted, his voice was still being heard.

But not any longer. God had closed the door on him. He was certain of it.

And who could blame Him? He had done a horrible, nasty thing. But surely God could see what he was up against, how he was being pulled one way and the other. Surely God could see some cause for forgiveness. Surely—

He closed his eyes. Sweat oozed from his pores. He could feel his pulse throbbing in his temples. He had sinned. Horribly so. Unforgivably so. God would never smile down on him again. He was an outcast. He was Cain in the land of Nod. Worse, really. Even Cain had never—

But couldn't God see how he had been tempted? How could any human being resist? At first, he thought God had forgiven him. He allowed Kirk's sister to be acquitted, right? Surely that was a sign of God's grace. Except now it was starting up all over again. If what he'd heard on the radio was true, she might not be safe after all. And neither was he. God was sending His demons to torment him. He couldn't sleep, he couldn't eat.

And he couldn't pray. He could try, but no one was listening. And what was the point of praying to a god who wouldn't hear?

Kirk flung himself out of the bed, collapsing on the floor.

He pounded his fist on the floorboards, sending a trembling throughout the small apartment. He had to get out of here, had to do something. He didn't know what, but he had to try something to wrench himself free of this pervasive guilt. He couldn't live with this, not much longer. He would rather die than live with this.

He pushed himself to his feet, scrounging for his coat. Surely there were answers somewhere, out on the street. Surely he could find some form of redemption. Some kind of relief, some peace of mind. He couldn't go on living like this, he just couldn't.

But if God wouldn't forgive him, who would?

* 6 *

Ben heard her footsteps long before she arrived; there were no secrets on a metal cage floor. He almost smiled with recognition of the quick, light sensible heels, tapping like Morse Code as she scurried down the passage. He'd been hearing that for years now. He thought he should sit up, push himself off the cot, greet her appropriately. But somehow that seemed like more work than he could manage at the moment.

"Ben?" He heard Christina's voice the instant the guard admitted her through the cell door. "Ben! What happened to you?"

He could tell she was beside him now. He tried to open his eyes—but only one of them worked.

A moment later, he felt her soft cool hand behind his neck. "Ben! Talk to me. Are you all right?"

His lips felt dry and cracked, probably because they were. His voice crackled when he tried to speak. "I'm fine."

"The hell you are. You've got a shiner the size of Kilimanjaro. Who did this to you?"

"I don't exactly know."

"By God, this is police brutality. I'll haul their butts up on charges. I can't believe this crap still goes on in this day and age. In a big city."

Ben shook his head, although the stiffness of his neck made it difficult. "It wasn't the police. Not the eye, anyway."

"Then who was it?"

"Another inmate. Temporarily lodged in my cell. I didn't get his name."

"What a coincidence. I bet they put him up to it."

"Likely." Braced by Christina's hand, Ben managed to pull himself upright. He was immediately embarrassed, remembering that he was wearing the formless bright orange coveralls. "But you'll never prove it."

"What about the cops? Have they been after you?"

"Well . . ."

"Ben! You have to file a complaint."

"C'mon, Christina. You've been around long enough to know how stupid that would be. Sad truth is, inmates get punched up in jail all the time. And if they make a fuss, they get an additional charge of assaulting an officer. 'I hated to hurt him, your honor, but it was self-defense.' " He glanced over his shoulder. "By the way, the inmates on either side of us are probably informants, so be careful what you say. The attorney-client privilege won't extend to them."

"Ben, I want the name of everyone who hit you."

He shook his head. "We've got more important things to investigate at the moment. By the way, how did you get in here? Shouldn't we be meeting in a visitor room?"

"That would take too long. I wanted to see you immediately. And I know one of the guards on duty . . ."

"Of course you do. You know everyone. So—do you have any idea what the hell is going on?"

"I know a little. I called the D.A."

That was his Christina. Straight to the top. "You mean the actual D.A.? Not an assistant?"

"Right. Woke LaBelle up in the middle of the night. Unfortunately, he didn't know much more than I did."

"What was the basis for the search warrant?"

"Anonymous tip."

"How convenient. Tape recording?"

"No. It didn't come over the phone. But Sergeant Matthews got it from a reliable source."

"Of course."

"Whom he refuses to name. Informant privilege."

"Naturally. He planned it out perfectly."

"Yeah. Except I still have two questions. How did the knife get in your file cabinet? And if it really is the murder weapon—where did it come from?" She touched her fingers lightly to the swollen blue-black bulge beneath Ben's left eye. "Is it tender?"

"Ouch!" He pulled away from her. "What do you think?"

"Sorry. I could get an ice pack . . ."

"Don't. I'd rather it was nice and dramatic when we appear before Judge Collier for the arraignment."

"But the police will deny—"

"Collier isn't an idiot."

"Are you going to be okay?" Christina asked. "I mean—really. You seem . . . subdued." She paused a moment. "Did they work you over?"

Ben nodded. "Like you wouldn't believe. They didn't miss a trick."

"Oh, Ben. I'm so sorry." She wrapped her arms around him. "It must've been awful."

"Not a Hallmark moment, for sure." She felt good against him. Soft but firm. Warm. "But I'm okay. Or would be if I got some sleep."

"You poor thing."

"Yeah, yeah. So did you find Mike? I'm sure he can sort this out."

"Mike is gone."

"Where the hell is he?"

"I don't know."

"We have to find out."

"That's a no go. Penelope says he's undercover. No one will tell me any more."

"Damn." Ben clenched his teeth. "He said he was leaving town for some new case. What lousy timing."

"I don't think it's a coincidence."

He jerked his head up. "What do you mean?"

"The cops show up to railroad you the second your close friend on the force goes under? That can't be just bad luck. They waited till he was gone."

Ben didn't like the idea at all, but he had to admit she was probably right. This was planned. And planned very well.

"So what's their goal here? What's the charge?"

"So far they've only charged you with concealing evidence. Aiding and abetting. Obstructing justice."

Ben pondered a moment. "That tells me they still think Keri is guilty. They're just using me to get to her."

"Probably."

"They'll never be able to make the concealment rap stick."

"I agree. I think the judge will kick it as soon as he learns you were the defendant's—and chief suspect's—attorney. I've done a little research." She popped open her brand-spanking-new briefcase and revealed a stack of photocopied cases so thick it barely fit inside.

Nothing like having a new grad on the team, Ben mused. Bundles of energy. "What's the aiding and abetting about?"

"Presumably they'll argue you helped Keri commit the crime. Or helped her cover it up."

"I suppose you could argue that, in a way, every defense attorney representing a guilty defendant helps them cover it up.

But I don't think they can make that a crime. Not without doing some serious damage to the Constitution."

"Ben . . . what you said. About Keri. Are you telling me she was . . ."

"Guilty? No. She convinced me she was innocent a long time ago. Not that it matters. Even guilty people are entitled to lawyers."

"But still . . ."

"Yeah." He stretched, straining his aching muscles. "Keri always said she'd been framed. That someone was out to get her. Which at the time I thought a trifle paranoid. Now I'm not so sure." He pondered a moment. "These charges against me are just preliminary. A device. They'll use this to reopen the case against Keri."

"What about double jeopardy?"

"There are ways around double jeopardy protection. And one of the best is to allege fraud on the part of the defendant. Or the defendant's lawyer."

"Like hiding key evidence in his file cabinet?"

"Exactly." The more he said it aloud, the more he realized it must be true. "That's what they're after. It's Keri they want."

"Maybe so," Christina said. "But I wouldn't discount anything. I hate to be the one to tell you, Ben, but every cop I talked to, everyone I tried to interview—they were all hostile. They loved Joe McNaughton, and they couldn't handle the verdict. I think some of these people are willing to do just about anything to get Keri convicted." She paused, then added, "And to teach you a lesson."

Ben's lip turned up at the edge. "I've already learned a lesson. But I'm not going to let them railroad my client."

"Which leads to my next important question." She pushed herself to her feet and began to pace. Ben marveled at how professional, how—*lawyerly* she looked. Snappy two-piece suit, briefcase, pinned-up hair, serious expression. She'd been out of school for less than twenty-four hours, but she already had the part down cold. "Whom do you want to represent you?"

Ben looked surprised. "What do you mean? I already have a lawyer. You."

"I'm serious, Ben."

"So am I."

"Ben, I just got my diploma. I haven't even passed the bar."

"You've already taken the multistate, haven't you? We'll get you a Rule 9 temporary permit."

"Ben, I'm not ready for this."

"You said you wanted to be tested. Tested by fire, in the courtroom. Right? Well, I think this qualifies."

"Ben—this is serious. These are major charges."

"I think they'll go away at the arraignment."

"But what if you're wrong?"

"If I'm wrong, we'll revisit the question. But as you know, I'm never wrong."

She rolled her eyes. "Oh, right. Only every other time."

"The truth is"—he reached out tentatively—"I don't want another attorney. I trust *you*."

Christina looked away. "This is crazy."

Ben laid back down on the cot. "I don't think so."

"Ben—I have to tell you the truth. I'm worried about you."

"Well, don't be. I'm not." Which was a major lie. The police were trying to frame him, he'd been mistreated and abused, and the one friend who might be able to help was not to be found. He knew all too well what the police could do. He'd seen it happen to his clients; had heard too many horror stories related by Mike. The truth—and the main reason Ben hadn't been able to sleep—was that he was scared to death.

But there was no point in letting Christina know that. "So go prep for the arraignment, slugger. My body's aching and I need a nap."

"Sure I can't bring you an ice pack?"

He closed his eyes. "I'm sure."

Christina crouched beside him. "I have something for you."

"What would that be?"

She leaned across and touched her lips lightly to his swollen eye. "All better?"

"All better," he whispered.

Her voice softened a bit. "Did I mention that you look very sexy in orange?"

For the first time in their conversation, he actually smiled. "Get out of here."

* 7 *

The very fact that Ben was being taken to court for his arraignment told him that this was not being handled like a run-of-the-mill case. These days, in Tulsa County, most defendants appeared for their arraignments by closed-circuit television from the jailhouse—what the cons called TV Court. It was simpler in many respects; it saved the sheriff's office the trouble and risk involved in hauling defendants out of the jail and across the plaza to the courtroom just so they could make a two-minute appearance that didn't amount to anything anyway. Arraignments were a vestigial holdover from the Constitution; they prevented arrestees from languishing in jail indefinitely, but didn't accomplish much else.

The second clue Ben received that this was not your garden-variety arraignment was that it was being handled for the prosecution by Nick Dexter—the same man who had tried Keri Dalcanton. Arraignments were typically handled by D.A. interns—law students, basically—which was another sign of how important everyone thought they were.

Except today. Today everything was different.

"The next case on the docket is *State versus Kincaid*." Judge Collier ripped through his docket like a speed reader; his only goal was to conclude before lunch. "Is this the defendant?"

"Yes, sir," Ben said, approaching the bench. He knew the judge recognized him. Ben had appeared before this judge on many previous occasions, although never as the defendant, and never in vivid orange coveralls.

"Are you represented by counsel?" Collier was young for a judge, only a few years older than Ben. He had dark hair and preppie eyeglasses; his skin was white to the point of being nearly translucent.

"Yes, sir, I am."

Christina stepped forward. "Christina McCall for the defense, your honor."

Collier peered through his glasses. "I don't believe I know you, Ms. McCall. Have you appeared before this court before?"

"No, sir. This is my first time." As a lawyer, anyway. She left out the part about having just graduated from law school yesterday.

The judge scrutinized her carefully, creating an atypical pause in the otherwise rushed proceeding. Ben knew what he was thinking. These were serious charges, and he was probably contemplating whether to advise the defendant that he might want to seek a more experienced attorney. Collier used to be a defense attorney himself; this is an issue he would care about.

But he apparently decided it was none of his business. "Very well. Mr. Kincaid, you've been charged with concealing evidence, aiding and abetting the commission of a felony, and obstruction of justice. Do you understand the charges?"

Ben nodded. "I understand them, yes."

"Will you waive the formal reading?"

It was tempting, given how he was being treated, to force the court to read and the prosecution to endure the painful and lengthy formal information. But his mother didn't raise him to be spiteful. "I'll waive."

"May I assume you wish to enter a plea of not guilty?"

"Darn tootin'."

"Plea of not guilty will be entered. Preliminary hearing is set for two weeks from now, Thursday at nine thirty A.M. Next case."

"Your honor," Christina cut in, "may I be heard?"

He shook his head. "Learn the rules, Ms. McCall. We don't take argument at the arraignment. I'll entertain motions at the preliminary."

"This is a little different, your honor."

"They always are. Next case."

"Your honor, Mr. Kincaid is an attorney."

"Lawyers have to follow procedure just like everybody else."

"Your honor, I don't think you quite understand." Ben knew Christina was trying the judge's patience, but he had to admire her for hanging in there. "Mr. Kincaid is an attorney charged with aiding and abetting his *client*. It's the defendant they're after. They botched that prosecution, so now they're going after the lawyer. It's all a ploy to reopen the case."

"Are you talking about the Dalcanton case?" Collier's face became stony. By the time he turned to Dexter, his eyes had narrowed significantly. "Is this true?"

Dexter was in his early thirties, handsome, with strong cheekbones that photographed well when he handled high profile cases. But none of that helped him at the moment. "That is not entirely correct, your honor."

Judge Collier drew himself up. "If one word of it is correct, you've got some serious explaining to do."

Dexter moved closer to the bench, an earnest expression on his face. "Your honor, we believe Mr. Kincaid aided and abetted Keri Dalcanton in the commission and cover-up of the violent murder of a police officer."

"So this *is* about the Dalcanton case?"

"Yes. We believe Mr. Kincaid suppressed evidence—"

"This is a crock, your honor," Christina said, interrupting.

"They lost the defendant, so they're going after the lawyer. It's a dog-and-pony show for the appeals court. And a revenge play."

"That's not so," Dexter insisted. "Kincaid's a bona fide defendant in his own right."

"Based on his alleged assistance to his client?" the judge asked.

"That's right."

"Who you were unable to convict."

"That's . . . right."

"Mr. Dexter, this does not look good." Collier appeared to have forgotten all about the other ten thousand cases on his docket. "How can you charge a defense attorney with concealing evidence against his own client? A defense attorney has no obligation to come forward with evidence against his client. To the contrary, he has an obligation to zealously defend and protect his client."

Ben nodded silently. Bad break for the D.A., drawing a former defense attorney for the arraignment judge. Collier knew the score.

"But your honor, no attorney has the right to conceal physical evidence."

"True. But the attorney can receive items in trust, can't he?"

"Well, yes, but he can't knowingly conceal—"

"Did the prosecution ever request that Mr. Kincaid turn over items presented to him by his client in trust?"

"Well, no. We didn't know—"

"Do you have affirmative evidence demonstrating that he was aware he was in possession of relevant evidence?"

"Well, no, but—"

"And what's this about aiding and abetting? How can we charge him with aiding and abetting someone you couldn't convict in the first place?"

Dexter's chiseled cheekbones began looking a trifle puffy. "Your honor, it's an independent charge. Before a different judge and a different jury, we could have a different result."

"So this man could be convicted for aiding and abetting his own client, who wasn't convicted herself? Mr. Dexter, this stinks to high heaven."

"It gets worse, your honor," Christina said, seizing her opportunity. "Certain police officers have been out to get Mr. Kincaid since he won the Dalcanton case. The search of his office was based on an anonymous tip, and they almost immediately turned up a knife no one had ever seen before. Worse, in the twelve hours Mr. Kincaid has been in custody, he's been intentionally mistreated and abused."

"Now that's a lie," Dexter barked.

"Look at his face!" Christina shot back. "Do you think he got that shiner by accident? Does that happen to every defendant who comes before this court?"

Collier's expression was grave. "Mr. Dexter, I do not like what I'm hearing."

"Your honor," Dexter pleaded, "I can assure you this prosecution is on the up-and-up."

"Frankly, Mr. Dexter, right now your assurances aren't worth a hill of beans. I can't let you go around locking up the defense attorney every time you lose a case."

"That isn't what this is about. I—"

"If you can't give me some independent charge against this man—something that doesn't hinge on your prior failed prosecution—I'm going to bounce him."

Dexter bit down on his lower lip. He glanced quickly at the back of the courtroom, then squared his jaw and addressed the judge. "Very well, your honor. I'd like to amend the charges against Mr. Kincaid in the information."

"To what?"

Dexter took a deep breath before answering. "Murder. In the first degree."

* 8 *

Ben and Christina reacted simultaneously. *"What?"*

The judge was barely a second later. "Mr. Dexter, what are you playing at?"

Dexter held up his hands. "I'm not playing, your honor. You wanted an independent charge; you got one. Forget about Keri Dalcanton. We'll go against Kincaid for murder one. The murder of Joe McNaughton."

Judge Collier was not placated. "Mr. Dexter, these are serious charges. If you file these without sufficient grounds—"

"Your honor, we found the murder weapon in his file cabinet. If Keri Dalcanton didn't do it, the only logical conclusion is that he did."

"Your honor," Christina said, "what possible motive could Mr. Kincaid have to kill that police officer? He didn't even know the man."

"A good question," the judge said. "Got an answer, Mr. Dexter?"

"We don't have to provide motive at the arraignment," Dexter said, squirming.

"True enough," the judge said, shaking his head.

"Frankly," Dexter continued, "we don't have to provide anything at this time, except the charge. So consider him charged."

"With murder?" Christina leaned across the bench. "Your honor, this is an outrage!"

"I'll take that as a plea of not guilty."

69

"And that's not all. We move to dismiss, your honor."

"Can't say that I'm surprised. But we can't handle that here. File your papers and bring it up at the preliminary."

"Your honor, they've brought frivolous murder charges just to perpetuate this petty vendetta against—"

"At the preliminary, Ms. McCall. There's nothing I can do here. And given the severity of the charge, I can't grant bail, either." The judge rapped his gavel. "Next case. And this time, I mean it!"

By the time they got outside the courtroom, the press had arrived in force. Ben didn't know who had tipped them, but as he was marched down the corridor toward the jail, the flashbulbs were flying.

"Mr. Kincaid! Comment?"

"Was it you all along?"

"Is it true you're Keri Dalcanton's lover? That she seduced you and made you kill Joe McNaughton?"

Times like these, the Fifth Amendment was Ben's favorite part of the whole creaky document. He kept his mouth buttoned for the whole ten-minute walk. He tried to keep his expression amiable and calm; the rest of the world didn't need to know that he was worried. Seriously worried. Because it now appeared that the D.A.'s office was as much a part of this as the police. And that they were willing to do almost anything to bring down Keri Dalcanton. And him.

Almost anything.

Nick Dexter was moving too fast as he hurried down the courtroom corridor. The Kincaid hearing had taken five times as long as they anticipated and had not gone at all as planned. There were people back at the office who would be very anxious to hear what had transpired; he didn't want to disappoint them by being late on top of everything else. But because he was hurrying, he was totally thrown off-balance when an arm suddenly shot out of one of the jury deliberation rooms and wrapped itself around his throat.

Dexter went crashing down toward the white marble tile floor. "What in the—"

He looked up and saw that pal of Kincaid's—the one with all the red hair—hovering over him.

"Where's the fire, Nick?"

Dexter stumbled back to his feet and brushed himself off. "What the hell do you think you're doing?"

"Getting your attention," Christina replied. "You seem to be in a big hurry. Got to report in to your masters?"

"I don't know what you mean."

"I'll bet you don't. Look, Nick, we need to talk."

His lip almost curled. "Make an appointment."

"Now. Before you report in to whoever is orchestrating this frame."

"You're in deep denial, Ms. McCall. Can't face up to the fact that your boss is scum."

Her face tightened. "I've known Ben Kincaid for years and I know damn well he wouldn't hide evidence, much less the murder weapon. Which leads me to the inescapable conclusion that the knife was planted. So get inside this room and talk."

"I don't take orders from some legal assistant."

Christina told herself she should count to ten, but she never made it past two. She grabbed him by the collar, slung him into the deliberation room, and slammed the door behind them.

"Listen to me, you twerp, and listen up good. I've got a diploma that looks just like yours, and I don't plan to take any grief because I was out busting my butt making a living while you were going to frat parties and panty raids. You're screwing around with two lives here—my client's and my friend's. So you damn well better be able to explain yourself."

"I don't have to tell you anything. I'm leaving."

It was possible, Christina mused, that she had not gotten this conference off to a terrific start. She *was* sometimes frustrated by Ben's mild, almost passive approach to these types of disputes—but she also knew that he usually got results. She, on the other hand, wasn't getting anywhere.

"Look," she said, blocking his exit. "Could we calm down and talk? Just for five minutes?"

Dexter somewhat reluctantly fell into a chair. "Okay, talk."

"Why are you bringing murder charges against Ben? You know damn well he didn't murder anyone."

"I don't know anything of the kind."

"Give me a break. He had no motive. He didn't even know McNaughton. Why do you want him?"

Dexter steepled his fingers, as if deep in thought. Christina could almost see the wheels churning, trying to decide how much he could safely say. "We don't. Not really."

"It's Keri Dalcanton you want. You're trying to reopen the case by claiming fraudulent concealment."

Dexter tilted his head to one side. "I'm not at liberty to discuss the prosecution strategy. Which will not be determined by me, at any rate."

"But that's the plan, right?"

"The thought has occurred to us."

"This is sleazy, Nick. Going after the defense attorney to get to the defendant. It stinks."

"Don't get all high-and-mighty with me. Don't you normally go after the prosecutors and the police when you're trying to get someone off?"

"That's different."

"Not to me it isn't."

"You know you can't make this murder charge stick."

"That's really not relevant. So long as people know the charges have been made."

"So you're just trying to attract media attention. Stir up public outrage. Get the press swarming. I suppose if you can create a big enough stink about this murder weapon in the file cabinet, the appeals court will almost have to grant your appeal and send the Dalcanton case back to the trial court."

Dexter smiled and spread wide his hands.

"Dismiss the charges against Ben, Nick."

"I'm afraid I can't do that."

"If you go forward, after we get the charges dismissed, we'll slap the city with the biggest civil suit you've ever seen."

"The answer is no."

"Why not? You've already done what you set out to do."

"I don't know that. And I have no objection to keeping your boss dangling for a good long while. Who knows—maybe we'll get two murder convictions."

"That's not acceptable, Nick. Ben shouldn't have to sit around in lockup while you play games with the appeals court. Cut him loose."

Dexter rose. "How can I get through to you? No!"

"Nick—"

"Your five minutes are up. I'm out of here."

Christina did not move away from the door. "Nick, you will dismiss the charges against Ben. If you don't, I'm calling a press conference. This afternoon."

"What a coincidence. I've already called a press conference. This afternoon."

"Yeah. But you won't like what I say at mine. I'll talk turkey; I'll expose your whole dirty game."

"You'll sound like a sleazy lawyer defending another sleazy lawyer who tried to put a vicious murderer back on the street."

"You'll sound like a manipulative prosecutor so desperate to compensate for the case you screwed up that you're willing to put innocent people behind bars."

Dexter's face tightened. "If you say anything like that, I'll file charges with the bar committee. I'll get your pretty little butt sanctioned."

On the job twenty-four hours, Christina thought, and people were already threatening to sanction her. Cool! "Nick, let me tell you something. I'm basically a very calm, collected woman. But you're starting to make me mad. And you know what? You won't like me when I'm mad." She leaned into his face. "Last warning, Nick. Dismiss the charges against Ben."

Dexter pushed past her and opened the door. "I'll pass along your recommendation to my superiors. Don't hold your breath."

A moment later he was gone.

* 9 *

Ben paced from one end to the other of the small visitor room. In truth, the worst aspect of being locked up was not the humiliation, or the squalor, or the confinement, or the company, or even the grotesque living conditions. The worst part of it was the stultifying boredom. There was absolutely nothing to do. So far, he'd been unsuccessful at getting any books, or any of his briefs, or anything else that could possibly divert him for a minute or two. Basically, all he could do was sit and wait. Small wonder people came out of prison embittered for life—and brain-dead. He'd rather be tortured and released than sit staring at these gray walls any longer.

Which explained why cons were so keen to get visitors. He only hoped Christina had some good news for him. Because he couldn't take this much longer.

He heard the click of the locked door outside which told him the guards were bringing in his visitor. "About time, Christina. I've been—"

He stopped short. It wasn't Christina. The woman who followed the guard into the cell was small and very well proportioned, with a glistening complexion and platinum blond hair that reached well below the shoulder blades.

"Keri! What are you doing here?"

Keri Dalcanton walked directly to him and clasped both his hands. "I had to come, Ben. I'm so sorry."

The guard looked particularly surly, and Ben could guess why. He knew who the visitor was. "I'll be just outside," he growled, closing the door behind him.

"Did they give you any trouble?" Ben asked.

Keri's eyes gave him the answer, but at the same time, they showed a steely toughness he had to admire. "What do you think?"

"Keri, you shouldn't have come."

"I had to, Ben. This is all my fault." She wrapped her arms around him and laid her head on his chest. "I'm so sorry."

"Don't be ridiculous." After a moment, he placed his hand gently on the back of her neck. "You're not the one who planted that knife in my file cabinet."

"But it's still my fault. This only happened because of me. It's me they want. And now, since they can't get me, they're going after you."

Ben didn't say anything, although that was pretty much his evaluation of the situation, too.

"Is there anything I can do, Ben?" She pressed all the closer.

"Keri, who might want to frame you—or me—for this murder?"

"I've told you already. Andrea McNaughton. You saw how she acted in the courtroom. And Joe's police buddies. They made up their minds I was guilty ten seconds after the body was found."

"Why?"

"Because they didn't approve of me. I worked in a strip joint. I wasn't one of the gang. I wasn't the nice housewife at home. I was the home wrecker. Never mind that Joe never told me he was married—until he used it as an excuse to break it off with me. Never mind that I only met Joe because he and his sanctimonious buddies came to the club to get drunk and shout obscenities at naked women. After he was killed, in such a horrible way, getting me became a crusade for them."

"I'm sure this has been hard for McNaughton's widow. Finding out about her husband's"—he stopped before he got to the word "affair"—"unfaithfulness. And having it exposed so publicly."

"I think she was the one who got the police worked up. At least initially."

"You think she wanted them to go after you?"

"Of course. What better revenge could there be against the 'other woman' than to sic a pack of ravenous cops—and the D.A.—on her trail? She hates me, Ben. She'll do anything to cause me pain."

A sobering thought. "Do you have any idea where that knife came from?"

Her shoulders heaved. "How could I? Knives are everywhere."

"I know. But it did have caked blood on it."

"Joe's blood?"

"I don't know yet. But I expect we both will soon."

"I just had a horrible thought. If that knife really is the murder weapon—and the police were able to produce it—what does that tell you?"

Ben looked at her wordlessly.

"Ben—is it possible they have another reason for wanting to frame me? At least some of them?"

"You mean—" Ben's brain raced a thousand miles a minute. He had never even considered that possibility. But it made perfect sense. It explained everything—even this current irrational desire to persecute and prosecute him. "But why would cops want to take out Joe? He was their friend. Their partner."

"That's what they say. But that doesn't necessarily mean it's true."

"Didn't you tell me Joe was working on a mob investigation just before he was killed?"

"That's right. He didn't like to talk about his work much—at least not when he was with me—but he told me a little. Said he was investigating Tony Catrona. Digging around in his past. Seeing what he could come up with."

Ben frowned. If only half the rumors he'd heard over the years were true, Catrona was a seriously bad news character. He'd swept into Oklahoma with the onset of pari-mutuel betting, but reportedly had expanded his operations well beyond the horse races—into drugs, prostitution, and murder for hire.

"Is it possible this could've been a mob hit?"

Keri shivered; Ben could feel her trembling softness against his chest. "I don't know. I don't even want to think about it. Poor Joe."

Poor Joe indeed. It seemed incredible—but it might explain some of the more extreme aspects of the killing. Like the humiliating public manner in which the body was strung up. And the severed penis in the mouth. Wasn't that something the mob did to squealers? People who talked too much? Or perhaps people they didn't want to talk at all.

"You've done so much for me," Keri said. "Back when this nightmare began, you were the only one who believed me. You were the only one who could get past the fact that I worked in a strip bar and see that I wasn't a murderer. And you were the only one who would help me. You were so kind. All my heart and—and—my love—for you—" She hugged him tighter. Ben could feel her heartbeat. "And now to see how they're making you pay for your kindness. I just can't stand it. Isn't there something I can do?"

"I don't think so. My legal—" Ben stopped himself. "My partner is working on the case. I'm hoping she'll be able to get these trumped-up charges dismissed."

"Christina?" He felt Keri's body stiffen slightly. "Has she graduated?"

"Yes. With flying colors."

"But—she's new, right? Maybe she should have co-counsel. Someone with more experience."

"She'll do fine. I trust her completely."

Keri tilted her head back. Ben could see her face was red and streaked with tears. "Maybe I should just confess. Tell them what they want. Tell them I killed Joe."

"Please don't do that."

"Why not? They'd have to let you go. And you said I can't be prosecuted again."

"I'm not sure they would let me go. They might try me as an accessory before or after the fact. And I'm not so sure about the last part, either."

"What?"

He hesitated. "Keri, I think they're going to try to use the discovery of the knife as a means of reopening the case against you. They'll claim one or both of us committed fraud—hid the murder weapon. They'll try to get a new trial. In fact, they're probably already at the Court of Appeals working on it."

Keri's eyes widened. The horror on her face was unmistakable. "But you told me about double jeopardy. You said that was impossible—"

Ben's chin lowered. "I know. I was wrong."

"You mean—it could start all over again? The whole— the—the trial and the publicity and—" Her voice cracked. "Oh, God, Ben. God. I don't think I could take that. I—I don't think I could survive it."

Ben tried to comfort her. "You'll survive it, Keri. You're tough." He felt her tears trickling onto his arm. "We'll survive it together."

"If—if you say so."

"I do. You didn't commit this crime. And I'm not going to let them railroad you—or me. We'll fight these people—and we'll win." He placed his thumb under her chin and tilted it upward. "I won't let them continue persecuting you, destroying your life. I won't allow it. And that's a promise."

* 10 *

"So," Christina said, "you've got the general picture?"

"I guess," her friend Karen said, scanning the seemingly endless pages bound in a loose-leaf notebook. "How do you keep track of all this stuff?"

"Comes with the territory," Christina replied. "Lawyers never forget anything." And she would know, of course, having been a lawyer now for—what? A day and a half?

Karen was a petite woman with a dress size that made Christina burn with envy. She was a little taller than Christina, but then, who wasn't? She wore her auburn hair in a bouncy blunt cut just above her shoulders. "Since you're the one with the steel-trap brain, why don't you do this yourself?"

"I can't. This is a press conference. I'm not a member of the press." Christina tossed back her strawberry-blond mane. "And there is the tiny matter of the ethical rules regarding pending criminal matters. Besides, it would just seem self-serving, coming from the attorney for the defense. But when *you* start asking the hard questions, people will listen."

Karen hesitated. "I don't know about this."

"Come on, Karen. You know Ben isn't a murderer. Hasn't he always shot straight with you?"

"Yes, he has. But I'm a journalist. I have to be impartial."

"You can be impartial. You can be impartially hard on everyone. I'm just suggesting one possible way of doing that."

"Well . . . I suppose that's true." She looked up and pointed a finger. "But you owe me, girlfriend."

"No way. We're even. I'm the one who leaked you the goods on the Barrett case, remember?"

"That was years ago."

Christina tapped the side of her head. "Lawyers never forget anything."

Christina took an unobtrusive seat on a bench in the back of the courtroom corridor where Nick Dexter was holding his press conference. She wanted to watch, but she didn't want to be noticed. It was fun to watch other people squirm—not so fun to do the squirming yourself.

In a matter of moments, reporters from all the local networks crowded just beyond the podium, each with two or three crewpersons huddled close behind with their minicams and boom microphones. Several print journalists were there, too, even though there was only one daily newspaper in Tulsa these days. Christina wondered if they were beginning to attract some regional or even national coverage. The newspaper reporters looked decidedly low-tech, scribbling away in their little notepads or holding up tape recorders, while their TV cousins worked in a swirl of electrical cords and blinking lights.

After a fashionable delay, Dexter walked briskly out of the clerk's office, two files tucked under his arm and a serious expression on his face. He looked the very picture of the determined young man on the move. Christina hoped he would slip and fall on his face.

But of course, he didn't. "Ladies and gentlemen, I have a brief statement. Then I'll take questions." He glanced down at his prepared text, never once breaking his solemn expression. "Two days ago, the Tulsa Police Department received reliable information leading them to believe that one Benjamin Jonah Kincaid, a Tulsa attorney, aided Keri Dalcanton not only in her successful evasion of criminal justice but also in the crime itself. Pursuant to a search warrant"—he glanced up here—"legally obtained pursuant to a proper showing of probable cause, a search of Kincaid's law office was conducted. During the search, a police officer found, hidden in a file cabinet, a bloodstained knife. Preliminary forensic reports indicate that the knife is the murder weapon, or one of them, that was used to kill career police officer Joe McNaughton. We understandably took Kincaid into custody and charged him. At the same time, we filed papers with the Court of Criminal Appeals asking to reopen the Keri Dalcanton prosecution based upon the fraudulent withholding of critical evidence during the first trial."

He swallowed, then peered out into the sea of faces. "Any questions?"

The petite brunette in the front row beat the others to the punch. "Karen Keith, Channel Two. I have a few questions."

Dexter nodded. "Fire away."

"What was the source of the information that led you to Mr. Kincaid?"

"I'm not at liberty to identify the source at this time."

"Was it an anonymous tip?"

"For present purposes, yes."

"If the source of the information is unknown, how could the judge issuing the warrant evaluate its reliability?"

Dexter paused a beat. "I never said the source was unknown. Only that I was not at liberty to reveal it."

Karen glanced down at a piece of paper in her hand. "Then the judge knew the source?"

"The judge was able to evaluate the information's reliability based upon the past reliability of the source." He inhaled deeply. "Is there . . . someone else?"

Another hand shot up in the air. A photogenic brunette with a microphone dangling over her head. "LeAnne Taylor, Channel Six. What charges have you brought against Mr. Kincaid?"

Dexter cleared his throat. "He's been charged with aiding and abetting, accessory after the fact, concealment of evidence, obstruction of justice, and, um, murder."

"Murder?" Taylor said. Dexter noticed that she, too, was reading from a sheet of prepared notes. "I thought the D.A.'s office believed Keri Dalcanton committed the murder?"

"We did. And we do," he added hastily.

"Well, which is it? Kincaid or Dalcanton?"

"We believe the two defendants may have acted . . . in concert."

"You're saying she called her lawyer and asked him to help her kill her boyfriend?"

Dexter coughed. "We're still gathering evidence at this time, Ms. Taylor. We don't necessarily know all the details of the crime yet. It's possible Mr. Kincaid's involvement was after the fact."

"Then he wouldn't actually be a murderer."

"In that scenario, no. But we're still—"

"So you're admitting you've charged someone with murder who might not have done it."

"I said, we're still exploring—"

"Shouldn't you do your exploring before you charge a man with murder?"

Dexter adjusted his tie. "I think I've said about all I have to say on this issue. Are there any other questions?"

"Yes. I have one." This time it was a young man, blond, in the traditional dark suit and white shirt. "Jeff Lea, Channel Eight. Other than the knife, do you have any evidence against Kincaid?"

Dexter mopped his brow. "Doesn't anyone have any questions about Keri Dalcanton?"

In the back, Christina had to force herself not to grin.

Lea shook his head. "We understand the case against her. But we don't understand why you're going after her attorney. Isn't this an infringement of the constitutional right to counsel?"

"If a lawyer commits a crime, he can be charged like anyone else."

"Yes—if he commits a crime. But representing his client isn't committing a crime."

"What is this, cross-ex?" Dexter's sudden outburst caught everyone by surprise, except the cameras, which were still rolling.

Lea kept plowing ahead. "No, this is a press conference. But as far as I've been able to ascertain, Mr. Kincaid has been a professional, respected, even admired member of the legal community."

Dexter made a sneering sound. "He's a defense lawyer."

"Yes, he's a defense lawyer," Lea said, reading from the piece of paper in his hand, "but he's never knowingly helped any client commit a crime or aided them in concealing a crime or their guilt. Why would he start now?"

Even Dexter's charismatic cheekbones couldn't help him now; he was beginning to look as if he were under siege. His face was red and he was sweating profusely. "We believe he may have been engaged in a relationship with his client. Beyond the lawyer-client relationship. More intimate."

"Do you have any evidence to support that accusation?" This from Karen Keith, right in the front row.

"Well, er, we're still gathering—"

"So, basically," LeAnne Taylor said, "you're just trashing his reputation to prop up your dubious case."

"That's not true. It's—it's just—we've only had the knife a few hours." He was floundering, digging himself in deeper with every word he spoke. "*You* did this!" He pointed over the heads of the reporters toward Christina, who was quietly sitting in the rear. "This is *your* fault!"

Christina pressed her fingers against her chest and smiled. Who, little ol' me?

There was a faint coughing noise from the direction of the clerk's office, behind the podium. Dexter whirled around—then jumped almost a foot into the air.

It was the D.A. himself—Thomas LaBelle. He was a sturdy, handsome man, broad-shouldered and slightly graying. His countenance emanated calm, mature strength. And he had a reputation for being unwilling to put up with any unprofessional behavior.

It was from bad to worse for Dexter, and he knew it. His mouth opened, but he couldn't seem to make any words come out.

"Nick, do you mind?" Not waiting for an answer, LaBelle stepped behind the podium, nudging Dexter into the background. "Why don't you return to your office, Nick? I'd like to have a few words with you, as soon as I'm done here."

Dexter obediently skulked away.

LaBelle adjusted the microphone for his greater height. "I've just been on the phone with the team I sent this morning to the Court of Criminal Appeals." In the space of a sentence, LaBelle had transformed the tenor of the press conference. Where before they'd had Dexter's blustering and fumbling, they now had LaBelle's considerable and imposing presence. No one was going to mess around with him. "I'm pleased to announce that the Court of Criminal Appeals has agreed that the apparent concealment of evidence, outside the control of the law-enforcement community, justifies the reopening of the Keri Dalcanton case."

Like the pro he was, LaBelle waited a few moments to allow the audience to absorb what he had said. "There will be a new trial. And we will do everything imaginable to see that justice prevails." He paused, making eye contact, not with the reporters, but with the cameras. "This time, I will handle the trial myself."

One newspaper reporter raised his hand, almost timidly. "What about the charges against Kincaid?"

LaBelle didn't blink. "Given this latest development, the murder charge will be dropped. We believe Keri Dalcanton is the murderer, and we will focus on her. We will continue to prosecute the charges of concealment of evidence and obstruction of justice against Mr. Kincaid. We will not oppose a defense motion to release Mr. Kincaid on bail."

Several more hands shot up, but a stony look from LaBelle was more than sufficient to tell them that, unlike Dexter, he was in charge, and he was not interested in messing around any further with their questions. "Thank you," he said curtly. Then he disappeared.

The crowd dispersed. Christina stopped Karen and LeAnne before they left. "Thanks for the help, girlfriends. Give my best to Jeff, too."

"Our pleasure," LeAnne said. "Nick definitely needed to be reminded of a few things. Like, say, the Constitution."

"Still, thanks."

"Hey," Karen said, "with your coaching, how could we go wrong? Nick should've known better than to take you on. Unless I miss my guess, he's now undergoing a major chewing out—and possibly losing his job."

Christina did not appear regretful. "I told the man he wouldn't like me mad."

Karen jabbed her in the arm. "Wait till Ben finds out. He'll be impressed."

"I'm not sure Ben would approve of this escapade. Even if it does mean he'll be brushing his teeth in his own bathroom tonight."

"Oh, of course he'll approve. Tell me something—have women always run the world, or does it just seem that way?"

Christina and LeAnne spoke as one. "Always."

"There is a problem, though, you know. Now LaBelle is on the case. And he's a million times tougher to beat than Nick Dexter ever thought about being. He's the best prosecutor in the state. Plus, after all this publicity, he'll have his whole reputation—and his chances for reelection—riding on this. He'll marshal all his resources to get a conviction. And his resources are pretty considerable."

Some of the light faded from Christina's eyes. "I know," she said, as she gathered up her briefcase and headed toward the jailhouse. "I know."

* * *

For some reason, Ben thought, as the officers shoved him down the corridor and repeatedly violated his personal space, not to mention his bruised and tender body, the police department did not seem as delighted as he was by the fact that he was being released. His jailer—Joe McNaughton's best friend, at least according to him—was downright surly. His eyes were cold and harsh. Most of the other officers' expressions were about the same.

"Yup," Ben said, as they handed him back his clothes, "I'm going to miss this place. And I'm going to miss all you sweet, good-hearted men. But most of all, I'm going to miss these lovely orange pajamas."

Once he was dressed, they took him to the Property Room and returned the belongings taken from him when he was arrested. *Almost* all of them—his wallet was empty and someone had drawn a mustache on the photo on his driver's license. But he wasn't about to complain.

The jailer personally led him to the exit. Through the window, Ben could see Christina waiting for him.

"Well, that's it then," Ben said, smiling. "Have a good life."

"You forgot something." Ben turned and, in the blink of an eye, the jailer landed a solid punch in the pit of his stomach. Ben doubled over, clutching himself.

"One to remember me by," the jailer whispered. "This isn't over," he added, as he unlocked the heavy steel door. "Not by a long shot. I'll be watching you." He paused, making sure Ben caught the malicious expression in his eyes. "We all will be."

* 11 *

Kirk hit the streets of the city at midnight, an hour when all good respectable folks are tucked away in bed—leaving the territory wide open for everyone neither good nor respectable. Just the place for me, Kirk thought miserably. Walking the streets with the rest of the Great Unwashed. The Unclean. The Unforgiven.

He was making his way down Brady when he saw three street punks collecting in front of a pawnshop. They were all wearing matching jackets. Were they Crips or Bloods? Or some local variant? He couldn't remember. They never had this sort of thing back in Stroud.

He knew they were bad news, no doubt about that. Anyone with half a brain in his head, anyone who didn't want trouble, would give them a wide berth.

Kirk kept walking.

The three punks, teenagers all, were acting casual, talking the talk, punching each other playfully, doing a little hip-hop dance. They were trying to act as if their presence here was strictly coincidence, but Kirk could see through that without any problem. He watched their eyes, gliding over the store-front window, inventorying its contents. He saw one of them position himself behind a wire mesh trash can next to a telephone pole.

Kirk knew what was going down. They were w___ ___ ___ the moment was right, the street was clear. The___ ___ ___ would toss the trash can through the window

Another one would grab the television in the window, and maybe some of the jewelry or whatever else he could stuff into his pockets. And then they'd run like hell. The whole thing would be over in twenty seconds. There was no way they could be caught. No alarm on earth could get the police here in time. The little thieves would get away scot-free. And there was nothing he or anyone else could do about it, not without getting seriously lacerated in the process.

Which did not deter him in the least. This is exactly what I need, Kirk realized. This is what I've been searching for.

I need to be punished.

He sauntered forward, just as he saw the punk in the rear laying his hands on the rim of the trash can. " 'Scuse me, gentlemen," Kirk said, affecting a lighthearted confidence he did not feel. "May I suggest that you give your plan of action a second thought?"

The punk in the middle, the largest and meanest looking of the lot, growled at him. "Get the hell out of here."

"You know," Kirk continued, "property crime is a terrible thing. It causes taxes to go up and strains the economy. It drains money away from valuable state endeavors like schools and libraries."

The kid at the trash can reached into his jacket pocket. A flash of silver emerged. "Last chance, punk. Leave!"

Kirk stared at the switchblade. Clearly, if he were going to make a break for it, this would be the time. If he wanted to escape the punishment.

But what would happen if he did? Would he be turning away from his only hope for redemption? Would he be thwarting God's plan for him? Let this cup pass from me, O Lord . . .

No, he couldn't do that. This was right. This was the path.

"I'm staying," Kirk said. "You're leaving."

The mean one in the middle grunted. "Case you haven't noticed, asswipe, there's three of us, and only one of you." He ͐·-ked his head toward the kid with the knife. "Waste him."

The kid lurched forward, carving a path for himself with his knife. Kirk tumbled backward, trying to get out of the way. The kid kept coming. Kirk moved as fast as he could, till he backed up against a telephone pole.

"You history, shit-for-brains." The kid grinned a little, then lurched forward like a soldier with a bayonet.

At the last possible moment, Kirk whirled out of the way. He did a complete circle, and as he came back around, he raised one leg and kicked the knife out of the kid's hand.

The kid fell down onto the pavement, surprised and knocked loopy by Kirk's slick move. He dove after his knife, but Kirk stopped him with another well-placed kick. He tumbled down, his chin thudding on the concrete. Another kick from Kirk and he was out of commission.

"Da-aamn," the big thug said, watching with a discernible degree of admiration, "this punkass can fight."

"Not two Crips at once," his companion replied. Another flash of silver, and he, too, was armed and ready.

This time, Kirk didn't wait for them to come to him. He knew his only chance was to go on the offensive, to take out the weapon and disable his attackers as quickly as possible. He'd studied martial arts, tae kwon do and kick-boxing especially, but he knew that fancy-schmancy stuff wasn't always helpful in a no-holds-barred street fight.

He launched himself toward the one with the knife, trying to knock it out of his hand. But this kid was ready for him. He moved himself and his knife out of the way, then slashed backward as Kirk flew past.

Kirk cried out in pain. The knife jabbed him just under the ribs. Not fatal, not by a long shot. But still plenty deep enough to hurt.

Kirk whirled around, trying to stop whatever came at him next. It was the big boy this time, reaching out with his hands. Kirk dropped, rolled, and managed to plant a solid punch in the soft part of his stomach. The kid felt it, too.

wasn't enough to slow him down. A split second later, one of those massive fists came crashing into Kirk's face.

He felt the skin over his left eye split. Blood spurted out, obscuring his vision. Another blow caught him between the legs, and he was down on his knees, coughing blood.

From that point on, it was a massacre. The punks kept coming at him, never stopping for a moment. Kirk was helpless, powerless to stop the relentless assault on every part of his body. Heavy boots crashed into his ribs, sending shock waves of pain throughout his body.

He felt something hard and metallic smash down on his head, knocking him flat against the sidewalk. After that, he couldn't feel the individual blows, just the horrible unending wave of pain and the salty bitter taste of his own blood.

"C'mon, man," he finally heard one of them say, "he's had it. Let's blow."

"One minute," his friend said.

Kirk felt his head being lifted up by the hair. Through blurred vision, he saw a cold blade sweep across his face. He cried out as, all at once, he experienced pain more intense than anything he had felt in his life, as the flesh of his forehead was rent apart.

"Now we can go," the kid growled. He let Kirk's head thud down onto the pavement.

Kirk heard the footsteps move away from him. The pummeling ended, but he could feel no difference. Cascading ripples of agony coursed through his abused and mutilated body. The blood streaming out of his head wound blinded him.

Have I suffered enough? he wondered. He wanted to cry out but couldn't find the strength. Have I been sufficiently punished? Is it over?

But there was no answer. No matter how much he pleaded, he got no response. No one was listening.

He began to cry, not because he hurt so badly, although he did, but because he realized now that it would make no difference. There would be no relief, no redemption.

He had suffered, but not nearly enough. Not for what he had done.

He still had to be punished.

* 12 *

When Ben arrived at his upstairs apartment, he found two envelopes tucked halfway under the door. Fan mail from some flounder? More likely death threats from an anonymous member of the Tulsa P.D. But when he opened the envelopes, he was pleasantly surprised. They contained the best of all possibilities: money.

Probably not a contribution to my legal defense fund, Ben mused, as he counted through the bills. Of course—today was the last day of the month, wasn't it? Time for all good tenants to pay their rent. And Mr. Perry had done so, promptly and invisibly, as always. The man had been in this building the entire time Ben had, and he had yet to meet him face-to-face. Mr. Perry was sort of like gravity; you knew it had to exist, but you never actually saw it.

The second envelope was not nearly as thick as the first. That would be from Mrs. Singleton, Ben surmised. Sure enough, at the back of the woefully inadequate envelope, there was a note: *I.O.U. $220. Sorry—short this month. Will pay when can.*

Which, of course, would be never. Ben'd been here before. If he could collect all the money that woman owed ﹍﹍ he could probably buy a country club membersh﹍ ﹍﹍ ﹍﹍ understood. Since her husband left her, Mrs. S﹍﹍﹍﹍

been the principal means of support for her twin daughters, one of whom was now in college, and two younger children besides. The room they rented was no bigger than Ben's; where all those people slept he had no idea. Mrs. Singleton worked in a factory assembling bits and pieces of machinery without even knowing what they were, and in the evenings, she took in laundry for extra cash. Making ends meet was a day-to-day struggle for her.

Ben took the I.O.U. and crumpled it in his hand. The last thing on earth this woman needed were worries about the rent. Mental note: If he ended up doing time on this trumped-up obstruction charge, Mrs. Singleton got the vacant room.

He shoved the two envelopes in his pocket and fumbled for his keys. Becoming a landlord had been an eye-opening experience. He had never imagined himself doing anything like this. He'd never imagined himself having investments, much less ones that actually earned money. And certainly not ones that put him in such direct and intimate contact with other people's lives. How was it, he wondered, that a person who was so pathetically poor at interacting with others could ever end up as a landlord—and a lawyer? Both jobs immersed him in other people's problems on a daily basis. Although there was this to say about landlording—it had never gotten him thrown behind bars.

Ben had lived in this upstairs apartment for years before he became the landlord. The original owner, Mrs. Marmelstein, had been a sweet, gentle, elderly woman. A little dotty, yes, even before the Alzheimer's set in, but Ben had loved her dearly. She'd been one of his earliest friends and supporters— in her own way—after he moved to Tulsa. She meant a lot to him. And in her declining years, Ben had been her principal means of support, both emotionally and financially.

Still and all, no one had been more surprised than Ben when Mrs. Marmelstein left him the boardinghouse in her will. All at once (or as long as it took to clear probate, anyway), he was transformed from a barely surviving attorney to a landed property owner. Actually, the impact on his bottom line was slight, but somehow, it made him feel more substantial, just knowing he owned something real and tangible. It had given him a sense of security, of location, that he had not previously known. It felt good.

Of course, Mrs. Marmelstein had known it would. Which was why she left it to him, God bless her sweet-hearted soul.

"Did they let you out, or are you on the lam?"

Ben glanced over his shoulder and spotted Joni Singleton, one of the Singleton twins—the college student and, at present, Ben's part-time handyman.

"I'm out on my own recognizance, pending the preliminary hearing on the charges."

"Oh." She stood for a good long moment before asking: "Is that good?"

"Well, it's better than spending another night in the holding cell." He pushed open his door. "Wanna come in for a minute?"

She considered. "You still got some of those little cheese puff things?"

"Tons."

"Totally rufus." Joni glided into his apartment, her overloaded tool belt bouncing around her slender hips. After several experiments, some more successful than others, her naturally curly brown hair had settled at just below shoulder-length, which, if Ben recalled correctly, was exactly where it had been before she started experimenting. She was an attractive young woman, just turned twenty. "Nothing like junk food to comfort a troubled soul."

Ben walked into the kitchen, retrieved the bag of cheese snacks, and poured them into a bowl. "Something wrong with the house?"

"No big. I fixed that flickering light in the hallway, oiled the creaking back door, and got Mrs. Slotznik's electricity running again."

"Sounds like a successful day in the life of a handyman. Handyperson. Whatever. So what's the problem?"

"It—doesn't have anything to do with work."

"School?"

"Nah. Boring, but bearable. Thanks to you." She gave him a quick wink. "No, it's boy troubles, I'm afraid."

"Something wrong with Boomer?"

"Boomer? Ben, get with it. He's like, three, four boyfriends ago."

"Sorry. I can't keep track."

"My main man these days is Milo."

"Milo?" Ben turned to look at her. "You're joking."

"Why does everyone act like that? It's a perfectly good name."

"Yeah, for a cat."

"Milo is a great guy. Very deep." She dipped her hand into the cheese treats. "He's majoring in poetry."

"Poetry? Can you major in that?"

"Well, literature, then. But he wants to be a poet. I'm not sure he knows how to go about it, though. You're an educated guy, Ben. You've written a book. What do you suggest?"

"I suggest he doesn't give up his day job."

"Ha ha." She twirled a strand of hair absently around her finger.

Ben sat down on the sofa beside her. "I'm sorry. Something's really bothering you, isn't it?"

She flipped her curls from one side to the other. "It's just that, well, Milo—he's really smart, you know what I mean? Like, major major-league smart."

"Ye-es . . ."

"And when he talks to me, he wants to have these deep conversations about symbolism and semi—semi—"

"Semiotics?"

"Yeah. That." Her voice dropped a notch. "I think. So he starts blabbing all this highbrow stuff and it's way over my head and I think, what kind of dummy must he think I am?"

"Joni, listen to me. You have no reason to feel inferior. You're as bright as anyone I know."

"Yeah, maybe, but we both know I wouldn't be in college if it hadn't been for you."

"Joni, all I did—"

"The point is, I can't talk all that hoity-toity talk. I don't know how. And I'm not likely to learn."

"So don't try."

Her face elongated. "What?"

"You heard me. Don't try." He took her firmly by the shoulders. "Joni, you're a smart, resourceful girl. You've got as much right to be at T.U. as anyone. You don't have to imitate other people."

"Yeah, but I can't rattle on about the use of horticulture in Shakespeare."

"And I'm willing to bet Milo couldn't rewire Mrs. Slotznik's electricity."

"Well, you may have something there . . ."

"Joni, I've known you for how many years now?"

"I dunno. Lots."

"Right. And I've never met anyone who knew you who didn't love you. Self included."

She bowed her head. "Aww, shucks."

"You were a great caregiver when I was keeping my nephew Joey. You did a superlative job of caring for Mrs. Marmelstein when she needed it. Heck, now you're taking care of the whole house. You're the most caring person I know. I can promise you Milo will see that. And if by chance he doesn't—then you need to find someone else who will."

Joni slowly raised her head a notch and smiled. "Thanks, Benjy. You're razor."

"Is that good?"

"The best. If there's ever anything I can do for you—"

He raised a finger. "Now that you mention it, I'm having a little trouble with my garbage disposal . . ."

*　　*　　*

Joni went back to her apartment around eight for dinner. She was ravenous, despite having eaten half a bag of cheese puffs, and she had some studying to do for a test tomorrow.

Which left Ben alone. Again.

To keep himself busy, he surfed aimlessly through the channels on his television, looked over some briefs he'd brought home from work, and fed his enormous cat, Giselle. How could he have lived in Tulsa so long and still be so perfectly, stupidly, alone? Imagine being his age, unmarried, living in a small apartment (even if he did own it now), essentially by himself. Sure, he had friends, coworkers, people he cared about and he believed cared about him—Joni, Clayton, Mike, Jones, Loving. And Christina. Especially Christina.

But when he turned out the lights at night, there was no one else around. No one but his spoiled and totally indifferent cat. What kind of a life was that for a grown man?

He would be the first to admit that when it came to socializing, he wasn't exactly gifted. More like the opposite of gifted, whatever that would be. Warmth impaired? Fraternizationally challenged? It wasn't that he didn't try. He made a real effort. But when all was said and done, other people were a mystery to him. He didn't get them. And all too often they didn't get him, either. Which, in a nutshell, was why he was going to bed alone tonight. Again.

He picked up the phone, thinking he would call Christina. But a moment later, he put it down again. What was the point? She probably wasn't at home, and even if she was, he would end up babbling about work or something. It was pointless. Christina didn't need him. She was a whirling dervish. In the past few years, while working full-time as a legal assistant, she'd gone to law school, plus been active in her church, the Norwegian Club, and a host of other civic organizations. She had friends all over the city. She didn't need any lame-o phone calls from him.

Keri? There was definitely something going on there,

every time she looked at him. Every time he felt those gorgeous blue eyes burning into his. It had a profound effect on him, one he'd probably best not even think about.

Or was he just being stupid? Sure, she was his client now, but this case wouldn't last forever. Of course, she was about half his age, but if she didn't mind, why should he?

What a dolt he was, he thought, as he galumphed off to his bedroom to cash it in for the night. As if she would be interested in him. As if anyone would.

Still, as he turned out the lights and stared, eyes open wide, into the darkness, he had to ask himself—Wouldn't it be better than this? Wouldn't anything be better than spending the rest of his life alone in a tiny apartment with a spoiled and—

He felt a furry nuzzling under his chin. Giselle was boring her way into the warm cranny betwixt chest and chin. Which was odd. She didn't usually do that. She didn't normally want anything to do with him at night, preferring her own cushioned wicker bed in the kitchen.

What made her come in here today? Did she sense how he was feeling? Did she know what he was thinking?

Don't be ridiculous, Ben told himself. Next you'll have her herding sheep or singing like Judy Garland. Still . . .

The cat snuggled in closer, and at long last, Ben closed his eyes. Someday, he had to take time out from solving other people's problems and fix his own life. After all, he thought (and these were the last thoughts he had before he drifted away), he didn't want to spend the entire rest of his life in a small apartment with a spoiled and, well, perhaps not totally indifferent cat.

* 13 *

Jones and Paula were squabbling over a chair.

"C'mon, punkin," Jones said. "I need to check my e-mails."

"E-mail, puddin' pie. The plural doesn't take an *s*." She brushed him back. "I'm on WestLaw. I'm trying to find a precedent for the Dalcanton reversal."

"But I'm expecting a very important message."

"From whom? Some cyberbimbo you met in a chat room?" Jones and Paula had first met in an Internet chat room, and everyone in the office knew it.

"It's about the case, Paula. I sent out several research requests and I need to check for replies."

"I'm not going to log off till I'm done," Paula said. "There's no point in incurring additional charges."

Jones grabbed her chair and swiveled it around. "I'm telling you, I need that chair!"

"And I'm telling you, no!"

Loving emerged from his office. "What in tarnation is goin' on out there?"

Jones coughed. "We're, uh, having a disagreement regarding the, uh, seating arrangements in the exterior office."

"Are you two geeks squabbling over the computer again? Jeez Louise, I'm gonna have to enroll you two in some twelve-step program for people who can't pry themselves away from the Internet."

"I'm trying to finish a report," Paula said huffily. "Ben said he wants it when he comes in."

98

"I'm trying to finish my research," Jones shot back. "Ben's going to want to know what I found, too."

Loving thrust his hands into his pockets. "Did I miss something here? I thought you two were supposed to be madly in love."

Jones and Paula looked at one another dubiously.

"Whoever heard of people madly in love fussin' over some silly gray box? You should be interactin' with each another, not some stupid Web browser."

"You know, he's right." Jones laid his hand gently on Paula's shoulder. "I'm sorry, sweet'ums."

"I'm sorry, too. I don't know what came over me." She stepped out of her chair and hugged him. "You're more important than some silly report."

"And you're more important than my research. I love you, punkin."

"I love you, too, puddin' pie."

"Good God," Loving growled. "I've created a monster."

Ben entered the office. Keri Dalcanton was barely a step behind him.

"Staff meeting," Ben announced, as he passed through the central office. "Conference room one. I want everyone there. Now."

A few minutes later, the entire staff had gathered in the largest conference room in Ben's office. He was still unaccustomed to having so much space and relative luxury at his disposal. After years of toiling away in his dive office downtown, these spacious new Two Warren Place digs seemed luxurious. Of course, compared to the jail cell he'd been residing in of late, his old office seemed luxurious.

Christina was the last to arrive. "How's the jailbird?" she said, smiling. "You're looking great for a guy who just got out of stir. I think I liked you better in orange, though."

Ben nodded graciously, but didn't smile. He couldn't, not with Keri right beside him. Her situation was too grim, and the possibility that she would be back in orange coveralls herself was all too real.

"As you probably already know," Ben began, "Keri's case is active again. The Court of Appeals has sanctioned a new trial. We're appealing that decision, of course, but I don't think our chances are good and in the meantime, the trial proceeds. Given the extraordinary circumstances, we've been able to keep Keri out of jail on bond, but we can't be sure that will last."

Paula shook her head. "This is asinine. She's already been through this once."

"But we have no recourse," Ben said. "We have to get ready. Let's face it—if the prosecutors fail again, they'll look like absolute fools. So they'll be pulling out all the stops to get a conviction."

"And LaBelle is going to handle the trial himself," Christina added.

"Which gives us even more to worry about." Ben turned slightly and saw Keri shrink back into her chair, like a frightened child trying to disappear.

He took her hand and squeezed. "But we're as good as any prosecutors. We've beaten the D.A.'s office before. And we'll do it again."

Keri tried to return his confident smile, but not much emerged. Ben could understand that. He only wished he could be half as confident as he sounded. But he knew LaBelle's reputation—and future political career—would be riding on this case. The eyes of the world would be upon them. The scary truth was, Ben had never had a case in which the prosecutors had shown such a willingness to do anything to get a conviction—or where he had so little to work with.

"The problem is, these charges pending against me, stupid as they are, create a potential conflict of interest. I know some defense attorneys will never represent codefendants because their interests may conflict; imagine the potential conflicts when the defense attorney *is* the codefendant. Keri has volunteered to waive the conflict; just the same, I can't try this case if I'm still a potential defendant. We need to get rid of the charges against me as soon as possible.

"And we're going to have to reopen our investigation," Ben continued. "Last time Keri was charged, we didn't have to put on a case. This time, we almost certainly will." He took a thick file folder out of his briefcase. "It's clear at this point that everything that's happened is more than just coincidence. Someone is actively trying to frame Keri."

"And you," Christina added.

Ben pressed ahead. "We have a couple of possibilities for who could be behind this. Keri thinks some of Joe McNaughton's buddies on the force may be behind it. She thinks it's possible McNaughton's widow, Andrea, may be pulling the strings."

"Did you see that woman's eyes in the courtroom? Even before she attacked Keri?" Jones asked. "I saw how she reacted every time Ben spoke on Keri's behalf. She's nursing a major grudge."

"Enough to make her sic some of Joe's buddies on Keri?" Ben asked.

"Oh yeah. And how much would it take, anyway? We know McNaughton was very popular. He was considered a cop's cop. He helped train half the guys on the force. She wouldn't have to do much to set those wheels in motion. A word would be enough. Maybe just a look."

"That would explain a hell of a lot," Loving said. "Like how the cops knew to search Ben's office. How they found that knife so damn fast."

"Loving," Ben said finally, "you're still in touch with some of the boys in black, aren't you?"

"I know a fair number, yeah."

"Think you could do a little investigating? See what you can find out about all this?"

"Well, Skipper, I don't think anyone's gonna admit that they're plantin' evidence to frame you and Keri."

"I realize that. But you might hear something. Learn something we don't know."

"Doubtful."

"It's always possible someone will talk."

Loving inflated his massive chest, then sighed. "I'll give it the ol' college try, Skipper. But I'm not holdin' my breath."

"That's all I can ask. Unfortunately, that's not the only possibility we need to check out. Keri also thinks it's possible there could be a mob connection."

Jones shot up out of his chair. "Mob connection? Are you kidding?"

" 'Fraid not. Apparently Joe McNaughton was investigating Tony Catrona at the time of his murder."

"Makes sense," Loving mused. "When you think about it, doesn't this whole thing look like a mob hit? Puttin' his body on display and mutilatin' it. That's got mob written all over it."

"Tony Catrona! Mob executions! Jiminy Christmas!" Jones bounced up and down. "How can I say this, Boss? Like—I'm outta here."

"Sit down, Shaggy. This is no time for faint hearts."

"Boss, we're talking about the *mob*. Those people would as soon blow you away as look at you. I'm not having anything to do with them."

"I agree," Paula interjected. "I don't want my puddin' pie messing around with any gangland thugs."

"Pity," Ben said quietly. "This could've been your big chance."

Jones's head turned slowly. "Big chance. Meaning?"

Ben shrugged. "Aren't you the one who's always telling me you want to do more investigating? Get out in the field?"

"Ye-essss . . ."

"Well, this is your opportunity. I need another investigator to figure out what all these people are up to."

"Ben Kincaid!" Paula said. "You should be ashamed of yourself! You're shamelessly manipulating him. *And* you ended a sentence with a preposition."

"It's a simple mathematical equation, Paula. I've got two lines of investigation that need to be pursued immediately. And I've only got one investigator. I need Jones to take up the slack. So, Jones—are you in?"

Jones frowned. "I'm in. Just tell me what to do."

"First, get up to speed on Catrona. Then find out what, if anything, Joe McNaughton had learned about him. Like something that might've gotten him rubbed out. But start your research in the usual ways: books, newspapers, Internet. Don't go anywhere near Catrona without my say-so."

"Yeah, yeah."

"I mean it, Jones. You report to me every day. I don't want you taking any unnecessary risks."

"But you know he will." Paula folded her arms, furious. "Ben, if anything happens, I'll never forgive you."

"Paula, I promise you I won't let him go up against Catrona or any of his associates. I just—"

"Ben, can I say something?" It was the first time Keri had spoken more than a word since the meeting had begun. It was almost startling, hearing that quiet, scared voice emerge from the folds of hair and clothing. "I have a brother."

"I know. Kirk. Met him in the courtroom."

"Yes. But what you don't know is—" She stared down at her hands. "What you don't know is that he's very hotheaded. I mean—sometimes—he just loses control. Especially when it comes to me."

Ben smiled. "It's only natural for him to be protective of his sister."

"There's more. He's—very religious. And he's disappeared. I haven't seen him for months. But when he finds out I'm being threatened again, I'm afraid he might do something . . . crazy."

Oh great, Ben thought. The only thing this case lacked was some whacked-out religious zealot. And now they had it. "We'll try to find him, Keri."

"Thanks." Keri sank back into her chair.

"Christina," Ben continued, "our new legal eagle, will be handling most of the law-related rigmarole. I can promise you the D.A.'s office will be pressing hard, on both cases. They've got a big staff over there, and they'll try to use that to their advantage. They'll be slinging motions and briefs, trying to keep us scrambling so we won't have time to investigate." He glanced her way. "But you're not going to let that happen."

"You bet your sweet bippy I'm not."

"And I have a few . . . miscellaneous matters I want to investigate. So, if there's nothing else—"

"Excuse me, den mother," Christina cut in, "but aren't you forgetting something?"

"Like . . . ?"

"Like, you're also a defendant, remember? You can't be investigating. It will look self-serving, like you're just trying to bail yourself out. Plus you've had way too much publicity. Anybody and everybody related to this case will recognize your face. No one's going to talk to you."

"That may be true, but I—"

"No buts about it, Danger Boy. Like it or not, you'll have to maintain a low profile. You can't run this case. Which means I will."

"Now, Christina, I—"

"Ben, this is the way it has to be and you know it. You can't be running all over town quizzing people when you're a defendant. If for no other reason, the judge might revoke your bail."

A disturbing possibility. "But I still think—"

"Forget it, Ben. You're out and I'm in. I'm taking over."

Ben drew in his chin. "You know, Christina, you should really consider getting some kind of assertiveness training. I hate to see someone with your talents being so mousy and reserved."

"Hardy-har-har. But you know I'm right."

"Sadly enough, I do." He leaned toward Keri. "You're the client; you get to make the final call. Is this all right with you?"

She hesitated for barely a moment, but it was not so brief that it was not noticed by both Ben and Christina. "Of course, Ben. Whatever you think."

"I still plan to handle your case at trial," Ben said. "Unless I'm behind bars at the time."

"I'm glad." She took his hand and squeezed it. She did not let go.

"That's it," Ben said. "Now get to work. We don't have much time. The second any of you turn anything up, I want to hear about it."

After the rest of them departed, Ben drew closer to Keri. Their hands were still linked.

"I'm sure this is all traumatic for you, Keri, and I'm sorry about that. But I want you to know that we're going to do everything possible to help you."

"But Ben—" Her eyes glistened. "You know I never had much money. And what I did have ran out a long time ago."

"It doesn't matter," he reassured her. "We'll figure something out. For the moment, we need to concentrate on getting you acquitted. Again."

She nodded, barely perceptibly. Ben could see she was trying to be brave, but the strain was too much. Tears came unbidden, tumbling forth from those vivid blue eyes.

"Ben . . . I'm so scared."

"I know you are."

"Please—hold me."

Ben drew her in and hugged her tight. The smell of her hair, her skin, overwhelmed him. There was no denying that he found her extremely attractive. Who wouldn't? But it wouldn't be right, not now, not when she was scared and vulnerable. Not while she was still his client.

But when she was so close, when her warm soft body pressed against his, it was impossible not to think about it.

"Don't let go," she whispered. "Please. Don't ever let go."

And had it been left entirely up to Ben, he never would have.

* 14 *

When Loving parked his pickup in the back lot behind Scene of the Crime, he saw two middle-aged men leaning against a lamppost, arms linked around one another's shoulders, obviously experiencing the elevated state of bliss denied to those who choose to remain sober all their lives. One of them was singing an Irish ditty, not especially well, and the other was sloshing lager all over his spiffy blue sport shirt. Both were mercifully ignorant of the existence of a world beyond themselves.

Definitely cops. Loving couldn't be too critical of them, though, even if they were making total asses of themselves. They had a hell of a hard job, in this wonderful world of drug pushers with 1-800 numbers and pimply teenagers bearing submachine guns. They were underpaid and little respected. No, Loving made a point of supporting the police whenever he could. Except, that is, when they were going after the Skipper.

He and Ben might be worlds apart, but that didn't in any way diminish the respect he had for the man. He'd never had so good a job, never been treated so well by a boss, and never felt like the work he was doing was so important. With Ben, every case was a holy crusade, and they were on the side of the angels. But this time, he suspected, he would have a hard time convincing anyone inside the bar of that.

Scene of the Crime was not just a cop bar—it was *the* cop bar. It was the numero uno watering hole for law-enforcement officers throughout the city, and most of the suburbs, for that matter. The top hangout used to be Harry's Squad Room, a place opened by a retired cop at Forty-first and Peoria, but since it shut down, Scene of the Crime got all the action. Anytime you wanted to find a cop who wasn't at home or on duty, Scene of the Crime was your best bet.

Loving understood why. Anyplace else the cops went, there was always a chance of being hassled by some sorry lowlife, the last thing on earth they wanted during their off-hours. Or they could be put in an awkward, uncomfortable position—i.e., when the guy at the next table decides to light up a joint.

Loving stepped inside. The decor was predictably black-and-white, like a cop car. Instead of pictures and paintings, the walls displayed handcuffs and billy clubs and truncheons and other such police accoutrements. Somehow, the owner had managed to get a full-length section of the grille from a patrol car behind the bar, where the mirror should have been. The placards on the tables offered mixed drinks with cute names like Police Blotter Punch and Book 'Em Banana Brandy, though Loving noticed almost everyone in the joint appeared to be drinking tap beer.

Truth was, Loving liked it here, and he came often, even when he wasn't fishing for information. Cops and private eyes shared a lot of the same interests and concerns. And no one had opened a private-eye bar yet.

Hey, Loving thought to himself. Maybe there's an idea for my retirement . . .

It was easy to see around. Whatever other vices these boys might have, smoking wasn't one of them. Presumably they had the intelligence not to ingest anything that would kill them that surely, or cut the speed that might be critical in a chase.

Loving spotted a familiar face and sidled up beside him. "Come here often, big boy?"

The face next-door went through a series of rapid-fire

changes: first, puzzlement, then understanding, then horror. "Loving! What the hell are you doing in here?"

"Gettin' a drink." He asked the bartender for a beer. "How 'bout you, Dodds?"

The paunchy man beside him did not seem to appreciate the joke. "But—I mean—*why* are you here?"

"I come here all the time. I like to swap stories."

"Maybe you used to. But no one's going to swap anything with you today."

Loving was unperturbed. "What'd I do, forget my underarm deodorant?"

The other man leaned close. "Everyone in here knows who you work with. You need to get out while you can still walk."

"Dodds, Dodds, Dodds. We're all friends. Nothing's gonna happen to me." He looked around. "See, no one cares about me."

"No one's noticed you're here. But as soon as they do, there'll be hell to pay."

"Ya think?" Loving pondered a moment. "Then I guess we should talk fast. I wanna know what's goin' down, Barry. I wanna know everythin'. And you're the one who's gonna tell me."

If Dodds could've segued into an alternate universe and disappeared, he surely would have. "I don't know what you're talking about."

"You do."

"I'm telling you, I don't."

"Barry, how long have we known each other?"

Dodds shrugged. "Since back when you drove a truck and were married to that piece of—"

Loving raised his hand. "Good enough. Now don't you think I've been around long enough to know when something's up?"

"Loving, one more time, I'm—"

"It's the Blue Squeeze, isn't it?"

Dodds's eyes diverted to his drink. "You're imagining things."

"I gave up my imagination when I was twelve." He grabbed Dodds and turned him around on his bar stool. "That's what it is, isn't it? The boys are puttin' the blue squeeze on my man Kincaid."

Dodds's voice dropped. "Could be."

"Why?"

"You know why. He helped that—that—"

"He did his job."

"Call it what you like. It's not going to go down any better."

"Ben has gotten perps acquitted lots of times—"

"This is different, Loving. Joe was a cop. We protect our own."

"So what have they done, Barry? Did they plant that knife in Ben's office? Is there more yet to come?"

"Who the hell are you talkin' to, Barry-boy?"

Loving did a slow pivot and found himself face-to-face with a stubble-faced, middle-aged man. He was tall and lean and had a practiced mean look that probably worked well with petty hoodlums. "He's talkin' to me. And it's a private conversation, if you catch my drift."

The other man didn't flinch. "We don't allow private conversations in here, sonny. If you catch my drift."

Loving made a point of being unimpressed. "You're Matthews, right?"

"Yup. Arlen Matthews, that's me. You can call me— Detective Sergeant Matthews."

"How 'bout I just don't call you?" Loving turned back toward the front of the bar.

Matthews grabbed Loving's arm and spun him around. A crowd began to gather.

"Let go of my arm," Loving said, in a low voice that bordered a growl. Personally, all this macho gamesmanship bored him to tears, but he knew if he didn't go through the motions no one here would ever talk to him.

Matthews let go of the arm, although as he did he let out a little sneer designed to let everyone know he wasn't intimidated.

A shorter man with a rounder face stepped forward. "I'm Mark Callery. And I know who you are."

"Great. Then we can skip the formal introductions—"

"You'd be smarter to skip this altogether. And leave."

"Who is he, Mark?" Matthews asked.

"Don't you recognize him? He's a P.I. Works with Kincaid."

"I knew it!" Matthews barreled toward Loving. "I knew it. You work with the cop killer!"

"I work with an attorney who never wanted to hurt anybody in his entire life," Loving said. "And frankly, jerkwad, you're not worthy to lick the dirt off his briefcase." A bold move, Loving realized, but one likely to command the attention of the room.

Matthews clenched and unclenched his fists, puffing his cheeks. "Joe McNaughton was my best friend."

"You know, I never knew Joe, but he must've been a hell of a guy, 'cause since he died, everyone I talk to turns out to have been his best friend."

"I don't like your attitude!" Matthews barked.

"And I don't like your breath, so why don't we both go back to our conversations and leave each other alone?"

Matthews gave Loving a little shove on the chest. "We want you out of here, and we don't want to see you again. You or your cop-killing boss."

"Is that right? Does that go for all of you?" Loving let his eyes scan the bar, even though he knew it was dangerous to take his eyes off this cretin for a minute. "Does that go for you, Barry?"

Dodds looked away.

"Ben Kincaid helped you out when you were hauled in front of IA, didn't he?" Loving asked. "Saved your butt, the way I remember it. What about you, Bert?" He pointed toward a gray-haired man in the back, who immediately looked away. "I kinda recall when the Board was tryin' to cancel your pension, just three weeks before you retired. Let me think, what was the name of the attorney who gave you your future back? Oh yeah, I remember now. Ben Kincaid."

Matthews shoved Loving again, this time harder. "We've had it with your games. Get the hell out of here before I throw you out on your ass!"

Loving glanced over his shoulder. He was hoping a manager or bartender might intervene, but no one was coming. It seemed the management was cowardly in the extreme—or perhaps, extremely on Matthews's side.

"You're pretty brave, aren't you?" Loving said, walking toward Matthews in slow steady steps. "You're a tower of strength—when you've got, oh, fifty or sixty other guys to back you up. But I wonder how brave you'd be if it were just you and me?"

For the first time, he saw Matthews blink. "I could take you standing on my head, but it doesn't matter, 'cause if you don't haul ass right now every damn one of us is going to be pounding your brains into pudding."

"I know what's going on," Loving said, in a much louder voice. "I know you've put the Blue Squeeze on Kincaid."

"You're hallucinating, chump."

Loving continued as if Matthews wasn't there. "I know you've framed him—some of you, anyway. And I want it to stop."

"And I want a Jaguar XJS. But that ain't gonna happen, either."

Loving felt his jaw tightening. Control, he reminded himself. You came here to open potential channels of communication. Not to start a barroom brawl. In which the odds against you would be roughly fifty to one. "All I want is the truth."

"Last chance. Leave now or pay the price."

"You know you can't keep this secret long," Loving said.

"Too many people know about it. Eventually someone will talk to me. And when they do—"

Loving never got to finish his sentence, because before he could, Matthews's fist materialized at the edge of his vision and slammed into his jaw. It was a good punch; it knocked him several steps back and would've done more if he hadn't seen it coming.

"Consider that a warning," Matthews said. "Now get the hell out."

Loving massaged his aching jaw. It would be so ... *pleasing* to deck Matthews, right here and now. But that wouldn't advance the investigation. He dropped a few bills on the bar and headed toward the door. "One of you is going to talk to me," he repeated quietly, just before he left. "It's just a matter of time. And when they do"—he cast a sharp eye in Matthews's direction—"I'll be back."

* 15 *

Christina found Andrea McNaughton at the John 3:16 soup kitchen, scooping red beans and rice onto tin trays. The priest at St. Dunstan's, Father Danney, after being assured that her intentions were honorable, had told Christina this is where Andrea would be. Even with forewarning, however, Christina found it hard to adjust reality to fit the preconceived mental image. Andrea McNaughton had been all over the newspapers for months, and she had been portrayed in a variety of roles. Grieving. Long-suffering. Betrayed. Most of the coverage in the *World* had suggested that she was the true victim of this sordid affair. Most of its readers, particularly the female ones, empathized with her and had elevated her to the status of tragic heroine, like Marilyn Monroe or Princess Diana.

Had they run pictures of the woman feeding the homeless, she might have attained sainthood.

Christina waited until Andrea finished serving lunch, which was a considerable wait. John 3:16 was the oldest and largest of the Tulsa shelters that undertook the monumental job of feeding the hungry; there were more than a hundred people, mostly elderly men, in line for a fundamental but life-preserving meal. Some had found a place to live in permanent shelters, but Christina knew far too many of them would return to the streets, a cardboard box under a bridge, a downtown gutter, or some other hellish place they called home. She strengthened her resolve to continue contributing to her retirement fund and to work the daily crossword to keep her mind sharp. Homelessness was not for sissies.

As soon as lunch was served, Christina tapped the shoulder of the woman behind the serving counter. "Mrs. McNaughton?"

Andrea looked at her warily. No doubt the past few months had taught her to be cautious about strangers who already knew her name. For that matter, even if she couldn't quite place the face, she probably recognized Christina from the courtroom. "Yes?"

Christina extended her hand. "My name's Christina McCall. I work with Ben Kincaid."

Not surprisingly, Andrea turned away. "We have nothing to talk about."

"I just have a few questions I'd like to ask you."

Andrea moved away, untying her apron. "Please. I don't want to talk."

Christina followed her into the kitchen. "I'm sure you don't. But it's very important."

Andrea continued walking away from her. "I've already said everything. Over and over again."

"Not to me."

Andrea whirled around, and in her eyes, Christina saw a sudden flash of anger. "Why can't you people just leave me alone!"

Instinctively, Christina reached out and took the woman's hand. "Please. Just give me a moment of your time. I know this must have been hideous for you—losing the man you loved. But now I'm about to lose my—someone I care about. Deeply. And I can't just stand by and let that happen."

"You're talking about Keri Dalcanton."

"No. I'm not. She's our client, but we don't have a personal relationship."

"Just as well. Let me give you a news flash, honey. Your client did it."

"I realize that's your opinion. Frankly, that's not why I'm here."

Andrea's face seemed to soften slightly. "You must be talking about the lawyer. Kincaid."

A slight tincture of pink appeared on Christina's cheeks. "I am."

Andrea drew in her breath, then released it, slow and full, as if purging demons from her soul. "It wasn't my idea to go after the lawyer. The D.A. came up with that one on his own. I thought it was a little extreme, even under these circumstances."

"It was a grandstand play. A desperate gambit to get the case reopened."

"But it worked."

Christina nodded. "Which is why I need to talk to you. Now more than ever."

Andrea's eyelids fluttered heavily. She seemed to relent, not so much from a sense of obligation as from weariness, from an inability to muster the strength to maintain the fight.

"Excuse me. Is everything all right in here?"

Christina turned and saw a white-bearded older man poking his head through the swinging kitchen doors.

"I'm fine," Andrea said. The man disappeared. "That was Father Danney, from St. Dunstan's."

"I know. He's a friend, right?"

"And then some. He likes to check on me. I get a lot of people wanting to talk to me, even this long after the murder. Spectators, the idle curious. Investigators. Actually, what I get most of all is other women who've been betrayed and think of me as some kind of soul sister. They want to tell me their stories. 'I was abused, too,' they say. 'My man done me wrong.' Which of course are the last things on earth I want to hear. So Father Danney keeps an eye out for me. He's a very kind, gentle man."

Andrea gestured toward the nearest table. "But that's not what you want to talk about. What is it I can tell you?"

Christina glanced down at the notes she'd made on her legal pad. "Did you know Keri Dalcanton? I mean, before the . . . incident." She mentally chastised herself for her awkwardness. Ben had warned her that talking to a woman about her dead murdered husband, not to mention the affair he'd had before his death, was not going to be easy. But the full truth of that statement didn't hit home until she was confronted with Andrea's large brown, doelike eyes. "Had you met?"

"Let me think," Andrea said, with a remarkably even temper. "Had I met a sleazy teenage big-boobed topless dancer from the bad part of town? I think that would be a no."

"But you did . . . find out about her. Right?"

"Oh, yes. Some concerned friend decided that I needed to know. Why, I can't imagine. People just can't resist the urge to butt into other people's business, can they? And they love to be the one who drops the big bombshell. It's like we're all still out on the playground. 'I know something you don't know,' " she said in a singsong voice.

"So who was it?"

"Marge Matthews. Another cop's wife. I guess everyone on the force knew about the affair for some time. I was the only one in the dark."

"What did you do when you found out?"

"First? I cried. Then I cried some more. Cried a whole Friday away. I was a basket case. We'd been married for almost fifteen years, you know? I mean, I've heard people use the word *betrayed*, but I never really knew what it meant, never felt it, until that day." Her hand, sculpted nails with bright red polish, rose to her forehead. "I'd probably still be crying, except that around eleven that night, he came home. That snapped me out of it."

"Did you confront him?"

"That would be one way of putting it, yes. I attacked him. I'm not exaggerating, either. Knocked him flat on his ass. Started pounding on his chest. He didn't know what hit him." She shook her head. "It was as if all that sadness, all that despair, suddenly converted into anger. Rage. I even bit him."

"Did he resist?"

"Not by much. 'Course, he was drunk. He'd been out with the boys. Might've been with . . . her . . . for all I know." Her eyelashes, dark with mascara, fluttered. "Poor snockered schmuck. He didn't know what was going on. At least not till he sobered up."

"Did he confess?"

"Eventually. Marge had been kind enough to give me many specific details. He couldn't possibly squirm out of it. He was busted."

"So what happened then?"

"I asked him to give her up. Stop cheating on me."

"And?"

"He refused. At that time. I'm sure it was a tough decision for him."

"How so?"

Andrea paused. It was evident that this was a difficult part of the story to tell, not because it was embarrassing but because she couldn't find the words to express it properly.

Andrea looked at Christina levelly. "You're a woman."

"Thanks."

"Are you married?"

Christina shook her head. "But I have been."

"Then you'll understand. Joe and I were very young when we married. Very, very young. Babies, really. I'd like to say we had a deep and profound spiritual linkage or something like that but, the truth is, I think it was mostly hormones."

Christina allowed herself a small smile. "I've been there."

"Yeah. Not that I didn't love him with all my heart and soul. But in the early days, he was a force to be reckoned with. Between the sheets. And I'm not exaggerating."

"Did that change?"

"Alas, yes. You know how it is. The nasty part of growing old together is that you also grow up. Our ... interests changed. His changed a lot. And so did mine, for that matter. We were still cordial and affectionate, but ... sexually ..." Her hands spread in a helpless manner. "We became distant. So it really shouldn't have been that much of a surprise that he was screwing around." She paused. "Shouldn't have been. But it was."

Christina nodded. Andrea appeared to be relaxing, settling into the story. She was relieved, and a bit flattered, that the woman felt comfortable enough to discuss these intimate and unpleasant matters with her. "So what did you do when he refused to break it off with Keri Dalcanton?"

Again the level look. "You're a woman. What would you do?"

"I'd have a few words with Keri Dalcanton."

Andrea brought her finger around to touch the tip of her nose. "Ding-ding-ding."

"That must've been hairy."

"It was. Caught her in that crummy apartment where she lived, where she and Joe used to go. She was watching some exercise program on the tube, working out. Wearing one of those sport bras with a matching headband. There she was, silvery hair, big boobs, the works. The child my husband chose to be unfaithful with. I just about died."

"Did you talk?"

"I thought she'd be reasonable. I thought once she knew there was another woman in the picture, one who wasn't going away, she'd back off."

"No such luck?"

"No. Instead I had to hear a lot of crap about what a pistol my man was, about how he and she were heartmates, whatever the hell that is. I think they must've carved their initials in a tree or something. I mean, she was talking like a teenager. Hell, she was a teenager. Except the man she was talking about was my husband."

"That must've stung."

"It got worse. 'You can't satisfy Joe.' That's what she said to me. 'You can't give him what he wants. He wants me.' " Her jaw stiffened. "It was—it was just more than I could take."

Christina reached across the table and squeezed Andrea's hand. "You hit her, didn't you?"

"How'd you know?"

" 'Cause I would've."

Andrea almost smiled. "It was more than just a slap on the chops, I'm afraid. I really went after her, just as I had gone after Joe. We had a regular catfight. We were rolling around on the floor, bumping into her exercise equipment. Tramp got her smelly sport bra all over me."

"How did it end?"

"The cavalry arrived, in the form of her brother, Kirk. He shares the apartment with her, or used to, anyway. He broke it up. Though not before I got a few good strokes in, I'm happy to say."

"So you left?"

"Not immediately. I had to put up with a tongue-lashing from Kirk first. Have you met him?"

"Not really," Christina answered. "I've seen him in the courtroom."

"We're talking about a man with major issues."

"Like what?"

"You name it. Sexual ambiguity. Inability to hold a job. Religious guilt. And he's absolutely irrational on the subject of his sister. He lives and breathes for that girl. There's nothing he won't do to protect her."

"So what did he say to you?"

"I don't remember the exact words, but the gist of it was, Get out and stay out. He thought I posed some kind of threat to Keri. And he wasn't far wrong, either."

"You had cause."

"Yeah, I thought so, but he didn't see it that way. So I scrammed. If this mess was going to get solved, I realized, it would be without the help of the teenage tramp and her psycho sibling."

"May I ask what you did?"

Andrea leaned back in her chair. "Hey, we've come this far together. I can't leave you hanging." She flashed a quick, if bitter, smile, and Christina got a brief taste of the luminescent beauty on which the papers had often remarked. "When Joe got home, I laid down the law. Told him I was going to talk to the lawyers and he was about to be divorced. He would be publicly branded an adulterer. Given the tender age of his chosen consort, he might even be kicked off the force. That was what did it, I think. That was when he caved."

"He agreed not to see her anymore?"

"He did. And he went straight over to her place to give her the bad news. And—well, you know what she did next."

"I'm not sure I do," Christina said. She didn't want to risk the relationship she was developing with this woman, but she had to be honest. "I've never been convinced by the so-called evidence the police had on Keri. I think she was just the obvious subject, The cops suspected her from the first and they trumped up some evidence to make it stick."

"You're wrong." Andrea glanced over her shoulder, as if making sure no one was listening. "Absolutely wrong."

"I know you think Keri is guilty, but—"

"I'm not talking about that. I mean about thinking Keri was the cops' first suspect. She wasn't. The obvious suspect was—me."

Christina's lips parted. This was the first she'd heard of this.

"I tried not to take it to heart. Any time a married person is killed, the cops' initial suspect is the spouse. And for a good reason—most of the time the spouse is the one who did it. And of course adultery is one of the most common reasons these crimes happen. And the other most common motive is money—which I stood to get a lot of when Joe died. So in many respects, I was the perfect suspect. Perfectly easy, anyway." She paused a moment. "But it still hurt, you know? To have this whole horrific event twisted around. To realize people who knew me thought I was capable of murder. That was painful."

"They must've realized relatively quickly that you weren't the killer."

"They got a better suspect, if that's what you mean. I think I might still be under investigation, if not in jail, if they hadn't found all that incriminating evidence in your client's apartment. Then she became Suspect Number One."

"Keri thinks you sent the cops out to her place. She thinks you encouraged the police to go after her, to get revenge for the affair."

"The girl is only nineteen. She thinks the whole world is one big soap opera."

"I gather . . . you don't care much for Keri?"

"Does it show?"

"Well, I saw you try to break her nose in the courtroom."

"I guess that was telling, wasn't it?" Andrea's lips pressed together pensively. "I suppose I should be grateful she didn't press charges."

"Ben convinced her it was not in her best interests. You should be grateful to them both."

"You're right, of course. But I'm not. I'm not grateful at

all. I hate her." Her delicate neck stiffened. "Honestly, who wouldn't? I mean, I know hate is a bad thing. I've talked to my priest about it, more than once. I've worried and I've prayed for help. But my God, if you can't hate the woman who slept with your husband, then killed him, who the hell can you hate?"

A point Christina was not prepared to argue. "I understand your late husband was investigating the Catrona crime family. Did you know anything about that?"

"Not much. No details. I do know Joe got a phone call at home, a few days before he was killed, that disturbed him very much. He was agitated enough to slam the phone down. But he didn't look angry. It was really more like he was—worried. Or scared."

"Didn't you ask what it was all about?"

"I did. But he didn't tell me. He grunted out, 'Catrona.' And that was the end of it. I probably would've brought it up again, later. Except your client killed him before I got the chance."

Christina folded up her legal pad. "I think that about covers it. Thank you very much for talking to me."

Andrea waved her hand in the air. "Sure. It wasn't that bad, actually. Not like some of them. You're a good ear."

Christina had been told this before, but it was still nice. "If I think of something else, may I call you?"

"Of course." She fell silent for a moment, and the light in her eyes faded. "I did love Joe, you understand that, don't you? We had our problems. We disagreed. We fought. Maybe I wasn't the perfect wife, maybe I didn't give him everything he wanted. Or even needed. Marriage is not a game of perfect. But even after I knew what Joe'd done, even after I knew I'd been betrayed—I still loved him. With all my heart. And I never wanted to see him come to any harm. Never. And certainly not"—she averted her eyes—"not, like it was. So gross and horrible and—public. No wife should have to endure that. No one should."

Christina laid her hand on the bereaved woman's shoulder and simply nodded. There was no arguing with that.

* 16 *

Ben had visited Tulsa's downtown police headquarters half a hundred times, but this was the first instance when he felt as if he were walking into enemy territory. Few times in his life had he had the opportunity to enter a building where he knew everyone present would view him as an absolute pariah. He had considered wearing some sort of disguise—dark glasses and a high collar, at least. But he knew that if he was spotted, that would only make matters worse. He passed on the disguise, but resolved to move as quickly and unobtrusively as possible.

He brushed down the fourth floor corridor till he found the cubicle belonging to Penelope, Mike's secretary. He ducked inside, avoiding detection.

As usual, Penelope's desk was piled high with paper and she appeared to be juggling three phone calls at once. As soon as she spotted Ben, however, she brought all conversations to an abrupt end.

"Ben!" It was almost like a hiss, because she was trying to be emphatic but to keep her voice down at the same time. "What in God's name are you doing here?"

Ben stared down at a spot on the carpet. "I, uh, need to review a file."

"Ben, you know I can't let you do that."

"I'm not talking about my case," Ben said hastily. "I wouldn't ask you to do anything inappropriate. This is something entirely unrelated. Something, uh . . . something Mike and I were working on. Before he had to go out of town." Not entirely true, of course. In fact, one might say it was totally false. But he felt certain Mike wouldn't object to the unauthorized use of his name and authority. Not too much, anyway.

"Mike didn't say anything to me," she said. Penelope had wide eyes and big brown frizzy hair that might make her seem ditzy and comical if you didn't know she was one of the most efficient and capable assistants who ever lived. "He didn't leave any instructions."

"He probably forgot. He had to disappear in a hurry."

"That's true enough." She gave Ben a long look. Her eyes seemed to soften. "What file do you need?"

"The file on the Catrona crime family."

Penelope winced. "Geez, Ben. You really know how to pick 'em, don't you? Haven't you got enough people who want to kill you already?"

Ben gave a small shrug. "It's . . . for a case." Well, that much was true, anyway.

"I didn't figure you wanted it for bedtime reading." She drummed her fingers for a moment. "Well, Mike has always told me to cooperate with you in the past."

"That's right."

"Of course, that was before you became a criminal defendant."

Ben pursed his lips. The woman's logic was relentless. "I only need it for an hour or so." Long enough to get to Kinko's and plug some quarters into the photocopier.

She pondered a few more moments. "I suppose there's no harm in that. I'll get the file. It'll take a few minutes. Let me warn you in advance—it's a thick one."

"Thanks, Penelope. You're an angel."

"Yes, but my halo's getting a bit tarnished. Too much contact with criminals. And their lawyers."

Ouch! Ben thought, but he could live with it—as long as she produced the file.

And quickly. Christina and the others were certain to return to the office soon, and he wanted to be back before they did. It would spare him answering a lot of unpleasant questions, and no doubt elongating his Pinocchio's nose. Christina had been firm about his staying out of the investigation, and she was probably right, but he couldn't just sit on his hands and do nothing, not while Keri's freedom was on the line—not to mention his own. Besides, Penelope would never give Christina or Loving the file; the only one who had a shot was him. Now if he could just get it and get outta here . . .

"I don't believe it. *You!*"

Ben felt his heart sinking and his blood pressure rising. He didn't have to turn his head to identify the owner of that belligerent voice.

Matthews. "Son of a bitch. Right here in our own offices." Matthews stomped directly in front of Ben. "What the hell do you think you're doing here?"

Ben took a deep breath, trying to remain cool. "This is a public building. I'm a taxpayer. I have as much right to be here as anyone."

"Like hell. You've got your snoop harassing us when we're off duty, and now you're shoving your stinking face around our offices. This is too damn much." Matthews glanced at the nameplate on the desk. "She's Morelli's secretary, isn't she? Trying to worm some favors out of your old college buddy? Maybe hide some more evidence to keep your sorry butt out of prison? That's what you do best, isn't it? Weaseling criminals out of their punishments."

"I'm not the one who botched his case with improperly obtained warrants. That was your stroke of genius."

"Don't give me any fancy lawyer talk. What are you doing here?"

"I don't have to explain myself to you. And I don't intend to."

His face contorted with anger, Matthews grabbed Ben by the collar and jerked him up to his feet. "Is that right? Let me tell you something. Joe McNaughton was my partner, and the best man I ever knew. The best. And his murder will not go unpunished. That little blond piece of ass you're protecting is gonna swing. And maybe you with her!"

"If you don't let go of me—*now*—I'll bring charges for assault. And I'm not just threatening, either. An undeniable case of police brutality right now could do nothing but help me."

Matthews shoved Ben back, his face twisted with disgust. "You revolting piece of—" He drew in his breath, fighting back the bile. "I'm not going to give you an excuse to pull more of your flashy lawyer tricks. Get the hell out."

"I've got business here. And it isn't over."

"Your buddy ain't here, Kincaid, got it? No one's gonna help you. There's no one here who wouldn't like to take you apart and drown the pieces. So for your own safety, get the hell out."

"I'm not fin—"

"Do you hear what I'm saying?" It would be impossible for Ben not to, as the man was barking directly in front of his face. "You just being here is an insult to Joe's memory. And I'm not gonna let that happen. So don't make me call security, chump. Get out!"

Ben carefully weighed his options, as much as was possible with the man literally breathing down his neck. He could stand fast, but the scene would only escalate, making it all the more impossible for Penelope to help him. Better to concede for now and hope to come back at a later date. When Matthews was somewhere else.

"I'll go." Ben turned and started toward the door, but apparently it offered Matthews a target he couldn't refuse. Just before he left the cubicle, Ben felt the flat of the man's shoe on his backside. The kick knocked him across the corridor.

Ben pulled himself together quickly and started toward the elevators. Unfortunately, Matthews's shouts had attracted too much attention; there was no chance of his getting out as surreptitiously as he got in. Practically everyone working on the fourth floor had emerged from their cubicles and stood at the openings. All over the office, people were scurrying for a better look, jockeying for position. Everyone was staring at him, and the stares did not contain much warmth.

It was like walking the gauntlet. True, no one was beating him with clubs as he passed by, but they were beating him with their eyes, pouring out malice with every glance, and in some ways, that was worse.

Ben had never felt such relief in his life as when he made it to the lobby. He decided waiting for the elevator was too slow, plus he might meet someone inside and start yet another unfortunate scene.

He opted for the stairs. He pushed open the pneumatic door to the stairwell . . .

And found Penelope waiting for him.

"Decide to get a little exercise?" she asked.

"You could say that. How'd you know I'd take the stairs?"

"Intuition. Also, I could hear Matthews ranting halfway across the building. Did he try to rough you up?"

"More intuition?"

"That, plus the imprint of his shoe on your butt." She held out a thick manila folder. "Here's the file. Just mail it back to me. They won't miss it for a day, and I don't think you want to come back here."

"You got that right." Ben took the file and tucked it under his arm. "Thanks, Penelope. I really appreciate this."

"Well, I know Mike thinks you're worth messing with, so I suppose I should honor his wishes. Anything else I can do?"

Ben hesitated. "I . . . don't suppose you'd like to tell me where Mike has gone?"

"Can't. Don't know."

"And I don't suppose you've heard any of the cops talking about visiting my office? Like maybe to plant a knife?"

Penelope shrugged. "I have no idea who might be behind that. But I do know this, Ben. These people are used to getting what they want. One way or another."

"Even if it means breaking the law?"

"They are the law, Ben. And as long as they believe the end result is just, they don't worry too much about the means." She took a step closer, her expression solemn. "Please be careful, Ben. Very careful."

* 17 *

Kirk stumbled down The Stroll, one foot after the other, no idea where he was going, or when, or for that matter, why. How many nights had he forced himself out like this? Prowling the worst parts of the city, late at night, looking for trouble, usually finding it. Brushing shoulders with hooligans and pushers and pimps and whores and—

He tried to erase the ugly word from his brain, without success. That was the word those bastards used to tarnish Keri, back in the courtroom. That was what they called her, just because she had to take her clothes off in that crummy club, just because she was dating that dirty cop. It wasn't right. She never did anything wrong, not really. She was a good girl, clean and pure, deep down. She was his sister, for God's sake. Those creeps didn't know what was in her heart. But he did. He knew. They—

Standing before him, he saw a heavenly vision, a shapely female figure barely over five feet tall, with platinum blond hair.

Keri? He couldn't see the face, but even from this distance, he knew she was gorgeous. He felt his knees weakening; his heart went out to her.

Keri! Had she come looking for him? Was she here to bring him back? Did she forgive him for what he'd done?

He rushed forward, hands outstretched. "Keri!" he shouted. "Keri, I—"

The young woman in the feather boa and fake-fur coat turned to face him. "Wanna date, sugah?"

"Keri?"

"You can call me Keri if you want, sugah. You can call me any li'l ol' thing you like."

It was not Keri. It was a prostitute. A whore. A real one.

"Sorry. I thought you were . . . somebody else."

"I can be somebody else, sugah. I'll be whatever—"

"Leave me alone!"

The young woman stepped back quickly, and her eyes darted upward to a third-story window in the building behind her. Where her pimp observed from a distance, no doubt. Or perhaps some big bruiser charged with protecting her. Either way, Kirk'd best disappear. Not that he'd mind a good fight. But he'd done that so much lately. His hand touched the scabrous slash across his forehead. He was ready for something new.

"Sorry," he muttered, then quickly scurried across the street. He turned right and headed off The Stroll, toward Cherry Street. Putting distance between himself and any immediate retribution.

Eleventh Street, particularly the section known as The Stroll, had a well-deserved reputation for being the sleaziest section of Tulsa. It was the easiest place in town to find a prostitute, in almost any price range, at almost any time of day. It was the simplest place to score drugs. Most of the other top vices thrived there as well. It was definitely the place to come when you were looking for action. Or, as in Kirk's case, when you were looking for punishment.

A neon sign with half the letters burned out illuminated the path before him. RAINBOW BOUTIQUE, it said, or used to, back when it was fully functional. And if the information he'd gotten from that old landlord back at the dump he now called home was correct, he'd be able to find another purveyor of il-legal vice there.

A tattoo artist.

Kirk pushed open a creaking door and stepped inside. The door stuck, making him wonder just how much business this place got these days. He scanned the smallish store. It was dark and dingy. The dust in the air was so thick it was hard to breathe. Or *was* that dust? . . .

By all immediate appearances, this was just a head shop. All kinds of drug paraphernalia stocked the shelves—hookahs, bongs, you name it. Incense was burning, adding to the generally heavy putrid atmosphere. Two scrawny men in their early twenties hung by one of the windows. Addicts no doubt. To them, visiting this place must be like going to Sears.

And all of this was perfectly legal, Kirk mused, as he strolled down the aisles. Selling drug paraphernalia was legal in Oklahoma, so long as you could claim some legal non-drug-related use for the equipment. Just as cockfighting was legal in Oklahoma. Pari-mutuel horse-race betting was legal in Oklahoma. Carrying a concealed weapon was legal in Oklahoma. But not tattooing. Tattooing was illegal. After all, we don't want to corrupt our youth.

Kirk spotted a doorway in the back with a curtain of cheap plastic multicolored beads obscuring the view. That might be just what he was looking for, he reasoned. He also noticed an extraordinarily fat man hunkering nearby, keeping an eye on the doorway. The bouncer, no doubt.

Kirk flashed the ogre a wave and a smile. "I'm not a cop."

Apparently the bouncer saw no reason to doubt him. He made a grunting sound, then returned his eyes to the skin mag he was drooling over.

Kirk pushed apart the beads and entered the inner sanctum. The light was dim, but not so much so that he couldn't make out a withered figure hunched over an art table. A single green-shaded lamp clipped to the top provided the only light in the tiny room.

And on the walls, just barely visible, were hundreds upon hundreds of tattoo designs, the full panoply, from anchors to butterflies to dear old MOTHER.

He was in the right place.

The man at the art board looked to be about three hundred and two, but Kirk figured spending your nights in this crappy room could probably age you in a New York minute. His chin and upper lip were covered with stubble; his mouth and face were dirty. There was a distinctive odor wafting from his direction which suggested the gent had not bathed since he was a sprightly youth of two hundred and twelve.

Not being much of a host, the man wasn't speaking to him. Kirk figured that left it to him to break the ice. "This the place to get a tattoo?"

"Body illustration." The man's jaw seemed to creak when he spoke. "Tattooing is illegal."

"Of course. Body illustration. That's what I want."

The man shifted slightly. He was taking a defensive posture, still keeping the art board between him and the newcomer. "What'd'ya have in mind?"

"Oh, I don't know." He waved his hand toward the walls. "Any of these. All of them. Whatever."

The man frowned. "Usually the customer picks the design."

"And isn't that crazy?" Kirk asked. "After all, what do I know about tattoos? You're the expert."

"Where'd'ya want it?"

Kirk considered a moment. "Where does it hurt most?"

"I don't do that kind of tattoo," the old man said, turning crabby. "No nipples, no genitalia. I'm a professional."

"How 'bout the back? Does that hurt?"

"Pretty much. Though the chest is worse." The old man's eyes narrowed. "Are you sayin' you want it to hurt?"

"Never mind. I'll go with the chest."

"Look, son, I'm not here to inflict pain. If that's how you

get off and you're lookin' for a quickie, let me recommend a little lady on The Stroll—"

"I don't sleep with whores!" Kirk shouted back at him. He looked away, embarrassed by his outburst. "I just want a tattoo."

"Fine. Customer is always right." The man reached for his needles, which were soaking in a muddy blue liquid. "Picture or letters?"

"Which of them . . ."

"Letters hurt the worst," the man answered, clicking his tongue as he dried the tips of his needles. "You wouldn't think so, but they do. 'Specially if you color in the letters."

"Then that's what I want, pal. On the chest." He took a hundred bucks out of his pocket and threw it on the art board. With a speed that would have suited an anaconda, the old man snatched it up and shoved it in his pocket.

Kirk gestured toward the padded chair in the corner. "That where I sit?"

"Right." The man came closer and, for the first time, took a good look at Kirk's face. "What the hell happened to you?"

Kirk touched his face, swollen in places, one eye still black, and a not nearly healed slash across his forehead. "I was in a fight."

"No joke. What'd you fight, a tractor?"

"No. Three punks trying to steal a TV."

The man pulled back. "Are you a cop?"

"Just a concerned citizen."

"With a death wish."

"Maybe," Kirk said quietly. "May be."

"Look, if you've got some kinda problem, I don't want—"

"Just do the damn tattoo already, okay?"

The man frowned a moment, then readied his needles and uncovered a few vats of dye. "So what do you want spelled out?"

"I don't know. Something long. With lots of big colored-in letters."

"Some people like to have their name. Or their lover's name."

"Too short," Kirk said. "Something else."

"Someone else's name? Your hero, maybe. A nickname?"

"No, no."

"Superman? Long John? Sex Machine?"

"No dirty stuff, old man."

He pushed himself to his feet. "What the hell is wrong with you, anyway? People come in here, they usually know what they want."

"What's it to you, you geezer? Just pick something."

"I'm an artist, goddamn it." He pounded his needles down on the table. "I take pride in my work!"

"An artist!" Kirk laughed. "You're a criminal, is what you are, you old crow. You're breaking the law, remember?"

"Get out of here," the man growled.

"No way, you old asshole. You took my money, now you'll give me what I want or I'll create such a stink you'll be shut down for a year."

"Who do you think—"

"I told you what to do!" Kirk bellowed. "Now *do it*!"

The old man's eyes fairly bulged out of their sockets. His fists clenched together so tightly Kirk thought those feeble bones might snap.

"Fine," the old man creaked, finally. He removed a bottle from a nearby shelf and poured something pungent onto a handkerchief. "I'll have to put you out for this."

"No!" Kirk shouted. "I want to feel this. I want to feel every—"

"Too damn bad." An instant later, the chloroformed cloth was over Kirk's mouth, and not ten seconds later, he was fast asleep.

Kirk awoke coughing. He was sitting in an uncomfortable chair in the main section of the Rainbow Boutique. The fat man was sitting opposite him, smoking a cigarillo. His nose was buried in yet another slick magazine with glossy photos of naked women in degrading poses.

"Where's the tattoo artist?" Kirk said, as soon as he could get his mouth to work.

"Tattoos are illegal," the man replied, not looking up.

"Okay, the body illustrator then."

"Gone. Won't be back any time soon."

"Son of a bitch." Kirk was beginning to feel a distinct itching on his chest. "Did he do it?"

The man shrugged. "You tell me."

The itching intensified. In fact, it was starting to ache. "My chest hurts."

"Wimp." A small smile played on his lips. "Mirror's over there." He nodded toward the nearest wall.

Kirk walked to the full-length mirror. He unbuttoned his shirt and opened it wide.

DICKLESS, it said, in big bold multicolored letters. Permanently.

He heard a wheezy laughing behind him. The fat man was watching, howling his head off. The two addicts in the corner were having a pretty good time, too.

"You know what the best part is," the immense man said, still chortling his heart out. "That little insult is going to hurt you for days."

Kirk gave him a look. "You got a tattoo?"

"Tattoos are for wimps. You want to feel something intense, go to the Body Beautiful, down The Stroll by Lewis."

Kirk glanced toward the beaded passageway. "Maybe after I have a word with your body illustrator."

The man rose up, blocking his path. "That isn't going to happen."

"Let me through, big boy."

The man placed his meaty fists firmly on his hips. "Aren't you hurting enough already, asshole?"

Kirk considered. He was, actually. Hurting pretty damn bad. The old creep probably did whatever he could to make it agonizing. Maybe even infected needles, who knew? His chest was burning like it was on fire. He was in serious pain.

He turned back toward the mirror and gazed at his reflection. The agony was washing over him, overwhelming him. But it wasn't enough.

Bad as it hurt, it still wasn't enough. Not for what he'd done.

* 18 *

Matthews left his office just after five and walked to his car in the underground parking garage behind police headquarters. He was meeting some of the boys at Scene of the Crime; they were going to plan out what to do next. So his mind was somewhat distracted when, all at once, a two-hundred-and-twenty-pound hurricane swept down out of nowhere and pinned him against his Toyota Celica.

"Wha—wha—" Matthews's eyes peeled open, wide and frightened. "What the hell is going on? Hel—"

A thick strong hand clamped down over his mouth. "Try that again, you little pissant, and I'll rip your tongue out. That's a promise."

Matthews's eyes lighted on the face. The hand on his mouth eased up just enough for him to talk.

It was the investigator, Loving. And he was mad.

"What are you doing here?" Matthews sputtered.

"I'm on my way to a baseball game, you schmuck. What do you think I'm doing here?"

"I guess your boss went home crying that I was mean to him. So he sent his enforcer out to fight his battles."

"As a matter of fact, I found out from someone else. Ben didn't mention it, and probably never will. And let me give you another clue, schmuck. Fighting his battles is my job. And I'm very good at my job." Loving lifted Matthews's body up into the air, then slammed it back down against the car.

Matthews was hurting, but he wasn't letting it show. "What is it you want, Loving?"

"I want you to back off, Matthews. Got it? What took place today on the fourth floor was totally unacceptable."

"That's a matter of opinion."

"There is no opinion. Except mine." Loving lifted him up and slammed him down again. "Kincaid is the man, understand? And no one touches the man."

"What's going on?" The loud echo of footsteps in the parking garage told them both they were no longer alone. Soon three other officers were crowding behind them—Dodds, Callery, The Hulk—most of them men Loving had seen at the bar a few days before.

Loving released Matthews. "We were just having a little chat, boys. That's all."

Matthews's lips curled. "He snuck up behind me and tried to jump me. Let's show him what happens to people who mess with the force!"

Loving didn't look scared. "You know, Matthews, you're a lot braver now that you've got three other guys backing you up. A minute ago, you looked as if you were gonna piss your pants. In fact, I think maybe you did."

"He was trying to rough me up," Matthews informed his friends. "Scare me off."

Loving rolled his eyes. "The only thing I'm tryin' to do is investigate. Which technically is the job of the police. But since you didn't do it, I have to."

Matthews was incensed. "Are we gonna put up with this kinda talk? *Are we?*"

Loving turned toward the others. "I'm just trying to find

out what happened to Joe McNaughton. What really happened. I'd think you boys might be interested in that, being friends of Joe's and all. But I guess you're more interested in railroading some little teenage girl. Or her attorney."

"That attorney tried to make us look like idiots," Callery said.

"That attorney just did what he's supposed to do. This business of puttin' the Squeeze on him is idiotic. Just because you've got one angry moron over here doesn't mean you all have to be angry morons."

"Are we gonna listen to this?" Matthews bellowed. "Are we gonna let this scumbag talk to us this way?"

"You're really desperate for a fight, aren't you?" Loving lowered his voice a notch. "Well, I tell you what, you little twerp. Maybe, just maybe, you're gonna get your wish. Except it ain't gonna be you and three buddies. It's gonna be you and me. Period." He smiled broadly. "Now that'll give you something to dream about at bedtime, won't it?"

Loving turned his attention to the others. "What I said before still goes. I know you know what's been goin' down. You ought to come clean. It's the right thing to do, and some of you owe it to Ben to do the right thing."

"You're full of crap," Matthews growled.

"Oh yeah? Well, I know this. If Kincaid knew something that could help you—any of you—when someone had trumped up charges against you, he wouldn't hesitate a second to come forward. No matter what the cost. If he could help you, he would." He paused, giving each of them a sharp look. "It's a pity none of you courageous do-gooders quite rises to his level."

Without warning, Loving swung around and jabbed the sole of his shoe into Matthews's backside. Matthews screamed, clutching his rear.

"Consider that payback," Loving said. He started moving away before any of the others felt honor bound to intervene.

"That hurt like hell!" Matthews shouted, still holding himself. "What are you wearing?"

Loving lifted his foot and turned his heel up so they could see. "Cleats, you sorry son of a bitch. Didn't I tell you I was on my way to a baseball game?"

* 19 *

"Learning anything?"

Ben felt delicate fingers light on his shoulders and give him a tender squeeze. "Christina, I'm glad you're—"

He turned. The woman standing behind him was not Christina, but his client, Keri Dalcanton.

He immediately stiffened, embarrassed. "Sorry. Didn't recognize your voice." He closed the Catrona file, which he'd been pouring through since he returned to his office.

He pushed away from the conference table. "I didn't know you were here. Kind of late, isn't it?"

She gave a little shrug, which did interesting things to her close-fitting white T-shirt. "I don't know. I guess I was feeling lonely and . . . well, worried. Thought I'd see how the case was going." Her eyes were hooded and her voice strained. She struck Ben as being troubled, and unhappy, and . . . vulnerable.

Ben reached out sympathetically. Like a typical lawyer, he sometimes got so wrapped up in the difficult and time-consuming business of preparing a case for trial that he forgot there was another person to whom the case was more important than it ever would be to him—the defendant. "This must be awfully rough for you."

She didn't argue. "I—I just miss having someone to talk to." Was it fear, Ben wondered, or uncertainty, or simply pervasive sadness—the strain of carrying an almost impossible burden for far too long. "You know I lost my job, and after all the publicity, none of the girls wanted to have anything to do with me. They were afraid the cops might go after them if they stood behind me, which was a real possibility. My parents are dead and Kirk has disappeared and I don't know my neighbors and . . . and . . . it gets lonely sometimes."

"I can imagine. I remember when I first moved to Tulsa. Didn't have a place to stay, didn't know anyone. Couldn't stand my job, not to mention most of my coworkers. I was pretty lonely. I only had one friend. Fortunately, it was Christina, and she came over about three times a day."

Keri smiled a little. "What's with you two anyway?"

"What do you mean?"

"You know what I mean. Are you . . . close?"

He shrugged. "Yeah. I think so."

"Intimate?"

"Me? And Christina?" Ben pressed a hand against his chest. "Oh, no. Just friends. Very good friends. We've been through a lot together."

"Is there . . . someone else in your life?"

"Sure. There's my mother, and my sister, my staff, my tenants . . ."

She laughed, then sat down in the chair beside him. "You know what I mean."

It felt to Ben as if the temperature in this small conference room was rising sharply. He decided to change the subject. "How did you end up in Tulsa?"

"Oh, you don't want to hear about me. It's so boring."

"You're wrong. I do. Please."

Keri cast her lovely blue eyes up toward the ceiling. "Well, you know I came from Stroud originally. You know where that is?"

"Sure. I see the signs every time I cross the turnpike."

"Just a little flyspeck, compared to Tulsa anyway, but that

was my hometown. My parents were killed in a car wreck while I was still in high school."

"That must've been horrible for you."

"It was. My daddy and I were close. I loved my mother, too, but—she was not like other mothers."

"How do you mean?"

"She had a—a—mean streak, and for some reason, she always took it out on me. She liked to do cruel things to me. Even—nasty things. Ugly. Even when I was barely old enough to walk."

"Keri—I—"

"It's all right. It's been a long time. Anyway, after they died, my brother Kirk and I got a job at the outlet mall. Probably half the town worked at the outlet mall."

"Till the tornado came."

"Right. I guess you've seen the pictures."

Ben had. They looked as if a giant hand had swept down from heaven and ripped the guts out of the entire mall. He had never seen such horrible damage from a natural phenomenon.

"I guess we're just lucky the tornado didn't come during working hours. After that, there were no jobs anywhere in Stroud. I didn't have anything to live on and neither did my brother. So we made our way to the 'big city.' Tulsa. Packed up everything I had in one suitcase and boarded a Greyhound. Except, as it turned out, there weren't many jobs in Tulsa, either. Least none my daddy would've approved of."

"How did you end up in that, um, gentlemen's club?"

"Well, it seemed better than becoming a hooker, which is what happens to most of the sweet young things that come to Tulsa and can't find work. I'd rather be bumping and grinding in a nice air-conditioned building than turning tricks on Eleventh Street."

"Good point."

"And to tell you the truth, I've always liked dancing, though I would've preferred to keep my shirt on. I love the music, the lights. It's exciting."

I'll bet it was, Ben thought. Especially when you were on the stage.

"The guy who ran the joint was basically a sleaze, as you might expect, but at least he kept his hands off the girls. And he paid regular. I got a tiny place on the south side where Kirk and I could live. He'd fallen in with some church group, which was fine for him, but it didn't bring any money home, so I was basically on my own."

"Till you met Joe McNaughton?"

Her eyes turned downward. "Yeah."

"How did you meet him?"

"Oh, pretty much like that cop was saying in court. He came to the club one night with a bunch of his buddies."

"Must've been a rowdy bunch."

"Oh, me and the girls always liked cops. They do tend to hoot and holler, but they don't get vulgar and they keep their hands to themselves and they tip well. Especially if you let 'em slip it under your G-string." Her face suddenly colored. "I'm sorry. I shouldn't have said that."

"Relax. I'm your friend." Ben placed his hand reassuringly on the side of her face and felt the warm smooth flow of her silvery hair. "So you met Joe at the club?"

"Outside, technically. After the show, after closing, he was waiting for me by the back door. I was almost out when I saw him in the alley."

"What did you do?"

"I slammed the door shut and locked it, that's what I did. Some of the other girls had had problems with stalkers, creeps who fall in love with them during the show and follow them around everywhere. I didn't want to end up on a slab at the morgue."

"But you must've changed your mind later."

"Yeah, I did. Stupid me, huh?" She looked down, and Ben saw a glistening in the corner of her eyes. "He talked to me through the door, assured me he didn't want to harm me. I opened the door a crack and he showed me his badge. Said he just wanted to get some coffee and talk. Said he'd meet me at the coffee shop if that would make me feel safer. Basically, he told me everything I needed to hear. Except for the minor detail that he was married."

"He left that out?"

She nodded. "That was my big mistake, see. I thought he wanted a girlfriend, maybe even a wife. But what he really wanted was . . ." She turned away and didn't finish her sentence.

"So you met him at the coffee shop?"

"Yeah. Denny's, actually. Gross, I know, but nothing else was open."

"What did you talk about?"

"Oh, he spun me some stories. Joe was a slick talker when he wanted to be. Knew how to charm a lady." She almost smiled, but the impulse faded.

"What did he tell you?"

"Oh, you can imagine. Said I had a lovely smile."

Yes . . .

"Told me I had the most beautiful eyes he'd ever seen."

Which, actually, you do . . .

"Said I had a perfect figure. Perfect! Can you imagine?"

Ben felt the inside of his mouth go dry. He'd had the same thought himself on many occasions.

"And here I was, still just eighteen, listening to all this sweet talk, seeing how strong and handsome he was, knowing he had a good job, knowing the thing I needed more than anything in the world was just—just a friend, you know? Someone I could . . . be with. So I wouldn't be alone all the time."

Ben felt an aching in his heart. All those lawyers, all those reporters, all those who had spilled so many words about this case—none of them had the slightest idea what this case was really about, or who Keri Dalcanton really was. She wasn't a shady harlot or a manipulative hussy or any of that crap. She was a poor lonely girl forced out on her own who made the mistake of trusting someone who was not worthy of her trust.

"How long before you started seeing him . . . regularly?"

She lowered her head. "Not long. He didn't make any bones about the fact that he wanted a—a—physical relationship. You know. And he wasn't talking about holding hands, either."

Ben's eye twitched.

"He explained to me that he was a special man, and a special man had special . . . tastes." She spoke the word as if it left an unpleasant residue in her mouth. "And slowly but surely, he started introducing me to his world of kinky sex. He liked it rough. Rough and weird. Raw. He wanted all the perverted stuff he couldn't get from his wife, although I didn't know about her at the time. Bondage. Whips and chains. Black leather."

She had to avert her eyes to continue talking. "And what did I know? I was just a little girl from Stroud. I didn't know anything about that stuff. I kept wondering: Is this what everyone does behind closed doors? He'd set up little plays, you know, and we'd act them out. Like, we pretend we've never met each other before. Or we pretend we're in some exotic locale. Didn't really matter—they all ended up the same place. I'd be the master and he'd be the slave. He'd be on his knees in front of me, begging for mercy. And I wouldn't give him any. We'd pretend that he'd been bad and had to be punished. That was the part I hated most. But he loved it. He needed it. It was the only thing that got him . . ." She closed her eyes. "You know."

Ben leaned closer. "Keri, you don't have to tell me this . . ."

"No, I want to. Really. I've kept so much locked up for so long, it feels good, in a strange way. To get it all out. To try to make someone understand. Those reporters and the D.A., they insinuated that I was the sex fiend, like I led him down the road to degradation. But it wasn't me. I hated wearing those costumes and . . . doing those things." Her head fell, and it seemed to Ben as if all the life had gone out of her. "But I loved Joe. I needed him."

"When did he finally tell you he was married?"

"He never did."

"What? But he must've—"

She shook her head. "I didn't find out until his wife, Andrea, showed up at my door."

Ben looked aghast. "No."

"Oh, yes. Oh, yes." A silver tear trickled down her cheek. "I had no idea it was coming. I was just watching television, doing my daily exercises. Believe me, when you have to take off your clothes in front of a crowd of guys every night, you have serious motivation to exercise. I went to the door and there she stood. Andrea. Full of fury and outrage, ready to tear me apart—and I didn't even know who she was or what she was talking about. She came over wanting to fight me, started hitting me and hurling insults, and all I could do was stand there and cry. Just stood there like a little baby and cried. I felt so betrayed, and so . . . used. Used up. She really wanted to hurt me, but she soon saw there was nothing she could do to me that would hurt me any worse than what Joe had done. Nothing in the whole world."

"What did she say?"

Keri brushed a tear from her eye. "Well, eliminating the profanity, what she basically wanted was for me to agree never to see her husband again. But I couldn't do it. I mean— I hadn't had enough time. Before that night, I'd been fantasizing that Joe would ask me to marry him. I'd only just found out he was married, and I still didn't quite believe it. Or didn't want to, anyway. I suppose I was in deep denial. Anyway, I wouldn't give the woman what she wanted. So she slugged me a few more times and made some ugly threats. Finally my brother Kirk showed up and pulled her off me. She left after that, when he wouldn't let her use me for a punching bag anymore."

She pressed her hand against her pink-blotched face. "I was a mess. I didn't know what to do. I couldn't believe it. I mean, I didn't have much of a life, but what life I'd had was totally turned upside down. I tried to call Joe, but he wouldn't answer the phone. My brother was yelling at me, telling me what a tramp I was to be messing around with this married man. Kirk hadn't been happy when he found out I was stripping, but when he learned about this new wrinkle, he just flipped. I had no place to go and no one to talk to. I was all alone, even worse than before, with not even my brother to help me."

"When did you see Joe again?"

"I never did. Not unless you count the pictures in the paper the next day. And you can imagine how I felt then. After that, it didn't matter if he was married or not. He was gone forever— gone from me, gone from Andrea. Gone from everyone."

"How did his badge and ID get under your bed?"

She shrugged. "I assume he left them the last time he was over. The cops kept saying that wasn't possible, but how else could it have happened?"

A disturbing question, and one to which Ben didn't know the answer. Yet. "And the bloodstained clothes?"

"I can't explain it. I mean, I can explain the leather suits— that was part of our regular routine. But the blood—I don't know how that happened. And I don't know how it got under the bed, either. I would never have put them there, blood-soaked or not."

She wiped away her tears, which fell on her blouse, dampening it. "I'm sorry. I don't know why I rattled on so long. You don't need to hear my sob story. It's my problem, not yours."

Ben reached out and took her hand. "You're wrong. It is my problem. It's our problem. And I—I care very much . . . about what happens to you."

Keri's head lifted, and once again her tears began to flow. "You're so kind. I could see that from the first moment I met you. I knew you were more than just a lawyer. That you wanted more than a paycheck. That you cared."

"I do," he said quietly.

"I need . . . someone. Someone who cares. I've been so alone. So scared."

"I'm here," Ben said, and standing, he pulled her into his arms.

"Oh, Ben. I'm so . . . I know I shouldn't, but . . . but . . ." A moment later she pressed her lips against his. Ben responded in kind, kissing her with an urgency he had never felt before. He pulled her close to him, feeling the warm press of her bosom against his chest.

This is wrong, a voice inside his head told him, but a thunderous throbbing throughout his body told him it couldn't possibly be wrong when it felt so right. When she needed him so much, and he so desperately needed her.

* 20 *

Barry Dodds took it slow and easy as he made his way home from Scene of the Crime. He was a short man, short and pudgy, to be honest about it. He hadn't always been that way. Back when he'd had a street beat, just after he finished college, he'd been downright buff. But after four years of that he accepted a promotion and a desk job downtown. Better for his blood pressure, if not for his waistline.

Dodds had a tendency to waddle when he walked, and never more so than when he'd had a bit too much to drink. And tonight he'd had much too much to drink. That seemed to be happening more and more of late, and the scary thing was, he had no idea why. He wasn't under any more stress than usual, he wasn't any busier than usual, and he hadn't had any traumatic incidents in his life. None that he recalled anyway. But something seemed to be bothering him. Either that, or he was slowly but surely becoming an alcoholic.

Ah, what the hell, he told himself. All this serious thinking was making his head hurt. Come to think of it, his head was throbbing, although he wasn't sure that could be blamed entirely on thinking. There was another possible explanation, and it rhymed with thinking, but . . .

He chuckled, then steered himself through Manion Park, the shortcut to the nice two-story he shared with his wife and three kids. A cool breeze caught him, easing his tension, and he felt himself relaxing, drifting into that lovely post-booze presleep quietude that could do a man a world of good . . .

"One too many, Barry?"

Dodds froze in his tracks. It was dark in this park. The lampposts shut off at nine o'clock.

"Who is it? Who's there?"

"Who do you think? The bogeyman?"

Dodds spun around in a circle, tripping over his own feet. "Where are you, damn it! I'm warning you—I'm a cop and I've got a gun!"

"No, you don't. Harry doesn't let people bring guns into the bar, and you didn't pick one up on the way out. I watched very carefully. So don't feed me any more baloney, okay?"

This time, he'd heard enough of the voice to get a fix. "Loving? Is that you?"

Loving stepped out of the shadows. "It is. Nice park you got here, Barry. Wanna play on the teeter-totter?"

Dodds wiped his brow. "You stupid fool. You had me scared to death."

"I don't know why," Loving replied. "I didn't do anythin' scary. Maybe you've got a guilty conscience."

"What in the—Is this about Kincaid? Because if it is, you can forget—"

"That your house?" Loving asked, pointing. "On the other side. The one with the white picket fence?"

Dodds's already tiny eyes narrowed. "What are you getting at? Is this some kind of a threat?"

"I bet that's a nice place to live," Loving continued, ignoring him. "Comfy. Bet your wife and kids like it there."

Dodds was still sweating. He didn't know whether he should run, shout, or fight, and given his current condition, he suspected he couldn't do any of them very effectively. "Yes, Loving, we like our house. I worked hard for that house. A long career catching bad guys. I *earned* that house."

"Earned that house. What a pompous ingrate." Loving walked closer to the much smaller man, his immense shadow dwarfing him. "You'd be living in a goddamn flophouse right now if it weren't for Ben Kincaid. Your wife would've left you years ago, and you'd never see your kids at all, except maybe once every other Saturday for a trip to the zoo."

"What are you talking about?"

"I'm talkin' about givin' a man his druthers, you pissant," Loving said, jabbing Dodds in the chest. "I'm sayin' you owe him."

"I don't owe that lousy cop killer anything."

"You do," Loving barked back. "And I'll tell you somethin' else. You owe me! I'm callin' in my markers."

"You're crazy, Loving. Delusional."

"You know damn well Internal Affairs had you dead to rights. Not that you'd really done anything wrong. Nothing major, anyway. Nothing half the force hadn't done. But they had you cold. More than enough of what passes for evidence these days to toss you right into the unemployment line, if not in prison. Ben Kincaid saved your sorry butt."

"He did his job and I paid him for it."

"You paid him peanuts. You couldn't afford a real attorney. Too much money blown at the bar and the bingo parlor. If Kincaid hadn't taken your case, you wouldn't've stood a chance. And if I may remind you, he took your lousy worthless case because I asked him to, as a personal favor." Loving squared his shoulders. "You owe him, and you owe me, Barry. And today is payback time."

Dodds moved away, reeling sideways. He grabbed the back of a park bench to steady himself. "Loving . . . I can't talk to you. You know what would happen."

"What? The Blue Mafia gonna put a horse head in your bed?"

"If Matthews and the boys knew I was talking to you—"

"They don't need to know. No one's gonna know but me, and I won't tell. I'm not askin' you to take the stand, Barry. I just need some background information. I need to know what's goin' on."

Dodds stared down at the park bench, his lips trembling, but no sounds coming out.

"It's the Blue Squeeze, right, Barry?"

Slowly, trembling, Dodds began to nod.

"Who's behind it? Who's doing it?"

"I—can't say—"

"C'mon, Barry, you can do better than that. It's Matthews, ain't it?"

"I don't know!" he shouted. The strength of his voice seemed to startle even himself. "I mean, I assume it is, but I don't know. I just hear whispers." Dodds started moving away, as fast as his rapidly sobering feet could carry him. "I can't say any more."

Loving grabbed his wrist and slung him around. "Talk to me!"

Dodds's eyes roamed wildly on all sides of him. It was pitch-black, the dead of night, and they were obviously alone, but none of that seemed to comfort him. "There's this secret group of cops, see."

Loving's face crinkled. "Like a special task force?"

"Yeah, sort of. Except it isn't official, if you get my drift. It's . . . private."

"And what exactly does this group try to do?"

"Fight crime. Right wrongs. Prevent injustice. All the things cops are supposed to do. Except . . . without the problems cops have. Without the obstacles."

"You're sayin' a bunch of the boys get together and play Dirty Harry in their off-hours?"

"You have to admit, Loving, things are pretty screwed up these days. Cops work their butts off, putting their lives on the line, taking all kinds of risks. We've got bad guys out there with Uzis, terrorist weapons, stuff that shouldn't even be allowed in a civilized nation, and they're out there taking potshots at us. And we hang in there like clay pigeons so we can catch the creeps and bring them to justice. And what happens then? Half the time some judge lets them go free on a technicality."

"Gimme a break. Outside of movies and TV, that rarely happens."

"The streets get more and more dangerous, and it gets harder and harder to convict anybody. So what are cops supposed to do? Watch all the bad guys get away? Or try to do something about it?"

"How long has this gang been operating?"

"I can't say for certain."

"What have they done?"

Dodds began wringing his hands. "I don't know how far it's gone. I thought it was mostly talk. You know, barroom bluster and poker table bravado. But then this thing with Joe McNaughton came up and . . . well, everything changed."

"They wanted to avenge Joe's death."

"Well—yeah. Of course. Everyone loved Joe. He was a great guy."

"So these clowns decided to hammer out some justice on their own?"

"Not at first. Everyone assumed the Dalcanton chick was going up the river, probably to death row. But after your boss pulled his fancy courtroom sleight-of-hand, and Joe's killer got set free . . . well, that was too much for anyone to take."

Loving grabbed Dodds by the arms roughly. He glared into the shorter man's eyes. "They planted the weapon, didn't they? They put that knife in Ben's file cabinet."

"I don't know anything about that." Dodds's trembling intensified. "Really."

Loving squeezed him harder. "I have to know, Barry."

"I'm telling you the truth. I don't know. I mean, it makes sense. All the tests show that the knife really is the murder weapon. You have to assume the killer didn't put it there. So who else would be likely to have the murder weapon except . . ."

"Except cops." Loving pushed Dodds away from him, disgusted. "Dirty, crooked cops." He paused. "But if they had the knife, why didn't they use it at trial? Didn't they want a conviction?"

"Of course they did. Everyone wanted a conviction. If they'd had the knife, they'd've made sure the D.A. used it." A silence fell. "Unless . . ."

"Unless somethin' about the way they found it didn't incriminate Keri Dalcanton. Unless it pointed to someone else. Then they would've hidden the weapon, at least until they could plant it somewhere that would bolster their case." Loving looked up abruptly. "Like in Dalcanton's lawyer's office."

"Could I be going now? My wife is expecting me before midnight, and if I don't show she'll be worried."

"Barry, I have to know who planted that knife."

"Y—You'll never find out from me."

"I'm serious, Barry."

"I don't know who did it!"

Unfortunately, he appeared to be telling the truth. "Can you find out?"

"No. Absolutely not."

"You still owe me, Barry."

"Correction—I owed you. I paid you back. We're square."

"We're not even close yet."

Dodds squirmed, trying to break free. "I'm telling you, I can't do it."

"And I'm tellin' you, you can." Loving's eyes burned like fire into Dodds's. "Ben Kincaid saved your life. And now you're going to save his."

* 21 *

"Where's Ben?" Christina said, as she whipped through the front doors of the office. She was looking frazzled. Between researching the legal precedents relating to the day's hearing and investigating the case itself, she was running herself ragged. Somehow, she had thought, once she finally got out of law school, things would slow down.

Wrong again.

"So where is he? We're due at the courthouse in ten minutes."

From his desk, Jones gave her a tight-lipped response. "I think he's in his office. Keri's here."

"Keri? This hearing's about him, not her. Why is she here?"

"Don't ask me," he said, slow and pointedly. "She's been hanging out at the office a lot lately."

Crinkles formed around Christina's eyes. "Why would she be—" She paused. "Jones, what's going on?"

He swiveled around in his chair. "Don't ask me. I'm just the office manager. I don't know anything. No one listens to me."

Christina rolled her eyes. "We've got a hearing. We can't be messing around." She marched toward Ben's interior office.

The door was closed. Without pausing a beat, she flung the door open . . .

Ben and Keri jumped away from one another, startled and embarrassed. Ben wiped his mouth dry. Keri readjusted the strap on her blouse.

Christina's jaw dropped low enough to tickle the carpet. "What in the name of—"

"Did you need something, Christina?" The look in Ben's eyes told her in unmistakable terms to keep her trap shut.

Christina spoke through clenched teeth. "We've got a hearing. We're going to be late."

Ben glanced at his watch, then at Keri. "She's right. I've got to go. I, uh, I'll call you."

"I'll wait here."

"Oh, you don't need—"

"I'd rather."

"Well . . ."

"Unless you don't want me to."

"No, it's not—"

Christina's eyeballs practically propelled themselves from their sockets. "Ben, we've got to go!"

"Right, right." He took a step toward Keri, hesitated, lowered his head toward hers, stopped, then finally patted her on the shoulder. "Be back soon."

The sound of four heels racing down the marble-tiled hallway of the county courthouse made a lot of noise, but it was nothing compared to the thunderous sound of Christina's voice.

"What the hell do you think you're doing?"

"Christina, please. It's . . . personal."

"It's not personal. She's your client."

"I am aware of that."

"Have you taken leave of your senses?"

Ben kept his eyes focused on the courtroom at the far end of the hallway. It was a lot easier than looking at her. "I really don't see that it's any of your business."

"You don't, huh? Well, let me remind you of something,

Lothario. We're partners now. I'm in the firm. That means she's my client, too."

"Technically, that's correct."

"Technically? It's a fact, period. And you're screwing around with my client!"

"Christina, keep your voice down!" His own voice dropped to a whisper. "We are not, as you so delicately put it, screwing around. We're just . . . very close."

"Very close? You were practically doing a tonsillectomy on her with your tongue!"

"Christina . . ."

"Not that she was exactly anesthetized. I guess that dance training really comes in handy."

"Christina, honestly. It was nothing."

Christina stopped dead in her tracks. "Nothing? Have you forgotten about the Rules of Professional Conduct which, last I checked, preclude lawyers from performing tonsillectomies on their clients?"

"The Rules don't absolutely forbid all relationships—"

"Don't get technical on me, buddy. What you're doing is wrong and you damn well know it." She started marching down the corridor again, leaving him in her wake.

Ben double-stepped to catch up to her. "Look, Christina, I didn't plan this. It just . . . happened."

She halted again, outside the courtroom door. "You've got to promise me this is not going to occur again."

His face took on a sickly expression. "Christina . . ."

"Promise me. Or I'm not walking into that courtroom."

"What are you, my mother?"

"No, Ben. I'm your lawyer. And I will not represent someone who's screwing around behind my back, endangering his case as well as someone else's. I wouldn't take that from a stranger and I certainly won't take it from you!"

"Christina, this is blackmail."

"You're damn straight it is. Now am I going in there or not?"

Ben inhaled deeply. "All right, I promise. I'll break it off with Keri. At least until our cases are over."

Christina grabbed the courtroom door and swung it open, her anger not subsided in the least. "That's damn white of you, Casanova."

Christina felt certain that Judge Cable already knew every single detail of the case currently before him, but he made a good show of acting as if it was no different than any other matter on his docket.

"*State versus Kincaid,* Case No. CJ-01-578C," he said, in a disinterested tone. Judge Cable was one of the older members of the Tulsa County judiciary. He sported gray hair and bifocals, and was known to be a staunch conservative—the last thing they needed on this case. "The defendant is charged with the concealment of evidence pertaining to a criminal investigation and obstruction of justice. This is the preliminary hearing, to determine whether the defendant should be bound over for trial. Is the defendant ready?"

Out of habit, Ben began to rise. Christina grabbed his shoulder and pushed him back down. "We are, your honor."

"Very well." He turned his attention to the prosecution table. "Will the prosecution be calling any witnesses?"

D.A. LaBelle rose, in a slow, dignified, fluid motion. "We will, your honor."

"Very well." Again, Judge Cable made no reaction. But as he and everyone else in the courtroom knew, the fact that LaBelle was handling this matter himself signified that it was an extraordinary case. "Proceed."

LaBelle called Sergeant Matthews to the stand. Matthews was relatively contained and quiet—for Matthews, anyway. Christina wasn't surprised. LaBelle was known for his attention to detail, his perfectionism. She imagined he'd had Matthews in the woodshed for a good long time, rehearsing his testimony and beating the obnoxious sarcasm out of him.

Matthews said what everyone expected. He refused to reveal the identity of his anonymous source, but claimed he had revealed the source to Judge Hart when obtaining the warrant to search Ben's office. He had no idea what he might find or where he might find it, but given that they were dealing with the murder of a police officer, he took no chances. He ordered backup, an SOT team, snipers, and the police helicopter. He and several other officers searched the office and soon found—in Ben Kincaid's file cabinet—the knife that was believed to be the weapon used to kill Joe McNaughton.

After LaBelle finished direct examination, Christina decided to try a little cross. Traditionally, defense attorneys don't cross much at preliminary hearings. They have little to gain, since defendants are almost always bound over for trial, so they prefer not to give the prosecution any advance warning of what they might do at trial. In this case, however, Christina thought the charges against Ben were so meritless that there was some chance, however remote, that she might get the charges dismissed before they went to trial. A long shot, to be sure, but one she was determined to try.

"What did you think you might find when you searched Mr. Kincaid's office?"

LaBelle didn't hesitate. "Objection. Calls for speculation." LaBelle was an imposing figure in the courtroom. Not only was he one of the best attorneys in the state, he looked good. He was tall and handsome, with just enough gray at the temples to appear distinguished without looking remotely old. There was something about the expression in his eyes, Christina noted, that made you want to believe what he said—even when you were on the other side of the case.

Judge Cable nodded. "Sustained."

Christina pursed her lips. Her first ever cross-ex question, and she'd already lost an objection. Great.

She tried again. "Were you surprised," she asked, "when your uniformed officer pulled that knife out of Mr. Kincaid's file cabinet?"

Matthews stayed calm and restrained his tendency to sneer. "Not especially."

"Why were you so sure you'd find something?"

"I wasn't sure. But obviously, I hoped we would. Otherwise, I wouldn't've been there."

"Did you obtain any evidence indicating how the knife got in the desk?"

"Well . . ." He smiled slightly. "It was in Kincaid's office. And he was her lawyer."

"So you think she gave him the knife and he hid it for her."

Matthews was too smart to be drawn into positively asserting something he couldn't prove. "That would be my assumption, yes."

"But why?"

"To keep it from the police, obviously."

"Why would Mr. Kincaid want to hide the knife from the police?"

"If you're asking me about motive, Ms. McCall, I could only speculate. We have had some indication that Mr. Kincaid's relationship with Ms. Dalcanton is . . . more than professional. It has also been suggested that he may have felt that a big win in such a high-profile case would be good for his somewhat . . . struggling career."

"So he puts the knife in his file cabinet? Does that make any sense? Not exactly a brilliant hiding place."

"I doubt if he expected his office to be searched."

"Are you aware that Mr. Kincaid has a safe in his office?"

Matthews paused a moment. "I do seem to recall seeing that, yes."

"Wouldn't the safe be a better place for something as incriminating as the knife?"

"I couldn't say. He probably didn't want anyone else in the office to know he had it."

"No, he wouldn't, would he? He probably wouldn't tell anyone about it."

"I would think not."

"No one else would know."

"That seems likely."

"No one except the person who put it there."

"Right."

Christina pivoted on one foot and moved as close to the witness stand as the judge was likely to allow. "Sergeant Matthews, what exactly did your anonymous informant tell you on the phone?"

"The informant said that if we searched Kincaid's office, we might find the weapon that killed Joe McNaughton."

"So the informant knew the weapon was there."

"Evidently."

"But Sergeant Matthews—didn't you just say that the only person likely to know the knife was in the file cabinet was the person who put it there?"

There was a considerable pause. "Well . . ."

"Surely you don't think your informant was Mr. Kincaid."

"Well . . ."

"Do you think Ben turned himself in?"

"No . . ."

"Then someone else must've known."

"I . . . hmm." She saw his eyes dart over to LaBelle. "I guess that's possible."

"But why else would someone know? Would Mr. Kincaid be likely to tell anyone he was stashing the murder weapon?"

"Well, it's poss—"

"Because just a few moments ago, of course, you agreed that he would not."

Matthews slowly released his breath. "No, I don't suppose he would."

"So the only way your informant could have known about the knife—was if he put it there himself!"

Matthews's lips tightened. "Perhaps the informant observed . . . something . . ."

"Sergeant Matthews," Christina said abruptly. "Who was your informant?"

"I've said before, his identity is confidential."

"Are you refusing to answer my question?"

"If you want to put it that way, fine. I'm not going to tell you who it was."

"Then I would suggest, Sergeant Matthews, that the only one who is guilty of concealing evidence or obstructing justice—is you!"

D.A. LaBelle rose to his feet. "Your honor, this has gone on long enough. Sergeant Matthews is not the defendant."

"No," Christina said, "but maybe he should be."

"I object!" LaBelle boomed.

Judge Cable cupped his fingers. "Approach."

At the bench, Christina didn't wait to be asked to speak. "Your honor, I move for the immediate dismissal of these charges. This is all trumped-up baloney and everyone here knows it."

"I must protest that inaccurate statement," LaBelle said. His deep resonant voice carried well even when they were whispering. "I've never filed or prosecuted charges I didn't believe in and I'm not about to start now."

The judge held up his hands. "People, please. Could we just talk about the witness at hand?"

"Your honor," Christina said, "the witness has admitted that another person—whom he refuses to name—must've been either involved in the planting of the evidence in Mr. Kincaid's office or acted as a coconspirator in the crime itself. And he refuses to name the person."

"I can't force him to identify a confidential informant, Ms. McCall."

"I know that, sir. But how can we prosecute one man for an alleged crime that might just as well have been performed by someone else, in whole or part?"

"Ms. McCall, this is just a preliminary hearing."

"I know that, your honor. But if we allow these charges to go forward, it will do incalculable damage to the career and reputation of a man who is guilty of nothing more than zealously defending a woman whom the law-enforcement community is desperate to crucify."

LaBelle leaned forward. "Your honor, if I may. I admire Ms. McCall's youthful enthusiasm, but she's tossing out about sixteen issues at once. The question at hand is whether there is sufficient evidence to bind the defendant over for trial."

"And whether this whole charge was cooked up by the police and their informants to punish Ben Kincaid for beating them in court," Christina added.

LaBelle steepled his fingers. "I remember when I was just out of law school. I, too, was full of excitement and zeal—"

"Don't patronize me!" Christina said, jabbing him with a long fingernail.

"—and I admire her support for the man who has, after all, been her employer for the past many years. But we cannot overlook the fact that the murder weapon was found in his file cabinet, and it didn't get there by itself."

"No," Christina shot back. "But you haven't got the least bit of evidence that it was put there by Ben Kincaid."

"She does have a point," the judge said, rubbing the rim of his glasses. Judge Cable was in his midfifties, craggy-faced, with patches of gray. He had a square chin and a no-nonsense gaze. "Your case is pretty thin."

"Your honor," LaBelle said calmly, "we both know the burden of proof at a preliminary hearing is light. All we need to show is the merest rational basis—"

"Not in this case," the judge said hastily. "Not in something that looks very much, whether it is or not, like a vengeance prosecution."

"But he had the knife," LaBelle insisted.

Christina cut in. "His file cabinet did, you mean. Remember, the Rules of Professional Conduct allow a lawyer to take and hold property from a client."

"You can't conceal evidence," LaBelle shot back.

"Well, the Rules are a bit murky on that point, aren't they? And you haven't established that he got the knife from Keri Dalcanton, or that he knew it was the murder weapon, or for that matter, that he ever saw it until the moment your man pulled it out of the files."

"I'm afraid I have to agree with Ms. McCall," Judge Cable said. "This doesn't smell good."

LaBelle drew himself up. "Your honor, with all due respect, we are both officers of this court and we have sworn an oath to uphold the Constitution and the laws of this state. The press and the government will be watching this proceeding carefully, so I know I can trust you to uphold your duty regardless of—"

"Now you listen to me," Judge Cable said, pointing his gavel. "You may be rich, and you may be popular, and you may be the D.A., but I'm the judge, and you will not threaten me in my courtroom."

LaBelle held up his hands. "No, no, Judge, you misunderstand me."

"I don't think I do."

LaBelle's steady calm seemed to be eroding a tad. "I—I didn't mean that as a threat."

"It sure sounded like one!"

"I assure you I didn't mean it that way."

Christina buttoned her lip and watched as the great man melted. There were miscalculations, and then there were miscalculations. And LaBelle's attempted power play had been a major miscalculation.

Not that she had been exactly lacking for confidence before, but if a great trial master like LaBelle could make such a bone-headed mistake, who could begrudge a little baby lawyer like her a few?

"Your honor," Christina said, "why don't we admit what we all already know? These charges were trumped up to suggest fraud in order to get the Dalcanton case reopened. Well, fine. It worked. Right or wrong, they succeeded, and Ms.

Dalcanton's life is on the line once more, despite the fact that the proceeding constitutes a gross violation of her Constitutional double jeopardy protection."

"Young lady," LaBelle said, "the Court of Criminal Appeals ruled—"

"I'm aware of how you weenied around double jeopardy. That's not what I'm here to argue. The point is, they've accomplished their mission. They've got their case back. They don't need to keep pushing these frivolous charges against Ben. Frankly, I think they would've dropped the charges as soon as they got the decision from the appeals court, except by that time there'd been a lot of press and to dismiss immediately would've been a tacit admission that the charges were bogus to begin with."

"Your honor," LaBelle protested, "that is not what happened."

Judge Cable ignored him. "I must admit, I've wondered if that wasn't what was going on here myself. The case seems so thin, and the prosecution is so weak, it's as if you're begging me to dismiss the case. Like maybe you know the charges should go away, but you're too cowardly to do it yourself."

"Your honor," LaBelle said, "let me make clear—"

"As Ms. McCall points out, if you dismissed the charges yourself, you'd probably take a lot of flak from the press. But if you can get me to do it, then you can blame the 'liberal judicial system' or 'revolving-door justice' or something like that."

LaBelle's voice sounded weaker with each protest. "I can guarantee that our prosecutorial motives were pure."

"Yeah." Judge Cable stacked his papers against the bench and pushed himself out of his chair. "Well, I don't see any reason to continue with this hearing."

Christina jumped forward. "Then you're going to dismiss the charges?"

Judge Cable hesitated. "I want to write this one down. I'll prepare an opinion. You'll have it tomorrow morning."

"With an apology?" Christina asked.

Cable squinted. "Excuse me?"

"An apology. From the D.A.'s office. Or the bench. Or both."

"Lady, your man should be grateful just to be off the hook."

"And I'm sure he will be, your honor. But I also think there should be an apology for the great injustice done to Mr. Kincaid, the damage to his career and reputation and so forth. I think it would be appropriate." She swallowed. "Under the circumstances."

Judge Cable pushed his eyeglasses down his nose and gave her a stern look. "You're not exactly shy, are you, Ms. McCall?"

"No, sir," she said, smiling. "Shy is Mr. Kincaid's thing. I've got a style all my own."

✳ 22 ✳

"All charges dismissed!" Christina cried, as she danced through the office lobby. "And 'the court regrets the inevitable inconvenience to the defendant.' We won!" She flung the judge's order into the air, then did a spritely jig around Ben. "We won, we won, we won!"

"That's great, Christina." Ben scooped the order off the office carpet. "No apology from the D.A.?"

"Did you think there would be?"

"I thought it unlikely, but you never know. After the turn you gave LaBelle in the courtroom, anything was possible. You had him quaking in his boots."

"Oh, right."

"You did. I bet he's never been so terrorized by a new grad doing her first prelim."

"Well, that's possible." She smiled. "The best part is, this frees you up to handle the Dalcanton trial."

"Christina, I want to thank you. You did a great job in that courtroom."

"Yeah, yeah. Just pay your bill on time, okay? Most of this firm's clients are total deadbeats."

"But seriously, Christina. I know you took on a big load in a short time, and I'm grateful."

She leaned into his ear and spoke in low dark tones. "If you want to show your gratitude—keep your lips zipped."

"Christina, I already promised you—"

"Do you think I don't know that woman is in your office? As we speak?"

"Christina, we've got a trial to prep. I have a million things to do—"

"Yeah, and she can't help you do any of them. She probably won't even take the stand. Since when did you have clients lurking around while you prepared a case?"

Ben squirmed a bit. "She's very unhappy right now, Christina. And . . . lonely. She has nowhere to go. She feels more comfortable being here."

"I'll just bet she does." She grabbed Ben by the shoulders. "You just remember what I said. If I get the slightest idea you're playing smoochy-goochums with our client, I'm out of here. I mean it. I'd rather go back to Raven, Tucker & Tubb than put up with that."

"Understood. And I will. I mean—I won't."

"Good." She marched off to her interior office.

Jones emerged from the storage room just in time to see Christina stomp past him. "Is this how Christina celebrates?"

"Apparently so."

Jones nodded. "I'll keep the champagne on ice."

Paula rushed out of one of the back offices. She wrapped

her arms around Jones, practically clubbing him with the papers clutched in her hands.

"Puddin', look what I found!" She was bouncing up and down with excitement.

Ben raised an eyebrow. "I assume it's either the winning Lotto ticket or an invitation to visit Buckingham Palace."

"No, silly. A new research file."

"And that's exciting?"

Jones shrugged. "It's a librarian thing." He took the papers out of her hands and scanned them. "Hey, this is hot stuff."

Ben couldn't resist any longer. He scrambled behind them. "What is it?"

"Joe McNaughton's employment file."

"I thought those were confidential."

The corner of Jones's mouth turned up. "Nothing is confidential when my honey-pie starts hacking. She can get anything. FBI files. Department of Defense secrets. She even hacked out the secret formula for Coca-Cola."

"You're joking."

Paula winked. "Come over to my house sometime. I've got my own still in the garage."

"Look at this," Jones said, pointing to a line on the top page. "Something happened to McNaughton about a year and a half ago."

"Something? Like what?"

"I don't know. But up till then he was rocketing through the ranks. Then all at once, he gets bucked back down to patrolman, no explanation given."

"But when he died—"

"And that's even more interesting. He only remains a patrolman for about two months. Then he gets promoted again— back to Sergeant!"

Ben squinted. "That makes no sense at all."

"No, it doesn't. But it's what happened. See for yourself. The promotion was formalized with a new employment contract. Witnessed by a Sergeant Bailey."

"Paula, can you follow up on this?" Ben asked. "Find out where this Bailey is at?"

"Of course. If you promise to never again end a sentence with *at*."

Ben dipped his chin. "I'll ask Loving to see what he can ferret out, too. This might have nothing to do with our case. But I'd still be happier if I knew what was going on with McNaughton before his death."

Paula scurried away just as quickly as she had come. Ben grabbed some papers from his in box and started down the corridor—when he saw an attractive, dark-haired woman making her way through the front office doors.

He recognized her immediately. And he felt the short hairs on the back of his neck stand on edge.

The woman seemed elegant and composed—almost too much so, as if she were making a concerted effort to keep something bottled up inside. "Excuse me," she said. "I'm Andrea McNaughton. Joe McNaughton's widow."

"I know. I remember." A stupid response, but at the moment, Ben's brain didn't seem to be functioning properly. He couldn't believe this woman had actually come to his office.

"I came to see Christina McCall. Is she in?"

"Uh . . . yes. Yes she is. May I ask . . . ?"

"She visited me not long ago. Asked me some questions. I tried to tell her everything I knew, but I remembered something after she left. Something that . . . could possibly be important. If she's available . . ."

Ben shook himself out of his stupor. "I'll get her."

Before he could so much as move, however, a woman emerged from one of the interior offices. Unfortunately, it was not Christina.

"You!" Keri ran forward, her eyes wide with disbelief—and anger. "What are you doing here?"

Ben tried to calm her. "Relax, Keri. She just wants to talk to Christina."

"To Christina? Why?"

"It has to do with the—"

"I thought you people were on my side," Keri said. "I thought I could trust you."

"You can, Keri. Take it easy."

Keri whipped her platinum blond hair behind her slender neck. "I want this woman out of here. Now!"

Andrea's face tightened, but she said nothing.

Ben tried to intervene. "Keri, be reasonable."

"Reasonable? This woman ruined my life!"

"Now wait a minute." Andrea's jaw clenched. Her eyes became small piercing points of light. "If you want to talk about who ruined lives—"

"I don't want to talk to you at all!"

"You stole my husband!" Andrea fired back at her. "First you took his love, then you took his life!"

"Ladies, please," Ben said, but to no avail.

"For your information," Keri said, "I didn't take anything. He gave me his love. He gave it to me because you evidently didn't want it."

"You little bitch." Andrea's nostrils flared. "Don't presume that you know anything—"

"Why else would he have needed me? He wouldn't've come to me in the first place if you were giving him what he wanted."

"That isn't true!" Andrea shouted, her voice choking. "I loved Joe. And he loved me till he met you. Till you forced yourself on him like the cheap whore you are!"

"That isn't what happened!"

"Like hell!"

"I'll bet Joe hated you! That's why he came to me. And it made you so crazy that you killed him yourself!"

Andrea sprang at her like a panther after its prey. Keri rocketed backward. Andrea slammed her against the wall so hard it knocked off a framed diploma. Although she was much smaller than Andrea, Keri fought back with considerable strength. She pounded the woman on the sides of her neck. Andrea's hands clenched around Keri's throat.

Ben raced behind Andrea and tried to break them up. He wrapped his arms around Andrea's waist. He managed to pull her back somewhat, but Andrea lurched forward again. She and Keri tumbled down to the carpet on top of one another, dragging Ben with them.

"Jones!" Ben shouted. "I need help!"

Although he looked distinctly uneager, Jones climbed out from behind his desk. Meanwhile, Andrea had Keri pinned to the floor, straddling her. Her hands were pressed down on Keri's head, twisting it sideways and mashing her face into the carpet. Keri began flailing her arms, pummeling Andrea on the chest and legs. Andrea removed one of her hands from Keri's face and drove it hard into her ribs. Keri screamed.

Ben wrapped his arms under Andrea's and finally managed to haul her off Keri. As soon as he had Andrea under control, however, Keri lunged at her, taking the opportunity to return the blow to the ribs. Andrea cried out in pain.

"Jones!" Ben shouted. "Get her under control!"

Jones tried, but Keri was moving too fast for him. Even as Ben tried to pull Andrea away, Keri followed them, swinging and jabbing every chance she got. Andrea tried to defend herself with her feet. Jones finally managed to wrap his arms around Keri, pinning her in a full nelson, but the instant Keri's arms were immobilized, Andrea hit her with a sharp kick to the gut.

"Stop it!" Ben shouted. "Both of you. Now!"

Ben and Jones yanked the two women to opposite ends of the office. The fighting finally subsided.

"Let go of me!" Andrea shrieked.

Ben refused. "Not till you've got a grip on yourself."

"I said, let go of me!"

"Do I have to call security? Because I will before I'll let you attack my client again."

"Did you hear what that woman said to me?"

"I don't care what she said. I advised Keri not to press charges the last time you attacked her. I won't do that again. So cool it!"

"But she said—she said—" All at once, as quickly as Andrea's rage had come on, it subsided. She crumbled into tears. She fell to her knees, weeping so loud and hard she couldn't seem to stop.

"She—took—my—husband—" she managed to spit out, in hard gasping breaths, wracked with sobs. "She—took—everything—"

"Excuse me, Boss," Jones said. The expression on his face alone was enough to inform Ben that he was not having a good time. He nodded toward Keri, who was still struggling to get free. "What should I do with this one?"

"Put her in my office," Ben grunted. "Lock the door, if necessary."

Jones steered Keri toward the office, still keeping her safely locked in his grip.

Andrea was practically convulsing. She seemed wracked with sorrow. Her head swung from side to side, her hands pressed between her legs.

"I loved him," she said, still gasping for breath. "Truly loved him."

"I'm sure you did," Ben replied. Gazing into her eyes at this moment, he couldn't doubt it.

Gradually, the wrenching sobs subsided. Ben gave her some tissues.

Andrea pushed herself back onto wobbly legs. "I—I think I'd best go now."

Ben held her elbow, steadying her. "Didn't you have something you wanted to tell Christina?"

She gave him a harsh look. "Not anymore."

On the street behind Two Warren Place, just below Ben Kincaid's office, two men sat alone in a motionless car. The one in the passenger seat, an immense man with an extreme buzz cut, was wolfing down Chinese food from tiny white carryout containers. The other, the man in the driver's seat, was peering through a pair of high-powered infrared binoculars.

"He's still in the office," Matthews murmured, eyes locked to the lenses. "Stargazing or something."

"Maybe he's wishin' upon a star," The Hulk suggested, barely comprehensibly, due to the quantity of moo goo gai pan in his mouth.

"Maybe he's thinking about throwing himself out the window." Matthews lowered the binoculars. "We can only hope."

"More likely thankin' his lucky star." The Hulk shoved some more noodles into his face. "I can't believe he weaseled out of those charges. Makes me sick."

"But we got the Dalcanton case reopened. It wasn't a total loss." Matthews lowered his binoculars. "We just need to think of some other way to nail Kincaid's ass to the wall."

"I don't know, Arlen. Maybe we ought to give it a rest."

"Would Joe McNaughton give it a rest?" Matthews's face tightened.

"Well . . . I don't—"

"No, he wouldn't. And neither will we."

"Arlen . . ."

"Joe saved your butt on more than one occasion, Frank, and you know it."

"Sure, I ain't sayin' otherwise, but it seems like there's a point—"

"Joe was my partner, did you know that?"

"Hell, yeah, Arlen. You mention it every day."

"I knew him before either one of us was on the force. We were best friends, right up to the day he died. If something had happened, he would've been there for me. And he wouldn't give up just because things got a little hairy."

"Well, sure, Arlen, but still—"

"I knew Andrea back then, too. Did you know that?" All at once, Matthews's hard-lined face seemed to soften. "She was a pretty thing back then, before she married Joe. Not that there's anything wrong with her now. I was the one who discovered her, you know? She was dating me first. We had some great times together. I mean, the girl had a temper, believe you me. But she was special, I could see that right away. We got really close, least I thought so. Then Joe entered the picture, and those two hit it off and . . . well, six months later they were married." He paused, and his voice took on an odd quavering tone. "I loved that Andrea."

He gazed out the car window. "So you see, Frank, I got two reasons for doing all this. I gotta do it for Joe. And I gotta do it for Andrea."

The car fell silent. The Hulk shifted his enormous bulk around to the edge of his seat and gazed at LaFortune Park. Without streetlights to illuminate the vast area, it seemed dark and foreboding, like the woods in a Grimm fairy tale, an unsafe place where the wary would not venture.

"You know, Arlen," The Hulk began, "I didn't want to tell you this, but I think Barry's been talkin'. To that Loving guy. You know. That works for Kincaid."

Matthews's eyes were glassy and fixed. "I know."

"You do?"

"Not much goes on in this town that I don't know about, Frank."

"But—if Barry's gonna be blabbing, I don't know how safe it is—"

"Barry doesn't know anything. Not really. Just rumors. Vague plans. He's on the outside."

"Well, sure. But if Kincaid gets wind of the Blue Squeeze and all—"

"It will be perfect."

Frank did a double take. "Excuse me?"

"Perfect. Exactly as I planned."

Frank pondered. "You know, Arlen, I'm really not as dumb as some people think. But I got no idea what you're talkin' about."

Matthews drew in his breath, then released it with a weary expression. "If Kincaid comes to believe that we were behind the knife in his office, and he has effectively defused that bomb by getting the charges dismissed, he will think he's safe. That he's escaped the Squeeze." He paused, turning to face his companion. "So he won't be expecting anything else. He won't, Barry won't, no one will." His eyes became dark and narrow. "And just when he feels safe, when he thinks there's nothing more we can do—that's when we'll crucify him."

* 23 *

His grandfather had loved racetracks, Ben recalled, as he paid his money and passed through the turnstile to Winchester Park. It was a bit of an odd dichotomy, now that he looked back on it. His grandfather was a sophisticated man; he'd managed to educate and advance himself from utter and abject poverty to a successful career in the medical arts. He was a stern man with a serious streak, but that was probably what was required to travel from the world in which he was born to the world in which he died. He didn't have much time for frivolity, and when free time did emerge, he usually preferred to spend it with a good book. He abstained from cards, dancing, smoking, loose women, and strong drink.

But he loved the racetrack.

When Ben was a boy, he and his sister Julia were not infrequently palmed off on one set of grandparents or the other while their parents vacationed in exotic foreign locales. If they went with their mother's parents, it meant treasure hunts and hikes in the lush wooded land surrounding their Arkansas farm. But if they were with their father's parents, it meant the horse races. They would all pack up in an RV that was gigantic (or so it seemed at the time) and head for Taos.

Not bad days, all in all. Ben had learned to read a racing form when he was six, and he was better at calculating odds than his grandfather or most of his friends, which made him somewhat popular in that set. The boy genius and his beautiful baby sister. It was fun to watch the horses run, and if he got bored, no one objected to his sitting in the rear of the stadium and reading comics—which was a refreshing change from the reception such activity received at home.

His grandfather had been to the track often enough that he knew everyone, and after a while, they tended to treat Ben and his sister like the track mascots. Probably half of those people were organized crime figures, but Ben didn't know that then. Not that it would've mattered.

His grandfather had died when Ben was fifteen, and after that there were no more trips to Taos . . . and things began to get really bad between Ben and his own father. It was probably just nostalgia, tinged by the tragedy of how things ended up with his dad, but Ben couldn't help but look back at those days at the track with a certain rosy fondness.

He hadn't been to Taos since his grandfather died, but in the interim, Oklahoma had legalized pari-mutuel betting. How his grandfather would've loved that, Ben had often thought. Today, his grandfather could spend an entire day soaking up the larger-than-life atmosphere, the sharks and touts and jockeys and all the other colorful characters, the smell of sawdust and horses and hot dogs—and still be home in time for dinner.

"Benjamin Kincaid! My old friend!" A hand slapped down on his back. "It's good to see you." The merry brown eyes suddenly telescoped. "I hope to God you're not looking for me."

"Actually, I'm not." Ben had no trouble recognizing Alberto

DeCarlo, gangland's youngest godfather. He had inherited the role from his father, who had taken it from his own father. Ben had crossed paths—and he did mean crossed—with DeCarlo a few years before during a murder investigation.

DeCarlo had changed since then; he'd traded the ponytail for an equally fashionable, but somewhat more contemporary buzz and goatee. It looked good on him, and probably also deaccentuated the bald spot and receding hairline. Not that Ben was one to give people grief about their hairlines.

"But it's good to see you," Ben continued. "How's Intercontinental Imports, Alberto?"

"Trey, call me Trey, remember?" Of course. Because he was actually Alberto DeCarlo the Third. "The company is doing wonderfully. Thanks for asking."

When DeCarlo took over the family businesses, Ben recalled, he had tried to modernize them. He had created a corporate entity, Intercontinental Imports, and invested in a number of legitimate enterprises—banking, real estate, and so forth. He maintained that their operations were now entirely legitimate, although Ben knew many at the police department considered Intercontinental Imports a mere sham and cover for the usual mob activities—prostitution, gambling, drug peddling. "I'm into antiques now. Did you know?"

"I didn't."

"You must come down to our showroom, Ben. Near Utica Square. I would imagine a sophisticated man such as you could appreciate some of these treasures."

"Sorry to disabuse you, but I wouldn't know an antique if it socked me in the face. And to tell you the truth, Trey, I'm rather busy these days."

A concerned expression came over DeCarlo's face. "I have read in the papers something about your troubles, Ben, and I'm sorry. I know what it is to be wrongfully persecuted. Could I help in some way?"

Ben's eyebrows rose of their own accord. Was he offering

to fix the case? Buy off the judge? Or maybe have him eliminated? "Thanks for the offer, but I'll have to pass."

"You know, Ben, I may not have told you this, but I was
very appreciative of how you handled that nasty business
after Tony Lombardi was killed. I'm sure you suspected I was
responsible. I know the police did. Nonetheless, you treated
me no differently than you did any other suspect. I won't
forget that. So if there's any way I can help you . . ."

Well, that was an offer he couldn't refuse. So to speak. "Do
you come to the racetrack often?"

"Actually no. I don't enjoy it much, plus, if I'm at any gambling establishment, people always suspect it's a mob opera-
tion. It's a cliché, but there you have it. Some people can't get
past the old stereotypes." Gazing into those deep-set brown
eyes, Ben could almost believe he was sincere. "My grandfather loved horse racing. Actually, he loved all kinds of gambling, which I suppose is what first brought him into his, uh,
line of work. But the horses were his favorite. Always he
would drag us out to Raton to see the horses. Every summer."

"Taos. With my grandfather, it was Taos."

"Really. Well, you see, Ben? We have more in common
than you imagined." His smile faded a touch. "I miss my
grandfather. Despite what you may have heard, he was a good
man and he cared about people. I could never say two words
to my own father without starting a fight, but my grandfather
always understood. You know what I mean, Ben?"

He certainly did. Life was full of surprises. He'd never expected to find himself standing around a racetrack waxing
philosophical with a Mafia kingpin. But there you have it.

"But enough of this talk. You must be here for a reason. If I
may be so bold as to inquire . . . ?"

"I'm looking for Antonio Catrona. I'm sure he's surrounded by security, and I probably don't have a chance, but I
had to try—"

"You want to see Tony? Say nothing more. I shall arrange it."

DeCarlo took Ben by the arm and led him like a dog on a

short leash through the stadium. A phalanx of horses sped past on the track beneath them, and a few moments later, half the stadium rose to their feet, cheering and shouting. It was a close finish, and some of the spectators seemed pleased with the result. But most, Ben noted, tore their tickets into pieces and pulled out their wallets to count what was left.

After taking the elevator to the top level, DeCarlo led Ben to a private glass-enclosed booth. He knocked twice. A burly man at the door let him in. Ben saw the security man give him a stony look, but apparently the fact that he was traveling with DeCarlo was good enough.

Ben peered through the huge glass window at the track below. These had to be the best seats in the house, and just to make them all the better, closed-circuit monitors had been placed all around the room, affording everyone an up-close view of the track. The booth was air-conditioned and sported a fully stocked bar. An attractive woman in a short black skirt stood at the side, waiting to fill orders for one and all.

DeCarlo tapped the shoulder of a large man sitting at the front. He turned, and Ben instantly recognized him from the photos in the police file. It was Antonio Catrona.

DeCarlo pointed Ben out, and a few minutes later, Catrona ambled toward him. He was not fat, not exactly, but he was large and Ben got the impression that walking was not as easy for him as it once might have been. His hair was thinning and gray, but it seemed appropriate to his rugged, scarred exterior.

"Hope you didn't bet the favorite," Catrona grunted.

Ben wasn't sure what to say. "No. I didn't bet at all."

"Smart man. No one ever got rich at the racetrack." An angular, lopsided grin broke out. "Well, no one but the owner, that is." He focused his eyes on Ben's face. "Al tells me I should talk to you, even if you are a lawyer."

"Al's a generous man."

"Yeah. Bit of a wimp, really, but he's smart as a tack, and frankly, these days we need all the smarts we can get. So what can I do for you?"

Ben swallowed. Maybe he'd just seen *The Godfather* too many times, but there was something about the man that was keenly intimidating. "My name's Ben Kincaid. I represent Keri Dalcanton and I'm investigating—"

"Yeah, yeah. I already know all about that. So you're asking if I know anything about that cop getting killed."

"In a nutshell, yes."

"And what would make you think I knew something about it?"

"Well, the . . . manner in which he was killed. The gruesomeness. The severing of his member."

"Sounds like a gangland execution to you, huh?" He chuckled. "You watch too many movies, kid."

"You're probably right. Still—"

"Listen to me. I didn't know this guy—what was his name?—McNaughton. Didn't know him at all. They tell me he was investigatin' me and my boys, but I didn't know anything about it."

"It's . . . hard to imagine that you wouldn't know . . ."

"Do you have any idea how many times I've been investigated? Let me tell you—a lot. They're always investigatin' me. Anytime they got something big, something they can't pin on anybody else, they come lookin' for me."

"Well, I'm sure they wouldn't—"

"You seen that movie, *Casablanca*?"

"Once or twice—"

"You remember when the French guy says, 'Round up the usual suspects'? That's like, the story of my life. Chief Blackwell says 'Round up the usual suspects.' And his boys all come scurrying to me."

"Still . . ." Ben knew he was venturing into dangerous waters, but it was hard to interview a Mafia kingpin without getting into the shark tank. "The police file shows Joe McNaughton had been investigating your organization for several months prior to his death. He must've thought he was onto something."

that thing. Problem is, your tongue does tend to lose some of its sensation after the cutting."

"I don't want that. I want to be able to feel everything."

"Doesn't have to be your tongue. I can split earlobes, lips. I even had one girl who wanted me to do her nose."

"Would that hurt?"

"It always comes back to the same thing for you, doesn't it?" He glanced down at his hand and, applying a sharp fingernail, pricked his own finger. Blood spurted out.

Kirk jumped out of his seat. "What are you doing?"

"Bloodletting. Good for you."

"You're kidding."

"This from the kid who goes around trying to get himself tortured. Look, pal, people have been bloodletting for centuries. It's healthy. Makes the body work a little. Freshens up the supply. You'll feel good afterward. I know I do."

Yes, Kirk thought, but you're soaking in your own urine.

"Look," the man said, "I've seen guys like you before. Want to mutilate themselves, cause themselves pain. This may not be in my best interests, but I'll give you a tip. You're making a mistake."

"Izzat so?"

"Yeah, it is. You think that if you punish yourself long enough, you'll be able to get past your guilt. Right?"

Kirk looked at him sideways but didn't answer.

"Thought so. Thing is—it won't work. It won't work because the only way to root out that guilt is to go after its source."

"Source?"

"Sure. I don't know what it is that's making you miserable. Your boss, your landlord, your car, your girl—"

"Why do you keep talking about a girl? I don't have a girl!"

"Uh-huh. Whatever. The point is—if you want to eliminate that guilt, you have to root out whatever is causing it. Nothing else will do. You can turn yourself into mincemeat, but it won't help."

"Who are you, Obi-Wan Kenobi?"

The blond man laughed. "No, I'm just a guy dripping blood from his finger who sees freaks like you every day. And I know what I'm talking about. You won't be cured until you confront the problem head on."

Kirk fell quiet. "I . . . can't do that."

"You mean you don't want to do that."

"I—I guess—" He hesitated. "It wouldn't be right."

"I can't say whether it would be right, not knowing what the hell we're talking about. But it's the only thing that will make you whole again."

Could he be right? Kirk wondered. He stared out the one small window on the north wall, seeing little but his own reflection. Is that what he should do? Was it even possible?

He turned back around, but the blond man's body seemed to be shimmering, fading. He was having a hard time focusing. He mumbled a few words, stumbled to his feet, and ran toward the door.

The night air was bracing, stark cold, but it didn't clear his head. He was so confused, so lost and angry and . . . messed up.

One thing the freak had said rang true, though. Maybe it was time to confront the source. Someone had to pay. Someone had to be punished before he would ever feel whole again.

And maybe, just maybe, that someone wasn't supposed to be him.

* 25 *

"Are we any closer to figuring out what the hell is going on?"

Christina was standing on the conference table, orchestrating the pretrial chaos all around her. She paced agitatedly from one end of the table to the other; a strand of hair was looped tightly around her finger. Normally, Ben thought, when you talk about someone pulling out their hair, it was just an expression. In the present case, Ben was afraid that if this kept up much longer, he wouldn't be the only lawyer in the firm with a bald spot.

"Do you people understand that we're going to trial? As in, tomorrow morning? On a capital charge?"

Jones and Loving did not appear impressed. "Yeah," Jones said. "And we've been here before. And we're never ready the night before trial. And we never will be. No one ever is. I think it's inherent in the nature of trials."

"Still," Loving grunted, "this is worse than usual. What's the deal?"

Jones took the bait. "It's because we used to have an aggressive, hyperefficient legal assistant, and now we've got a second lawyer. So we're getting about half as much work done." He turned toward Ben. "Boss, now that she's a lawyer, can we hire a new Christina?"

Ben arched an eyebrow. "I'll check the budget."

Jones cringed. "Don't bother."

Christina looked distinctly annoyed. "Listen up, you muggles. This is serious business. I can promise you LaBelle will have his ducks in a row, not to mention a staff of thirty or so people supporting him. He's going to make us look like amateurs. And that's not acceptable. A woman's life is on the line."

Jones fluttered his eyelashes. "Not to mention your brand-new professional reputation."

She gave him a look that would chill fire. "Listen to me, you—"

Ben rose from his chair. "Perhaps this would be a good time for me to get the updates I didn't get earlier—"

"Because you were off trying to get yourself killed strong-arming major mafiosi."

Ben ignored her. "Did you ever find out what Andrea wanted to tell you, Christina?"

"No. After the big catfight in our lobby, she's not talking to any of us. Not even me. Wouldn't even come to the door."

"Great. Don't stop trying."

"Of course not. Goodness knows I have nothing else to do but to harass widows."

"What's your take on her, anyway? You know, Keri thinks she's Suspect Number One."

Christina thought before answering. "It's hard to say. She's very sympathetic when she tells her story. She's going to be devastating on the stand, unless maybe we can get her to lose her temper and slug somebody." She hesitated. "There's something else, though. I had a real sense that something is . . . bothering her. Something she's not telling us. Or anyone, probably. But I have no idea what that would be."

Interesting, Ben thought. But not helpful, unfortunately. "Does anyone know where Keri is? I called and asked her to be here."

Christina nodded. "I called and asked her not to be here."

Ben did a double take. "What?"

"You heard me."

"And why may I ask did you take it upon yourself to do this?"

"Because we have a lot of work to get done," Christina fired back, "and we can't get it done if you two are off making—"

"Excuse me! I think your law degree has gone to your head."

"Baloney. I just know we won't get anywhere if you're busy groping—"

"Hey!" He glanced at Jones's and Loving's attentive and somewhat astonished faces. "Not in front of the children."

Christina shook her head, exasperated. "Loving, have you heard any more from your cop informant? Barry whatsit?"

Loving shook his head. "We've talked, but he ain't said much."

"Is he worried about retaliation?"

"Yeah. But I think he's pretty much told me everything he knows."

"So . . . have we seen the last of the Blue Squeeze routine?"

"I wouldn't count on it. I don't think it'll end until Matthews has a heart attack or Keri Dalcanton gets convicted."

"Which isn't going to happen," Ben said firmly. "Not if I can help it."

"Unfortunately," Jones said quietly, "that's a big *if*."

"Where's your one true love, Jones?"

"Search me. Paula's probably at the library. Trying to get more dope on McNaughton. The mystery of his sudden fall and rise in the police department."

Ben nodded. "I'll be interested to hear what she learns. Everything Catrona told me suggested there was something dirty going on in the police department. Something involving McNaughton. Or maybe Matthews and his Blue Squeeze brigade. Or both."

"I got a question about that, Skipper," Loving said.

"Which is?"

"If some of the boys were on the take, or tied in with Catrona somehow, why would Catrona be so eager to tell you about it?"

"A good question," Ben said, stroking the side of his face. "But alas one to which I don't know the answer." He glanced at Christina, who had climbed down from the table and started plowing through the document bags. "Is my trial notebook ready?"

She gave him a stern look. "Yes, Ben, *our* trial notebooks are ready."

Whoops. This was going to take some getting used to. "Exhibits?"

"Oh yeah. I just wish some of them were our exhibits rather than the State's exhibits."

Ben nodded. "Then I'd say we've done about all we can do tonight."

Christina glared at him. "Are you kidding me? Ben—we don't have a defense! We don't have an alternate explanation for what happened to McNaughton. We don't even have a decent alibi."

"No, and we're not going to get one tonight, either. It'll take LaBelle at least a week to put on his case, and we'll continue to investigate. Maybe we'll get lucky."

"And if we don't?"

Ben drummed his fingers on the tabletop. "Excuse me, but aren't I suppose to be the worried one and you the supportive one?"

"That was before I got my law degree. Now I can wring my hands with the best of them."

"Pity. I'd rather have someone hold my hand than wring it."

"Well, that's why you've got your cute little client."

Ben's expression was indescribable.

"Look, we're not doing any good here." Ben checked his watch. "It's late, we're tired, we're cranky, and we're getting on one another's nerves. Some of us are getting snappish"— he cast a harsh look in Christina's direction—"and I'm sure it's making everyone else uncomfortable."

"Actually," Jones said, "I'm rather enjoying it."

"We're not going to get anything more done tonight. So

let's go home and get a good night's sleep for once. It's the best thing, really."

"I'm not ready to call it quits," Christina said, almost immediately. "I want to review the witness outlines."

"You've already reviewed those things so many times you can probably recite them from memory."

"I'd just feel better if I looked everything over again. Made sure we haven't missed anything."

"That's not necessary."

She looked down. "You . . . just don't understand."

"I do. I remember my first trial. How nervous I was. How sure I was I'd do something wrong. Which I did. But I got through it, and you will, too. Are you feeling sick yet?"

"Seriously. Haven't been able to keep anything down."

"Knees knocking?"

"Like pistons." She looked up. "Does it get any better, after you've got a few trials under your belt?"

"Not really. But you do learn when it's time to go home and get some sleep."

She grinned. "All right. I'll bow to the voice of experience."

"Good. Lights out in five minutes. Anyone caught on the premises is docked to half pay."

Jones pushed himself out of his chair. "Half nothing is still nothing."

She stepped out of the elevator and moved down the darkened corridor, a thick bundle of papers under her arms. The front doors to the office were locked, but she had her own key. Quietly, she turned the tumblers and stepped inside, not locking them behind her. She was only going to be here a minute.

She knew Ben would be angry if he knew she was here, but she had something she had to check and it couldn't wait until morning. Besides, as well she knew, her chances of getting any sleep tonight were about nil. If she had some little detail nagging at her that she couldn't resolve, she'd toss and turn till sunup.

She pushed the power button on Jones's computer. The sudden blue illumination reminded her that she hadn't turned on the lights. Probably just as well, since she wasn't supposed to be here. Still, she would need something. She flicked the switch on the lamp hanging over Jones's desk blotter. The sixty-watt bulb helped a little, but not nearly enough.

"That's just not going to cut it," she murmured. She started away from the desk—then stopped dead in her tracks.

"Is someone in here?" She couldn't explain why, but for some reason she suddenly had the distinct, almost certain feeling that she was not alone.

Had she heard something? That wasn't it, not exactly. It was more like she . . . felt something. Like she sensed a presence. A warm body emanating from . . . somewhere. But if someone was here, why on earth didn't they answer?

"I said, is somebody here? Answer me!"

There was no response. But she was certain she was not alone.

Springing away from the desk, she ran toward the light switch on the opposite wall. Before she arrived, however, she collided. With something. Something that shouldn't be there.

Not something. Someone.

"Who *are* you?"

She felt two powerful arms grip her, pinning her against the wall. She peered at the person before her, but in the near-total darkness, she was unable to make out her assailant's features.

She pounded her fists against her attacker's chest, not that it did any good. "Who is it? Who are you?"

When at last the intruder spoke, the voice was eerily soft, almost as if it were drifting in from a distant location. "Call me the strong right arm of justice."

"And what the hell is that supposed to mean?" She continued to struggle, but to no avail.

"Justice has not been served." The soft flat voice made the hairs rise on the back of her neck. There was something inhuman about it, something rough but cutting, like a dull knife.

"Look, I don't know who you are or what you're doing here, but—"

"It's time justice took a firmer hand."

An instant later, she felt the intruder's right hand leave her arm. She thought this might be her chance to break away, but before she could, the hand came back and slammed hard into her abdomen.

She doubled over, the pain so sharp and abrupt she couldn't immediately tell what had happened to her. She pressed her hands over the place on her stomach where he had hit her.

There was blood on her hands. Lots of it.

The shock was enormous, more than she could bear, more than her brain could catalog. The intruder released her and she crumpled to the floor.

"Who . . . are . . ." She pulled her hands away from her abdomen. They felt warm and sticky. Even in this darkness, she knew she was losing blood, lots of it, fast. She heard footsteps on the carpet and realized with some relief that the intruder must be leaving.

"Who . . . why . . . ?" The blood was forming a large puddle all around her crumpled body. She tried to cry for help, but found she had no strength for it. All she could do was lie there, helpless, gushing blood.

And then, all at once, the pain kicked in. She felt the full force of what had happened to her, her gut ripped open, her insides torn apart.

She clenched her teeth together, trying to block out the pain. She had never felt anything like this, never in her entire life. It was as if she had been broken, eviscerated, as if she had been violated in some permanent, elemental way.

Her head throbbed. She imagined she could feel her blood

flowing through her heart, pumping past her temples and oozing out onto the floor. She felt her strength flowing with it. Sleep was coming on, or something like it. She told herself to fight it. Don't give in, she said to herself. If you sleep now, you'll never wake.

Another flash of pain coursed through her body. What did that person do to her? She couldn't conceive of anything that would hurt like this. Her eyes watered from the anguish but there was nothing she could do to stop it.

Was this what it was like to die? she wondered. Was this how it felt?

"Please . . . help . . ." she said, but she knew there was no chance that anyone would hear. Her eyelids were too heavy to keep open. Her eyes closed and she was glad. She didn't know whether she would ever wake again, but at this point, any kind of sleep seemed like a blissful retreat.

Her head fell back and she was gone. Blood continued to ooze out of her wound, spreading all around her, swirling and flowing until at last it soaked her dress and her hose and her name tag, the standard Tulsa City-County Library identifier, and the five letters of her first name.

William Bernhardt

TWO

* *

The Strong Right Arm
of Justice

* 26 *

"Paula!"

Jones raced down the hospital corridor, his overcoat flapping behind him. He rounded a corner, skidded, reoriented himself, then peeled off in the next direction.

"Sir!" The nurse behind the receiving desk shot out of her chair, but she was much too slow to stop him. Jones was halfway down the corridor before she felt the breeze of his passing.

Jones kept racing, tracing the numbers posted by each door. 510, 512, 514 . . . There it was. 522.

He practically dove toward the door, but a uniformed security officer interceded before he had quite reached the threshold. "Excuse me, sir. That's a private room."

Jones tried to push past him, but the officer wouldn't budge. "Is Paula Connelly in there?"

The officer's eyes narrowed slightly. "May I see some identification, sir?"

"I don't have time for this! I need to see her!"

The officer raised a firm hand, restraining. "I have instructions to prevent any unauthorized persons from entering the room."

"I'm not unauthorized. I'm Jones!"

The officer pulled a list from his shirt pocket and scanned it. "First name?"

"Jones. Just Jones."

"And your relationship with Ms. Connelly?"

"I'm her, er, boyfriend. I guess. Look, I've got to get in there!" The hospital room door opened slightly and a familiar face emerged. "Ben! Tell this lug to let me in."

Ben gave the officer a nod. "He's okay." The officer relaxed and stepped away from the door.

Jones surged forward. "What's his deal, anyway? Why the guard?"

"You'll understand in a minute."

Jones entered the room. Christina was seated next to the bed. And in the bed . . .

Her face was a ghastly white; even her lips seemed colorless. Her face was marred by blue-black bruises in several places. An IV was connected to her wrist; an emergency respirator covered her mouth.

Jones broke down on the spot. He crumbled beside the bed, his eyes wide and watery. "What happened?"

"We don't know exactly," Ben answered, in a quiet, solemn voice. "Someone attacked her when she came back to the office. Left her for dead. We don't know how long she lay bleeding. No one found her till Christina came in this morning. Fortunately, she came in about four-thirty."

Jones gently tugged back the edge of the sheet covering Paula's pale fragile body. "What did they do to her?"

"She was stabbed. At least twice."

Jones clenched his eyes shut. "With what?"

"We don't know exactly. A knife, probably." Ben turned his head. "A big one."

"Is she . . . is she . . . ?"

"We just don't know, Jones," Christina said softly. "The doctors haven't told us anything. The wounds themselves were serious enough. She was barely breathing, and probably wouldn't be now without the respirator. And she'd lost so much blood by the time I found her . . ." She shook her head, not finishing the sentence. Not that it was necessary.

Tears tumbled out of Jones's eyes, one after the other, like a waterfall. "This is all my fault."

"What?"

"She wanted to get married. I knew she did. She never said as much, but . . . I knew. And the crazy thing is—I wanted to get married, too. I just couldn't bring myself to say the words. And now . . . now . . ."

Ben placed his hand on Jones's shoulder. "Jones, don't torture yourself. You couldn't have known."

"I should've known. I should've known that life is precious. And short. I shouldn't've wasted so much time."

Christina walked to the opposite side of the bed and wrapped her arms around him.

Ben stood silently by his friend. Which at a time like this, was about all he could do. Certainly words were useless.

After a long spate, Jones lifted his head and wiped the grief from his eyes. "Ben . . . I won't be in the courtroom today."

"Understood."

"All your trial materials are ready and waiting for you. You shouldn't have any problems . . ."

"Don't even think about it, Jones."

"I have to stay with her. I have to. Just in case. If there's even a chance."

"I know. I took that for granted." Which was true. He had known Jones would want to remain here, even if the trial started without him, and even if Paula's chances were . . . remote at best.

"Why?" Jones said, as if that single syllable spoke volumes. His fist clenched the bed sheet. "Why would anyone do this?"

"We don't know," Ben answered. "But she was attacked in the office. There was no sign of forced entry."

"She was a librarian, for God's sake!" Jones cried out. "She never did anything to anyone. She'd die before she'd hurt someone. How could anyone possibly be so cruel?"

"I don't have the answers, Jones—"

"Do you think it has something to do with your damned Dalcanton case?"

Ben hesitated before answering. Hard words to say, but he couldn't lie to Jones at a time like this. "I have to assume her attacker thought she was a member of my staff. Or Keri. Or me."

Jones's voice flattened. "That's what I thought."

"That's what I think, too."

Ben turned slowly and found, standing behind him, to his horror and disgust, Detective Sergeant Matthews.

"What in the name of God are you doing here?"

"I'm a detective, remember? I've been assigned to this case."

Ben's face was stony. "No way. No way in hell."

"It's already done."

Ben glanced back at Jones. He didn't need any more trauma in his life. He grabbed Matthews by the coat sleeve and jerked him outside the hospital room.

In the corridor, Ben pushed Matthews up against the wall and got quite literally in his face. "I don't know what you're trying to do here, Matthews, but—"

"The only thing I'm trying to do is my job. I've been told to investigate. So I'm investigating."

"You can't handle this case. You're too close. You have too much animosity toward me—and my staff."

"Says who?"

"Don't play games. We both know it's true. And that goes for you and all your Blue Squeeze buddies."

"I don't know what you're talking about."

"Bull. Listen to my words, Matthews. I do not want you on this case."

"Then file a complaint. Ain't gonna break my heart if I have one less case to handle. But until I'm transferred, if I'm transferred, I have to do my job."

"I'm taking this straight to Chief Blackwell."

Matthews chuckled. "Oh yeah, that'll do it. You two are so close and all. Listen to me for a minute, Kincaid, before you go flying off the handle. I know you don't like me, and that's okay. You ain't exactly at the top of my hit parade, either. But understand this—I'm a cop. And I'm a good cop. Always have been. I get the job done. And I don't like seeing crooks and killers get away unpunished. That was true with Joe McNaughton. And that's true with this librarian woman, too. If you care anything about catching the bastard who cut her, you should be glad I'm on the case."

"That sounds great in theory," Ben said, his words even and measured. "But what if the bastard who did this *is* one of your cop buddies?" He leaned in so close Matthews couldn't possibly escape his gaze. "Or you."

* 27 *

The first day of trial was always Ben's least favorite, although in a case like this, picking a favorite was like trying to choose the least offensive from a smorgasbord of deadly poisons. All his usual nemeses were present: the reporters stalking a sound bite, the spectators fighting off boredom by entangling themselves in the drama of other people's tragedies, the judge who would rather be anywhere else, and of course, the district attorney, who acts as if his prosecution is God's Own Work, a characterization which inevitably casts the defense attorney in the role of the Prince of Darkness.

Well, Ben was feeling rather satanic at the moment, as the judge rattled through the preliminaries that launched the monster modern-day trials have become. Christina was sitting at the defense table—between Ben and Keri. Every time Keri so much as leaned in Ben's direction, Christina shot her an evil look that could probably hold back an advance of the demons of hell. LaBelle was keeping his distance, not shaking Ben's hand, not even glancing in his direction, as if his very touch or gaze might somehow contaminate him. Ben knew it was a show for the benefit of any potential jurors who might be around or any potential voters who might be watching on television, but it didn't make him love the judicial system.

Judge Cable seemed particularly crabby this morning and Ben didn't know why. It was impossible to tell with judges. It could be that he didn't get the kind of cereal he liked for breakfast that morning. Or it could be his unhappiness at actually having to hear this miserable Take-Two case. Ben had been trying to contact Mike, but no one was willing to give him any information about where his friend had gone. He was beginning to doubt that anyone knew. And even though he needed to focus his full and total attention on the trial at hand, it was almost impossible not to keep thinking back to the hospital room where Paula's life hung in a delicate balance.

For Ben, getting into the trial mind-set was a process of submersion. It was as if the courtroom was a submarine, and the further the trial progressed, the deeper they sank beneath the waves. The whole trial experience was one of separation, apartness from the real world. As Ben became more and more consumed by the incredibly complex trial process, he lost touch with almost everything that was a part of his normal life: fun, friends, family—hell, even his cat.

Why did he do it? Ben had asked himself on more than one occasion. In many respects—in most respects—he hated being in trial. And yet, at the same time, there was something elusively thrilling about it. Granted, there was the opportunity to actually do some good in the world, to be of service to other people, and Ben knew he had been, on more than one occasion. But there was something else, something hidden away beneath all the objections and legal obscurities and lies. Being in the courtroom was like being in the arena. It was unmasked conflict, one man against another. It was a small sort of warfare, and yet it was sanctioned by law. If it was true that all men, even civilized sorts like Ben, had a spark of the warrior in their heart, this was an occasion when that instinct was truly revealed.

Whether Ben cared to admit it or not, being in trial was like nothing else in the world.

"*The State versus Keri Louise Dalcanton*, Case No. C-01-874." Judge Cable rattled the papers from which he read. "Court is now in session. Are the parties ready to proceed?"

Ben and LaBelle both indicated that they were.

"Gentlemen, let's pick a jury." He redirected his attention to the bailiff. "Please call out the first twenty names on the list, Brent."

Brent the bailiff called out the names of the potential jurors—"driver's licenses," lawyers liked to call them, because of the keenly scientific basis by which they were chosen. Brent had a clear, bass voice; he would've been good on radio, Ben mused. But in the courtroom, his voice gave a sense of authority and gravity to what was basically a mundane procedural matter.

The lucky twenty took their seats in and around the jury box. They knew the case for which they were being called. Ben could see it in their eyes; he could feel it in their movements, in the way they carried themselves, the way they looked at one another.

LaBelle knew it, too, and he made no bones about the fact when he began his juror examinations. "You know why you're here," he said, positioned still as a statue just beyond the rail demarking the jury box. "I won't go into a lot of details about the cruel, inhuman crime that lies at the heart of this case. You'll hear plenty enough about it later; I won't describe the horror any sooner than necessary. It isn't fair to you."

That, Ben thought, plus it would draw an immediate sustained objection and mess up his whole voir dire.

"You know why you're here, but do you know *why* you're here?" LaBelle paused, letting the words sink in, as if he had uttered some great profundity. "You're here because you have been asked to be part of the most important branch of our government. The branch that keeps us safe. The branch that strives to see that justice is done, that virtue is rewarded, that evil is punished."

This was a bit heavy-handed, even for LaBelle, Ben thought. He wondered if the man was making a tactical error, coming on so strong when the evidence wasn't yet on the table. Still, LaBelle had tried more cases than he had; Ben had to assume he knew what he was doing.

"When you become a part of the judicial process, you enter something larger than yourself, something greater than all of us combined. You become a part of society's quest for correction and perfection. A never-ending battle. A crusade, if you will. You probably already know this, but I want to remind you of it now, at the outset, so you will remember that you must take your duties seriously and perform them to your utmost ability, with honesty and fearlessness. In short, you must not be afraid to do what is right."

Christina leaned into Ben's ear and whispered. "The trial hasn't started and he's already pressuring them to convict. Shouldn't we object?"

"No," Ben whispered back. "The jury will be suspicious if you try to shut him down every time he starts to talk about the defendant, and Judge Cable is the sort of judge who is only going to tolerate so many objections, whether they're right or wrong. Save it for something that matters."

LaBelle began his direct questioning of the jurors, first as a group, then individually, particularly when a raised hand gave him answers he didn't like. Most of his questions appeared designed to weed out potential bias and preconceived ideas that might not be to his advantage. "I want you to understand that I'm not accusing anyone of anything," he emphasized. "But my job is to root out candidates who might not be appropriate for this jury. Doesn't mean you're a bad person. Just means this isn't the right trial for you to hear."

Because you're a bigoted moron, presumably, but LaBelle omitted that part.

He mercilessly quizzed anyone who'd had prior problems with law enforcement, or anyone who'd witnessed such troubles in their immediate families. He trolled for jurors with grudges against police officers—a sensible precaution, since most of his witnesses would be cops. And he looked for people who didn't believe in the trial process, either for philosophical or religious reasons. When Juror Number Fourteen, a heavyset woman in her late forties, explained that she believed all people should follow the Word of the Lord and "turn the other cheek," Ben knew she would be the first one LaBelle yanked. Forgiveness was not on his agenda.

Some of the prejudices LaBelle tried to unearth were not exactly on the standard ACLU list. "Now there's another subject I need to address with you good people," LaBelle explained. "This is a delicate subject, and I apologize in advance if this discussion causes you any discomfort. It's always awkward to discuss matters that are . . . sexual in nature, but I'm afraid in this case, it can't be avoided." This, of course, was an introduction that ensured every juror would be listening to him with rapt attention.

"This relates to the defendant, Keri Dalcanton," LaBelle continued. "As the subsequent evidence will show, prior to this trial, and at the time of the crime in question, Ms. Dalcanton was employed as . . ." He let his head hang low, as if he somehow bore part of her great shame. ". . . as a stripper. For those of you who don't know what a stripper is—"

Ben rolled his eyes. Right.

"—a stripper is a woman who removes her clothing—in a public place in front of a group of men—for money. Usually this takes place in a smoky crowded bar that does not exactly cater to the highest strata of our society. It's my understanding that loud music and, well, frankly erotic dancing are usually a part of this performance."

Christina looked at Ben sharply. "Would this perhaps be the time to object?"

Ben shook his head. "Not yet. She was a stripper, like it or not, and they're going to find out sometime."

LaBelle continued. "But I must caution you, ladies and gentlemen of the jury, that no matter how distasteful you find these . . . elements of the defendant's life, you must not let them prejudice you. The decision that you ultimately reach—that I am confident you will reach—must be based upon the evidence, and nothing else. I want to make sure you do not allow these unpleasant realities to bias your verdict unfairly."

Which of course was a gigantic crock. LaBelle was bringing up Keri's status as stripper for the sole purpose of prejudicing the jury—principally composed of older women—against her. He knew they wouldn't "meet" Keri, so to speak, on the witness stand, until well after he had finished putting on his case—and maybe not even then. He would take advantage of that fact by attacking her well before she could defend herself. He wanted the jury disliking her from the get-go.

"Ben," Christina said, "I think this is getting—"

"Not yet."

LaBelle placed his hand against his brow, his expression suggesting that there were even more unpleasant topics yet to come.

"Unfortunately," he continued, "our discussion of matters pertaining to . . . sex . . . cannot end there. In the trial to follow, there will be considerable discussion of . . . uh, sexual activities involving the defendant and the victim, which could be equally prejudicial. The evidence will show that Ms. Dalcanton regularly enjoyed sexual practices that many of you will find strange or even . . . aberrant. That she promoted and enjoyed—"

"Now?" Christina asked.

"Oh yeah," Ben replied.

Christina jumped to her feet. "Objection, your honor. This has gone well past the scope of proper voir dire."

The judge agreed. After a brief bench conference, Cable instructed LaBelle to get off the defendant and back to his own case. LaBelle acquiesced easily. Presumably he knew he was on dubious ground and was just trying to see how far he could get.

LaBelle questioned the jury on a few more miscellaneous topics, then finished up with a tremendous push-and-pressure routine on the subject of the death penalty. Needless to say, with a gruesome, public, torture-murder and dismemberment, LaBelle wanted the ultimate sanction, and he was determined to uproot any juror not capable of delivering.

"Most of us are, at heart, I believe, good Christian people," LaBelle opined. "We are generous and forgiving. We want to be kind. And therefore, it goes against the grain to issue the greatest of all penalties the law allows, the one that permits no second chance. And statistics show we are particularly hesitant to issue that sanction when the defendant is a woman." He paused, leaning against the rail for dramatic effect. "But I will suggest to you, ladies and gentlemen, that it is not the gender of the defendant that matters, not the goodness of your hearts. There are some crimes so extreme—so abominable—that they cry out for justice. An eye for an eye. To preserve our principles—and our safety—there are times when the death penalty cannot, and should not, be avoided."

He called for a show of hands of those who would, if the right facts were presented, be capable of delivering the death penalty. He was not disappointed. He quizzed many of them personally, leaning on them ever so subtly. Again, he was not disappointed.

When all was said and done, LaBelle had the death-qualified panel he wanted.

Ben's questioning was considerably briefer than LaBelle's had been, but by the time he got the jury, they were tired of this routine and most of the obvious inquiries had already been made. And at heart, even though he knew other attorneys would never agree with him, or admit it publicly anyway, he thought the whole jury-selection process was a big crap shoot. He could question these people for a month; he'd still not really know anything about them. He couldn't predict how they would rule in a trial; no one could. All he could do was watch their eyes, listen to their answers, and hope for the best.

He started with his usual spiel on the importance of the four magic words: *beyond a reasonable doubt.* It might not be exciting stuff, but Ben knew it was the most important point he could make at this stage of the trial—maybe at any stage of the trial. LaBelle could rant about the death penalty all he wanted; if Ben could convince these twenty people that the defendant really was presumed innocent, and that the burden of proving guilt beyond a reasonable doubt was as tough a standard as it sounded, the penalty stage could become irrelevant.

Unfortunately, what he soon learned was that virtually everyone on the jury already had, via the media, some passing familiarity with Keri Dalcanton—and that they didn't need LaBelle's influence to dislike her.

"I heard she was after the guy's money," Juror Number Eight admitted, after Ben pressed her for details on what she had read about this case. What he got from the other jurors was no more encouraging.

"I knew a woman who stripped once. She was nasty."

"A nice girl would not have been involved with a married man."

"She had to be pissed when he broke it off with her. Look what happened to the body."

"My cousin's girlfriend's mother saw her once in a restaurant. She said she was wearing black leather."

"I heard this wasn't the first. Like she's got chained and dismembered victims buried all over the state."

Ben tried to suppress the deep despair he felt. The media saturation on this case was greater than he had imagined. Keri Dalcanton appeared to have been turned into some kind of nouveau urban legend. He didn't have nearly enough preemptory challenges to remove all the problems on this jury panel.

Ben questioned those who had negative preconceptions about whether they could still be fair and unprejudiced. If anyone indicated that they could not, Ben could get the judge to remove them for cause, thus saving his precious and limited preemptory challenges. But so long as they indicated they thought they could be fair, no matter how unlikely that seemed, the judge would not remove them from the jury panel. One woman admitted she might have troubles (probably because she had other things to do and wanted off the jury), but the others insisted they thought they could still evaluate the case without prejudice. Which ironically enough, at that point, was exactly what Ben did not want to hear.

By the end of the day, the jury had been selected. LaBelle predictably removed young females and anyone else he thought might be wobbly on the death penalty. Ben removed older women and people with strong fundamentalist leanings—anyone whom he suspected might never get past the fact that Keri was a stripper with an active sex life. When all the shouting was done, fourteen people remained—a jury of twelve, plus two alternates.

Ben had done the best he could, but he knew this jury was far from ideal. Many of them had come into the courtroom assuming Keri was guilty. He saw them looking at her, catching furtive glances, like children who didn't want to be caught staring at the scarlet lady. Sometimes, Ben knew, impressions were more important than evidence, and this could well be one of them. As long as they thought Keri was a bad person, a harlot, a temptress, a Jezebel—all negative female stereotypes LaBelle would be reinforcing at every opportunity—Keri didn't stand a chance.

28

Kirk fell to his knees and flung himself prostrate across the stone bench that flanked the north side of the prayer garden. His arms cradled his head. He thrashed back and forth, riddled with torment, unable to stop the flow of tears that poured forth from his eyes.

"My God, my God," he moaned to himself. "What have I done?"

He turned his head up, just enough to see the statuette of St. Francis of Assisi. The saint had kindly eyes; he seemed to look at Kirk sympathetically, as if he truly cared about him, as if he shared the torment that wracked Kirk's soul. St. Francis loved the little animals, right? Would he love Kirk, too? He felt like an animal, torn and battered, barely surviving from one day to the next, isolated from everyone he ever knew or . . . loved.

He tossed his head back, peering upward, like a wolf howling at the moon. The reminders of his sins were everywhere, all around him. Sins of commission, sins of omission. The first sin was perhaps the worst, but certainly that was forgivable, wasn't it? The second sin was an atrocity, but given what had gone before, what choice did he have? Surely most people—even St. Francis—could understand where he had been, why it had happened. But the third sin—no one could forgive that. Not even God.

He turned his head, peering into the deep-set stony eyes of the saint. Would you forgive me? he wondered. Could you forgive me?

He felt wasted and empty. Is this what it's come to? Talking to garden figurines? Begging forgiveness from statuary? He was in even worse shape than he had imagined.

"God hears your prayers," a voice said softly. "He knows you're suffering and he wants to help you."

Kirk's head shot up. Did the statue—?

He relaxed. No miracles this night. The tall bearded man hovering over him was entirely corporeal and all too present.

"I'm Father Danney," he said, He was wearing a beret, cocked at a jaunty angle. "Can I possibly be of help?"

"Why are you here?" Kirk growled. Don't be so damn rude, he thought to himself, almost simultaneously, but the deed was already done.

"This is my church," Danney explained. He didn't seem put off in the least by the insolence. "I work here at St. Dunstan's."

"Kind of late to be out priesting, isn't it?"

Danney smiled. "Paperwork," he explained. "It gets the best of us, even in the ministry. And I do like to walk the garden at night."

"I don't think you can help me, Father."

"Why don't you give me a try?"

"You can't imagine what I've done." He turned away, unable to meet the man's glimmering eyes. "I've done something horrible."

"We all have, son."

Kirk shook his head. "Not like this."

"You might be surprised."

"I've made a terrible mistake. An unforgivable error. And it's like I can't stop somehow. Everything I do, I follow up with something even more terrible. Like I think that might make it better. Might cancel it out. But it never does. It just makes everything worse. Much, much worse."

Father Danney crouched beside him. "Are you sure you wouldn't like to come inside? We could get something warm to drink. Maybe pop open a bottle of wine."

Kirk looked at him coldly. "Should a holy man be drinking wine?"

"I'm an Episcopalian, son. We love wine."

Kirk turned away. "I prefer to stay where I am."

"Well, fine. I adore this garden. Always have. Even after all these years, after so many people I loved have passed away and had their ashes buried here. I still love this place."

"You're a flower freak. You're into the smell of honeysuckle."

Danney shook his head. "I feel the presence of God here. Don't you?"

"No," Kirk said quietly. "Not for a long time."

Father Danney gently laid his hand on Kirk's shoulder. "You know, my friend, God knows what you've done. And no matter what it was, He understands. And He's waiting to forgive you."

"Not this time," Kirk said, shrugging his hand off. He pushed himself to his feet. "I shouldn't have come here. I'm leaving, Father."

Danney clasped his arm. "You can't keep running forever."

"Watch me." Kirk gave the priest a hard shove, sending him reeling backward into an azalea. Kirk turned and ran, full out, as hard as he could manage, leaving the meddling holy man far behind.

But not his guilt. Never that. No matter what he tried, no matter what he did to himself, he could never escape that.

He had shoved the priest hard, trying to push him out of his life, out of his mind, but even as he ran, he knew he had not been successful. The man was back in the bushes, but his words remained, haunting Kirk, just like everything else.

You can't keep running forever, he had said. Because eventually, they'll find you.

Which was true, Kirk knew, even as he tore down Seventy-first. Eventually they would find him.

Unless he made it impossible for them to find him. For anyone to find him.

But that wasn't the worst thing the priest had said. That wasn't what haunted Kirk most, even as he sweated and cried and sent fresh shock waves of pain rippling through his tortured body.

God knows what you've done.

That was more than a mere pronouncement. That was a curse. That meant no matter what Kirk did, what pain he caused himself, what torture he endured, it would never make any difference. God would always know.

And so would he.

* 29 *

Day Two—The Siege Continues, Ben thought, as he left the parking garage and headed toward the county courthouse. As usual, a throng of reporters were lying in wait; as soon as he approached they surrounded him, blocking his way, forcing him to push past them just to get inside. The minicam lights were on him every step of the way as the reporters tossed out questions one after another.

"How do you think the case is going for you?" one of the reporters shouted above the fray.

"The Rules of Professional Conduct discourage lawyers from giving public statements regarding pending criminal actions."

"District Attorney LaBelle gave a press conference this morning."

Ben's lips pinched together. "No comment."

Another reporter inched forward. She was female and, if

he wasn't mistaken, one of Christina's buddies, not that that was doing him any good this morning.

"Do you think your client will be able to overcome her past life?"

Ben looked at her levelly. "I think she already has."

"Don't you think it will be hard to get people to listen to Keri Dalcanton's story when there's so much public antipathy toward strippers?"

Ben shrugged. "People don't like reporters, either. But they still listen to you every night at six and ten."

The reporter placed one hand firmly on her hip. "I think there's a little difference between a reporter and a stripper."

"True. Strippers provide a public service."

Ben blazed a trail to the elevators. Probably not a smart move, he thought, as he glanced back and saw the reporter's gaping expression. But it certainly was fun.

Christina and Keri were waiting at the defendant's table when he arrived. Ben waved Christina aside.

"How is she this morning?" he asked.

Christina shook her head. "Two words: *basket case.*"

Ben approached Keri and laid his hand gently on her shoulder. A second thereafter he caught Christina's stony stare and removed it. "How are you doing?"

Keri's eyes were red and puffy; she had obviously been crying. "I . . . didn't sleep well."

"That's understandable." And it was, but why today? Most defendants got their worst case of jitters on the first day. Keri had seemed fine yesterday. What had happened? "Did you see something or . . . read something?"

"No. Nothing like that." She pinched the bridge of her nose, pressing so hard she left a mark. "It just sunk in, that's all."

"What did?"

"LaBelle. What he was saying all day yesterday. He . . . he didn't use these exact words, but basically, he was trying to get the jury to kill me. That's what it amounted to. He wants me dead."

Ben tried to be comforting, but he knew that if he were in her shoes he'd be just as traumatized. "Well, he's the prosecutor. Since you wouldn't plea bargain, and this case has gotten so much publicity, he probably feels he has to push for the maximum sentence."

"Maximum sentence? We're not talking about some fine, here, Ben. We're talking about a man who wants me killed!" She brushed away a fresh batch of tears. "And he's standing right in front of me, trying to get other people to do it!"

"I'm sorry, Keri. I know this must be rough. But I have to warn you—it's going to get a lot worse."

Keri's head fell. "Do I have to be here?"

"I'm afraid you do."

"Every day?"

"Absolutely. It's required. And we wouldn't want the jurors to get the impression you didn't think it was important."

Keri sighed, long and mournfully. "I suppose you're right. But, God, it hurts. It hurts being so afraid." She turned her face away, hiding the tears. "And it hurts not . . . not knowing."

Ben mentally finished the sentence for her: Not knowing whether you're going to live or die. Everything depended on the outcome of this trial, this preposterously creaky, unscientific way of determining whether a human being should be executed.

"We're not going to give LaBelle what he wants," he said, whispering softly into her ear. "He has to get a verdict before he can get a penalty. And we're going to do everything possible to stop that from happening."

"But—but—what if that's not enough?"

Ben didn't bother responding. To some questions, there was simply no good answer.

After the preliminaries, Judge Cable invited LaBelle to deliver his opening statement. LaBelle took center stage, his arms locked behind his back. If his expression had been serious the day before, it was positively grim today.

"Ladies and gentlemen of the jury, I won't insult you by shilly-shallying around the truth or trying to cushion the blows. You know there is a horror lurking at the heart of this case. Let's confront that horror now, so we can get past the inevitable initial shock and decide what needs to be done about it.

"The horror took place on the evening of March the fourteenth, right here in Tulsa, Oklahoma. The defendant, Keri Dalcanton, had left her job at a south side club where, as you already know, she took off her clothes for a living. It was very late, but when she returned to her apartment, no one else was there—not her brother, who lived with her, and not her married lover, Joe McNaughton, who often met her at her place after she got off work.

"All was not well between the two lovers. As the evidence will show, Keri Dalcanton had been visited earlier by Joe McNaughton's wife, Andrea. Harsh words were exchanged. Ms. Dalcanton actually attacked Andrea, hitting her repeatedly, pummeling her with blows that left Andrea bruised and battered. Andrea had asked Ms. Dalcanton to break off the affair with her husband of twelve years—and she refused.

"But now the tables were turned. Ms. Dalcanton was the one who was listening—and she didn't like what she heard. Joe McNaughton arrived and informed her that he was breaking it off. That he was returning to the loving arms of his wife. That it was over."

LaBelle paused, making them wait a bit before he delivered the clincher. "That was when—and why—she killed him."

LaBelle stepped away from the rail. "Some of you, I suspect, may well feel sympathetic toward Keri Dalcanton and her plight. Perhaps some of you have been jettisoned by a lover after the relationship became old or inconvenient. But none of you took the step Keri Dalcanton did. She is not on trial today because she was dumped. She's on trial because she killed the man who dumped her.

"Is there any doubt—any at all—that Keri Dalcanton committed this crime? Not in my mind, and by the end of this trial, I predict, not in yours. You will hear from the police officers who investigated the crime, who found the evidence that clearly proved she was the murderer. You'll hear incontrovertible evidence that Joe McNaughton went to her apartment that night—a fact she later denied. You'll hear from the coroner, whose findings are totally consistent with the police evidence. And you'll hear from the victim's poor wife—the truly wronged woman in this case. After you've heard her testimony, any lingering doubts you may have harbored will be gone. You will know with certainty what I know with certainty—that Keri Dalcanton murdered Joe McNaughton in a fit of jealousy and rage.

"Who else could've done it? Who else would've done it, especially in such a gruesome and barbaric fashion? When Joe McNaughton's body was found, crucified and pilloried in the center of Bartlett Square, he had been stripped naked and bound with chains—chains previously used by Keri Dalcanton during her fetishistic and perverted sex play. He had been stabbed over twenty times, bloodied with a large sharp knife, obvious proof that this was a murder of rage and vengeance. Worse, he had been mutilated, his male member severed and stuffed into his mouth, obviously suggesting that the murder had a sexual motivation. And finally, after he was dead, the word 'faithless' was written across his chest in his own blood. When Keri Dalcanton did that, she might as well have signed her own name."

LaBelle stepped closer to the jury box, his head lowered and his hands clasped, almost as if in prayer. "I know this is a difficult thing I ask you to do. Most of you are kind, understanding people. You want to forgive, not to punish. But when an abomination of this magnitude occurs, forgiveness is not an option. You must put that instinct out of your mind. You must become, if you will, machines. Logical, rational, truth-seeking machines. Because if we are to have any sense of security in our society, any semblance that justice is done, we cannot allow this heinous crime to go unpunished. When you swore your oath and accepted your role as juror, you became a part of a great machine, a machine that keeps us safe, that keeps society moving forward. Please don't take that role lightly. You must do your duty." He paused and looked at them levelly. "When all the evidence is in, hard as it may be, you must find the defendant guilty of murder in the first degree."

Since he'd never had a partner before, deciding who would do what was a new and strange experience for Ben. His choices had to be realistic; he had the utmost confidence in Christina and her abilities, but this was her first trial, and a woman's life was hanging in the balance. Ultimately, he decided to give her opening statement, while reserving closing argument for himself. Many attorneys, he knew, thought opening statement was more important, since first impressions are so critical and it is the lawyer's first chance to discuss the meat of the case with the jury. Ben disagreed, at least in this instance. The jury would learn little about the case in the opening that they didn't already know. What they needed now was someone who could elicit sympathy and urge them to keep their minds open until they had heard all the evidence. Ben knew Christina was much better at understanding and touching human hearts than he was ever likely to be. So she got the job.

"I'm in agreement with Mr. LaBelle on one point," Christina said, almost too quietly. Her voice quivered a bit as she approached the jurors. "All I ask is that you listen to the evidence, judge it fairly, and then look into your hearts and render the verdict you know is right." She cleared her throat, adjusted her pitch. She was learning as she went. "But I also differ with Mr. LaBelle. I don't think it takes much courage in this case to deliver a guilty verdict. That's what he wants you to do. That's what everyone wants you to do. To go against the grain—that's hard. But that's what I'm going to be asking you to do. Because Keri Dalcanton is not guilty. She did not commit this crime."

Christina repositioned herself slightly. When her voice returned, most of the nervousness was gone. "Contrary to Mr. LaBelle's suggestion, most of the so-called facts he presented to you are keenly in dispute. Most of them are entirely unproved—they are suppositions. Guesses. The real evidence will paint a significantly different picture. Keri Dalcanton is not an evil woman. Basically, she's a scared little girl from Stroud, Oklahoma. The evidence will show that she was only eighteen when she left her hometown, after the tornado devastated it and she couldn't find work. Except she couldn't find work in Tulsa, either, not enough to support her and her brother, not with her limited skills. She lived in a tiny apartment at a level of near abject poverty, barely able to feed herself for months. Maybe becoming a stripper wasn't the best choice, but the fact is, she was a child, and children make mistakes. Maybe getting involved with Joe McNaughton wasn't the smartest move either, but if you'd been in her situation, if you'd found a man offering to take care of you and solve your many problems, wouldn't you have been tempted? I know I would've been."

Christina moved ever so slightly closer to the jury, drawing them in both physically and verbally. "It's true, as Mr. LaBelle said, that she had a sexual relationship with Joe McNaughton, a married man, although she didn't know he was married at the time and the relationship was neither so unusual or so aberrant as he suggests. Here's the truth, ladies and gentlemen—Keri loved Joe McNaughton. Maybe she shouldn't've, but she did. With all her heart. He was her protector, her savior. She was devastated when he tried to break up with her. But she still loved him, and as the evidence will show, she wouldn't've hurt him. Not then. Not ever.

"The prosecution has no real evidence that she committed this crime and they never will. Because she didn't. They can make suggestions, they can trot out circumstantial indicators. But they have no proof. And that's of critical importance. Because as my partner told you yesterday, the burden of proof is entirely on the prosecution. They must prove her guilt beyond a reasonable doubt—a very high standard. If they fail to do so—and they will—then you have no choice under the law but to find her not guilty. No choice whatsoever. That's what the law says you must do. And what I'm confident you will do."

She paused, started to turn away, then stopped again. As far as Ben knew, this was the end of her opening, at least as they had practiced it. But it seemed Christina had something more she wanted to say.

"And let's get one more thing straight before I sit down, okay? This court is not a machine. Keri Dalcanton is not a machine. *You* are not a machine, and I hope to God you won't act like one. This case is not about machines. We could probably program computers to be jurors, if measuring evidence was all there was to it. But we choose to use real people because that's what trials are about. Real people. Only people can understand what goes on in the human heart. Only people can consider circumstances, can separate truth from fiction. And only people can stand up and do what they know is right, even in the most difficult of circumstances. We are not machines and God willing we never will be. We're human beings. So let's act like it."

* 30 *

Ben walked Keri to the door, squeezed her hand (after he made sure Christina wasn't watching), and told her to go home and get some rest. "We're likely to be prepping well into the night. You need to get some sleep."

"Me?" she said. "But I don't even do anything."

"Whether you do or not, the jurors' eyes are on you, constantly. You need to look sharp, confident, and very not guilty. So go home."

Instead of moving away, she took a step closer. Her fingers brushed against his. "Ben . . . thank you." Her lips turned up toward his.

Ben backed away. "Keri . . . I told you . . ."

"I know. I'm sorry."

"After the trial, it will be different—"

"It's just so hard . . . being close to you, all day long, and not being able to . . . show you how I feel."

Ben felt a sudden dryness in his throat. "I know how you feel. Intimately. But we have to wait."

She nodded, unhappy but understanding, and left the office.

When Ben returned to the central lobby, he found Loving and Christina waiting for him.

To his relief, Christina made no comment on what she had probably just witnessed at the door. "Are you taking the first witness tomorrow?"

Fine. As long as they stuck to trial strategy, there should be no problems. "If LaBelle calls the cops first—and I think he will—yes. After all, I cross-exed them before, during the first trial."

"Makes sense. But wouldn't LaBelle be smarter to lead with a strong fact witness?"

"The truth is, LaBelle doesn't have that many fact witnesses. He's got a strong case, but it's mostly made up of circumstantial evidence and evidence collected after the fact. What few eyewitnesses he has, he'll save for a big finish. That's what I would do, anyway." He paused. As long as Christina was being nice to him, he might as well return the favor. "By the way, I thought your opening was terrific."

Christina looked away, almost blushing. "Oh, you're just being nice."

"Christina, you know me well enough to know that I'm never just being nice."

"Oh right. I forgot." Her face turned an even deeper red. This was a reaction Ben had never observed on the normally ultraconfident Christina, but it was a charming change. "You heard that opening so many times before the trial, you must be sick to death of it."

"Not at all. And you improvised several additions, I noticed."

"Was that all right?"

"I thought it was brilliant."

"I didn't come off too strident?"

Ben almost laughed. To hear this from Christina was amazing. She was normally so strong and unruffled it was easy to forget she was as likely to be nervous during her first trial as anyone else. "I thought you were perfect."

Ben could see she was pleased. Which was good. She had put an enormous amount of work into this case, and all too often he forgot to appreciate what an invaluable associate she was.

He turned toward Loving. "Speaking of cases, do we have one yet?"

Loving heaved his enormous shoulders. "Sorry, Skipper. No news on my front."

"No more information from your pal Barry?"

"I don't think he knows nothin' more to tell. And all my other police contacts have clammed up. I know this Blue Squeeze thing is real, and I know they want Keri—and you—bad. But that's about it."

"We know Matthews is involved, right? Maybe if you followed him around . . ."

"Tail a cop?" Loving shrugged. "Can't hurt."

"Agreed. And if we get any real proof that he's behind all the . . . problems we've had in this office of late, I could use that against him on cross-examination."

"I'm on it, Skipper."

"What about Catrona? Have you found anything on him? I still think he was hinting to me about some kind of involvement with Joe McNaughton. I just don't know what it was."

" 'Fraid I've been a bust there, too. No one's talkin'. The Omerta, you know."

Ben did know. The Omerta was the mob code of silence. Penalties for those who violated the Omerta were extreme. And lethal.

"The thing is," Ben said, "the man didn't have to tell me anything. I had nothing over him. But there he was, blabbing away between races. It was almost as if he wanted me to find something out. But what?"

"Sorry, Skipper, I don't know. And I don't know how you're ever gonna find out, neither."

Ben fell silent for a moment, his finger tapping his temple. "What about . . . a subpoena?"

"Against some mob guy?"

"Against Catrona himself."

Christina stepped between them. "Ben, are you kidding? You're talking about a major mob chieftain!"

"Mob chieftains have to obey subpoenae just like everyone else."

"Skipper," Loving said, "you're playin' with dynamite here."

"Why? He's an American citizen, isn't he? If he knows something, he should tell us."

"Ben," Christina said, "this is suicide."

"Maybe so. But if we don't win this case, it's death for Keri Dalcanton."

"Ben—"

"We tried being nice guys, and it didn't get us anywhere. He won't talk, the cops won't talk. All these people know something, maybe many things. But they're not talking. They're playing games, and Keri's life is on the line." He pounded his fist on the table. "Catrona's going to talk to us, one way or another."

"Ben, listen to reason—"

He didn't. "Does anyone know if Paula discovered anything? I mean, before the . . . the . . ." He didn't need to say more. A pallor fell over the assemblage, just from the mention of her name.

"Jones thought she had something," Christina explained. "Apparently, she called him earlier, very excited. But she didn't tell him what it was. And now . . ."

"Did you look through her papers?"

"Extensively. There was a huge pile of stuff on the floor, near her body when she fell. A lot of it was soaked in . . . in . . ." Christina looked away, batting her eyes. It must be hard to remain professional, Ben thought, when the mere thought of something brought tears. ". . . in her blood. But I still read it all. There were no surprises, though. Whatever she discovered, it's locked up in her head."

"Which we can't get into, at the moment. What are the doctors saying?"

Christina frowned. "They're not . . . optimistic. She hasn't regained consciousness and . . . well, she's just barely hanging on."

"Damn. Have the police got any leads on Paula's attacker?"

"They've got nada," Loving said. His voice seemed a little

hoarser than usual. "They say they're working on it, but given how they feel about this office . . . who knows?"

"Damn, damn, damn." Ben pressed his hand against his forehead. "How's Jones holding up?"

"He's doing okay, all things considered," Christina said. "But he won't leave her side. Not that I blame him. But it leaves a big gap in our trial team. I'm doing the work of two, basically."

"Christina, you always do the work of two. This time, you're probably doing the work of a regiment. But we can't let up. Once LaBelle starts putting on his witnesses, it's going to be war in that courtroom. LaBelle and the police will stop at nothing—absolutely nothing—to see that Keri Dalcanton is convicted. The only thing, the absolute only thing in the world that stands between her and a lethal injection—is us."

The stale, artificial smell of Styrofoam pervaded the small car. Steam rose from the cup and fogged the closed windows. Actually, Frank, better known as The Hulk, didn't think of Styrofoam as having a smell, most of the time. But tonight it did. Tonight it was all around him, inescapable, perhaps because there was no competition. The coffee was stale and tasteless; it was hot, but nothing else. Matthews's car was so old it bore no scent at all, unless you pressed your nose up against the vinyl. Frank suspected his clothes probably did have a scent, this late in the day, but he preferred not to dwell on that.

Matthews was staring straight ahead, his eyes locked on the lights in the offices on the seventh floor. His eyes never seemed to wander; he barely blinked.

Frank checked his watch. Well past the time he'd told his wife he'd be home. He was going to have to have that talk with Matthews—the one he'd been putting off for far too long.

"Arlen, did you ever think maybe . . . just maybe . . . we've pushed this thing about as far as it needs to go?"

Matthews's eyes didn't waver. "What kinda crap is this?"

"I just think maybe . . . maybe we've about reached the limit."

Matthews grunted. "Don't think, Frank. You're not used to it, and you're not good at it."

Frank pursed his lips together. Yeah, that was the standard line. Frank, the force's likeable lump. The gentle giant. The amiable lummox. Except, Frank did think, on occasion, and he'd been thinking a lot of late.

"Arlen, you know I feel the same as you. About Joe and all. I want to see justice done. But it's back in the courts, where it ought to be. Why are we still out here?"

"It ain't over till it's over. I don't like leaving a job half done."

"But I'm tellin' you, Arlen, this is wrong. It's no good anymore."

"I'll be the judge of that."

"What the hell are we doin', anyway? Tailin' Kincaid and scopin' out his office? What's the point? The case is re-opened, Kincaid's got a judge who's ready to hang the Dalcanton chick, he's got a member of his team nearly dead and another one watchin' over her. What are we goin' to accomplish out here?"

Matthews paused a few beats before answering. "I don't know exactly. But there's no telling what Kincaid might try. We need to keep our eyes open. Maybe we can tip LaBelle off to the next big trick up his sleeve."

"Arlen, you're dreamin'."

"Fine. Let me dream."

"Arlen—I gotta tell you—my wife's been complainin'. 'Bout me bein' gone all the time."

"What kind of pathetic little pussy-whipped pissant are you, anyway?"

"Arlen—you know I don't like that kind of talk."

"Fine. Let's stop talking."

"Arlen—are you hearin' what I'm sayin'? It doesn't make sense anymore. You don't know what you're doin'. Or why."

Matthews whipped his head around to face Frank. "Don't tell me I don't know why I'm doing this. I sure as hell do know! I'm doing it for Joe!"

"Arlen, be reasonable. I knew Joe, too, remember? I loved him like a brother. But this—this stuff we're doin'—this is crazy. Even Joe wouldn't want this!"

"Don't tell me what my own partner would want!"

"I'm right, Arlen! You know I am! Joe believed criminals should be punished. But he never wanted to hurt anyone. He wouldn't stand around and let anyone else get hurt, either! And he didn't like it when people messed with him."

"You don't know what you're talking about."

"I think I do, Arlen. I still remember."

"You're babbling."

"You may've got the files expunged, but I've got a long memory. I know why Joe got bucked down to patrolman. And I know why he got bucked back up again, too."

When Matthews's voice returned, it was slow and . . . different. "What exactly are you saying, Frank?"

"You know what I'm saying. I'm saying this has gone on long enough."

"Are you threatening me?"

"No, I'm not threatening you, you thick-headed moron! I'm trying to get through to you. I thought this was a good idea when we started. I wanted to see justice done. I wanted to see Joe avenged. But it's over now. The case is back in the courts. Our work is done. But you won't let go of it!"

"I'm very concerned about—"

"You're not concerned. You're obsessed!"

Matthews slowly turned away until he once again faced forward, staring at the lights on the seventh floor. His calm demeanor was belied by the rapid rise and fall of his chest. "Get the fuck out of my car."

"Arlen—"

"You heard me."

"Arlen, you gotta listen to reason. You—"

"Get outta my car!" Matthews pounded Frank with his fists, slamming him on his neck and shoulders and face. Frank tried to deflect the blows, but in such a tiny space, there was little room to maneuver.

"Arlen, get a grip!"

"Get out!" Matthews was screaming now, his fists still flying. "Get outta my car!"

"All right!" Frank popped open the car door and shifted his enormous frame forward, but—

Someone was standing just outside his door.

"Smile!"

A moment later, a blinding white flash of light erupted in their eyes.

"What the—" Frank fell back onto the car seat, his arm covering his eyes. "What's going on?" Another bright white flash illuminated the darkness.

"Who the hell is it?" Matthews bellowed. A few moments later, enough of his vision had returned to answer the question for himself. "Loving!"

Loving was holding a palm-size camera in his hands. "At your service. Poker game break up early tonight, boys?"

"What are you doing here?"

"I work here," Loving replied. "Shouldn't I be askin' what *you're* doin' here?"

"None of your goddamned business!"

"I think it is." Loving leaned forward, not intimidated in the least by the hulk he had to cross over to get near Matthews. "I think you've been tailin' my man Kincaid. And God knows what else. You should've taken the warning I gave you back in the parking garage."

"Get stuffed."

"I'll tell you somethin' else," Loving continued. "If I find out you're behind some of the troubles Ben's been havin' lately, I'll be comin' to you for payback." His voice dropped a notch. "And I find out you were the son of a bitch who attacked Paula Connelly, you're a dead man."

"Very scary, Loving. I'm trembling."

"You should be, Matthews." He slowly pulled out of the car. "Now if you've got any sense at all in that tiny little pea brain of yours, which unfortunately I'm not sure you do, you'll take your friend's advice. Let the courts do their job and leave Kincaid alone."

"How long have you been eavesdropping?"

"You see, Matthews, it ain't eavesdroppin' when I'm supposed to be here—and you ain't." Loving took a step back, then raised the camera again and snapped another picture. "See you in court, Matthews. Don't let the bedbugs bite."

* 31 *

"Where are the Matthews exhibits?" Ben said, ripping through the notebooks scattered across the defense table. "I need those exhibits."

"I think they're in one of the bankers' boxes," Christina offered.

Ben scanned the stacks and stacks of boxes beside their table in the courtroom. "That's helpful. Which one?"

"If I recall correctly, the blue one."

"There is no blue one."

"Uh-oh."

Ben looked at her with unforgiving eyes. "How could this happen?"

"Beats me. I'm the new grad, remember? How do lawyers normally keep track of their exhibits?"

"Normally their legal assistant takes care of that. Unfortunately, mine just got a law degree." He glanced over his shoulder. The bailiff was coming in, which meant the judge would not be far behind. "Christina, could you run to the pay phone in the corridor and call Loving? The box must be back at the office."

"Phone's broken. And I didn't bring my cell phone. I didn't think Judge Cable would be amused if it started playing 'La Vie en Rose' in the middle of the trial. I could run downstairs—"

"No way. I need you here." He snapped his fingers. "I know what to do. I've been looking for an excuse to use this." He popped open his briefcase and took out a small Palm Pilot. "Christmas present from my mother."

Christina watched over his shoulder. "Going to look up the office phone number?"

"Hey, this baby's wireless. I can send e-mail."

"Loving doesn't have a computer."

Ben punched the tiny keys on the palm-sized keyboard. "I'm sending the message to a company called myFax. They'll receive the message and fax it to Loving. Isn't that incredible?"

Christina rolled her eyes. "Boys and their toys."

LaBelle started the testimonial phase of the trial predictably enough by calling back to the stand Sergeant Mark Callery, the young cop who was the first on the scene to discover Joe McNaughton's body. He recounted the whole incident in gory detail. Ben thought he was much more persuasive than he had been at the first trial; as with all things, he supposed, practice makes perfect. Callery painted the picture with an artist's exactitude. All the grisly details were included; not so much as a single blood splatter was left to the jury's imagination.

The effect on the jurors was immediate and apparent. They already knew what had happened to the unfortunate Joe McNaughton. But it was another thing again to hear it described in court, in minute detail, with pictures no less. The true horror of the crime hit home with a force Ben knew would linger for days. This was no longer a hypothetical matter. A man had been killed, horribly so, and according to LaBelle, Keri Dalcanton was the monster who did it.

Ben cross-exed, principally on the subject of physical strength. Unfortunately, Callery was ready for this line of questioning, having already heard it once before, and had his answers polished and ready. One of the flaws with retrying a case, Ben thought—one of many such flaws—was the fact that it was almost impossible to surprise anyone. As he had before, Callery opined that someone had driven the body to Bartlett Square, then dragged it to the fountain and somehow mustered the strength to hog-tie it with the chains. As for the severing of the male member, that was an easy stroke, Callery said. Anyone could have done it. Callery had no opinion on why the word FAITHLESS had been smeared across his chest.

When Ben sat down after cross, Christina leaned close. "I don't think that hurt us," she said. "All he did was establish that a crime occurred. Which we've never denied."

"That's not all he did," Ben whispered back. "He etched into the jurors' brains the visceral nature of this crime—that only a truly sick, twisted, sociopath could have committed."

"Still, he didn't—"

"Have you noticed how the jurors are looking at Keri?"

Christina turned her head. In fact, many of the select fourteen did appear to be looking her way.

"They're scrutinizing her, trying to get a fix on what kind of person they think she is. Whether she's capable of committing this atrocity."

"We have to convince them that she's not."

Ben nodded. "Which is going to be pretty damn hard to do, if she doesn't take the stand. And she says she doesn't want to."

Given all that had transpired since the last trial began, Ben wasn't sure whether LaBelle would recall Matthews to the stand or not. A few minutes after Callery departed, though, LaBelle answered the question. He did.

Matthews studiously avoided making eye contact with Ben as he strolled confidently to the witness box. Just as well. There was no love lost between the two; that much was certain. And Ben might've been tempted to show him the photograph tucked inside his manila folder.

Not ten minutes into Matthews's testimony, it became clear that he, unlike Callery, would be singing a very different tune this time around. Despite the fact that the previous trial had been mooted on grounds of alleged fraud, there was no reason to believe Judge Cable would rule any differently on the subject of the improperly obtained warrant to search Keri Dalcanton's apartment. To the contrary, LaBelle knew the ruling would be no different, so he avoided the subject altogether. If the search of the apartment was invalid, then all the evidence obtained during the search, including Keri's testimony, was inadmissible.

This time, Matthews told the story of his midnight raid on an unspecified law office with a valid search warrant, and how his men had turned up the murder weapon.

This line of questioning had been the subject of intense debate during the pretrial hearings. Ben wanted it excluded altogether; Matthews's story could only cast negative aspersions on the defendant's counsel, which was not an acceptable trial tactic. After all, no one had proved Ben had done anything wrong and the charges against him had been dropped. Telling this story could force the defense attorney to testify—to exonerate himself by telling the jury he did not put the knife in his files. This, too, Ben argued, was unacceptable.

LaBelle had argued just as strongly that the evidence had to be admitted. After all, Matthews couldn't introduce the weapon without explaining when and how it had been found. The murder weapon was a critical part of the defense case and it wasn't reasonable to expect him to proceed without it. There was nothing illegal about the manner in which it had been obtained; therefore, there was no justification for excluding it.

As judges usually do when confronted with such imponderable contradictions, Judge Cable compromised. Matthews could explain that the weapon had been found in the office of one of Ms. Dalcanton's legal representatives, but he was precluded from mentioning the attorney's name. Both LaBelle and Matthews were precluded from suggesting that there was anything improper about the knife being where it was. That's just where it was, period, no smirks or smart remarks. Like most judicial compromises, it pleased no one, and worse, created a logical gap in the facts that the jury would wonder about for the rest of the trial. Ben hated it when judges precluded the jury from knowing something they were desperate to know; it usually resulted in their imagining something far more complicated and dirty than the reality, and almost always at the defendant's expense.

"What did you do after you discovered the weapon?" LaBelle asked.

"While wearing gloves, I placed it in a plastic bag to prevent any trace evidence from being lost, then I immediately returned to our downtown headquarters." Ben noted that Matthews was omitting the minor detail of arresting the attorney on trumped-up charges later dismissed, as well as the police helicopter, the SOT team, and all the other evidence of his obsessive overkill. "I logged in the evidence, assigned it a number which was recorded in two different places, tagged it, lockered it." Matthews was trying to establish a chain of custody sufficient to thwart any cross-ex attempts to suggest the evidence could have been tampered with after it was found.

"What was done with the weapon after it arrived at police headquarters?" LaBelle asked.

"A battery of tests were performed to determine if it was the murder weapon, and to examine it for any trace evidence, such as blood or fingerprints."

"Do you know what the results of those tests were?"

What did they take him for? "Objection," Ben said. "Did Sergeant Matthews perform the tests? I don't think so."

"Sustained," Judge Cable said.

LaBelle continued undaunted. "Have you been able to determine whether that knife was in fact the weapon used to kill Joe McNaughton?"

"Yes," Matthews said hastily, barely waiting a breath, which was a signal to Ben that the answer was probably improper and he knew it. "The coroner determined conclusively—"

"Objection," Ben said. "This is not within the witness's scope of knowledge."

"Sustained," Judge Cable said wearily. "Mr. LaBelle, please put the proper evidence on with the proper witness, and stop trying to get everything in with this one much too eager witness."

"As you wish, your honor," LaBelle replied, as if he hadn't actually violated any evidentiary rules but was simply humoring a personal peccadillo of the judge's. "That's all I have."

"Thank you," the judge said. "Mr. Kincaid?"

As Ben approached the podium, he thought perhaps he detected the tiniest crack in Matthews's armor, his permaplaqued obnoxious exterior. Could it be Matthews was actually afraid of him? That he was dreading this cross? It would be nice to think so. Of course, the last time Ben had crossed Matthews, he'd gotten the whole case dismissed. If that happened again, Matthews would probably be out of a job.

Alas, no such miracles were in the cards. There was precious little Ben could do, since what Matthews had said was true and wasn't especially incriminating (at least, not yet). He was tempted to whip out the photo in his folder and accuse Matthews of harassing him and his staff, even planting evidence. But what was the point of impeaching a witness who hadn't said anything false or incriminating? Ben decided to save that ammo for a time when it would do him more good. He hated to let the creep get off so easily, but when all was said and done, Ben simply asked a few perfunctory questions and let Matthews retake his seat.

The real battle would be fought, not with these remnants from the past trial, but with the new witnesses in the current one because, Ben knew, their testimony would be much more damaging.

* 32 *

"The State calls Corporal James Wesley Jr. to the stand."

Normally, in Ben's experience, the first witness after the lunch break had the toughest job—keeping the jurors awake. With this witness, however, Ben knew that wouldn't be an issue.

In a brief expanse of time, LaBelle established that Wesley was a sixteen-year member of the force, that he was a good friend of Joe McNaughton's, and that he had worked with McNaughton not long before his death. It seemed that La-Belle, like the jury, was in a hurry to get to the good stuff.

"Did Sergeant McNaughton ever mention Ms. Dalcanton in your presence?" LaBelle asked.

"Oh yeah." Although Wesley had to be in his forties, he looked much younger, almost baby-faced. "That he did. Repeatedly."

"Did he ever describe the . . . uh, nature of their relationship?" This was hearsay, but the judge had ruled before trial that he would allow it, since the declarant was deceased and, therefore, somewhat unavailable.

"Yup. He didn't make any bones about it. He was boink— uh, uh—" He closed his eyes for a moment. "Excuse me, your honor. He was engaging in a sexual relationship. With the defendant. Ms. Dalcanton."

"You're certain about this?"

"Oh yeah. Joe did occasionally tend to brag and even exaggerate, but there's no way he could have invented all these details. And man, did he give me lots of details."

"Like what?"

"Objection." Ben knew this was a loser, but he at least wanted to register his displeasure. "This is not relevant. He's just hoping to introduce a lot of embarrassing details to smear the defendant."

"That's not true," LaBelle shot back. "The sex life of Ms. Dalcanton and the deceased is, regrettably, keenly relevant to the case, as it explains the chains, the black leather, some of the deceased's wounds and, as we will show, the defendant's motive."

"I'll allow it," Judge Cable said. "But try to keep it under control, would you? This is a courtroom, not a tabloid TV show."

"I'll do my best," LaBelle said, which Ben suspected would count for precious little. "Please proceed, Corporal Wesley."

"Well, from the start, Joe knew that this chi—um, this young woman, had unusual tastes. She liked it kinky, if you know what I mean."

"Perhaps you could explain."

"Well, she liked to pretend. Joe told me time and time again about how she got off on that dominatrix stuff. You know, she'd dress up in black leather, or he would, or both. And she'd get out the whips and chains. Sometimes he'd wear a dog collar and pretend to be her slave. That sort of thing."

Ben tried to look disinterested. Just another day in Mayberry, right?

"They had this routine they went through. I guess it started the first night he took her back to her apartment from the strip joint, and it continued right up until the time he broke it off.

She'd play the master. She'd use the whips and she'd call him
dirty names. She'd spank him or punish him in a variety of
ways. According to Joe, she got off on the playacting; she'd
really work up a lather."

"How long would this continue?"

"Until she'd had enough, or he had. Then gradually, he'd
rebel, so to speak. He'd become more aggressive."

"Does that mean he took over the whips?"

"No, no, that was her thing. He'd start by—" His face
flushed red. "I'm sorry, this is kind of embarrassing."

Like the rest of it hasn't been? Ben wondered.

"Please continue," LaBelle urged him.

Wesley drew in his breath. "He'd suck her little toe."

"And was this . . . pleasurable to her?"

"Ooooh, yeah. A thousand times yeah. Joe said she really
went into spasms over that one. Apparently she thought it was
like, well, the equivalent of a . . ." He coughed. ". . . A similar
procedure she sometimes performed for him."

"I see. Then what happened?"

"Well, as Joe told it, after he'd pushed that button as far as
he could, he'd do other things. She loved it when he kissed the
back of her neck. When he put his hot tongue on her wrist. So
he'd do that sort of stuff until she'd totally transformed from
the dominatrix to a puddle of jelly. She was like a kitten. A
sex slave. She'd do whatever he wanted."

"Did Joe enjoy this?"

"Well, he liked this part better, yeah. He said he didn't
much care for all the kinky whips and chains stuff, but it was
worth it to get her to the sex-slave stage."

"And why was that?"

Wesley tucked in his chin. "Well . . . this is a bit indelicate."

"We understand. But you're under oath."

"Well . . . according to Joe . . . she was really put—I mean,
she was, um, great. You know, like—sexually. Good in
bed, except actually, they rarely did it in a bed. The best he'd
ever had, Joe said. By a large margin. And she wanted it

constantly. Couldn't get enough, like she was addicted to it. He said she was a—a—what's the word? You know, a nympho. So to him, it was worth the crud to get to the cream. So to speak."

"Your honor," Ben said, rising. "I renew my objection. This can't possibly be relevant to the question of who committed the murder."

Judge Cable frowned. It was probably a hard thing for the old geezer to do—cutting off such a stimulating line of questioning. "I do think we've pursued long enough the question of . . . what exactly the two parties did. Let's move on."

"As you wish," LaBelle said congenially. He'd already gotten what he wanted. "Corporal Wesley, were you aware that Joe McNaughton was married?"

"Of course."

"And yet, he had this rather . . . extensive affair."

"Yeah. You gotta understand Joe. He knew he was married and I think he loved his wife. But at the same time . . . things hadn't been so good between him and Andrea for many years. I mean, not in the sex department. And Joe was a man, and a man's gotta do what he's gotta do."

Ben turned his head slightly, just enough to see Andrea McNaughton in the courtroom, burying her face. Listening to the sordid details of her errant husband's sex play probably hadn't been fun, but this was just too much. A hand covering her face, she ran down the aisle and out of the courtroom.

"I see." LaBelle's expression registered his comprehension, though not his approval, Ben noted. The district attorney hadn't forgotten that the plurality of the jury behind that rail was female. "Corporal Wesley, are you aware that when Sergeant McNaughton's body was found he was bound up—by chains?"

Wesley ran a hand through a shock of brown hair. "I think everyone knows that."

"So let me ask you again—are you sure Joe told you that Ms. Dalcanton liked to use chains in their sex play?"

"Oh yeah. I'm sure. Plus, I saw them over at her place."

Ben sat bolt upright. What the hell—?

LaBelle seemed surprised, too, although Ben suspected that was an act for the jury's sake. "You were in her apartment?"

"Well . . . I was never actually inside. But I saw inside. Through the window." He paused, turning his eyes toward the gallery. "And I took pictures."

An audible ripple ran through the courtroom, as each spectator's lurid imagination speculated on what exactly those pictures might portray.

"Pictures?" LaBelle asked. "Do you have them with you?"

"Oh yeah." Wesley reached inside his sport jacket and removed a packet of photos.

"Your honor," Ben said, with as much indignation as he could muster. "I've had no advance notice of this and I've never seen these pictures before in my life."

The judge looked more tired than annoyed. "Great. Approach."

Both Ben and LaBelle rushed to the bench. The judge shut off the microphone.

"What's going on here?" Ben said angrily. "He can't spring new evidence on us at trial. At the second trial, for that matter."

"Your honor," LaBelle said, addressing the judge, not Ben. "I apologize for this inconvenience. I only learned of this evidence myself last night."

"Oh give me a break," Ben said.

LaBelle gave Ben a harsh look. "Your honor, I think you've known me long enough to realize that I don't play games and that my word is good. I've filed an affidavit testifying to the last-minute discovery of these photographs."

Judge Cable removed his glasses and tapped them against the bench. "What's in these photos, anyway?"

LaBelle removed them from the envelope. Ben nearly gasped.

They were worse than anything he could've possibly

imagined. Not that they revealed any new evidence, exactly. It was already well established that McNaughton and Dalcanton had a sexual relationship, and Ben didn't imagine that anyone doubted it was true. They had even been told that the nature of that sexual relationship was somewhat . . . outré. But to hear about it was one thing. To actually see it, right before your eyes, was quite another.

Wordlessly, Ben thumbed through the photos. Wesley must've used a zoom lens, because he didn't miss much. There was Keri, all decked out in a black leather bustier. There she was again, wielding a cat o'nine tails. And there she was again, wrapping heavy chains around Joe McNaughton's throat—and acting as if she enjoyed it.

It was like a step-by-step pictorial of their secret sex lives. The snapshots showed it all. Toe-sucking. French-kissing. Oral sex. And penetration. Nothing was left to the imagination.

There was no doubt in Ben's mind about the potential consequences of these photos. If the jury saw these, rehabilitating Keri would be a thousand times more difficult. Once they had these graphic, pornographic pictures in their heads, they'd never be able to look at Keri with an open mind again. If they ever had to begin with.

"Your honor, I must protest the admission of these photos in the strongest possible terms. Bad enough that they weren't presented to the defense in advance of trial. Bad enough that they constitute a gross invasion of privacy. But furthermore, they are not relevant to the question of Ms. Dalcanton's culpability for murder. The potential prejudice stemming from these photos vastly outweighs their purported probative value. The D.A. is just engaging in visual slander, hoping the jury will be so put off they'll convict her of anything, whether the evidence is there or not."

"Obviously, I disagree," LaBelle said calmly. "These photos are graphic, but they also remove all doubt as to whether the defendant was engaged in, um, unusual sexual practices with the deceased, which clearly relates to motive.

They also show that she possessed chains similar if not identical to the ones used to string up McNaughton's corpse. The pictures show her engaging in violent fantasies and, in my opinion, rather enjoying it."

"This is not evidence!" Ben said. "This is a peep show!"

"Now, Mr. Kincaid—"

"This is beyond the pale, your honor. Trying to smear a young woman by showing her enjoying herself sexually—it's just a cheap ploy to turn the jury against her. It's sexist and disgusting!"

"I certainly agree with the disgusting part," LaBelle said under his breath.

"Gentlemen, please." Judge Cable held up his hands. "I don't believe in trial by ambush and I don't like last-minute evidence and I especially don't like"—his face pinched together—"smut of this variety in my courtroom. But I can't deny that it's relevant. I'm going to allow it. If the defense needs additional time to prepare its response, I'll grant it."

Ben's eyes flared. "Your honor—"

"I've ruled, counsel."

"This is an appeal issue, your honor. And I'm moving for a mistrial."

"I can't say that I'm surprised. But the trial goes on. With the photos."

"Your honor, I—"

"Don't get yourself thrown into jail," Judge Cable snapped. "Your new associate seems very capable, but I'd hate to see her have to try this case by herself, wouldn't you?"

Ben was furious, but he buttoned his lip. The judge's ruling was wrong, flat-out wrong, and the damage this would do to Keri's case was incalculable.

Silently, he watched as the bailiff passed the photos to the jury so they could examine them one by one. The reactions were varied—shock, embarrassment, horror, revulsion. They were all a little different. But none of them was good.

*   *   *

Once the judge gave him the nod to start cross-ex, Ben didn't hold back.

"Are you a professional Peeping Tom, or was this a first for you?"

LaBelle was on his feet. "Your honor, that's grossly offensive."

"I find this witness grossly offensive!" Ben returned.

Judge Cable raised his gavel. "Mr. Kincaid, watch yourself," he warned. "I think you're entitled to inquire into the circumstances surrounding the taking of these photos. Just be careful how you do it."

Ben took a deep breath and started again. "Would you please explain to the jury how you came to be snapping pictures through the window of two private citizens having consensual sex?"

Wesley was unruffled, although some of the boyish élan seemed to have drained out of his face. "I was on assignment."

Ben blinked. "An assignment—from the police?"

"That's correct."

"Before the murder? Why would the police department have been investigating Keri Dalcanton?"

"We weren't. We were investigating Joe McNaughton."

Ben was pleased to hear the buzz from the gallery. It was comforting to think he wasn't the only one who was totally and utterly confused. "Why would they be investigating one of their own officers?"

"The investigation was instigated by Internal Affairs."

"And why?"

He hesitated. "It pertained to McNaughton's investigation of Antonio Catrona."

Curiouser and curiouser. "Did they think McNaughton was on the take?"

"Frankly, I don't know what they thought, and they didn't explain it to me. Whenever someone investigates an organized crime figure—excuse me, an alleged organized crime figure—there's a concern that the officer might be turned. It's happened before."

"Did you have any evidence that Joe McNaughton had been bought off?"

"No. None. But he had begun an intense affair with a woman half his age with unusual sexual proclivities—shortly after he initiated the investigation. The young woman was known to work in a strip club operated by a holding company believed to be owned by Antonio Catrona. Something of a coincidence, don't you think? My superiors perceived this as, at the very least, an area of . . . weakness. A way that he could be influenced. So they asked me to investigate."

"And you did? You and your little camera?"

"I'm a cop. I follow orders."

"So you conducted a secret investigation of your friend."

"Yes. I've said that already."

"Do you realize you probably broke about a dozen laws when you took these shots? Like invasion of privacy laws?"

"I'm a cop, not a lawyer. I try to solve crimes, not cover them up."

Ben let that pass. "Why didn't you show anyone these pictures before last night?"

Wesley shrugged. "After Joe's death, the IA investigation was naturally terminated. I put the pics in storage. I didn't see any use for them at that point, and I didn't want them to cause any unnecessary grief to Joe's widow."

"What changed your mind?"

Wesley nodded toward the prosecution table. "D.A. La-Belle. I told him about the photos last night while we were preparing for trial. He insisted that I collect them and bring them to court."

I'll bet he did, Ben thought. "Did it not bother you that you were spying on your alleged friend and colleague? That you were betraying his trust?"

"Who was betraying anyone? I didn't think for a minute

that Joe did anything wrong and I expected my investigation to prove it."

"I doubt if Joe would've been so sanguine about it if he'd known you were photographing him having sex."

"Oh, I don't know. Remember, he'd told me all about it in great detail. He didn't have to, but he did. He was having sex—great sex—with a very young woman, doing new things, getting it regular. You know how it is. Guys like to brag about that sort of thing." He glanced down at the packet of pictures. "I don't think Joe would've minded so much. In fact, I think he might've put them up in his locker."

There was no graceful segue out of this cross-ex, so Ben just ended it. Judge Cable recessed for the day, and the reporters raced out the back, happily toting several salacious tidbits for the evening news.

"You've got a lawsuit against that creep," Ben told Keri, "and against the Tulsa P.D. for authorizing him. Invasion of privacy. It's a slam-dunk, and I'll be happy to file it for you."

She nodded. "But that's not going to do me much good, is it? Not if I'm in prison."

Or worse, Ben thought but did not say. "Let's meet back at the office in one hour," Ben told Christina. "Strategy meeting."

He began gathering his materials, thinking about what they might do next. Honestly, what could they do? Ben wondered, as he watched the jurors file out of the courtroom. Even those who suspected she was guilty could not possibly have loathed her with the intensity that they did now. They would never forget those photographs. They would never like her. No matter what Ben did or said, they would always see the cheap amoral slut who pleasured herself in bizarre ways. Who got her jollies pretending to inflict pain. Who had a taste for violence.

Or, in other words, exactly the sort of person who would commit murder.

* 33 *

"Ben, I'm worried."

Ben glanced up from his desk. Christina was standing in the doorway, her shoulders drooping, her head hung low. She was her usual cute strawberry blond self, one of the few women he had ever known who actually looked good in a business suit. But the inevitable toil of trial was beginning to wear on her. She looked stressed, tired.

What time was it, anyway? A quick glance at the digital readout on his phone gave him the bad news. It was well past his bedtime—and hers, too.

"You've got nothing to worry about," he said reassuringly. "Go home and get some rest."

"I'm concerned about the coroner," she said, as if she hadn't heard him. "He's going to be an important witness for the prosecution. Maybe the most important one."

Ben shook his head. As long as Andrea McNaughton remained on the witness list, there was no way the coroner could be the "most important." Still, he would be critical to the prosecution's effort to tie the murder to Keri. "So what's your worry?"

"I don't think I should do this witness. He's too important. You take him."

Ben pushed away from his desk. "Christina, you'll be fine. I have every confidence in you."

"Yeah, but that's just because you're a nice guy. I've never done this before and we both know it."

"You've watched me do it a hundred times. And you've watched some good attorneys, too. You'll be fine."

"What if I freeze up? What if I clutch? What if the coroner makes me look like a fool?"

"Bob? He won't."

"You don't know that. This case is too important to be taking risks."

"Putting you in charge of a witness isn't a risk. It's a sure bet."

"You don't know that."

"I do." He reached out and lightly touched her shoulder. "There's no one I'd rather be trying this case with. Seriously."

She smiled a little, but did not appear much comforted.

All right. Then he'd try the bad-cop routine. "Look, Christina, are you going to be my partner or not? Because if you are, you're going to have to earn your keep."

"Excuse me?"

"You heard me. I've got no use for a partner who chokes every time a trial gets hairy. Because as you well know, every trial gets hairy, at one point or another. That's why people hire lawyers."

"But—"

"No buts. You'll be great. Assuming you don't develop an ulcer between now and tomorrow morning. So go home and get some rest, okay?"

She shook her head. "I think I'll review my cross-ex outline again."

"Read my lips, Christina. Go home."

"I just want to make sure I haven't missed anything."

He twirled her around and gave her a gentle push toward the door. "Leave. Depart. Vamoose. That's an order."

She smiled slightly, then nodded. "All right." She looked up at him, then tentatively reached out, her fingers brushing the side of his face. "Thanks."

"No problem."

She hesitated another moment, her eyes locked on his. Finally, she turned and headed for the outer door.

Then stopped. "Hey, who said you could give me orders, anyway? We're partners, remember?"

"My apologies. It's just an expression."

"Well . . . okay. But don't let it happen again."

"Ben, I'm worried."

Once again, Ben looked up from his desk. Was he experiencing déjà vu? Or was he caught in some pretrial time loop?

Neither, as it turned out. The words were the same, but the woman standing in his doorway this time was platinum blond rather than strawberry blond and she was his client, not his partner.

Keri looked as if she had been exercising. She was wearing a halter top with an exposed midriff, short shorts, and sneakers. He could see beads of perspiration in various places all over her body.

Sweat. Sexy sweat.

"I'm sorry if I'm disturbing you," she said. "I was just in the neighborhood."

"The neighborhood of the seventh floor?"

"Seriously. I was out jogging, and Warren Place is a good location for it. Well lit."

"Why on earth would you be jogging at this time of night?"

She shrugged, and Ben tried not to notice the effect that had on her sport bra. "I had to burn off some steam. Couldn't sleep. And . . ."

"Yes?"

Keri twisted her fingers around themselves. "And to be honest . . . I wanted to see you."

Ben crossed his office to her, although he was careful to keep a few feet between them. "What's wrong, Keri?"

"I don't know exactly. I guess it's—all those things La-Belle said in court today. The way he tried to make me look like—well, you know. Some kind of tramp. Like I spend my whole life dreaming up new kinds of kinky sex."

Kinky sex was not a phrase Ben ever needed to hear coming out of her mouth. Especially when they were in the office alone. "Don't let it get to you. It's a standard prosecution technique."

"Yes, but it's working. I saw the way the jurors looked at me when they filed out of the courtroom today. Not that they've ever looked at me with eyes of love. But today was . . . different. Worse. Before, it was like, 'I wonder if you're capable of murder.' But today it was more like, 'I wonder if there's anything you're *not* capable of.' "

"It always looks bleak during the prosecution phase. After all, I can cross, but that only goes so far. Things will improve once the defense starts."

"I hope so. But still, I—I—" All at once, she surged forward. She wrapped her arms around him and buried her face against his chest. "Ben, I'm so scared."

Ben gently laid his hand atop her silver hair, trying to pretend he didn't feel a reaction the instant they made contact. "I'm sure this is difficult for you. But you have to be strong."

"It's more than just hard. I can't sleep. I can't eat. I wake up every morning with a horrible burning sensation in my stomach. I—I—really don't know if I can stand it much longer." She squeezed closer, her tear-stained cheek burning against his shirt.

Ben felt his pulse racing. "I'm sorry," he whispered. "This must be awful for you." He could feel her warm breasts heaving against him, her warm lips pressed against his neck. "Please know that we're doing everything we can to give you the best possible defense."

"I know that," she said, her voice cracked and broken. "But I'm still scared."

"Keri, when we put on our case—"

"Which is what exactly? Do we even have a case?" Her

words came out in broken gasps. "I've told you this before, Ben—I can't testify. I just can't do it."

"You don't necessarily have to . . ."

"You say that, but who else can deny all those awful things they said in court today? Who else can tell them what really happened?"

"We don't have to answer this question yet," Ben said, knowing that would not be much comfort. "When the prosecution rests, we'll see where we are then."

"Oh, Ben. I'm so scared. So so scared. I need—I *need*—"

A moment later, their lips were locked in a passionate, intense kiss. Ben pulled her close to him, swallowing her up, embracing her in every way possible. Keri's lips broke away from his, then began kissing him everywhere, on his neck, his forehead, his ear. Ben's hands slipped under her halter top. She began fumbling with the buttons on his shirt.

They fell back against his desk, knocking off reams of paper. "I need you," she said breathlessly. "I need you so much."

"We can't do this," Ben said, but his voice wasn't convincing, not even to himself.

"Please," she whispered, pulling him closer.

"No." Ben broke away, bracing himself against a chair. "We can't do this."

"But *why*?"

"You know why. It isn't right. Not now. Not till the trial is over."

"But, Ben," she cried, "if you knew how I feel—"

"I feel the same way, Keri. But we can't." He walked away from her, to the opposite side of the room, an effort which required more strength than anything he'd ever done in his life. "Keri—I'll see you in court tomorrow morning."

"Is this your way of dismissing me?"

"I think it's best. You know how important this trial is. To you, more than anyone. I have to keep a clear head."

She pushed off the desk, rearranging her scant clothing. "You're right. I don't know what came over me. I just lost control." She laughed bitterly. "Maybe what LaBelle says about me is true."

"Don't say that. Not even in jest. You're a beautiful person, Keri. I can't imagine how you've survived all that you've been through. And when this trial is over—well, things will be different. But for now, we have to focus on the trial. The trial, and nothing but the trial."

"I know. I'll go." She finished pulling herself together and started toward the door. Before she left, though, she quietly crossed the room and planted her lips softly on Ben's cheek.

"I love you," she whispered.

* 34 *

Kirk was crouched in an alleyway beside a Dumpster, his forehead pressed against his knees. He was not having a pleasant evening. Too many inescapable truths hounded his brain. There was no hope for him, he realized now. The priest had been right. God knew what Kirk had done. He would always know. Somehow, Kirk had fooled himself into thinking he could erase his crimes, eliminate all the traces, but now he realized that had been a child's fantasy. No amount of pain or self-inflicted misery could ever alter the truth.

He was damned, pure and simple.

He saw something glistening at the other end of the alley. Winking at him. Something translucent and . . . sharp.

A broken bottle, if he wasn't mistaken. A green-tinted

jagged edge, just waiting for someone to come close enough for it to do some permanent damage.

The idea formed in Kirk's brain with such immediate clarity that he wondered why it hadn't occurred to him before. Enough with these halfway gestures—picking fights and mutilating his body. One swift stroke across the jugular with that bottle and he would be out of his misery permanently.

Unless the priest was right. Unless there really was a God, and he really did punish those who committed sins. Like suicide. The unforgivable sin, that was what his Sunday school teacher used to call it. Unforgivable—because you were dead before you had a chance to ask.

But to be free of this torment, released . . .

Kirk was distracted by the sound of footsteps at the other end of the alley. Clicking footsteps, light and even.

Stiletto heels, as it turned out.

"Jeez Lou-*ise*. You really are a mess."

Kirk peered upward through hooded lids. She was a black woman decked out in a tight white dress cut practically down to the nipple, blowsy hair, and the legs of a sixteen-year-old. Not that she was much older than that.

A prostitute. Had to be.

"So anyway," the woman continued, "my girlfriend, she says, 'Girlfriend, don't you be goin' over to see that boy. He a mess.' And I says, 'Well, I don't see much goin' on out here.' And she says, 'Girlfriend, I don't care how slow things are on The Stroll. That boy be trouble.' "

"What do you want?" Kirk's voice was harsh and raspy.

She smiled, a broad smile that might have been called toothy but for the fact that so many of her teeth were missing. "Why, honey, ain't you figured that out yet? I got the cure for what ails you."

He lowered his head. "Go away."

"Forgive me for bein' crass, but I am a little concerned about the money thing. See, my girlfriend, she says, 'Girlfriend, he don't look like he got two pennies to rub together.'

But I say to her, I say, 'Girlfriend, don't you be jumpin' to no conclusions there. The boy's down in the dumps, sure. He's had some bad knocks. But that don't mean he's poor.' " She took a baby step closer. "Does it?"

Kirk reached into the pocket of his jeans and pulled out a big wad of money, including several hundreds. "Now will you leave me alone?"

Far from causing her to leave him alone, the display of wealth had precisely the opposite effect. "Why lookee there. Boy, you got all kinds of money on you!" She gave him a sideways leering grin. "I think we can do business, handsome."

"I want you to leave me alone."

"Now don't you go all unsociable on me. I got the cure, remember? I'm eager and willin' to please. And I'm very flexible. If you know what I mean."

"You can't help me."

"Now you don't know that till you've given me a try."

"Look—"

"Maybe I should properly introduce myself. My name's Chantelle. I'm a professional, know what I mean? Very experienced." She ran a long black nail slowly down the curve of her hip. "And I think I could do you a world of good."

"You're wrong."

"Look, baby, I ain't no priest—"

"Lucky for you."

"—but I can see you got troubles. Somebody done you wrong, right? I don't know exactly who it was. Maybe yo' mama done you wrong. Maybe it was your wife, your girlfriend. Your mistress. Your fiancée, even. I don't know. But I know this. Whoever it was, I can make it better."

"No one can make it better. Not even God."

"Well, I got to be honest with you. I don't know much about God. But it's just possible I've got a few tricks in my bag He don't have."

Kirk turned his head up, teeth clenched. "Leave me alone!"

When she saw his face, Chantelle's eyes went wide. "Honey!

What happened to you?" She bent down and cradled his head in her hands. "You look like someone done you but good."

Kirk almost laughed. "Wait'll you see my chest."

"Honey, you need someone to be good to you. Someone to make the hurt stop hurtin'." She pulled him closer and pressed his head against her breasts. "I'll take good care of you, sweet thing. Promise I will."

The heat of her body warmed him. He felt the chain reaction it sent cascading through his body. And he panicked.

"Get away from me, you filthy whore!" He rocked her backward, sending her rolling across the alley. "I'm not like that. I'm not!"

Chantelle held up her hands defensively. "All right, boy, stay calm. Just stay calm."

"I'm not like that!" he bellowed again. "Just because I—it doesn't mean—" He broke down. He jammed his face against his fists, bending over, thrashing from side to side.

Chantelle pushed herself to her feet. "My friend, you are in sorry shape. Truly sorry shape." She walked to the end of the alley. "I'm prob'ly crazy to do this, but here I go anyway. Most nights you can find me right here, on The Stroll. But I've also got a place, a little room just above that pawn shop on the corner of Lewis. Room 12. Anytime you decide you want to see Chantelle, you just come on up there."

She gave him a long look, shook her head a few more times, then clickety-clacked out of the alleyway.

Kirk wanted to tear his eyes out. As his fingers pressed hard against his eyeballs, he gave it serious thought. Why couldn't he make anyone understand? It only happened once. He wasn't like that!

Or maybe he was. Maybe that was what really bothered him. The knowledge that he was the sinner who did that horrible thing. And what's worse, that he did it because he wanted to. Because he enjoyed it.

He flung himself down on the pavement, pummeling himself

against the concrete. His head clanged against the Dumpster, then against the brick wall, then back again and again and again, beating his head into a bloody pulp.

God, God, God, he cried, sobbing silently. Why couldn't he make this torment end? Why couldn't he finish it, once and for all?

* 35 *

As promised, D.A. LaBelle started the next day of trial with the state medical examiner, Bob Barkley. Barkley was relatively new and this was the first time Ben had seen him in court. His predecessor, Dr. Koregai, had passed away from a heart attack several months before.

Barkley was young, energetic, buoyant—a complete contrast to Koregai. Koregai had always been serious and dignified, had always treated his job with enormous gravity. To Barkley, it was more like an all-night party. His infectious enthusiasm suggested that he thought being a coroner was, well, a good time. He seemed to adore rattling on about body parts and blood splatters.

It was quite a change. Koregai had always been so intelligent and commanding that jurors treated his opinions with respect, even if his testimony tended to induce premature napping. Barkley was much better at keeping them awake. The question was how much respect the jury would give the opinions of a coroner who came off more like a surfer dude.

After the preliminary elicitation of Barkley's background and credentials, LaBelle brought him to the case at hand.

"Did you perform a forensic examination on the remains of Joe McNaughton?"

"I sure did," Barkley answered, sort of like, Gee whiz, Mom, I remembered to take out the trash.

"And did you reach any conclusions regarding the cause of death?"

"Absolutely."

"Would you describe those conclusions to the jury?"

"Of course." Taking the cue, Barkley shifted himself slightly so he could make eye contact with the jurors. "The cause of death was the twenty to thirty stab wounds inflicted by a knife, perhaps an inch to an inch and a fourth, with a serrated blade. It's a common configuration; a kitchen knife would fit. The blows landed all over the victim's body—torso, arms, legs, neck, face—even one eye."

Ben saw two of the jurors wince.

"The wounds punctured several critical arteries and caused excessive bleeding, which resulted in the victim's eventual death."

"Would this have been a quick death, Dr. Barkley?"

"Probably not. There were no fatal blows to vital organs, although, of course, the penis was severed. Neither the jugular vein nor the carotid artery were slashed. The process of bleeding to death could have taken anywhere from half an hour to two hours."

"And would the victim have been conscious while bleeding to death?"

"For most of it, yes. Conscious, and in extraordinary pain."

This portion of the testimony was totally irrelevant to the question of who murdered McNaughton, but it was keenly relevant to LaBelle's desire to whip the jury into such a frenzy that they would convict anyone he told them to convict.

"Is there any way of . . . quantifying the pain McNaughton would've experienced? Before his death?"

Barkley pondered a moment. "Have you ever cut your finger?" he asked, to the jury, not LaBelle. "Maybe the knife slipped while you were chopping vegetables? Maybe even just a paper cut. It hurts like heck, doesn't it? For a brief moment, the pain is so intense you can't think of anything else. But with those minor injuries, the pain passes, because the body's healing agents take over. Seratonin is released; the wound reseals; the blood coagulates. But with Joe McNaughton, with injuries of such extraordinary number and degree, there was no hope of healing before his body had drained itself dry. That intense, unbearable pain stayed with him till the moment he died."

The courtroom fell quiet for a moment, as all present contemplated something that was, in fact, too horrible to contemplate.

When he was ready to proceed again, LaBelle held up a knife in a plastic evidence bag. During Matthews's turn on the stand, it had been admitted and labeled Exhibit Fourteen.

"I'm holding an exhibit that has been previously identified as a knife found in the file cabinet of an attorney working for the defendant, Keri Dalcanton. Have you seen this knife before?"

"I have."

"And have you had an opportunity to examine this knife in conjunction with your autopsy of Joe McNaughton?"

"I didn't have the knife when I performed my autopsy. But when I did receive the knife, I compared it to the notes I had made previously regarding the cause and instrumentality of death."

"And did you reach any conclusions regarding the knife?" LaBelle was being more than usually careful not to lead the witness, Ben noticed. Presumably he thought he was on a roll and didn't want it interrupted by objections from the defense.

"I did."

"Dr. Barkley, in your expert opinion, is this knife consistent with the wounds you examined on Joe McNaughton?"

"It is."

"And by that, do you mean that this knife could have been the weapon that caused McNaughton's death?"

"I do," Barkley said eagerly, "but I can go even further than that. Given the blood splatters on the knife and their shape, and the fact that the blood type is the same as McNaughton's, and the matches between the serration pattern on the knife and striation pattern in the wounds, I think it is highly likely that this is the murder weapon. To a medical certainty, in fact."

"Thank you, Dr. Barkley. I appreciate your candor."

Was that candor? Ben wondered. Seemed more like blatant sucking up to him.

"Were there any other wounds on the body, other than those that led to death?"

"Oh yes. And many of them were gruesome in their own right, even if nonfatal."

"Could you describe those injuries, please?"

"Well, I've already mentioned the penectomy. And there were horrendous scrapes and abrasions all over the body."

"Would these abrasions be consistent with the body being dragged over a concrete or gravel surface?"

"Precisely so. I don't think there's any doubt but that's what happened. And remember, the body had been stripped naked, so the effect of being dragged was profound."

"Were there any other injuries?"

"Yes. The victim had suffered a severe contusion to the head, discoloring the left side of his face."

"Anything else?"

"Yes. There were several broken bones. When the body was chained to the fountain, both arms and one of the legs were stretched in unnatural, painful positions. One of the arms snapped, either when chained up or when removed."

More than one juror shook his or her head.

"Would it be fair to say, Doctor, that the killer did not treat the victim with much care?"

Barkley frowned. "I think it would be fair to say that the killer treated the body with intentional disrespect and cruelty."

"Let me ask you another question, sir. There's been a considerable discussion of physical strength in this trial. And in particular, whether the defendant, a small young woman—although one who exercised regularly and was in particularly good shape—could have accomplished the murder. Do you have an opinion on this subject?"

Ben gave Christina a nudge.

"Objection," Christina said, springing to her feet. "Outside the scope of the witness's expertise."

"Not so," LaBelle replied. "Who can speak more expertly on this subject than the doctor? He knows the precise weight of the deceased's body. He knows exactly what rigors the body was put through. He knows what the human body is capable of doing. I believe this falls squarely within his field of specialty."

"Well, it's a little on the fringe," Cable said, grudgingly acknowledging that Christina's objection had some merit, "but I can't say that it's totally outside. I'll allow it."

Christina sat down, frowning. "Should I have argued more?"

"No," Ben whispered. "Save your egregious conduct for when it really matters."

"You may answer the question," LaBelle told his witness obligingly.

"Thank you." Barkley turned back toward the jury. "My opinion is that there was nothing involved in this murder that could not have been accomplished by any adult person of reasonable strength."

"Even moving the body?"

"Yes. Remember, the body was dragged, not carried. A dead body is heavy, but dragging it isn't that hard, particularly if you don't care what happens to it along the way."

"What about chaining the body to the fountain?" LaBelle was asking the hard questions himself, rather than leaving it to the defense. A smart strategy, especially since he and Barkley had undoubtedly already prepared answers.

"Admittedly, that would've been harder, but I still don't believe it was outside the abilities of the average adult. The chains could have been used for leverage; that is, once they were tied to the body and wrapped around the fountain, a sort of rudimentary pulley system could've made it possible to get the body in place. And bearing in mind what the killer did to the body, I think it's fair to assume there was some major adrenaline pumping, which always increases strength. Almost anyone could've done it, really."

"Even a five-foot-three female weighing a hundred and three pounds?"

"Yes. Even her." For the first time, Barkley glanced toward Keri. "Especially given her overall fitness and the undoubted rage she felt at the time."

"Objection!" Christina said. This time she didn't need nudging. "Definitely outside the scope."

"Sustained," Judge Cable replied calmly. "The jury will disregard."

But as Ben and Christina both well knew, the damage was already done. The jury had heard it, and all the instructions in the world would not make them forget it.

"Dr. Barkley," LaBelle continued, "were there any other indications you uncovered during your autopsy regarding the identity of the killer?"

"Yes. I discovered tiny yet discernible traces of skin under the victim's fingernails."

"Skin under the fingernails," LaBelle repeated. "Tell me, Doctor, is there any way to determine conclusively whose skin it was?"

"There is now. DNA analysis."

"And was any DNA testing done?"

"Yes. Fortunately, I discovered a sufficient quantity to be testable. My work was checked by an independent agency—CellTech, in Dallas." He quickly added: "There is no doubt about the results. The DNA matches exemplars taken after arrest from the defendant, Keri Dalcanton."

The good doctor had rushed ahead, Ben realized, because he and LaBelle both knew the question would draw an objection. If Barkley didn't do the testing himself, he had no business announcing the results.

"Should I?" Christina whispered.

"Don't bother. The word is out. And they would only call their CellTech rep to the stand to say the same thing. It's getting in, one way or the other."

LaBelle followed up equally quickly. "Is there any possibility of error on these DNA tests, Doctor?"

"Virtually none. The results were checked and double-checked, both by me and CellTech. There's no doubt about it. Keri Dalcanton's skin was under his fingernails. There was probably a struggle while she was stabbing him—"

"Objection!" Christina said.

"Sustained," Judge Cable said. "The witness will refrain from speculating."

"Let me ask it this way," LaBelle said. "Was the location of the skin consistent with what you would expect when a man was trying to protect himself from a killer?"

"Of course. Perfectly."

LaBelle nodded toward the defense table. "Your witness."

Christina tried to act as if she wasn't nervous about this, but she knew she wasn't fooling anyone, least of all herself. Not that she hadn't spoken out in court before, but cross-exing a major witness in a capital trial was a different matter altogether. She kept humming "I am strong, I am invincible" under her breath, but it wasn't making much difference. She was terrified.

"Dr. Barkley, you're the coroner, right?" It was a safe question, surely. How could he disagree?

"Actually no."

Christina did a double take.

"My title is state medical examiner. That's the terminology we use in Oklahoma, don't ask me why. So to call me a coroner is technically incorrect."

"But the descriptions are the same."

"More or less, yes."

Great start, Christina thought to herself. Maybe next I could get his name wrong or something. "As the medical examiner, do you perform autopsies on a regular basis?"

"Of course."

"How often?"

He shrugged. "On average? Maybe a dozen a week."

"And when you're doing your dozen a week, do you normally speculate on how much pain the victim suffered? Is that a standard part of the medical examiner's work-up?"

"Well . . . no."

"Then why did you do it in this case?"

Barkley appeared slightly off guard. "I just answered the questions that were put to me."

"Yes. And why did Mr. LaBelle want everyone to hear that? Is it relevant to determining how and when the victim died?"

"No."

"Of course it isn't. But it makes for a dramatic story, doesn't it? Certain to fill the jury with contempt and loathing."

"Objection," LaBelle said. Christina wondered what had taken him so long. "Is that a question?"

"A good point," Judge Cable replied. "You're up there to ask questions, Ms. McCall. Not to give speeches. That part comes later."

Oh, thank you so very much. "Doctor, your answer to the questions regarding pain and suffering were entirely speculative, weren't they?"

Barkley appeared indignant. "They were based upon my medical examination."

"Sir, isn't it possible that the man went into shock, then unconsciousness, with the first blow? Or with that head blow, which might have come before the stabbing?"

"In my opinion—"

"I didn't ask you for a self-serving opinion, Doctor. You're not my expert." Out of the corner of her eye, Christina could see LaBelle start to rise, but he ultimately decided to let it go. Better to let the good doctor take care of himself. "I asked if it was possible he went into shock or unconsciousness with the first blow."

"I suppose it's conceivable—"

"Or to put it in Mr. LaBelle's terms—would that be consistent with the evidence?"

"Well, I suppose it's an outside possibility, but—"

"So your answer is yes. Why didn't you inform the jury of this possibility?"

"Excuse me?"

"You've admitted that there were two possible results. At least. And yet you chose to tell the jury about one possibility, and to ignore the other. Why did you mislead the jury? Is that because dying in pain is so much more dramatic than instant unconsciousness?"

Barkley sat up straight. "Mr. LaBelle asked me what I thought happened. I told him."

"And I never once heard you admit the possibility of other results. You just told the jury what you wanted them to know."

"That's absurd. I—"

"What I wonder is, how many other alternate possibilities did you fail to tell the jury about?"

"Objection," LaBelle said. It seemed restraint was at an end.

"Sustained," the judge said sharply. "Counsel, move on to something else."

Which she was happy to do, since she was finished anyway. The jury heard what she wanted them to hear. Hot dog, Christina thought, barely suppressing a smile. This cross-ex stuff wasn't as bad as she thought. In fact, she kinda got a charge out of it.

"On the subject of other possibilities you didn't mention to the jury, Doctor, let's talk about that knife. You claim that Exhibit Fourteen is the murder weapon, right?"

"That was my testimony, yes."

"But didn't you also say that the shape of the knife was a common configuration?"

"Yes . . ."

"Which, translated to English, means a lot of people probably have this very same knife."

"Not covered with blood."

"C'mon, Doctor, there are a lot of ways a knife could get covered with blood, aren't there? I mean, it is a knife, after all."

"I suppose. But this blood was of McNaughton's type—"

"Which is O, correct?"

"I believe that's—"

"Which is the most common blood type in the world, right?"

He tilted his head to one side. "That is correct."

"So contrary to what you told the jury—you don't know if this is the knife that killed Joe McNaughton. All you can say for sure is that it's the kind of knife that killed Joe McNaughton."

"I hardly think it likely—"

"That it could be another knife?" Christina didn't give him a moment to come up for air. "Is that based on your medical examination? Or what the police told you about where the knife was found?"

"Well . . . I suppose . . ."

"Doctor, are you testifying based on your medical expertise, or are you just regurgitating what the police told you?"

"Objection," LaBelle said. "This is inappropriate."

To Christina's amazement, the judge did not immediately agree. "I don't know, counsel. I think she is making a point."

"She's impugning the character and professionalism of the state medical examiner!"

"Well, that's more or less her job here, isn't it? Overruled."

Christina wanted to jump into the air and give the judge a high five, but she managed to restrain herself. "Once again, Doctor, you failed to apprise the jury of all the possibilities. The murder could've been committed with a different knife, right?"

This was a point of keen importance, because if it was another knife, there was no link to Keri.

"But this knife had finger—"

"Excuse me, Doctor, are you testifying outside the scope of your examination again?" Christina was well aware there was bad news to come about the knife with the next witness, but he was Ben's problem, not hers.

Barkley drew in his breath. "It is remotely possible that another knife was involved."

"Thank you very much, Doctor." *Yes!* Could she cook, or could she? "Speaking of the knife, Doctor, we're not even certain that the knife—any knife—was the cause of death, are we?"

"The body had between twenty and thirty wounds—"

"Yes, but that doesn't necessarily mean it was the cause of death, does it?"

"No one could sustain—"

"Did the body also suffer a severe blow to the head?"

"Yes . . ."

Christina checked her notes. "A contusion sufficient to dislodge the skull, correct?"

"Yes . . ."

"That's a rather serious blow. Couldn't that be fatal?"

"Given the evidence of bleeding—"

"You're not answering my question, Doctor. Could that have been fatal?"

"I suppose it's possible. But I don't think—"

"And if that was the cause of death, then the knife had nothing to do with it."

"The knife wounds were there!"

"Yes, but if they didn't kill the man—if the blow to the head already did it—then the person who wielded the knife may have mutilated the body, but was not necessarily the killer." There you go, Ben, she thought. Something for the next witness. Don't say I never gave you anything.

"Based on the blood flow, I believe—"

"For that matter, the victim also suffered at least one severely broken limb, correct?"

"That's true." Barkley was looking less boyish and exuberant by the minute.

"Couldn't that cause internal bleeding? Couldn't that be fatal, too?"

"It could. But the external bleeding would've killed him first."

"You're assuming that all the injuries happened at about the same time. But we don't know that, do we?"

He squirmed a bit. "Well . . . it seems logical."

"Doctor, are you up there to testify as a logician?"

"Obviously not."

"Then please don't. The truth is, any of these things I've mentioned could have been the cause of death, right?"

"It's . . . possible. But what difference—"

"Doctor, do you have any way of knowing whether the person who stabbed Sergeant McNaughton was also the same person who broke his arm or bashed him on the head?"

"Well, I assume—"

"But you don't know, do you?"

"No."

"So there could've been a second person. Someone who didn't touch the knife." Someone other than Keri, in other words.

Barkley was starting to cave. Evidently, he'd had enough. "I suppose it's possible."

"Thank you. As long as there's room for doubt, it's important for the jury to know it." The operative word, of course, being *doubt*. As in reasonable. "Doctor, you said the skin sample found under the victim's nails matched a sample taken from Keri Dalcanton. Some people might think that means they were exactly alike. But that isn't so, is it?"

"It means the similarities between the two were sufficient to establish to a medical certainty—"

"Doctor, I've seen the analysis," Christina said, holding a

long strip of scrolled paper above her head. "They are not exactly alike, are they?"

"Not exactly, no."

"So once again, what you're actually saying, is not that you're certain the skin came from Keri, but that it might have come from Keri."

"The odds against it being anyone else—"

"This isn't Vegas, Doctor. I'm not interested in the odds. I'm interested in telling the jury the truth. And the truth is, the skin might've come from Keri—but it could've come from someone else. It isn't like fingerprints. You can't say where it came from with absolute certainty."

"DNA analysis never does," Barkley protested. "But it can establish that the odds against the sample coming from anyone else are so—"

"Yes or no, Doctor—is it possible the sample came from someone else?"

"It's possible, but—"

"Thank you for answering my question. It's important that we separate the truth from the speculation."

"Your honor," LaBelle said. "She's speechifying again."

"I have warned you," Judge Cable said, looking at Christina sternly. "Don't let it happen again, young lady."

I'll try not to, old man. And watch the sexist remarks. "Speaking of speculation—that was a handy bit where you told the jury the skin must've gotten under his fingernails when McNaughton fought off his attacker. The truth is, you have no idea how that skin got there, do you?"

Barkley hesitated before answering. After being burned four times, he was undoubtedly reluctant to defend another assumption. "Given the circumstances, it seems reasonable—"

"You don't know how it happened. You're guessing again. Your testimony has been nothing but guesses strung together to support the prosecution's unsubstantiated case."

LaBelle started to object, but Barkley jumped in before he

could. "Well, how else could it have gotten there!" he shouted. "It was her skin!"

"Were you in the courtroom yesterday, Doctor?"

"You know I was."

"Then you undoubtedly heard the lurid and unnecessary testimony about the victim's unusual sexual tastes."

"I thought it was the defendant's—"

"And you heard that he allegedly participated in . . . rough sex."

Barkley's face began to color. Apparently rough sex was not a topic LaBelle had prepared him to discuss. "So?"

"Well I'm not an expert, Doctor, but if two people are having rough sex—don't you think it's possible he might get her skin under his nails?"

"Well . . . how would—"

"Maybe a long scrape down the back during a moment of passion? A firm grip on the buttocks?"

Bentley was beet red. "How would I know?"

Christina smiled. "That's just the point, Doctor. You don't. That skin sample might've come from consensual sex—it might have nothing to do with the murder. You don't know how the skin got there, just as you don't know whether this knife is the murder weapon or whether the victim suffered much pain or even what precisely was the cause of death. You're just guessing. And the jury is entitled to know that."

LaBelle redirected, naturally, but after that whirlwind cross, there was only so much he could do. He'd made his points and Christina had made hers. The jury was ready for a new witness. And since he had a doozy waiting in the wings, it probably seemed smarter to move on.

During the recess between witnesses, Christina couldn't resist asking. "So, Ben—I know this is kinda like the insecure guy who wants to know, Was it good for you, too?, but I have to ask anyway—what did you think of my first cross?"

"I only wish I'd been that good when I started," Ben replied.

"You mean it? You thought I did okay? I mean, I thought I did okay, but maybe I'm too close to be objective."

Ben smiled and gave her a punch on the shoulder. "It was good for me, too."

* 36 *

After the lunch break, LaBelle called a series of so-called experts. Ben knew that most of them were required, in order to establish one legal criterion or another, but none of them was very sexy, which was no doubt why LaBelle scheduled them during nap time.

LaBelle called the hair-and-fiber expert who testified to the precautions taken to secure the crime scene after the police arrived. The evidence custodian testified regarding the chain of custody for all prosecution evidence. He was about as interesting as the ingredients label on a carton of milk, but the testimony fulfilled the legal need to establish that the evidence could not have been corrupted. The jury also heard from another DNA expert, an expert on knives, and the civilian who first found McNaughton's body in Bartlett Square and called in the police.

Just after the midafternoon break, LaBelle called Chester Isaac Bare, Tulsa P.D.'s top man on fingerprints. Ben had heard Bare testify so many times he could have done it for him, but he forced himself to remain attentive, just in case LaBelle tried to slip something past him.

Before they got to any of the evidence relating to the case at bar, LaBelle and Bare gave the jury an almost hour-long lecture on everything you ever wanted to know about fingerprints, but not really. Bare waxed on about latents and patents, curls, smudges, line patterns, the thirty-two key indicia of print matching, the roles computers play in the identification process, the FBI database, and on and on and on. Ostensibly, this testimony was relevant because it would help the jury understand his later testimony—as if there was anyone on earth who didn't know about fingerprints already. The real purpose, Ben knew, was to establish Bare as the unquestioned expert in his field—so the jury would believe what he said and resist any efforts by the defense to challenge his findings.

Bare actually seemed to bounce up and down in his seat as he extolled the "virtually infallible computerized print extrapolation programs," which could accurately create an entire print from a smudgy partial. In some respects, Bare, who was balding and wore thick black glasses, was like a Hollywood stereotype of the egghead professor, waxing on enthusiastically about a subject that could not possibly be of interest to anyone other than himself.

Until they got to the McNaughton case. In a fraction of the time it had taken them to establish the man's credentials, LaBelle and Bare told the jury why this information was important—because both the chains that bound the body of Joe McNaughton and the murder weapon itself bore the fingerprints of Keri Dalcanton.

"Is there any question about your findings?" LaBelle asked, summing up.

"Absolutely not. There were three perfectly clear unsmudged prints on the chains, and two on the murder weapon."

"Are you saying it's likely Keri Dalcanton touched those chains?" It seemed LaBelle was learning from the previous cross.

"No. I'm saying that it is an absolute certainty. This isn't like DNA analysis, where ultimately you can only say that the chances of the sample belonging to anyone but the defendant are astronomical. No two people ever born anywhere on planet Earth have ever had the same fingerprints. Never. Those prints were made by Keri Dalcanton. Period."

LaBelle continued debunking any theories Ben might advance. "Is there some way those fingerprints could have been . . . planted?"

"No. Despite what you might have read in Dick Tracy or Batman comics or something, there's no way to fake a fingerprint. Ms. Dalcanton's fingers made contact with the chains and the knife. Unquestionably."

"Thank you," LaBelle said. "I'll conclude and let Mr. Kincaid examine the witness. If he thinks there's any point."

Hard to turn down an invite like that, Ben thought, as he pushed himself to his feet. He sensed that the jury was not going to be responsive to any Simpsonesque theories of how the police could've planted the fingerprints. The expressions on their faces suggested that they believed Bare, and indeed, they had no reason not to trust him. Ben would have to do the best he could with the facts as they were.

"Mr. Bare, were you in the courtroom during the testimony of Corporal Wesley?"

"Yes, I was."

"Then you heard the evidence regarding alleged sexual activities between the defendant and the deceased." He hated to keep reminding the jury about the most lascivious aspect of the case, but it was better than letting this damning fingerprint testimony go unrebutted.

"Oh yes. Hard to miss that."

"Then you understand that there has been a suggestion that chains such as those found on the dead body were used on occasion in these sexual activities." Somehow, it sounded worse when he used these euphemisms than it would if he just came out with it.

"I kind of got that idea."

"So it's entirely possible that the chains used did in fact belong to Keri Dalcanton, or were kept in her apartment. In fact, we saw chains in a photograph taken in her apartment."

"Okay."

"For that matter, lots of people keep chains in their homes for other reasons."

"They do?"

"Ever heard of snow chains?"

"In Tulsa?" He shrugged. "I guess it's possible."

LaBelle rose. "Your honor . . . I fail to see the relevance . . ."

Judge Cable fingered his glasses. "I'm a bit mystified myself, Mr. Kincaid. Could you please get to the point?"

"Certainly. Mr. Bare . . . if the chains belonged to Keri Dalcanton, is it any big surprise that her fingerprints were on them?"

Bare gave a sidewise glance toward some of his police buddies in the gallery. "It was no surprise to me, that's for sure." A mild round of laughter followed.

"I don't think you quite take my meaning. If I went into your apartment and started dusting your personal belongings, wouldn't I likely find your fingerprints on them?"

"Yes."

"And similarly, when you dusted Keri Dalcanton's belongings, you found her prints. But that doesn't prove she killed anyone, does it?"

"If you ask me—"

"All it proves is that at some time or another, she touched the chains. Which is hardly unusual, if they belonged to her."

"But there were no other prints found on the chains or the knife."

"So the killer used gloves. It hardly takes a rocket scientist to work that out."

"I don't think so. Gloves would prevent someone from leaving prints, but would also probably smudge existing prints. I found clear unsmudged prints on both items."

"Sir, how long was the chain in question? The one on which you found the prints."

Bare's expansive forehead crinkled. "Oh, gosh. I don't know exactly. Twenty or thirty feet."

"So someone else could have held the chain—in another place—and neither left prints nor smudged the existing ones."

"I suppose it's possible," Bare said grudgingly. "But what about the knife? The handle is palm-sized. Keri Dalcanton's prints are there, unsmudged, vivid and unmistakable. If someone else had held the knife after she did, even wearing gloves, the prints would be smudged. In fact, I feel comfortable saying not only that Keri Dalcanton held that knife, but moreover, that she was the *last* person to hold that knife."

Ben frowned. He needed to figure some way around this. Everything Bare was saying made perfect sense.

He glanced out of the corner of his eye toward the defense table. C'mon, cocounsel, help me out here. Think of something.

A moment later, Christina began making a strange movement with her right hand, under the table where the judge couldn't see. Was this some sort of obscene gesture? From sweet little Christina? Surely not.

He watched more carefully. She was making a stabbing motion, like she was holding a knife. But when she thrust out, she shook her head. When she moved her hand inward, she nodded.

Ben's eyes lighted. Clever girl.

"Tell me, Mr. Bare. You say you're certain Keri was the last person to touch the knife?"

"Definitely."

"Does that necessarily mean she was the one who stabbed him?"

"I'd say there's—"

"Let's think about this before we jump to any conclusions. You say you know Keri touched the knife. But that doesn't prove she was the one who put the knife into Joe McNaughton's body." He paused. "Maybe she was the one who took it out."

Bare frowned. "What are you talking about?"

"Why wasn't the knife in the body when it was found?"

"Well, I'm sure I don't—"

"Obviously, someone removed it."

"True, but—"

"And that person—not the killer—would be the last one to touch the knife."

Bare straightened. "I have always assumed—as would any logical person—that the person who plunged the knife into the body was also the person who took it out."

"Yes, you assumed," Ben shot back, "but as we've already learned so many times in this trial, what the police assume for convenience is not necessarily what happened. Isn't it possible that someone else killed Joe McNaughton—and that Keri discovered the body and removed the knife?"

"But why?"

"Maybe he wasn't dead yet. Maybe she wasn't thinking logically. Maybe it was her knife and she wanted to prevent the police from making the obvious assumption—the wrong assumption. Or maybe the killer removed the knife but Keri found it and picked it up. My point, sir, is that the evidence doesn't necessarily lead to your conclusion."

"I think this is all very far-fetched."

"No doubt. You're a policeman. But answer this one question for the jury—and please tell them the truth. Isn't it possible that the last person to hold the knife—the person who left prints on it—was someone other than the person who killed Joe McNaughton?"

Bare squirmed a bit. "I suppose it's remotely possible—"

"And therefore, the fact that Keri's prints are on the knife does not necessarily—does not utterly without doubt—mean that she is the killer. Right?"

"I suppose there is a remote—"

"Which is not at all what you said before. But I appreciate the fact that you've told us the truth now, sir. And I think the jury does, too."

⋆ 37 ⋆

The clock on the courtroom wall indicated that it was past four, and given that Judge Cable would never dream of working past five, and LaBelle didn't like to split a witness's testimony over two days (because it gave the defense all night to prepare a cross based on the direct they had already heard), Ben felt sure LaBelle would call for a recess. But once again, he was wrong.

"The State calls Sergeant Frank Bailey to the stand."

Ben had met Bailey during the prelim for the first trial, but he was still taken aback by the man's immense frame. He was even larger than Loving, something Ben would not have previously thought possible. Shoulder to shoulder, he filled the witness box and then some. In the words of the immortal Jim Croce, he was "built like a 'frigerator with a head."

With a quick flurry of questions, LaBelle established that the man was a career member of the police force with a wife and six children. Bailey answered questions in the traditional cop manner—short and to the point. As Ben knew, police officers were coached by the D.A.'s office to testify in that Jack Webb nothing-but-the-facts manner. The idea, of course, was that the less they said, the less likely the defense attorney would be to trip them up. As Mike had told Ben a thousand times, cops were not prepared for trial with a lecture about the exalted search for truth. They were trained like soldiers preparing for combat. It was us-against-them—the *them* being the defense lawyers, who would at every possible opportunity be trying to make the police officer look like Bozo the Clown.

After he finished with the preliminaries, LaBelle cut to the heart of the matter. "Sir, in the course of your work for the police department, did you ever have occasion to know a man named Joe McNaughton?"

"Of course," Bailey said matter-of-factly. "I knew Joe for years."

"Did you work with him?"

"Yeah. I saw him almost every day, till he got shifted over to the Catrona investigation."

"Did you feel that you knew Sergeant McNaughton well?"

"Like he was my brother."

"Were you in contact with him prior to his death?"

"Constantly. We weren't working together, but we saw each other around. And we talked."

LaBelle turned a page in his notebook, signaling to the jury that he was moving on to a new and more interesting subject. "Were you aware that Sergeant McNaughton was engaged in a, uh, liaison with Keri Dalcanton?"

"Oh sure. Lots of the boys knew about her. I was at the club the night he met her."

"And you were aware that the two developed a . . . relationship? A sexual relationship."

"Sure." Bailey shifted his bulky frame. "He told me about it. Repeatedly."

"What did he say?"

"Objection, hearsay." Ben knew he was going to get creamed, but he had to make the gallant effort, just the same.

"Your honor," LaBelle explained tiredly, as if Ben's petty little objections were the most wearisome thing in the world, "as with Corporal Wesley, these statements come from the deceased, a witness who is obviously unavailable, and given the circumstances surrounding the statements and the utter absence of any motivation for falsehood, I ask that the court accept these statements as evidence just as it did the previous ones."

"Your honor," Ben jumped in, "these statements are different because—"

Too late. "I'll allow it," Judge Cable said, cutting him off. "Overruled."

LaBelle nodded toward his witness. "You may answer the question."

Bailey did. "Basically, he said she was a pistol. A real hot potato. Always ready and eager to please. He liked that."

Well, who wouldn't, Ben wondered. Except, perhaps, McNaughton's widow. A quick glance into the gallery told him she wasn't pleased at all.

"Did he have any concerns regarding the relationship?"

"Well, I know he worried a little about her age. She claimed she was eighteen, but she was awful young looking, and he didn't want to get into any trouble with the law."

How noble, Ben thought. Of course, this concern didn't stop him from dropping by her apartment every night for another go with the whips and chains.

"Did he have any other concerns?"

"Yeah. More than once he told me that he was worried about . . . well, this is kinda delicate."

"I understand it's hard to talk about private matters you were told in secret," LaBelle said. "But I must assure you, it's for the best. Please answer the question."

"Well," Bailey said, his massive frame drooping a bit, "he did tell me he was worried about Keri's . . . fondness for violence."

"For violence?" LaBelle said, as if surprised. "Was she violent?"

"Oh, yeah. Well, you can understand, if you've seen those pictures . . ." He nodded toward the graphic exhibits resting on the edge of the judge's bench. "Or if you'd heard Joe talk about . . . some of the things she liked to do. Really weird stuff. Weird and violent."

"Was her taste for violence restricted to sexual activities?"

"Unfortunately, no. I think Joe could've lived with that. He didn't like it, but it was worth it to get . . . well, you know. But it wasn't just the kinky sex. She had a horrible temper—that's what he told me. Said she used to fly off the handle with the least excuse, screamin' and yellin' and throwin' things. Said she got all red in the face and crazy, like she totally lost her head or something. One time, she even came at him with a knife."

Someone in the jury box gasped. The word *knife* had the effect for which LaBelle had undoubtedly been hoping.

Keri leaned close and whispered in Ben's ear. "This is not how it happened. Not at all."

Ben patted her hand. The time for explanations would come later.

"A knife?" LaBelle repeated, making sure every juror got it. "McNaughton told you she came at him with a knife?"

"Yes, sir."

"Are you sure about this? It's very important."

"I'm sure. It's not the sort of thing you're likely to forget. Something about her wantin' to go out barhoppin', but he had to go home and do somethin' with his wife, and she just lost it. Grabbed a knife out of the kitchen and tried to stop him. He said he thought she would've killed him if he hadn't seen her comin'."

"If he hadn't seen her coming," LaBelle murmured meaningfully. "That time."

"Your honor!" Ben said, jumping up.

Judge Cable nodded. "Mr. LaBelle, please stick to the questions and keep your comments to yourself."

"Of course, your honor," he said. "Sorry." Although Ben did not detect much sorrow in his face or voice. He turned another page in his notebook. "Sergeant Bailey, did you have occasion to talk to Joe McNaughton in the early evening of the night he was killed?"

"Yes. I saw him at headquarters. We talked."

"Did Sergeant McNaughton mention Ms. Dalcanton on this occasion?"

"Yes, he did."

"What did he say?"

"Said there'd been a big blowup. With both his wife and his—Keri Dalcanton. Said his whole life was fallin' apart all around him."

"How so?"

Bailey inched ever so subtly toward the jury box. "I didn't get all the details, but somehow, his wife found out about the affair. She was mad. She was talking about divorce, talking about takin' him to the cleaners. As I think you know, Joe didn't work for money—he was actually quite well off. At the same time, Keri Dalcanton was having a major tantrum, demanding that he come back to her, threatenin' him."

"Threatening him?"

"Oh yeah. In no uncertain terms. Joe told me she said that if he dumped her, he'd be very sorry."

Ben heard Keri whispering under her breath. "It isn't true. I didn't even know yet."

Christina cautioned her to remain quiet.

"He would be sorry," LaBelle repeated. "What exactly did that mean, Sergeant?"

"Joe didn't know. But given her fondness for violence, he was worried about it."

"Was there anything else?"

"Yeah. When he told her that his wife knew and all, she apparently went kinda crazy. Started screamin' and shoutin' and spittin'. Throwin' things at him. He said he finally had to leave. She was nuts—screamin' the same word over and over again."

"Indeed. And what was that word?"

Bailey took a deep breath before answering. "*Faithless.* That's what she called him. That's what she said over and over again. *Faithless.*"

Ben watched the reaction on the jurors' faces as they heard

the dreaded magic word. The word the killer had painted on McNaughton's chest in his own blood.

LaBelle pivoted and gave Keri a long look—thus inviting the jury to do the same.

A considerable period of time elapsed before he spoke again. "I have no more questions, your honor."

As Ben scrambled to the podium, he could think of at least ten different ways to start the cross of this witness. But he had to pick one. And it needed to be the right one, because the testimony this man delivered had been keenly incriminating.

Ben cranked up the volume so he could be sure his first question hit home. "Have you been following me?"

Bailey blinked several times rapidly. "I . . . excuse me?"

"You heard the question. Have you been following me?"

"I . . . uh . . . I don't know what . . ." Ben was pleased—and relieved—to see the witness stumbling around. Evidently he had managed to choose the one subject on which LaBelle had not known to prepare him.

LaBelle tried to bail him out. "Objection, your honor. Lack of relevance."

"Lack of relevance?" Ben shot back. "Like it's not relevant whether the police have been harassing and stalking the defense team? Believe me, your honor, I'll tie it up."

Judge Cable rubbed the bridge of his nose unhappily. "Well . . ."

"Furthermore," LaBelle added, "I object on grounds that this exceeds the scope of the direct examination."

"I think it will soon be evident," Ben said, "that this is keenly relevant to the credibility of every word this man has ever said."

Judge Cable sighed heavily. "I will give you some leeway to quickly and firmly establish the relevance of this line of questioning, Mr. Kincaid. Don't disappoint me."

Ben turned back toward the witness. "Let's try it again, Sergeant Bailey. Have you been following me?"

He coughed. His words came slowly. "I, um, I still don't see . . ."

"Maybe I can help you." Ben whipped a photo out of his notebook. "This was taken by my investigator a few nights ago just outside my office building. It clearly shows you and another officer, Arlen Matthews, who coincidentally has also testified against my client, watching my office. So let me ask again, Sergeant. Have you been following me?"

Bailey inhaled, lifting his massive chest, then letting it fall. "Yes."

Hallelujah. "For how long?"

Another long pause. "Since the first dismissal of this case."

"You and Arlen Matthews?"

"Like it shows in the picture."

"Anyone else?"

He nodded. "At times."

"And was this an official police assignment?"

"No."

Too bad, Ben thought. A *yes* might've gotten this case dismissed again. "So why were you there? Why were you stalking me? Why were you surveilling my office?"

Bailey craned his neck. "We were concerned because . . . we felt that you had gotten Joe's killer off by underhanded means and . . . we wanted to make sure it didn't happen again."

"So you invaded my privacy. Carried on illegal surveillance."

"Now wait a minute. We never did anything illegal."

"I wonder. Were you watching the night the police found the alleged murder weapon in my office?" This question would, of course, remove the carefully drawn curtain of anonymity around the identity of the lawyer who had the knife, but Ben thought it was worth it to follow up this line of questioning.

Bailey frowned. "I was."

"And Matthews?"

"For a while. Then he got an anonymous call, which caused him to get the warrant to search your office."

"Did you actually hear this anonymous call?"

"Well . . ."

"No. Matthews just told you there had been such a call, right?"

Another long pause. "That's right. But—"

"And were you and your buddies also on hand a few nights ago when a young woman was brutally stabbed in my office?"

"No. Absolutely not."

"Are you sure? Because my investigator—"

"We were there that night. But we left before . . . the incident. We thought everyone had left."

"But you *were* there that night."

"Yes. But we—"

"Just answer the questions, Sergeant." He assumed the man would not admit he was behind the stabbing, so he moved on. "Would you please explain to the jury the meaning of the phrase 'the Blue Squeeze'?"

Bailey hesitated, giving LaBelle time to try to bail him out. "Your honor, Mr. Kincaid promised us he would establish the relevance of this questioning and he has failed to do so. He's just trying to tarnish the reputations of our valiant police officers in a cheap attempt—"

"I'm trying to tarnish the reputations of the stalkers who have been illegally hounding me and my staff," Ben replied. "And if he doesn't see the relevance, he needs to be shipped back to first-year law school!"

Judge Cable pointed a gavel. "Mr. Kincaid, watch your tongue."

"Your honor, this is gross misconduct of the worst sort by police officers who have passed themselves off as disinterested witnesses. I should be asking for a mistrial."

Ben saw Judge Cable's face lose its color. The last thing on earth he wanted was to see this case boomerang back again. "I'll allow this to continue. But get to the point."

"Your honor," LaBelle said, "for the record, I must protest—"

"Sit down!" Cable snapped.

Ben and Christina exchanged a look. Cable going after the prosecutor? Was it possible he was beginning to smell a rat, too?

"I'll repeat the question," Ben said to Bailey, "and don't pretend you don't know the answer. What's the Blue Squeeze?"

Another heavy sigh. "The Blue Squeeze is a term some people use when police officers decide to—well, put the squeeze on someone."

"We're not talking about official police business, right?"

Bailey nodded. "This would be a . . . private matter."

"And after the first trial ended, you put the Blue Squeeze on me and my staff, didn't you?"

"It wasn't my idea—"

"Matthews then. Whoever. But the Blue Squeeze was on, right?"

Bailey glanced at LaBelle, but there was no way the prosecutor could help him now. "Right. The Blue Squeeze was on. I didn't think it was necessary, or even a particularly good idea. But some of the other boys—"

"I'm sure they dragged you kicking and screaming."

"Mr. Kincaid!" Judge Cable bellowed.

"Sorry, your honor. I'll withdraw that." As if it mattered. "You admit the Blue Squeeze was on. You admit you were following me and my staff around, watching our movements, watching our office—"

"But we didn't do anythin'," Bailey insisted. "We just wanted to make sure you didn't try anythin' underhanded. We just watched."

"You just watched. And we're supposed to believe that it's just a coincidence that while you were watching, the knife turned up in my office."

"I don't think it's a coincidence," Bailey said. "I think you—"

"And it was just a coincidence that Paula Connelly, who was working with me on Keri Dalcanton's defense, was brutally attacked—while you were watching."

"I don't know anything about—"

"For all we know, you might've planted every piece of evidence in this case. It's clear that you and your friends were so determined to see my client convicted, you were willing to do anything!"

LaBelle rose. "Is that a question?"

Well, Ben had done about all he could here anyway. It was time to move on. "I'll withdraw it." He flipped to the next page of his outline. "Can you explain to me why Joe McNaughton was demoted, several months before he was killed?"

Bailey seemed startled by the abrupt change of subject. "Why—what?"

"You've told us you and Joe were buddies, that you talked to him all the time. Surely you know why he was demoted."

"It was my understanding that . . . Internal Affairs was concerned that he might've gotten . . . too close to the subject of his investigation."

"That would be Antonio Catrona?"

"Yes."

"And can you then explain why sometime later his rank was restored?"

Bailey shrugged. "I assume the IA investigation cleared him."

"Really?" Ben arched an eyebrow. "If IA cleared him, why was Corporal Wesley running around taking pictures of McNaughton through the windowpane?"

Bailey paused. "I don't know."

"Could it be that he wasn't really cleared—because he really was tangled up with Catrona? Could that unfortunate connection possibly be the real reason he was killed?"

"I don't think it's—"

"Is—it—possible? " Ben asked, practically shouting.

"I couldn't say," Bailey replied.

"Then you don't really know who killed Joe McNaughton, do you?"

"No," he said finally. "I guess I don't."

"That's right," Ben said, walking away from the podium. "And neither does anyone else."

* 38 *

It was late, well past visiting hours at St. John's, but Ben still wanted to stop by the hospital before he went home. It had been an exhausting day at trial, and tomorrow would be no better—but this was something he had to do. He owed it to Jones—and to Paula.

After sweet-talking his way past the admissions desk, he quietly pushed open the door to room 522 and tiptoed inside.

Jones was sitting at the side of the bed, his head resting against the iron railing. His eyes were closed, but Ben knew he was not asleep.

"How goes it?" Ben asked quietly.

Jones did not look up. "No change."

Ben stepped carefully around the end of the bed, glancing at the chart as he passed. "Christina told me the doctors say she's stable."

"Sort of," Jones mumbled. "Stable, but critical. They've got her blood level normal again. They've patched up the wound. They're feeding her intravenously. But she won't wake up."

Ben glanced at Paula's recumbent form, lying atop the bed like Sleeping Beauty, alive but deep in slumber. She looked as if she had been that way forever. The rubber bag attached to her respirator slowly filled and emptied, but there was no other sign of life. "Is she in a coma?"

Jones shrugged. "They don't know what it is exactly. They say she should come around. But she doesn't. She may have gone too close to the edge. She was very low on blood before they got her to the hospital. It may have been too—"

"Don't talk that way," Ben said, cutting him off. "Don't even think it. She just needs time, that's all. She suffered a grievous injury and she needs time to recover. Build her strength. I was in a coma once, and I know—"

"Ben, stop." Slowly, Jones's head rose from the railing. His eyes were red and lined and tired. A pink smudge showed where the iron bar had imprinted upon his cheek. "You're not telling me anything I don't already know. That I haven't already thought about. Constantly." He stood up, but his legs seemed wobbly and insubstantial. "How goes the trial?"

Ben shrugged. The trial was a matter of life and death to Keri, but at the moment, in this room, it seemed almost trivial. "Not well. But it always looks dark when the prosecution is putting on their case."

"I heard you put some major dents in LaBelle's witnesses on cross-ex."

Evidently Christina, the eternal optimist, had preceded him. "I think I established that some members of the police department were willing to do anything to put Keri Dalcanton behind bars. And that helps. And Christina did a great job with the coroner. But did either of us prove Keri didn't commit the murder? No."

"It's early days yet."

"Yeah." That was what defense attorneys always said. It'll get better, once we're putting on our case. Ben just hoped it was true. "Seen Matthews around?"

"Some. Not much."

Ben swore under his breath. "I filed a formal protest,

asking that Paula's case be reassigned, but it doesn't seem to have done much good. I don't have much pull with Tulsa P.D. these days. I wish to God Mike were around. But he isn't, and no one's telling where he is."

Jones's jaw tightened. "They're never going to find out who did this to Paula, are they?"

He couldn't lie. "I don't know. But I won't let them give up without trying. And I've got Loving looking into it, too."

That seemed to cheer Jones, at least a little. "That's good. Loving will make a serious effort. He——" His voice choked. "He liked Paula, too."

"Don't talk about her in the past tense, Jones."

"I didn't mean to. I just——I——" His voice dwindled away to nothing.

Ben walked to the door. He had felt it was important to stop in, but he had no sense that his presence was a comfort to Jones—almost the opposite, in fact. He wondered if his being here reminded Jones of how this tragedy came about—and whose fault it was.

"Is there anything I can do?" Ben asked.

Jones's eyes turned toward the still figure on the hospital bed. "Got a miracle in your pocket?"

" 'Fraid not." He shoved his hands deep inside his coat. "I do have some leftover cheese puffs, though."

Jones almost smiled. "Then I guess that'll have to do."

* 39 *

Kirk had barely ten seconds to wait after he knocked on the faded, warped-wood door of apartment 12.

She smiled. "I knew you'd be back."

Kirk entered the room. He did not make eye contact, but chose instead to walk right past her, sullen and silent.

"And you couldn'ta chosen a better time. I was thinkin' 'bout going back out. I called my girlfriend, but she said, 'Girlfriend, whatchoo wanna go out there now for? There's no one out this time of night. No one you wanna see, leastwise.' "

Kirk jabbed his hand into his tight jeans pocket and withdrew what seemed like a huge wad of cash. He tossed it down on the end table beside her sofa. "That's for you."

The expression on Chantelle's face, which had been lively from the start, became positively animated. "Why, you generous boy." She untied the scarf from her neck and wrapped it around the back of his head, tugging him closer. "For that kind of money, my little man, you can do anything you want. Anything at all."

"Glad to hear it," Kirk grunted. A second later, he was on top of her. There was nothing subtle about this approach. His mouth was on hers, pressing hard. His arms were flailing all over her, probing, groping, half fighting against hers. Their teeth actually scraped, then Chantelle opened her mouth wider. Kirk's tongue plunged inside, exploring with an urgency that almost gagged her.

"Whoa, slow down, boy," she said, as soon as she was able,

but Kirk did not comply. She had told him he could do anything he wanted, and he meant to do it. There was nothing tender about what they were doing, in his mind. There was no pretense that this was lovemaking. This was brutal, animal, and he wanted it to show. He wanted to feel what was happening to them. He wanted it to hurt.

He slung Chantelle backward, missing the sofa by inches. She fell onto the floor, which fortunately for her was carpeted. He pounced on top of her again. He was breathing hard and audibly now; they could feel one another's breath.

"My, my, you are in a hurry, sugah." Despite her position, she did not seem in great distress. She had seen it all before, Kirk supposed. A small smile creased her face and she nuzzled into the crook of his neck and waited to see what would come next.

Kirk bit her. Hard.

Chantelle screamed. It was perhaps a scream more of surprise than pain, but at any rate, it sent her into action. Her hips rocked; her legs locked around his.

"Now don't you be damaging the goods," Chantelle said, rubbing the place on her neck where he'd bitten her. "Don't want you gettin' in trouble with my main man."

"You said I could do anything I wanted," Kirk growled. He pushed himself up with one strong arm and, bringing the other around faster than she could follow, slapped her hard on the side of the face.

She screamed again, and this time she meant it.

Kirk began ripping off her clothes, her dress, her panties, her bra. When he couldn't figure out the clasp, he tore it apart. I've paid for this several times over, he told himself. This belongs to me. He clawed at her relentlessly, never resting until she was totally naked. Using one hand to undress, while the other kept her firmly pinned in place, he soon had his clothes off as well.

She raised an arm against him, but he knocked it away effortlessly. She followed up with a raised knee, but he stopped that with another sharp blow to the side of her face. He was stronger than her, plus he had a fury inside him that she couldn't hope to match. She was powerless against him.

He came at her like a hurricane, wrapping himself around her, enveloping her. She eventually realized she could not fight him, so she clutched him and held on tight, just trying to minimize the damage. He pounded and pounded her, sex as violence, pummeling her with his raw passion. At last, he entered her, hips locking, and he began thrusting and thrusting, beating at her, bruising her, coming at her with all the finesse of a drunken teenager. He continued ramming himself against her, over and over again, and to his surprise, Chantelle's resistance evaporated. Her eyes became wide and interested; her back arched against his stomach. Soon she was rocking with him, back and forth, back and forth. The intensity magnified until all at once, she let out a brief shuddering cry, part sob, part ecstasy. Kirk thumped away, finishing, shouting out his release in her ear.

And then, all at once, the frenzied motion was over. They lay beside one another on the floor, chests heaving, struggling for breath. They were both wet with sweat, naked bodies glistening under the subdued light.

A few moments later, Kirk was surprised to feel Chantelle's fingers tickling the back of his neck, then the spider's touch of her lips pressed against his cheek.

"Je-suss," she whispered into his ear. "I ain't felt nothin' like that in ages." He heard a small chuckle in the back of her throat. "But next time, give a girl some warnin', okay? We'll get out the handcuffs and ropes and do this thing proper."

"Don't talk dirty," Kirk gasped, between breaths.

"Course not." She snuggled closer to him. "You just keep comin' to see me, sugah. I'll make you forget all about . . . whoever it was."

"Don't," Kirk said. His heavy breathing intensified. "Don't."

"Just relax," Chantelle said, licking his shoulder. "I'll take her place. I'll be whatever she was to you."

"No!" Kirk jumped to his feet, screaming. He gathered his clothes as quickly as possible and ran out the door. As he tumbled down the stairs, he felt an aching in his gut, intense and unavoidable. It was back again, back with a vengeance, back with such intensity that he knew in his heart he could never be free of it. He had forgotten it for a moment. He had managed to put it out of his mind. But it was back—back to stay. No matter what he tried. No matter what he did to whom. No matter what.

He raced all the way to his delapidated apartment building, ran up the stairs, raced inside, and slammed the door shut. He pressed himself against the inside of the door, as if blocking the path to the demons he knew lurked beyond.

It didn't work.

"You can run, Kirk, but you can never hide."

Kirk's eyes exploded. "Who is that?"

"Aren't you tired of this game, Kirk? The running, the hiding. Punishing yourself. As if that could ever make a difference."

"Who is that?" He paused, then felt the most horrible clutching at his heart. *"You!"*

"Yes, me. The realization of your worst fears."

"But, you—I—are you—are you real?"

"Well, that's a problem for your sick little brain to work out, isn't it?"

Kirk pressed harder against the door, clinging to the woodwork. "Wh-Why are you here?"

"I've come to see what the hell is taking you so long."

"I—I don't know what you mean."

"Yes, you do. I thought you'd be dead long before now. How long are you going to go on with this foolishness? Punishing yourself. Punishing others. Pretending that it might somehow make you feel better. When you know damn well that nothing is ever going to make you feel better."

"That isn't so!"

"It is. There's only one thing that will ever give you any relief. And you know what it is. So why don't you get on with it?"

"No! I—I don't have that—that guilt anymore. I—I got rid of it. I—"

"Rid of it?" the voice said incredulously. "Kirk, have you been doing something naughty tonight?"

"No! I—I—"

"Kirk, tell me the truth."

Kirk covered his face with his hands.

"And you thought that would make things better? All you've done is make it worse. All you've done is prove you can never compensate for what you've done." The voice took on a tone of harsh finality. "It's over, Kirk. End it."

"Noooo!" Kirk flung open the door and ran, ran like the devil was chasing him. He tumbled down the stairs, taking them three at a time. The crotchety landlord emerged from his room, shouting something about the noise, but Kirk didn't stop for him or anyone else. He ran and ran into the night, never stopping.

But where could he go? There was nowhere left to run, he knew that now. Nothing left to try. It was over, just as the voice in the dark had told him. It was done.

There was nothing else left for him, no alternative. It was time to end it. Once and for all.

* 40 *

Keri seemed calmer this morning, although Ben sensed it was only a temporary respite, like a wounded sparrow clinging tenuously to a slippery eave. The pressure bearing down on all of them was more intense than ever. Ben could literally feel the burning gaze of the jurors as they constantly scrutinized Keri's face, checking her reactions, looking for insight on an insoluble problem. Keri might be steady, but she was not strong, and Ben knew she could break down altogether at any moment.

"This one still mine?" Christina asked, as she nestled between them at the defendant's table.

"With my compliments," Ben replied.

"Is that because you think I'd be particularly good at crossing her, or because you particularly don't want to do it yourself?"

The corner of Ben's mouth turned upward. "Am I under oath?"

"The State calls Dr. Margaret Fulbright to the stand," LaBelle announced, as soon as Judge Cable was in the courtroom.

Immediately thereafter, a surprisingly attractive woman began the long walk to the witness stand. She was thin and delicate in appearance, with long brunette hair that fell behind her shoulders. She was dressed professionally but not unattractively and she walked with a calm, if slightly uncertain, manner.

Not exactly your stereotypical psychiatrist, Ben thought. A quick glance told him similar thoughts were running through Christina's brain as well. This could call for a change in strategy.

After Dr. Fulbright stated her name and established her professional credentials, LaBelle drew her into the case at hand. "Are you currently practicing, Dr. Fulbright?"

"I am. I have a private clinic for psychotherapeutic analysis and consultation in the Medical Arts building near Seventy-first and Yale."

"And do you see patients at your office?"

"I do."

"And do you by chance know the defendant, Keri Dalcanton?"

"I do. She's one of my patients. Or was, anyway."

The response from the jury was subtle but nonetheless discernible. The prosecution had been suggesting all along that Keri was aberrant and disturbed. This was undoubtedly where they'd try to prove it.

"And why were you seeing Ms. Dalcanton?"

"Objection," Christina said, even though she knew it was hopeless. "This is protected by the patient-doctor privilege."

"We've already discussed this, counsel," Judge Cable replied. "I'm letting it in. Overruled."

"But your honor, the prejudice—"

"Overruled," he repeated emphatically. "Sit down."

The witness answered. "Initially, I saw Ms. Dalcanton because she was suffering from a variety of anxiety-related difficulties. What you might call nervous problems, but in reality they represent a far more complex and interrelated series of psychological disturbances."

"How did she come to be your patient?"

"She was referred to me by a doctor at Social Services. She was picked up on a minor criminal offense—shoplifting, I believe—"

"Objection," Christina said again. "Evidence of prior bad acts is inadmissible."

"Inadmissible to prove a likelihood to act in conformity at a later time," LaBelle quickly replied. "Here, it's just being mentioned to establish a basis for the expert witness's expert conclusions."

Judge Cable nodded. "I'll allow it for this limited purpose."

Ben frowned. As if the purported purpose mattered. If the jury heard it, they heard it.

Dr. Fulbright continued. "The doctors at Social Services perceived Keri as suffering from psychological distress. She was unable to pay for professional help, so they sent her to me." She paused, then added by way of explanation, "I try to do a certain amount of pro bono work each year."

"I see. How much time did you spend with Ms. Dalcanton?"

"I met with her regularly—at least once a week—for approximately five months." Her voice was calm and assured. "She was suffering from some serious problems, in my opinion."

"Objection," Christina said strenuously. Perhaps if she tried a different basis she would have more luck. "No foundation has been laid for that opinion."

LaBelle gave her a patronizing look. "We will do so shortly, your honor. Unlike law school, in real life, not everything can happen in perfect order."

Christina shot daggers at him with her eyes. "Law school or real world, you still have to follow the rules. Foundation first, conclusion second."

Judge Cable held up his hands. "I'm sure Mr. LaBelle will go into the basis for the expert's opinion in detail. I'm going to give him some leeway. Overruled."

LaBelle nodded. "Dr. Fulbright, during this period when you treated Ms. Dalcanton, did you keep any notes?"

"Of course."

"Do you have them with you today?"

She reached down toward her feet and retrieved a dark brown folder. "I do."

"Fine. Feel free to refer to them. Could you please explain to the jury exactly what Ms. Dalcanton's problems were? Or perhaps I should say—are."

"Objection!" Christina said, rising to her feet. "I must say again—this violates the doctor-patient privilege. She's not only revealing secrets but making recourse to confidential files."

"The privilege is ended," LaBelle replied.

"The privilege," Christina shot back, "can only be waived by the patient—Keri Dalcanton."

"Not so," LaBelle rejoined. He was obviously ready for this. "According to both the canons of the AMA and the case law of this court, the privilege can be dissolved whenever there is serious threat of bodily harm to a patient or third party, or where the patient has engaged in a criminal act. In this case, both exceptions apply."

Christina started to speak, but Judge Cable stopped her with a wave of his hand. "Don't waste your breath, counsel. I'm going to allow it. Please continue."

LaBelle thanked the judge, then turned back to the witness. "Again, please tell the jury what Ms. Dalcanton's problems were during the time you saw her."

"Objection!" Christina said. The jury was probably getting tired of her interruptions, but this testimony was too damaging to allow without a fight. "Lack of foundation. Lack of specificity. More prejudicial than probative."

"Three very different objections," Judge Cable said, nodding. "And all of them overruled. Proceed, Mr. LaBelle."

Dr. Fulbright nodded. "Initially, she was suffering from a variety of anxiety-related problems. As you may know, she was living in Stroud when the Level Five tornado hit a little more than a year ago. Her place of work was destroyed; many of her friends lost their homes and a few lost their lives. Close in time and proximity, she lost her parents, in a sudden and traumatic traffic accident. The psychological scars left by these incidents were profound. She suffered symptoms of anxiety, paranoia, and severe neurosis."

Fulbright glanced down at her notes before continuing. "Shortly after the tornado eliminated her place of employment, she moved to Tulsa, a much larger city than she had ever lived in before. From a psychological standpoint, this was a major error in judgment; it simply added additional stress to a psyche already crippled and dysfunctional. She had far more trouble finding work here, ironically, than she would've had in Stroud. After a series of stressful failures and an arrest for shoplifting, she ended up working as a stripper, and if I'm not mistaken, worked as a prostitute on the side for additional income."

"That's not true!" Keri said. Her voice rippled through the

courtroom. Her eyes were wide with horror and outrage. "It's a lie!"

Judge Cable pounded his gavel. "Mr. Kincaid, control your client!"

"I will, your honor." He leaned close to Keri. "Quiet now. We'll get our chance."

LaBelle continued. "What was the effect of this . . . difficult lifestyle on Ms. Dalcanton, Doctor? In your expert opinion."

Fulbright straightened slightly. "Clearly, the stress of living in a shameful way, of taking her clothes off and exposing herself, several times a night, over and over again, combined with the previous bereavement and trauma, took a psychological toll on her. This was intensified by her younger brother, who lived with her, was quite religious, and did not approve of her new occupation. His repeated comments only intensified the guilt and shame she was already experiencing."

"To what effect, doctor?"

She paused before answering. "To the effect that Keri Dalcanton was a seriously disturbed human being. Unstable. And deeply psychotic."

"Objection!" Christina said, letting her anger show. She wondered if her objections were doing more harm than good, flagging all the important parts for the jury and making them unforgettable. Still, she had to try. "Speculation. Lack of foundation."

"This is an expert witness, not a fact witness," Judge Cable answered. "She's allowed to give us her expert opinion, even if it is speculative. Overruled."

LaBelle continued. "Doctor, could this condition potentially be . . . dangerous?"

"Definitely. And particularly so in the case of Keri Dalcanton."

"Why?"

"Because Ms. Dalcanton has an extreme penchant for violence. One of the worst I've ever seen."

The buzz in the courtroom was audible. And to Ben, most disturbing.

"Isn't a taste for violence inconsistent with the rather fragile psyche you've described, Doctor?"

"Not in the least. It is precisely people like Keri Dalcanton, people with damaged or fragile egos, who end up committing most acts of sudden, irrational violence. The least provocation could've caused her to commit acts of depravity and extreme cruelty."

LaBelle walked to the easel and uncovered the enlarged photo of Joe McNaughton's mutilated body chained to the fountain. "Even this?" he asked.

Christina jumped to her feet. "Objection! This is not a fact witness, remember?"

"Sustained," Judge Cable said, nodding. But the point had been made.

Ben watched LaBelle carefully as he glanced down at his notes, trying to decide where to go next. LaBelle was walking a narrow tightrope, and they both knew it. If he made Keri appear to be crazy, Ben might go for a verdict of not guilty by reason of insanity. On the other hand, if he didn't make her seem seriously off-kilter, how could he possibly explain the enormous violence done to Joe McNaughton—even after his death? After all, Joe was not the first man who ever dumped his girlfriend. But he was the first one who ever got chained to the fountain in Bartlett Square.

"What's your basis for your statement that Ms. Dalcanton had proclivities for extreme violence?" LaBelle asked finally.

"Her taste for the extreme is evident throughout her life and lifestyle. Take her sex life, for instance—"

"Objection," Christina said. "That is not relevant here."

Dr. Fulbright turned toward the judge. "I don't agree, your honor. I believe it is."

Judge Cable nodded. "You may speak."

Fulbright turned back toward the jury. "From the start, Ms. Dalcanton's sexual relationship with Joe McNaughton was shaped by her personal psychoses. They had, not just aberrant, but violent sex. Frequently. This is a manifestation of her proclivity for violence, a fondness she tried to suppress in everyday life, but which revealed itself during these moments of unbridled passion."

"Your honor," Christina said, "I must protest. This is simply an attempt to alienate the jury with repeated references to the defendant's private sexual practices."

"Not so," LaBelle said. "This is keenly relevant to the matter of Keri Dalcanton's thirst for violence—and the relevance of that is obvious."

"Quite correct," Judge Cable said. "Proceed."

You dirty old man, Ben thought, even though he knew he shouldn't. You're enjoying this. You may pretend to be dismayed and above it all, but you're really getting your rocks off with all this sin and sex stuff. You're going to let it all in, prejudicial as it is, 'cause you enjoy listening to it.

"Were there any other indications that Ms. Dalcanton was suppressing a tendency toward violence?" LaBelle continued.

"Yes." Again the good doctor glanced at her notes. "As I said, it was exemplified in her behavior. But it was also manifested in her words. Particularly in what she said during our therapy sessions."

"I have to object again," Christina said, her anger evident. "This is absolutely privileged. When my client went to this doctor, she presumed that what she said was confidential and would not be repeated—"

Judge Cable didn't wait for LaBelle to respond. "I've already ruled, counsel."

"But your honor, this goes to her most private—"

"I've already ruled, counsel," the judge repeated, much louder than before. "If you interrupt again, I'll hold you in contempt!"

Realizing it was useless, Christina sat down. "Did I push too far?" she whispered into Ben's ear.

"There's no such thing," he replied.

"As I was saying," Dr. Fulbright continued, "she was frequently preoccupied with violent fantasies."

"Can you give us some examples?"

Dr. Fulbright paused, perhaps for the first time exhibiting some regret or concern for her former client. "She had a recurring fantasy in which she killed her parents, paying them back for the imagined cruelty they perpetrated on her during her childhood."

Sitting next to Ben, Keri actually gasped.

Dr. Fulbright continued. "This was of course impossible, since her parents were already dead, but it didn't stop her from fantasizing about it. She also, perhaps more pertinently, fantasized about killing her lover, Joe McNaughton."

"Excuse me? Did you say Keri Dalcanton daydreamed about killing Joe McNaughton?"

"Yes."

"Even before McNaughton's wife broke up their relationship?"

"Well before. You have to understand that a sexual relationship in a personality as damaged as Keri Dalcanton's is always complex. Her relationship with a much older, married man was a classic love-hate relationship. She slept with him, she felt dependent on him. But the feeling of dependence did not make her love him more. To the contrary, it made her, at some base level, hate and fear him."

"That's not true," Keri said, so loudly everyone in the courtroom could hear. Her eyes were wide and teary. "It's a lie! Make her stop lying!"

Judge Cable rapped his gavel. "Mr. Kincaid, you must control your client!"

Ben was so angry he could barely speak. I'll control my client, he thought, when you control the courtroom and stop admitting this offensive testimony. "I'll do my best," he managed.

Fulbright continued. "She feared Joe McNaughton would leave her, just as her parents had done, and she resented feeling dependent. Her violent instincts were never far beneath the surface. All she needed was a trigger."

"And the trigger came when Joe McNaughton tried to break off the relationship."

"That would be my evaluation of the situation, yes. She was confronted simultaneously with the loss of a man upon whom she had become dependent and a betrayal by the man she loved. Those barely suppressed violent urges rose to the surface and consumed her. Resulting in the tragedy at Bartlett Square."

"Thank you, Doctor," LaBelle said, "no more questions."

Ben looked at Christina gravely. The weight on her shoulders now was enormous. The witness they had both thought would be minor had turned out to be more important than they could've dreamed. Before, perhaps the best thing the defense team had going for it was the fact that McNaughton's murder was so horrendous that it was all but impossible to imagine that pretty little Keri Dalcanton could have done it. But Fulbright had turned all that around. Her testimony had succeeded in taking a near impossibility and making it psychologically plausible, if not probable—at least for the jurors, who did not know Keri as well as he did.

Christina leaned close and whispered. "Should I try to fight Fulbright on her own ground?"

Ben shook his head. "You heard the way this woman talks. All you'll get is a lot of jargon and psychobabble. If you're going to put a dent in her testimony—and you must—you're going to have to carve out some ground of your own."

"Got it." She paused, then added, "Got any suggestions?"

Ben's head moved slowly from side to side. "Haven't a clue."

"Is it traditional for psychiatrists to reveal their patients' secrets in a public forum?" Christina asked when she reached the podium.

Fulbright's lips pursed slightly. She was undoubtedly expecting this question, but that didn't make it any more pleasant. "No."

"When your patients come to you for help, don't they expect you will keep what they tell you confidential?"

"No doubt. And I normally do keep patient secrets confidential."

"But you made an exception for Keri Dalcanton."

"I made an exception for murder!" Fulbright said forcefully. "Besides, the District Attorney's office subpoenaed and collected my records, so my verbal testimony didn't tell them anything they didn't already know."

"So that makes it all right?" Christina knew she'd never get a confession of wrongdoing out of this witness, but she did want to reemphasize for the jury what a traitor this doctor had been to her client. They might care. Maybe they've told their doctors a secret or two, also.

"Lives are in danger. That changes everything."

"Joe McNaughton is already dead."

"That's right. And I want to make sure no one else joins him. I have a responsibility to society, as well as my clients."

Ouch. One question too many. The nods from the jury box told Christina she had made a tactical error. She tried to recover. "Speaking of your responsibility to society, why didn't you come forward with this information sooner?"

"I . . . don't think I follow you."

"You said you believed months ago that Keri had these violent tendencies, that they were barely suppressed, that she talked about killing her boyfriend. So why didn't you warn him?"

Her words came slowly. "Well, there's the confidentiality problem—"

"Please, Doctor, we can all see how seriously you take that. Why didn't you warn Joe McNaughton that his life was in danger?"

"I . . ." She paused for a moment. "To be honest, I didn't realize he was in danger."

"Even after you heard Keri's alleged fantasies?"

"Fantasies of this sort are not uncommon, particularly with disturbed personalities. In most cases, however, they turn out to be harmless. Delusions."

"So at the time, you thought Keri was having harmless delusions."

"I didn't say—"

"When did you change your mind, Doctor?"

"Well, after the tragic events unfolded—"

"But why would that change your mind?"

"When it became obvious that Keri had acted on these—"

"Ah." Christina leaned forward. "So you only changed your mind after the murder happened—because you *assumed* Keri had done it."

"Well . . . given the circumstances . . ."

"Dr. Fulbright, Keri Dalcanton has not been convicted of this crime."

"Perhaps not, but it's obvious—"

"It's obvious that you're assuming she's guilty. Even though she hasn't been convicted."

"I just—"

"So the truth is, you're testifying against her, not based upon what she said, which you thought was harmless at the time, but based upon your assumption—your *guess*—that she's guilty."

Fulbright frowned. "I wouldn't put it like that."

"I'm sure you wouldn't, but that's the truth of the matter. You thought Keri's fantasies were harmless. Only after the murder did you think they were significant."

"But who wouldn't—"

"Doctor, let's assume, just for the moment, that Keri is innocent, and that someone else committed the crime. In that case, Keri's fantasies would go back to being harmless delusions, wouldn't they?"

"I suppose, but—"

"So the truth is—your testimony doesn't prove anything—except maybe that you can't be trusted to keep your patient's secrets secret."

"Your honor," LaBelle said, jumping to his feet. "That's uncalled for."

"Never mind," Christina said. "I think I've made my point." Or she hoped she had, at any rate. Because it was the only one she was likely to make. But she wanted to go out with a bang, and she had a pretty good idea how to do it. "Tell me, Dr. Fulbright—do you like kinky sex?"

"Objection!" LaBelle shouted. "This is outrageous!"

Christina plowed ahead before the judge had a chance to rule against her. "It's a fair question. What about it, Doc? You look as if you might like it rough. You sure talk about it enough."

"Again I object!" LaBelle bellowed.

"Excuse me," Christina said, "but a minute ago, when I objected to the same line of inquiry, I was told it was relevant to the credibility of the witness's testimony. Apparently if you engage in sex in any way but the missionary position in the dark, you're not trustworthy. So, since I'm inquiring into the veracity of *this* witness's testimony, I think I'm entitled to ask the same questions."

"The objection is sustained," Judge Cable said, not amused. "This witness is not on trial."

"I never said she was," Christina replied. "I'm just trying to find out if she's an honest person. Maybe she has some barely suppressed violence in her, too."

"Your honor," LaBelle protested, "this is beyond the bounds."

"Really? Well, then let me rephrase." She turned back toward Dr. Fulbright. "Do you like doing it with chains? Handcuffs? Maybe the occasional threesome? Maybe by yourself in the shower?"

"That's none of your business!" Fulbright answered angrily.

"That's exactly right," Christina shouted, over the pounding of the judge's gavel. "It's nobody's business but your own. It doesn't mean you're a bad person if you do, and it certainly doesn't mean you're a murderer." She paused, glancing at the jury. "And the same thing goes for Keri Dalcanton."

* 41 *

There was a discernible change in Keri as she watched the wife of her deceased lover approach the witness stand. Ben could feel it from where he was sitting, even with the tangible barrier of Christina between them. There was a certain stiffening, a detectable apprehension, as she watched the tall slender figure of Andrea McNaughton approach. There was an electric moment, as Andrea passed through the gate separating the gallery from the front of the courtroom. Neither woman looked at the other, but Ben knew each was keenly aware of the other's presence. The hostility was palpable—and understandable. Both had shared the same man—and each apparently suspected the other had killed him.

There was a discernible change in the jurors as well, Ben noted. Their eyes were now filled with anticipation. Ben supposed that should be no surprise. The prosecution could go on for days with forensic evidence, police officers, and rabid psychologists, but when all was said and done, there were two witnesses the jury wanted to hear from, two witnesses who would make the greatest impact on their ultimate decision. And given the ever-present Fifth Amendment, they might never hear from one of them. That left Andrea McNaughton the star attraction.

Ben leaned across Christina to whisper into Keri's ear. "Remember, whatever she says, whatever happens, you do not react."

Keri didn't answer. Her eyes were still focused front and center, on the witness box.

"We can't have any more outbursts. The judge won't tolerate it and the jury won't like it. You have to seem interested but unconcerned. You don't agree with what she says, but you don't act defensive about it. You are innocent. You remain above the fray."

Keri still didn't respond.

"Do you understand me?"

Keri's lips seemed to move more slowly than usual. "That woman hates me," she said, her eyes never wavering. "She absolutely hates me. It's so strong I can feel it."

"Stay calm, Keri."

"Don't you understand? She could say anything. Anything at all."

D.A. LaBelle took Andrea on a leisurely tour of her early life, giving the jury an opportunity to feel as if they knew the woman in the witness box. Andrea answered in a firm, if somewhat halting voice. This was clearly an emotional experience for her, but she was struggling to keep herself together.

The testimony only began to be directly relevant when Andrea described how she first met her late husband. "Joe and I met in high school, out in Broken Arrow. He was on the football team—first-string quarterback. I was in the Pep Squad. We fell in love and decided to get married. Both of our parents opposed it, but of course we wouldn't listen. It's an old story. I realize now that we should've waited to get married, but who listens at that age? We were in love, Joe had an entry-level job with the police department, and our hormones were raging. So we got married."

Despite their youth, as Andrea described it, the early years of their marriage were happy ones. "Sure, we had problems, just like everyone else, but nothing we couldn't work through. Joe felt strongly that I shouldn't work. 'I don't want to see my wife slinging burgers,' that's what he used to say. It was a matter of personal pride to him. And I think he wanted me to be free, in the event we should be blessed with children. We never were." Her head tilted lower, and for the first time Ben heard a slight tremor in her voice. "The doctors said we were both healthy and capable, but it never happened. That was probably our greatest disappointment, but we were still young and we both believed it would come in time. Except now," she added softly. "Now it never will."

Gradually, LaBelle brought her to the present, the twelfth and final year of their marriage. "A marriage changes over time. People change. It's part of life. But we still had a happy marriage. We were still close. We were still . . . intimate. We were important to each other. We went out on dates—and we called them dates, just like when we were kids. We laughed and played and giggled. Joe had a real silly streak in him. I suppose his friends at work didn't see much of it. But I did. I loved that about him." She turned her face away, but Ben could still see the tiny twitch of her lips. "I loved everything about him."

LaBelle cleared his throat. "When did you first suspect there was something wrong in your marriage?"

"When did I suspect? Never." Her neck craned unnaturally. "I was such an idiot. I never had the slightest inkling. I thought everything was perfect." She shook her head. "A fool in paradise."

"When did you learn otherwise?"

"At lunch. That final day. I was visited by the wife of one of Joe's partners on the force. Marge Matthews. I believe you've already met her husband, Arlen Matthews. I only slightly knew Marge, but for some reason she still felt it was incumbent upon her to spill my husband's dark secret. She kept saying I had a right to know, which was a crock. She wasn't there because I had a right to know. She was there because she wanted the dirty pleasure of being the one to tell me. To tell me what everyone else already knew."

"What was that?"

Ben knew this question technically called for hearsay, but he saw no purpose in objecting. Everyone already knew the answer.

"She told me my husband was having an affair. That he had been having an affair for some months. With a teenager. A young girl the—well, the same age I was when he married me. All those years ago."

"What was your reaction?"

"Oh, I went through the typical stages. At first I didn't believe it. Deep denial. But Marge kept pounding away at me, inundating me with details. Where they met. Where they slept together. How often they did it. She even knew the dates, for God's sake. And sure enough, the dates Marge said he'd been sleeping with this child were the same dates he claimed he'd been in Oklahoma City working on some big new investigation. After a while, I had to give in. It was obviously true. Joe had betrayed me."

"What did you do?"

She turned her head away again, and for a moment, Ben was certain they were going to see tears, but Andrea managed to fight them back and continue. "I cried for the better part of the day. I walked into the shower, fully clothed, and screamed for an hour at the top of my lungs. I stared into the mirror and hurled insults at myself. I just felt so . . . cheap. So used. So pathetic."

Ben dutifully made his check of the eyes of the jurors and saw that many of them—especially the women—were deeply affected.

"How long did this continue?"

"Too long. I was punishing myself. Finally I realized that this was not the right approach. After all, had I done anything wrong? No. I needed to stop tearing myself apart, and to start gathering my strength. So I confronted Joe."

"What happened?"

"He didn't deny it, but he wouldn't agree to stop seeing her, either. I think he was embarrassed, ashamed. Like a little boy who got caught with his hand in the cookie jar. Anyway, his pride got in the way and he refused to break it off. So I went to see her."

"And by her you mean . . ."

"The defendant. Keri Dalcanton." Her eyes moved to the defendant's table only fleetingly, but the anger and hatred Ben felt as those eyes swept past was frightening in its intensity. "I rummaged through Joe's address book till I found out where she lived. Then I hopped into my car and went over to see her."

"When exactly was this?"

"After dark. About nine P.M. The night before he turned up in Bartlett Square."

LaBelle nodded solemnly. The grim spectre of Bartlett Square awaited them, but apparently LaBelle wanted to postpone that for later. "What happened when you arrived at her apartment?"

"At first, it was almost comic. You see, she didn't know who I was. I guess Joe never showed her my picture, which is understandable, I suppose. I showed up, ranting and raving and demanding that she break it off, and she didn't even know who the hell I was. She was totally confused—until I said the W word. 'I'm Joe's *wife,*' I told her. The instant I said that, she became hostile and threatening.

"She was wearing some kind of exercise suit," Andrea continued. "A skimpy thing—not much to it. Her little teenage heart was pounding away in her chest. She was sweaty and breathing hard—but not as hard as once we started talking."

"Did you ask her to break it off?" LaBelle asked.

"No, I didn't ask her to break it off. I *told* her it was over."

"And her reaction?"

"She laughed at me." Andrea's jaw tightened. "Do you understand what I'm saying? She laughed at me. Laughed in my face."

"This is not true," Keri murmured, under her breath. She was being careful not to let her face betray her feelings, but Ben could hear her just the same. "This never happened."

When Andrea's face turned up again, a single tear was tracing its way down her cheek. "She was so heartless. So . . . smug. She told me that I couldn't satisfy Joe. That he loved her. That they had done things together that . . . that I never dreamed of doing. She held nothing back. She wanted to destroy me."

LaBelle took a step forward. "I'm sorry to make you relive this, ma'am. If you need a break—"

"No," Andrea insisted, "I want to go on." She swallowed hard. "I told her she couldn't have my husband. She laughed and said he wasn't my husband anymore. Nothing was mine anymore, she said. 'Everything you have is mine.' And then, just to make her point, she whipped back her hand and slapped me, right across the cheek."

"This is a lie," Keri whispered, back at the defendant's table. "A complete fabrication."

LaBelle continued the questioning. "And what happened after she assaulted you?"

Andrea licked her lips, then wiped the tear from her face. "I lost it. Just totally lost it. I slapped her back. And then we were fighting."

"By fighting, you mean—"

"I mean the real thing. Not just words. A real knock-down-drag-out. She grabbed me by the shoulders and slung me onto the carpet. I remember I fell on some exercise machine she had—felt like I'd broken my spine. We rolled around on top of each other, clawing and scratching and hitting. She even bit me." She held out her wrist. "You can still see traces of it, after all these months. It left a scar, for God's sake. It was a serious fight."

"When did it end?"

"When her brother Kirk came home. If not for that, we might still be fighting. Or one of us would be dead, more likely. I was bleeding from half a dozen places when he finally pulled us apart. And she wasn't in the greatest shape herself."

"Did anything else happen before you left?"

"Yes. As I stumbled out the door, she spat at me. Really truly spat at me. Her brother held her arms behind her back, but she struggled and shouted."

"What did she say?"

Andrea drew in her breath. "The last thing she said was, 'If I can't have him, no one can!'"

The effect of these words on the jury was profound. Ben watched as, one after another, the jurors turned, shocked and appalled, to scrutinize the face of the woman who had allegedly spewed out these incriminating words.

LaBelle had been trying to establish a motive for murder, but now he had even more. This was not just a mere motive. It was more like a promise.

"And what did you do then?"

"I went home. It was obvious that I was going to get nothing out of her. It would have to be Joe that broke it off. So I waited for him."

LaBelle nodded sympathetically. Ben had to marvel at his sensitive performance; he was more like a daytime talk-show host than a district attorney. "What happened when Joe got home?"

Andrea waited a long while before answering, as if gathering her strength, mustering her control, choosing her words. "I'm sure you can imagine," she said slowly, "that it was not a pleasant experience. Do you really want all the details?"

"I'm afraid I do," LaBelle said.

"Very well." She brushed her dark hair back behind her ears. "I had managed to collect myself enough to be at least somewhat rational. I didn't scream and shout. I simply told him what I knew and what I expected to happen next, in no uncertain terms."

"Did he agree?"

"Not at first. He was a man, after all. He puffed up his chest and told me no one could boss him around, yadda yadda yadda. But I gave him no choice. I told him it was her or me. If he didn't break it off, I'd leave him. We'd be divorced—and everyone would know why. Everyone would know how young his little whore was, too—which I didn't think would exactly contribute to his advancement on the force."

Ben felt the heat rising from Keri when she heard the word "whore." She too appeared to be struggling to maintain control—struggling to keep her face from revealing the bitterness she felt inside.

"So in the end," Andrea continued, "he agreed to break it off. He wanted to wait till the next day to tell his little tramp the bad news, but I wouldn't hear of it. 'It ends today,' I said. 'You'll tell her now.' So he went over to her place to do just that." She paused. "And I never saw him alive again."

She turned away, and tears tumbled out of her eyes like the spray of a fountain. "The next morning, the police woke me up and told me—told me—" The anguish in her voice was so intense it hurt to hear it. "Told me he was dead. Not just dead—but dead in such a horrible, inhuman way. I was devastated. Just the day before, I learned I had lost his heart. Now—I'd lost everything." Her hand covered her face. "And through it all, I just kept thinking of what that horrible woman had said to me. 'If I can't have him,' she'd said, 'no one can.' And after that—no one did."

The judge, bless his heart, called for a recess after LaBelle finished his direct examination. After that emotionally draining testimony, everyone needed a break, not just Andrea but every warm body in the courtroom. During the five-minute respite, Ben chatted briefly with his client.

"It didn't happen like that," Keri said. "I swear. It wasn't like that at all."

Ben nodded. "I know. I'll try to bring that out on cross."

"But she made me seem so—evil. It wasn't like that."

"I understand. But I have to tell you, Keri—I was watching the jurors while she testified. And they believed her. She was very convincing."

"You have to tell them the truth," Keri said. "Make them understand."

"I'll do my best. But I think we have to face reality at this point. Only one person can tell them what really happened. Only one person can make them believe it. And that's you, Keri."

She turned her head away. "I've told you this already, Ben. I can't testify. Absolutely not."

"Keri, I don't like putting my defendant on the stand, either, but there are times when I realize it's necessary, and this is one of them."

"I can't."

"Why not?"

"I just—can't."

Ben broke off the conversation. All it was doing was escalating his frustration level. For now, he needed to be concentrating on his cross.

After Judge Cable called the court back to order, Ben dutifully walked to the podium. As he approached, he wondered if he should have let Christina handle this one. It was an important cross, true—probably the most important one in the trial. But she was a woman, and a woman crossing another woman might play better with the jury. Having a big gruff man go after this obviously tormented, bereaved widow might be too much; they might be so sympathetic to her and so antagonistic to him that it wouldn't matter what he said or got her to say.

Well, the decision was made, and it was too late to turn back now. He would have to make the best of it. He knew he would never get Andrea to recant any of her testimony, and the jury would hate him if he started browbeating her in the attempt. The best he could hope for was to plant a few seeds in the jurors' minds—a few seeds of doubt he could nurture during closing argument.

"You mentioned that your husband was involved in an investigation in Oklahoma City. Could you tell us what exactly he was investigating?"

"To tell you the truth, we didn't talk much about his work."

Probably true, but he wasn't about to let her off that easily. "Nonetheless, you did know the general nature of his investigation, did you not?"

"I never got into the details. He's not allowed to talk about—"

Ben cut her off. "He was investigating organized crime, wasn't he?"

Her lips pursed slightly. "I believe that was the gist of it, yes."

"Do you think investigating organized crime could conceivably be . . . dangerous?"

"Objection," LaBelle said. "Calls for speculation. She has no personal knowledge."

"Sustained," Judge Cable said.

"Your honor," Ben protested, "we're discussing a man who was subjected to an extremely violent murder. If he was engaged in dangerous activities, anything that might lead to extreme retaliation, I think I'm entitled to pursue that."

"With the proper witness, perhaps. But you have not established that this is the proper witness."

Ben took a deep breath and regrouped. "Do you know who was the target of your husband's investigation into organized crime?"

"I've heard some names. I would only be speculating." It seemed Andrea was smart enough to pick up on cues from the judge.

"Would Antonio Catrona be one of those names?"

"I have heard the name."

"You've heard the name because he was the subject of the investigation, right?"

She still hesitated.

"If there's some doubt in your mind, we could call up some of the other police officers to confirm this."

"I think that is correct," she said.

"And you also had reason to believe that the investigation of Catrona could be dangerous, didn't you?"

"All investigations are dangerous," Andrea said. "Criminals are criminals. They don't like to be caught."

A valiant attempt to derail this line of questioning. But Ben wasn't going to allow it. "We're not talking about petty theft here, ma'am. We're talking about organized crime."

LaBelle rose. "Your honor, I must protest. Asked and answered. This badgering of a bereaved woman is unconscionable."

"The question has been answered," Judge Cable said.

"But not truthfully," Ben replied.

Judge Cable pointed his gavel. "Counsel, I'm warning you—"

Ben switched back to the witness. "Mrs. McNaughton, isn't it true that shortly before your husband was killed, you received a threatening phone call that you believed came from Antonio Catrona or someone working for him?"

The jurors' chins rose, a sure sign that their interest level was increasing. Good.

"Joe did receive a phone call that . . . disturbed him. But I don't know who called."

That's it, Ben thought. Keep being evasive. The more you play games, the easier it will be for me to poke holes in your story. "You may not have known with absolute certainty, but you believed—at the time—that it came from Catrona or his associates. You believed they were threatening retaliation against your husband."

"I . . . don't know if I would exactly . . ."

"You're under oath, ma'am."

She bristled slightly. "I'm well aware of that. But I still don't think I'd say—"

"That's what you told my associate, Ms. McCall."

"I was just speculating—"

"If you're having trouble remembering what you said, I can call Ms. McCall to the witness stand. She has a very good memory."

"That's not necessary." Andrea straightened slightly, folding her hands in her lap. "It's true, at the time, I thought the call must've come from the mob. But I don't think that now. Now I realize that—"

"Thank you, ma'am. You've answered the question."

Andrea wasn't going to be stopped that easily. "Now I realize that the threats must've come from Keri Dalcanton."

Technically, Ben should've moved to strike, but he decided to go with a frontal assault instead. "Do you know that for a fact, Mrs. McNaughton?"

"There's not the slightest doubt in my mind."

"You're not answering my question. Do you know that for a fact?"

She frowned. "No."

"You're just assuming it was Keri, because you assume she's guilty of this crime."

"I think it's obvious to any unbiased observer—"

"But you don't have any proof that Keri made those calls, just as the D.A. doesn't have any proof that she committed the murder, right?"

LaBelle was quickly on his feet. "Your honor, I object!"

"I'll rephrase." Ben tried again. "Do you have any proof that the phone call that frightened your husband was made by Keri Dalcanton?"

"No proof," she said defiantly. "Just common sense."

"Common sense. Common sense," Ben repeated. He knew he'd get slammed by the judge, but he sensed this might be the time to make his point in an unmistakable way. "We're talking about the brutal sadistic murder of a strong adult male, a man who was overcome, dragged a long distance, and chained to a fountain. What does common sense tell us is more likely to be the cause of this tragedy? A hundred-and-three pound teenager? Or a mob hitman?"

"Your honor!" LaBelle said, pounding the table. "Did I miss the call for closing argument?"

My, my, Ben thought, the D.A. made a jokie-poo. Surprises never cease. "Your honor, the witness was the one who brought up common sense."

"And you twisted it around into an improper diatribe," Judge Cable replied. "The objection is sustained. And if you can't stick to questions, Mr. Kincaid, I'll cut this cross off now."

"Sorry, your honor. That won't be necessary." Duly chastened, Ben proceeded to the next part of his cross, knowing full well the judge would like it no better than he had the preceding. "Mrs. McNaughton . . . you don't like Keri Dalcanton much, do you?"

She seemed somewhat taken aback by the question. "I'm . . . not sure what you mean."

"It's a pretty simple question, ma'am. I think everyone else gets it. In fact, I think everyone else already knows the answer. You don't like Keri Dalcanton much, do you?"

"I suppose not."

"In fact—you hate her. Right?"

"I wouldn't put it like that . . ."

"I would. You despise her. And you would do anything to see her put away for life. Or worse."

"That's not true. I don't know why you would say that."

"Oh, I don't know. Possibly because I watched you try to break her nose in the courtroom."

"That was an—I didn't mean—"

"And because I watched you knock her to the floor in my own office."

"That was unfortunate, but—"

"And because almost every time you mention her, you resort to unkind, untrue, words like *whore* and *tramp*."

"The woman killed my husband!" The words erupted out of her, like a sudden burst from a volcano. "She's a killer!"

"Accused," Ben added.

"Even before she killed him," Andrea continued, "she stole him from me. Stole his affection. Stole his . . . love."

"You hated her, didn't you?" Ben said quietly but insistently. "You still hate her."

"Yes, I hate her," Andrea admitted, her voice dark and low. "Why shouldn't I? Don't I have that right?"

"Perhaps," Ben said. "But what I've noticed is that, in addition to being full of hate, you also . . . have a very violent temper."

Several heads rose, both in the gallery and the jury box.

Andrea seemed somewhat shaken. "I don't know why you would—"

"C'mon, ma'am. Your testimony is replete with instances of violence. All of them instigated by you."

"That isn't so!"

"You attacked my client in the courtroom, in front of hundreds of witnesses."

Red blotches began to spot her face. "My husband's killer was being released scot-free!"

"You attacked her again in my office."

"Do you remember what she said to me?"

"You told my associate, Ms. McCall, that you attacked your own husband, mere hours before he was killed."

"I didn't attack him. I just—I—"

Ben made a point of reading directly from his notebook, so the jury would know he wasn't making this up. "When he came home you confronted him with your knowledge of his affair. In your own words, you totally lost it. You hit him repeatedly on his chest. You scratched his face with your fingernails. You even bit him."

"But—But—!"

"On the right arm. In fact, the marks were still visible when the coroner performed his autopsy. I can show you the report, if you like."

"I was *angry*!" Andrea shouted, so loud it split the courtroom. "He betrayed me! For a—a—child!"

"So you attacked him."

"He wouldn't listen to me!" Her voice trembled. "I tried to talk to him, but he wouldn't listen! He wouldn't let that whore go!"

"Did you hate him, too?"

"Did I—but—I—*no*!"

"But you attacked him. You hit him over and over again."

"I was terrified! And so angry!"

"Yes, you were. Your anger at him was so strong you lost control." Ben paused just a hair before delivering his clincher. "And a few hours later, he was dead."

Andrea's mouth froze. "Wha—what are you saying?"

"You had a motive to kill your husband, didn't you, Mrs. McNaughton? You had the motive, the opportunity—and the burning hatred necessary to do it."

LaBelle jumped up. "Your honor—this is grotesque!"

"What's more," Ben continued, "you had the temper and the established penchant for violence that would be needed to bring off such a horrendous and brutal crime."

"No!" Andrea cried. Tears spewed forth from her face. "It's not true! I wouldn't—"

"Your honor!" LaBelle shouted. "This is outrageous! The witness is not on trial."

"Maybe she should be," Ben replied.

LaBelle whirled on him. "You have sunk to some shameless tactics in your tawdry little career, Kincaid, but this time you've hit a new low."

"Your honor," Ben said, ignoring him, "the D.A. is interfering with my cross."

"I'm making an objection!" LaBelle bellowed. "I'm objecting to this repellent line of questioning, this revolting assault on a woman who is still grieving the loss of her husband. And most of all I'm objecting to this disgusting defense attorney!"

"Personal attack on the opposing attorney, impugning his credibility," Ben said, moving toward the bench. "I move for a mistrial."

LaBelle threw up his hands. "More sleazy tactics!"

"There's case law, your honor," Ben said. "It's automatic. You know it as well as I do."

Judge Cable rose from his black cushioned chair. "Both of you—*be quiet*! Approach the bench!" He slung his gavel with such vigor that Ben ducked.

Cautiously, both Ben and LaBelle made their way to the front. "I will not put up with this in my courtroom!"

Ben held up his hands. "All I'm trying to do is cross-ex the witness."

LaBelle pressed forward. "He's trying to accuse a grieving widow of murder!"

"Silence!" Cable was so angry his whole body shook. He remained on his feet, towering over them like the Colossus of Rhodes. "I will not permit this to continue. I'm cutting you both off now."

"But your honor," LaBelle insisted, "he's trying to suggest that the wife murdered her own husband. It's incredible!"

"Oh, right," Ben said. "That never happens." He leaned across the bench. "Your honor, I'm permitted to explore alternate explanations for the crime. And that includes alternate suspects. In fact, as defense attorney, it's my duty to do so."

The judge gave him a harsh glare. "And you really think Mrs. McNaughton is the murderer?"

"What I think is not relevant."

The judge's face tightened like a fist. "I continue to be astonished by what attorneys are willing to do these days. Impugn the reputation of an innocent person just to exonerate their client. It's offensive and I won't have any more of it."

"Your honor," Ben protested. "Under the Rules of Professional Conduct, I have an obligation to provide a zealous defense. If there's another possible suspect, I have to bring that out."

"Which you've done. Do you have anything more to add?"

"Well . . ."

"I thought not. So sit down and stop your speechifying." He turned his loaded gavel toward LaBelle. "Do you want to redirect?"

"Of course!"

"So stop bellyaching and get to it. Now!" Ben and LaBelle scampered away from the judge's ire, Ben to his table, LaBelle to the podium.

"First of all," LaBelle said to Andrea, "let me express my deepest regret that you were subjected to this disturbing, unnecessary, and disgusting accusation."

In the witness box, Andrea was still crying profusely. Her cheeks were flushed red and her mascara had streaked all over her face. Her hands were shaking.

"I have just a few more questions for you, ma'am, and then you may go. I don't think anyone in this room has any problem understanding why you might bear the defendant some animosity. But the critical question is—"

"I didn't lie," Andrea said, cutting him off. "I wouldn't. Sure, I don't like what that teenager did, but I wouldn't say something about her if I didn't think it was true."

"I appreciate that, ma'am. Now let me ask you another indelicate question. Forgive me for being blunt, but we all know the . . . defense attorney . . ." He said it as if it were a dirty word. ". . . has suggested that you are the murderer. So let me ask you straight out, Mrs. McNaughton. Did you kill your husband?"

"No. Of course not." Her voice cracked as she spoke. "I couldn't. Couldn't possibly."

"I know. But I had to ask. You see, what the defense attorney forgets is that, to commit this particularly gruesome murder, you would have to have more than anger. You would need all the specialized equipment. Tell me, ma'am, at the time of the murder, did you posses any heavy chains such as were used on your husband?"

"No, I didn't."

"And did you own any black leather outfits?"

"No."

"Did you have any knives similar to those that were used?"

"No."

"Right. The only person who had those things—certainly the only person who had all of them—was the defendant. You couldn't've committed this murder. And no cheap tricks can ever prove otherwise." He lowered his voice. "I'm sorry you've been put through this, Mrs. McNaughton. I'm sorry for your loss, and I'm sorry you had to be here today."

He glanced up at the judge. "No more questions, your honor. I think it's perfectly clear what happened at Bartlett Square last March. The prosecution rests."

* 42 *

After dinner, back at Ben's office, the mood was universally glum. Usually, the conclusion of the prosecution case, which heralded the opening of the defense case, was a happy time for the defense team. But not tonight. Tonight, Andrea's McNaughton's testimony had cast a pallor over everything.

Including the conversation in the main conference room. Ben and Christina and Keri were all three gathered together again, but this time, instead of Christina being strategically positioned between them, Keri was in the middle, feeling the pressure mounting on both sides.

"You promised I wouldn't have to testify!" Keri said. She was kneading her hands with such vigor that she left white marks long after her fingers were gone. "You promised."

"And you don't," Ben replied. "The Fifth Amendment takes care of that. But what I'm saying now is—I think you should."

Keri's fingers pressed against her temples. "Why?"

Christina jumped in. "Keri, we can't minimize the impact of Andrea McNaughton's testimony. The jury heard what she was saying and for the most part, I think they believed it."

"I thought Ben did a good job on cross," Keri said.

"I do, too. The best he could, given the circumstances. But the fact remains—she's a tragic figure, a bereaved widow. People's hearts naturally go out to her. And while Ben successfully planted the possibility of another killer, I don't think anyone believes Andrea could kill her own husband."

"I believe it!" Keri said. "You'd believe it, too, if she'd knocked you to the floor a few times."

"Just the same," Ben said, "as your defense attorneys, we have to assume the worst. We have to assume the jury believes Andrea McNaughton. We have to believe they were persuaded by the prosecution evidence. It may be circumstantial—but a lot of circumstantial can add up to 'beyond a reasonable doubt.' "

Keri's fingers combed through her platinum hair, so forcefully it looked as if she might tear it out by the roots. "But why do I have to testify? Surely we have other witnesses."

"Other witnesses, yes," Ben said. "But no one who can tell the story of what really happened the night Joe died. No one else knows."

"Plus," Christina added, "the jury needs to hear it from you. They need to hear you say that you did not kill Joe. Thanks to Andrea's testimony, this case has become a sort of showdown between her and you. The jury can only believe one of you; they have to choose. They heard Andrea say that you killed Joe, and like it or not, she was convincing. You need to be equally convincing. Or more so."

"But what about the cross-examination?" Keri asked. Her eyes looked frightened. Ben had to remind himself how young Keri was—how terrifying and unfamiliar this must be to her. "I hate that man—LaBelle. He'll start asking me questions. Things I don't know. He'll try to trick me."

"Yes," Ben agreed, "he will. No doubt about it—there's risk involved. But I think we should take the risk. I think we have to."

The conference room fell silent for a moment. Keri looked down, elbows on the table, hands pressed against the sides of her head.

"I know what you think," she said finally. "You think if I don't testify, they'll convict me. You think they'll sentence me to death."

Ben could not make eye contact with her. "It's a possibility," he said quietly. "A very real possibility."

"I'm sorry," she said. "I'm sorry to both of you. But I can't. I won't."

Christina reached out. "Keri, think about this before—"

"You heard what I said. I won't do it. I've told you that all along, and nothing has changed."

"But Keri—why?"

"I just—I don't—" She turned away. "I can't explain. But I can't testify. I won't."

Christina pushed away from the table and started pacing around the room. "I don't get this at all. Why can't you testify, if you—you—"

"If you're innocent?" Keri said sharply. "Because you don't think I am, do you? You never did. Ben believes me, but you don't. You think I killed Joe."

"I didn't say that."

"You didn't have to."

Ben tried to wedge himself between them. "Keri, I'm sure Christina didn't mean that."

"She did."

"But it *is* frustrating. If you didn't do it, why not tell the jury that? Why can't you testify?"

"I'm tired of talking about this," Keri said. For the first time, some of her fear and sorrow faded—and was replaced by anger. "I've given you my decision. You work for me, right? So you need to figure out something else to do in the courtroom tomorrow. Because I'm not testifying."

"And neither am I."

Ben whipped his head around. His eyes widened when he saw the dark menacing figure in the corridor—surrounded by three bodyguards. "Catrona!"

Instinctively, Christina and Keri backed away from the doorway as Catrona slowly sauntered in. His escorts followed close behind.

Ben could feel his knees knocking. "Why are you here?"

"I'm here because you wanted me, right?" Catrona said, his voice like gravel. He reached into his coat pocket and withdrew an official looking single-page sealed document. "I got this subpoena."

Ben swallowed. "That's for the courtroom. Tomorrow."

"I thought we should talk tonight." He moved forward, his eyes never leaving Ben's. "You know what? I've been in business almost twenty-three years. I've been the subject of a dozen investigations. But this is the first time anyone's had the balls to slap me with a subpoena."

Christina's fingers were frantically curling her hair. "I guess you have to admire someone with that kind of courage, huh?"

Catrona gave her a brief but harsh look. "No. I think I need to teach him a lesson in respect." He crumpled up the subpoena and shoved it into Ben's shirt pocket. "You want to talk to me, you come and talk to me. Like you did before. But keep your crappy papers to yourself." He moved even closer. "If you can't learn some manners on your own, I'll have my boys teach 'em to you."

"You don't scare me," Ben said, delivering what was easily the biggest lie he'd told since the second grade.

"I should." Catrona pressed his index finger against Ben's chest. "Now listen to me. I knew that McNaughton clown was investigating me. I had some boys working on him, even. But I did not kill him. I didn't do it; I didn't order it done. I had nothing to do with it."

"I don't know that I can believe that," Ben said defiantly.

"Kincaid, your lack of respect is seriously getting on my nerves. Don't push your luck."

"Who else would kill McNaughton in such a horrible way? Who else would make such a show of it?"

"Like I'd want that? Listen, creep, you've been to the movies too much. You think I want publicity? I don't. Hell, everything I do depends on having as little publicity as possible. So I don't blow up buildings, I don't put horse's heads in people's beds, and I don't chain corpses to fountains."

"Fine," Ben said. "Then that's what you'll tell the jury. The important thing is that I have a chance to ask you the questions in a public forum."

"You're not listening to me, punk." He gave Ben a shove, just for emphasis. "You are not going to call me to the stand. I don't need or want this publicity, I don't need to be subjected to whatever questions the D.A. might care to ask, and if you like your life, and your friends' lives, you won't mess with me."

"I have an obligation to defend my client to the best of my ability."

"I got that. Why the hell do you think I talked to you in the first place? I didn't have to give you anything back at the racetrack, and I don't have to give you anything now. I'm doing it because I feel sorry for your client. I think she's getting a bum rap; I told you that already. I know you want to turn me into some cartoon mobster, but I got feelings just like everyone else. So I gave you some help. And how do you reward me? With a subpoena!"

Ben drew in his breath. "If my client's case depends on your testimony—"

"Let's imagine for a moment that you don't have the sense God gave a lamppost and you actually do call me to the stand. Am I going to admit I killed McNaughton? No. But I will reveal that he was on the take, which is why he got demoted. They couldn't prove anything; I'm much too careful for that. But they knew, just the same, and that's why they bucked him down."

"If that's true, why was he reinstated?"

Catrona leaned back, thumbs hooked in his lapel. "I'm not without a certain influence in this town, Kincaid. Even in the police department."

"I don't believe—"

"You believe what you want. The point is this. If you haul me up on the stand, I'll repeat what Joe McNaughton told one of my lieutenants the last time he saw him. He said that he was afraid your little girl was going to kill him."

"That's not true!" Keri cried.

"In fact, he said she came at him with a knife and said she was going to cut him into a million pieces and hang him out where everyone could see what a faithless toad he was."

"I don't believe a word of this," Ben said. "That's a lie."

"Maybe it is, and maybe it ain't. But if you haul me up on the stand, that's what I'm going to say. So you just think about this, Kincaid, and you think about it real good. Do you really want me up on that witness stand? 'Cause I don't think you do." He gave Ben a good hard push, enough to knock him back against the wall. Then he jerked his head around. "C'mon, boys. Let's go home."

Eleven P.M. Several hours had passed in the main conference room, but for all intents and purposes, the persons sitting inside were no further along than they had been before.

"I'm lost, Ben," Christina said. "I'm sorry to be so clueless, but I don't know what we're going to do."

"We're going to call Catrona, just like we planned."

Christina's eyes fairly bulged. "Did you hear what that man said to you?"

"I'm not worried about his threats."

"You should be! Even if you don't have the sense to understand that you're endangering yourself and your friends, you should understand that he plans to commit perjury. He's going to tell all kinds of lies."

"I'll be questioning him as a hostile witness. I'll prove he's lying."

"You mean, you'll try. He's not a stupid man, Ben. Not by a long shot."

"Well, we have to do something!" Ben slapped his hand down on the table. "Maybe they didn't cover this in Trial Tactics 101, but after the prosecution finishes its case, the defense starts. That means tomorrow morning at nine A.M., Judge Cable is going to ask me to call my first witness. And I'd damn well better have one!"

Loving rushed into the conference room carrying a cordless phone. "Skipper—we got a phone call. From Sergeant Matthews."

"What does that son of a—"

"It's not for you," Loving said breathlessly. "It's for Keri."

Slowly, Keri's head lifted. "Wha—"

"They've found your brother."

"Kirk?" Her lips and mouth opened, in a strange, mixed expression. "Where is he?"

"He's on the roof of the Bank of Oklahoma Tower. And he says he's going to jump."

* 43 *

Three armed police officers led Ben and Keri through the cordon surrounding the Bank of Oklahoma Tower which, at fifty-plus stories, was the tallest building in Tulsa. They took the elevator to the highest level, then rushed up the stairs to the roof.

When Ben emerged through the hatch, he felt as if he had entered another world. Two helicopters were hovering overhead, casting focused beams of light on the otherwise dark tableau. Police officers were swarming over the roof, though they kept a respectful distance from the lone man at the far edge. Only one plainclothes officer stood within twenty paces of the man, an electronic bullhorn dangling from one hand.

Arlen Matthews, of course. Flung into Ben's face once more, like a cancerous scab that just wouldn't heal.

The whole scene was all too eerie for Ben, too reminiscent of the night he had been arrested—the copters, the cops, Matthews. That night, of course, it had been a show Matthews and his buddies put on to scare and intimidate him. This time, however, it was all too real. Kirk Dalcanton stood poised on the edge of the roof threatening to jump. One baby step is all it would take. He could do it long before anyone got close to him. No one could possibly stop him.

"Get him!" Keri screamed, as soon as her eyes had adjusted enough to understand what she was seeing. "Someone stop him!"

"They're trying, ma'am," a nearby uniform explained.

"But there's not much they can do. He says if they come any closer, he'll jump. And he looks like he could do it."

"How did he get up on the roof?" Ben asked.

"No clue," the officer replied. "We think he must've snuck in during office hours, then hid in the stairwell till after most of the security officers got off. But that's just a guess."

"But why here?" Ben asked. "There must be other places where it would be easier to kill yourself."

"Easier, yes. But few more certain." The officer cast his gaze toward the horizon. "If he takes that step off the edge of the building, ain't no power on earth that can save him."

"Someone has to help him!" Keri cried. "Please!"

Officer Matthews spoke into his bullhorn. "Kirk, your sister is here."

The effect on Kirk, on his lone silhouette poised on the edge of space, was immediate. "No! Send her away! I don't want her here!"

"Kirk, she cares about you." The electronics made Matthews's voice seem weird, inhuman. "She doesn't want to see you come to any harm."

"I said, keep her away! I—I don't want her to see me like this."

"Then come away from the edge. Let us take you home."

"There's nothing for me there. There's nothing for me anywhere." All at once, Kirk fell to his knees. "It's all over for me."

"Don't talk like that, Kirk. It's never over. Not unless you make it over."

Ben watched the terrifying tableau from the rear. Keri clung tightly to him.

"What's going on?" Ben asked her. "Do you know what he's so upset about?"

Keri did not immediately respond.

"Keri?" He took her by the shoulders and lifted her up to his eye level. "Keri, if you know something, you've got to tell the police."

Her voice was quiet. "I know what's wrong with him."

He pulled her closer. "Keri, does this have something to do with the case?"

He was interrupted by Sergeant Matthews. "Can you give me some hint what to say to him? Something that might persuade him to step away from the edge?"

Keri hesitated before answering. "Tell him he's forgiven."

"Forgiven? What did he do?"

She shook her head. "Just tell him—tell him it doesn't matter anymore. That it's all over."

Matthews frowned. "Could you give me a little to go on here? The more information I have, the better able I am to do my job."

"That's all I can say."

Matthews frowned, then returned to his previous position, the closest he could come to Kirk without sending him into a panic. "Kirk . . . listen to me."

Kirk's head jerked up. "What?"

"Kirk . . . you've been forgiven."

"You're wrong," he shouted back. His face was wet, illuminated in the cascading beams of light from the helicopters circling overhead. "I can never be forgiven. No punishment is enough. Even God has turned His back on me."

"Now listen to me, Kirk, I don't know what church you went to, but when I was growing up, they taught me that God never turns His back on anyone. We're all sinners. But God forgives us."

"Not this time." His eyes slowly turned toward the edge of the building. "Not now."

"Don't do anything crazy, Kirk. Let's just talk awhile. There's no hurry."

"It's over," Kirk said, monotone. He inched closer to the edge. "Time to end it." His body swayed back and forth, teetering on the brink.

"Kirk, listen to me!" Matthews was turning one way, then the other, looking anywhere for help. "We'll do whatever you want. We've got your sister here. Look, I'll send her out to talk to you. She—"

"No!" he shouted, and a second later, he was gone.

Ben and Keri rushed to the edge, just in time to see his body dropping out of sight, drifting downward like a skydiver without a parachute, plummeting silently out of their view toward the harsh reality of the pavement fifty stories below.

"Kirk!" Keri screamed. She fell, her face cradled in her hands. Ben knelt beside her, steadying her, holding her tight. *"Kirk!"*

But it was much too late. No one could do anything for Kirk now, not Keri, not Ben, not Sergeant Matthews, not even God. There was nothing in Kirk's future now but a cold hard death and, if Father Danney was right, the afterlife, which no matter what form or shape it took could not possibly be crueler to Kirk than the life he had finally left behind.

It was hours later, back at police headquarters, before Keri had recovered sufficiently that she could even speak intelligently. Her face was red and swollen from crying. Her eyes were so weary she could barely keep them open.

"Come on," Ben said, wrapping his arm around her. "Let me take you home."

She shook her head, with what little energy she had left. "No. We need to talk."

"About . . . us?"

"About the trial."

"Keri, I don't think this is the time. I'll get a continuance—"

"I can testify now."

Ben stared at her, lips parted. "I don't understand . . ."

"I can testify now. I want to testify now."

"But you said before—"

"Don't you see?" She raised her head and her eyes turned upward, pleadingly, toward the heavens. "Everything has changed now. Everything."

* 44 *

The courtroom was quiet as a funeral as Keri Dalcanton took her place in the witness box. To say that there was some interest in her testimony was like saying there were animals at the zoo. All eyes were focused on Keri. Everyone had the same suspicion as Ben—that the outcome of this trial would depend on what happened in the next few minutes.

Judge Cable had called a two-day recess after Kirk's death, and he had explained to the jury that the defendant had unexpectedly lost her brother, so Ben knew they would have some understanding of the altered figure who now sat before them at center stage. Keri's eyes were bloodshot and lined in red; too much crying and too little sleep. Although she had usually conducted herself with calm and sobriety in the courtroom, there had also always been a bounce in her step, a liveliness in her eyes. She was nineteen, after all. But not today. Today she moved with slow care, like the flow of a river, heavy and deliberate. She sat before the jury unadorned, almost as if she was helpless to do anything but respond to the questions put to her—the questions that she told Ben she could now answer truthfully, for the very first time.

"When did you leave Stroud and come to Tulsa?" Ben asked, after they finished the preliminaries.

"Just after the Level Five tornado hit. Little over a year ago." Her voice was flat and uninflected, and yet at the same time packed with raw emotion. "It had been a hard year. For both me and my brother."

"What had happened?"

"We . . . lost our parents." Again, the fact that she was not overtly emotional, that she was obviously fighting it back, made what she had to say all the more tragic. "They were young—early fifties—but there was a tragedy. A traffic accident. They were driving late at night and a truck came out of nowhere at an intersection and—" As she paused, Ben could almost see the strain, the furious energy it took to suppress her anguish. "They were killed instantly."

"Where did that leave you?" Ben asked.

"In a mess. Kirk and I didn't know what to do. I was only eighteen, then—I hadn't even finished high school. We both worked at the Tanger Outlet Mall. For two kids living at home, that was fine. But once Dad was gone—and there was no insurance—we couldn't make ends meet. And then after the tornado hit and destroyed the mall—" Her head drooped slightly. "Well, that just seemed to be the killing stroke. There was nothing left for us in Stroud. So we came to Tulsa."

Ben kept the pace of the questioning slow and easy. She was doing great so far, but he knew it would not take much to push her over the brink. "That must have been a difficult decision."

"To leave everything you've ever known and come to an unfamiliar city full of strangers? Yes, you could say that." She looked up, and for the first time, a tiny spark of fire seemed to light in her eyes. "At the same time, it was an adventure, if you know what I mean. We were starting fresh, leaving the pain of the past behind." She paused a moment. "I heard what that . . . psychologist said about me, about how the repeated traumas and the change of environment unbalanced my mind or something. But she's got it all wrong. I still had Kirk, and I had my head together, and it's not as if I was moving to the moon, after all. I had to get out of Stroud. If I'd stayed, I would've been much worse off. Even now, I still know that."

"What happened when you got to Tulsa?" Ben asked. He appreciated her unwillingness to play the martyr, and her defensiveness about being called crazy, but at the same time, if the jury was going to sympathize with her, they needed to understand the full horror of her situation. "Did everything go as planned?"

"No. Nothing went as planned. Everything was harder than I anticipated. Couldn't find an affordable place to stay. Couldn't find work. It seemed like the only jobs available were minimum wage—burger joints, that sort of thing. We couldn't make it in Stroud on that kind of money—what were our chances of making it in the big city? Plus, Kirk wasn't working at all. He was having some serious emotional problems. He took the death of our parents hard, and the trauma of the tornado even harder. He still talked to Mom and Dad as if they were in the room with us, and he used to sleep in the bathtub at night—because he figured that would be the safest place to be if a tornado hit. He had always been . . . confused, and everything just seemed to get worse for him. He was in a bad way. So there was no chance of him working. I was on my own."

"That's why you ended up working at a stripper club, isn't it?"

"It was the only thing I could find that paid a decent wage—not counting those jobs that were illegal and a lot more disgusting than stripping. Contrary to what you've heard, I never worked as a hooker and I never would. I didn't like stripping—it was humiliating and, frankly, hard work. Dressing up like a nurse or a schoolteacher or whatever, then peeling off your clothes in front of a bunch of drooling men. But it did pay enough to get a small apartment for me and Kirk. And some of the other girls became friends. I can't tell you what a difference that made. Say what you like about those girls—when you're all alone in the big city, it's good to have friends. Any friends."

"Were you happy at this time?"

"Happy might be stretching it. I was surviving. I was eating regularly. At the same time, I had zero security. One missed check would've been enough to put us on the skids. I started having trouble sleeping, worrying about what might happen if I lost my job." She paused thoughtfully. "No, I can't say I was happy. I was walking a very thin tightrope, and I knew that the tightrope could snap at any moment. Still, it was better than before."

As always, Ben kept a careful watch on the faces in the jury box. They seemed attentive; they seemed to be absorbing what she had to say. There were no expressions of outright disbelief or contempt. At the same time, he knew that he was going to have to give them more than this if he hoped to undo the tremendous damage done by Andrea McNaughton and the rest of the prosecution case. "Keri, would you please tell the jury when you met Joe McNaughton?"

A tiny involuntary shudder signaled to all present that this subject was more difficult, more unpleasant than what they had previously discussed. But she dutifully pressed forward.

"It was about four months after I started working at the gentlemen's club. He came in with a group of cop buddies. I'd seen him watching me while I did my act, but I didn't think anything of it. They were all watching me. But there was something more . . . intense about Joe. Something that stood out in your memory."

"Did you contact him during your . . . work?"

"Oh no. I finished my show in the usual way and forgot all about him. Until I left to go home that night, just after midnight." A moment's hesitation. "He was waiting for me in the alley behind the club."

"Did you talk to him?"

"Not at first. I ran back into the club and locked the door. I might be from Stroud, but I'm no idiot. When you find a man lurking in the alley, you run."

"But that changed."

"Yes. He talked to me, through the door. Assured me he wasn't going to harm me or force himself on me. Showed me his badge. Said he'd seen me during the show and he'd been taken with me—that was his phrase. 'Taken with me.' He

asked if I would do him the honor of allowing him to escort
me to my car. He was really very charming. And in time . . . I
gave into it."

"You let him escort you back to your car?"

"Oh yeah. And the next night, he showed up at the club
again. And this time he drove me home. And one thing led to
another . . ."

"And you became lovers?" Ben and Christina had spent
about an hour and a half debating what was the best word to
use, one that didn't seemed coyly euphemistic but at the same
time didn't make it sound any worse than necessary.

"We did." Her head rose. "But bear in mind—I didn't
know the man was married. He didn't wear a ring and he
never mentioned it. He even talked about us getting married
sometime in the near future. And Joe was such a comfort to
me. I had been on edge, worried, uncertain, for so long. But
Joe made everything better. It seemed as though he could fix
anything. He was fun, comforting. He told me he had a lot of
money. He said that once we were married, I wouldn't have to
strip anymore. He said he'd take care of me. He'd take care of
everything." Ben saw the tiniest crack in her facade, a deep
and heartfelt twinge of pain. "You can't imagine how good
that sounded to me. You just can't imagine."

"How long did this relationship continue?"

"For a little over two months."

"And in that time . . ." Ben licked his lips and reconsidered.
This was a delicate subject, and although it had to be addressed (better him than LaBelle) he had to be careful how he
did it. "Was there any aspect of your relationship that bothered you?"

"Yes," she said bluntly. "The sex. I'm not pretending that I
was some kind of prude. From Stroud or not, I knew the way
of the world. Still, the things Joe liked to do . . . well, they
shocked me. Horrified me, even. I guess I'm a small-town girl
at heart. I'd never heard of anything like what he wanted to
do—what with the whips and chains and leather and all. My

mama never told me about anything like that, believe me. And he wanted to do it all the time, every possible opportunity. Which could be awkward. Especially when my brother was also in the apartment." Her hands fell on the rim of the witness box, and she leaned forward slightly. "Of course, now I realize that he wanted to do those things with me—because his wife refused. He was getting from me what he couldn't get from her. But I didn't know that at the time."

"Did you learn to ... enjoy these activities with Joe McNaughton?"

"No, never. I know what the prosecution witnesses have been saying. That I had all these weird kinky tastes. That I was some kind of sex addict. But it isn't true. Joe was the one who wanted it that way. All I wanted—" Her voice dropped so low as to be nearly inaudible. "All I wanted was someone to take care of me."

"Keri, some of Joe McNaughton's coworkers have testified that you were the instigator of these sexual activities."

"I know. But were they there? No. I don't know why they say those things. I don't know what Joe told his macho buddies when I wasn't around. Joe lied to me; maybe he lied to them, too. Men have been known to brag about sex to their friends. Making it sound like he was such a stud I couldn't get enough of him. That probably would've scored him some points down at the police station."

In the jury box, Ben saw an older woman on the top row slowly nodding her head. She understood what Keri was saying. But did she believe it?

"Those police officers," Keri continued, "those so-called friends of Joe's—they've been out to get me from the moment his body turned up in Bartlett Square. I don't mean to sound paranoid, but it's true. They all knew about me, and they didn't like me. I'm not sure why. Maybe they were jealous, maybe they were friends of Joe's wife. I don't know. They probably thought I was mistreating the wife I didn't even know existed. I know this, though—they were at my apartment less than an hour after Joe's body was found. They were determined to prove that I had killed him. And they haven't let up since—even to the point of following me around, stalking my attorney, planting knives—"

"Objection," LaBelle said, for the first time breaking the spell Keri was weaving. "It has not been proven that the police planted that knife."

"Well, who else—" Keri began, but the judge silenced her.

"She's the witness," Ben rejoined, "not Mr. LaBelle."

"I'll sustain the objection," Judge Cable said. "Let's stick to the facts. What you actually saw and heard."

"Yes, your honor," Keri said quietly.

"Keri," Ben asked, "despite your reservations, did you want your relationship with Joe to continue?"

"Of course I did. Even in that short time, I had come to depend on him for so much. And he was talking about marrying me. It was like a dream come true. It was all I ever thought about."

"Would you say he was serious about it?"

"We looked at rings!" Keri said, straining against the edge of the witness box. "We picked a church. We even talked about a date. He said he wanted to wait until June, because that was when his mother was married. Of course, now I realize he was probably just stalling. Stringing me on as long as possible until I learned the truth."

Ben stepped away from the podium. "Keri, when did you find out Joe was married?"

"When Andrea McNaughton showed up at my door."

Ben paused a moment, letting the full horror of that moment sink into the jurors' consciousnesses. "And before that, you had no idea she even existed?"

"None whatsoever. I was stunned. Stunned and—shattered." Her hand covered her eyes. "I didn't know what to think," she said, barely above a whisper. "I couldn't believe it."

"What did Mrs. McNaughton say?"

Keri sniffed, wiped her eyes, and carried on. "After she

convinced me she really was who she said she was, she insisted that I break off my relationship with her husband."

"And what was your response?"

"I'm not even sure. I was so totally overwhelmed. Please try to understand—I had pinned all my hopes, all my dreams, all my future, on that man. And now, this woman showed up at my door and wanted to rip it all away, everything I had, or everything I thought I had, in a split second. I—I just couldn't deal with it."

"Did you agree to stop seeing Joe?"

"How could I? I had my whole world wrapped up in him. But I didn't say any of those awful things she claimed I said. Mostly I just stood there like a dummy, not knowing what to say."

"And what was her response when you declined to break off the relationship?"

"She hit me," Keri said. "Hard." Once again, the slightest trace of an edge crept into her voice. "She knocked me down on the floor, then she started kicking me. Left bruises that stayed for days. I thought she'd cracked a rib, that's how bad it felt."

"Did you fight back?"

"I tried to, but she was out of my league. It wasn't at all like she described. I wouldn't attack her. She came after me. She totally lost control. I thought she was going to kill me."

Again, Ben surreptitiously checked the jury. This testimony directly contradicted what Andrea had told them. Who would they believe? "How did you get away?"

"Kirk came home. And thank goodness for it. No doubt in my mind—I'd be dead now if he hadn't shown up. He pulled her off me and shoved her out the door. Even as he did it, though, she was screaming and cursing, scratching at him, pummeling him with her fists. She was out of her head. I remember as she left, Kirk said, 'If she isn't locked up soon, that woman's going to kill someone.' "

"Your honor, I have to object." LaBelle jumped to his feet.

"That's hearsay. Moreover, as much as we're all enjoying the defendant's little story, this nonsense is nothing but a blatant attempt to slander Andrea McNaughton."

"Your honor," Ben said, "she's entitled to tell the jury what really happened."

"Maybe so," LaBelle said, "but she's not entitled to push guilt off herself by implicating an innocent woman."

"As I've said before and everyone in this courtroom knows, the defense is entitled to advance alternative theories of how the crime was committed."

"There's right, and there's wrong," LaBelle answered, his voice ringing through the courtroom. "And what they're trying to do here is wrong. Andrea McNaughton is a victim. This is nothing but a sleazy attempt by the defendant to get herself off the hook by suggesting that Mrs. McNaughton is the killer."

To the surprise of both attorneys, Keri spoke from the witness box. "Oh no, your honor. That's not right. That isn't it at all."

Judge Cable peered down at her, pushing his bifocals a few notches down his nose. "Excuse me? What isn't right?"

"What he's saying," Keri replied. "That I'm trying to blame Mrs. McNaughton for the murder."

"You're not?"

"No, I'm not. I'll admit, I did that before. Not that I ever actually accused her, but I suggested the possibility. But I know she didn't do it. And as much as she hates me, I don't want her to suffer for a crime she didn't commit. I know what that's like, and I wouldn't wish it on anyone."

Judge Cable followed up. "And how is it you're so certain she didn't kill her husband?"

Keri swallowed, then looked directly at him. "Because I know who did. It wasn't me, and it wasn't Andrea McNaughton." She paused, and the suspended silence in the courtroom was deafening. "It was my brother. Kirk Dalcanton."

* 45 *

The jury was not alone in having stunned expressions plastered across their faces. Everyone in the courtroom—spectators, witnesses, and workers alike—evinced equal surprise. Half the reporters in the press row leaped to their feet and headed toward the back, cell phones in hand, to phone in this latest development. The judge pounded his gavel furiously, trying to bring the courtroom back to some semblance of order.

"If I don't have silence I'll clear the courtroom!" he bellowed. A few moments later, Judge Cable peered down at the witness, his face a mixture of suspicion and concern. "Young lady, do you realize what you're saying?"

"I do, your honor. But it's true. I couldn't say so before, but now that Kirk's gone, I have to be honest. I don't want to go to prison for something I didn't do, and I don't want Andrea McNaughton to go to prison for something she didn't do, either. It was Kirk, God bless his soul. Kirk did it."

Ben returned to his position behind the podium to continue the examination. "Keri, perhaps you could step back a bit and explain to everyone exactly what happened. After Andrea McNaughton left your apartment. The night Joe was killed."

"Joe showed up at my place about an hour after she left. About midnight. Apparently Andrea'd gone home and pretty much read him the riot act. Left him with no choice. I don't think he wanted to break it off—not yet, anyway. He figured he had several more months of . . . using me . . . before he'd

341

have to end it. But Andrea forced his hand. So he came over and told me in no uncertain terms that he was ending it. That it was over. That there would be no marriage. That I would never see him again."

"And how did you take this news?"

"Not well, obviously. But my reaction was nothing compared to Kirk's."

"Please explain."

"Kirk was still there, and he was a little high from that encounter with Mrs. McNaughton. Ever since he tossed her out of the place, he'd been badmouthing both of them, really working up a froth. You see—Kirk and I were very close. Always have been. And he was very protective of me. He considered it his job to take care of me. And one other thing you should understand—just as I looked forward to marrying Joe, as much as I saw it as my salvation—so did Kirk."

"Had Kirk had any history of . . . emotional problems?"

"Oh yes. That's why he was thrown out of high school. He'd been picked up by the cops a few times, back in Stroud, for vandalism and other minor offenses. I knew he needed help, but how could we afford that? We could barely afford to eat." She drew in her breath. "He had a hyperparanoid feeling that everyone was out to get him—or me. And he had a lot of . . . sexual issues, too. I never understood if he was gay or bi or what exactly—and I don't think he did, either. He was confused. Add in all our other stresses and you had a bad situation. Much as I loved Kirk—he was very sick. And when Joe waltzed in and told me it was all over—well, that was just the end. He snapped."

"Did he attack Joe at your apartment?"

"He tried. We all struggled for a while. I imagine that's when Joe got my skin under his fingernails. But Joe was bigger and stronger and a much better fighter. Joe pushed him away and made his exit."

"What happened next?"

"Kirk had a total breakdown. I mean, I'd never seen him

like that before in my life. He was screaming uncontrollably. 'No one treats my sister like that! You turned my sister into a whore!' Crazy stuff. Crazy. And then he looks at me, with the most horrible expression I've ever seen in my life, and he says, 'Keri, I'm going to kill that bastard. I'm going to cut him up until there's nothing left.' "

The emotional stoicism of her previous testimony had disappeared. Keri's eyes were wide and alive. Her chest was heaving and her hands were trembling. "I tried to stop him, I really did. But there was nothing I could do. He put on a pair of gloves, then ran into the kitchen and grabbed one of my knives. The D.A. was right—it was my knife, and my chains, too. Kirk took them from my bedroom. I tried to block his way, but he was too strong for me, and, and—" Her voice cracked. "He left ranting about how he was going to kill that faithless son-of-a-bitch cop. How he was going to make him pay."

"Did you call anyone?"

"No. I wish to God I had. But I didn't want to get my brother in trouble. Even though he'd been convicted of only minor crimes, he had two on his record. You know Oklahoma law—if he'd been convicted again, he could get twenty years. And I didn't really think he'd do anything. I thought he would cool off in a few minutes, or he wouldn't find Joe, or even if he did, Joe would be too strong for him. But Kirk must've caught him by surprise and—and—"

She broke down, flinging her head into her lap. "Kirk wasn't a bad person, he really wasn't," she said, sobbing. "He was just confused. So confused. But when I heard what had happened, when I heard how violent it was, how the corpse had been mutilated and 'faithless' had been written across his chest in blood, I knew it was Kirk. I knew it."

Ben paused, giving everyone a breather. "When did you last see Kirk?"

"He never came back to our apartment after the murder. And after my first trial, he disappeared altogether—till he turned up on the roof of the Bank of Oklahoma Tower. I think he must've been riddled with guilt about what he'd done. And the fact that he'd gotten me in trouble probably only made it worse. It must've been tearing him apart."

"Which is what led him to kill himself."

She nodded, her head still bowed. "Poor sweet Kirk. He loved me so much. And now he's gone. Just like everyone else. They're—they're—" All at once, she broke down in tears. The emotional wall she had built to get herself through this testimony crumbled, like ancient masonry. All her sorrow came pouring out.

"I have no more questions, your honor," Ben said.

D.A. LaBelle, however, did.

"Very well," Judge Cable said, after giving Keri a few moments to collect herself. "Any redirect?"

"Yes," LaBelle said, stumbling to his feet. Never in Ben's life had he seen a man look less like he wanted to do a cross-examination than LaBelle did at this moment. Trying to follow an emotional testament like that one—trying to be hard on the young girl who had been through so much—was not a job anyone could envy.

"Forgive me for saying so," LaBelle began, "but I can't help but think that this eleventh-hour confession of someone else's guilt is terribly convenient." Ben knew he was trying to be obnoxious, but his heart wasn't in it. "Your brother dies a tragic death, and then, presto-chango, he becomes the murderer."

"It's what happened."

"I find that very difficult to believe."

"You weren't there!" Keri lifted her tear-streaked face. "I was. I saw the look in his eyes."

"And do you have any proof of his guilt?"

"*You* have all the proof," Keri shot back, "but you were so determined to railroad me you missed the obvious. You kept saying only one person had access to the chains, the knife. But two people lived in that apartment—me *and* Kirk. I couldn't have killed Joe. I wasn't strong enough to drag his body around and chain him to a fountain. But Kirk was. And he did."

LaBelle drummed his fingers on the podium. "Forgive me for saying so, ma'am, but as you yourself pointed out, you've been a suspect almost since the crime was committed. You've been tried, not once but twice for this offense. If convicted you could be executed. If you knew who the killer was, why on earth didn't you say so before now?"

Keri looked at him, her eyes wide, tears streaming. "He was my brother."

After that, nothing LaBelle said mattered. He tried to make a few more points, but no one was interested, not even La-Belle. He soon gave up and sat down.

"Very well," Judge Cable said. "I assume this completes the defense case."

Ben shook his head. "Not quite, your honor."

Christina leaned toward him. "What are you saying? Keri's testimony was great. I think the jury believes her."

"We can do better," Ben whispered back.

"Ben, nothing personal, but don't screw up what we've got here. This is the time to submit the case to the jury. If you call another witness, you just risk—"

"We have one more witness, your honor." Ben turned to face the gallery. "The defense recalls Andrea McNaughton."

* 46 *

Christina tugged at Ben's shirt sleeve. "Have you lost your mind?"

Ben held her at bay. "I know what I'm doing."

"Ben, she's the worst witness against us!"

"Which is why we have to bring her back."

"Ben—"

"I know what I'm doing."

Judge Cable wrinkled his brow. "Counsel, have you notified Ms. McNaughton that she would be called as a witness today?"

"No, sir. But she is on the witness list—thanks to the prosecution—and she is in the courtroom."

LaBelle joined in. "Judge, he's already had an opportunity to crossexamine."

"True, your honor. But now I want to introduce new topics, not rebut matters raised on direct. And I want to reexamine her in light of the new information that has arisen."

Cable ran his fingers through his graying hair. "I suppose he has that right. Mrs. McNaughton, would you please return to the witness box?"

In the third row of the gallery, Andrea McNaughton pushed herself up on uncertain legs. "Sir, I . . . don't . . . want to."

"I'm sorry," Judge Cable said. "I can imagine the pain this must cause you. But I'm afraid you have no choice."

"I've already said everything I have to say."

"And if Mr. Kincaid starts repeating matters that have

already been addressed, I can assure you I'll shut him down. But for now I must insist that you come to the witness box. Bailiff."

On cue, Brent, the bailiff, walked up the aisle beside Andrea. Taking her elbow, he gently escorted her to the front of the courtroom.

The judge nodded. "Thank you, Mrs. McNaughton. I'll remind you that you're still under oath."

"Of course." Her voice seemed hollow and hoarse.

Ben approached the podium. He had no notes for this cross. He was winging it, pure and simple, which was unfortunate, because he knew that everything depended on what happened next.

"Mrs. McNaughton, you were in the courtroom while Keri Dalcanton testified, weren't you?"

"Oh yes. I heard it all." Her voice left little doubt but that she was not persuaded by what she had heard. At the same time, it had a fragile quality, a vulnerability that had not been there before.

"Then you're aware that her testimony differs from yours on several key points."

She twisted her neck awkwardly. "Is that really a surprise?"

"No, it isn't. You and Keri have been antagonists from the outset. In some respects, this whole case has been a conflict between you and her. But it leaves the jury in a bit of a fix. Because both of you can't be telling the truth. So they have to determine who is—and who isn't."

"She's lying," Andrea said. "She's lying to save her scrawny neck."

"So you've been saying. But something about your story has always bothered me, something I couldn't quite put my finger on. Until just a few minutes ago, when I heard Keri testify. When I heard her talk about what a hard life she had after she moved to Tulsa."

"Is there a question in here somewhere?" LaBelle asked.

"I'm getting there," Ben replied. He turned his attention to

Andrea. "I remembered your account of your visit to Keri's apartment, just before your husband was found dead. You said she attacked you—"

"She did."

"—which she denies. In the struggle, you said she threw you down on some kind of exercise equipment and you hurt yourself. The problem is—I've been to Keri's apartment. And there's no exercise equipment."

"I don't know exactly what it was. One of those fancy high-tech things—"

"You heard how poor she's been. There's no way she could afford some Nautilus equipment or rowing machine."

"She probably thought it was worth the cost to keep up her shapely figure. That's important when you make your living as a whore."

Ben took a deep breath. "It's not there, Mrs. McNaughton."

"She probably got rid of it after she murdered my—"

"This is a copy of the police inventory," Ben said, waving a sheet of paper in the air, "taken when the police arrived at her apartment, less than one hour after your husband's body was discovered. It lists everything they found there. Which is not much. And there is certainly no exercise equipment."

"Maybe they didn't think—"

"Here is a sheaf of photos I pulled out of the file," Ben said, passing them to the bailiff. "The police photographed Keri's apartment in every room from every possible angle. Standard operating procedure—at the time, they thought the murder might've occurred there." He watched as the bailiff passed the photos to Andrea. "Take your time and look through them, ma'am. There's a lot to see. But I can tell you one thing you won't see—exercise equipment. Because she didn't have any."

Andrea rifled furiously through the pictures. "Well, maybe it was a table or cabinet . . ."

"Ah, but now you're changing your story. Before, it was a fancy high-tech exercise machine."

"It all happened very quickly. I could've been confused."

"Confused? Is that a way of saying you lied?"

"I did not lie!" Her face flushed. "All right, maybe I did make that part up. I made a mistake."

Ben shook his head. "You didn't make a mistake. You invented the exercise equipment because it fit the image you were trying to create, the image of this young husband-stealing bimbo living in the lap of sin and luxury. The problem is—none of it is true."

"Your honor," LaBelle said angrily. "He's speechifying again. He's already made his point."

"Have I?" Ben asked. "The point is—she's admitted she lied once. How can we believe anything else she had to say?"

"Your honor—"

"Given the knowledge that you lied once," Ben continued, "it's now easier to resolve all the other conflicts between your testimony and Keri's. For instance, you say that when you came to her apartment and identified yourself, she greeted you with contempt and hostility. But why would she? Remember—she didn't even know Joe had a wife. Her principal reaction was shock."

"That's her story. If you want to believe it."

"No one has ever given us any reason not to believe it. Not even you. You say that she attacked you."

"She did."

"And Keri says you attacked her. Now which is more likely? That the attack would be initiated by a nineteen-year-old girl who's just found out her boyfriend is married? Or the betrayed married woman with an acknowledged proclivity for violence? The woman who subsequently attacked Keri twice in front of witnesses. The woman we know has already lied once."

"That's not true! I didn't—"

"I've seen you attack Keri myself. You admitted you attacked your husband. And I think you did it in Keri's apartment, too. You obviously have a problem with your temper, ma'am. And although I'm no psychiatrist, I suspect your problems go even deeper than that."

"How dare you! You don't know what happened—"

"I think I do. You claim Keri made a lot of hateful threats to you as you were dragged out of the apartment by her brother. But why would she? She may have been shocked to learn that Joe had a wife, but she had no reason to believe he would leave her. He refused when you first asked him, something you've already admitted. And something you told Keri when you were at her apartment. He didn't change his mind until later—after you worked on him some more. So what reason did Keri have to be making threats to you? None. None at all." Ben leaned in closer. "I think you made it up, Mrs. McNaughton. You made it up because you hate Keri Dalcanton and you want to see her die."

"That isn't true!"

"I think it is. In fact, I know it is. The truth is, Keri has no reason to be telling lies about you. But you have every reason to tell lies about her. Because, as you've already admitted to the jury—you hate her."

"That's not so!" Andrea rose out of her chair. "Make him stop saying that!"

"You did lie, Mrs. McNaughton. You lied about the exercise machine and the threats and everything else. Anything that would make the police arrest Keri and pursue her relentlessly. Which they did. Because they felt they owed it to Joe's poor widow."

"Make him stop!" Andrea was screaming, almost out of control with rage. "Make him stop lying!"

"Your honor—"

Ben cut LaBelle off before he had a chance to interrupt. "And you told all those lies, Mrs. McNaughton, you stirred up the whole police department, because you hated that woman, you hated her with every ounce of your body, hated her so much you were willing to do anything—"

"She stole my husband!" Andrea's impassioned screech

reverberated across the courtroom. She leaned across the rail, almost flinging herself out of the box. *"She stole my husband!"*

Ben allowed the horrible silence following her outburst to fester. Andrea placed her hand against her temple, brushing the hair from her eyes, and lowered herself back to her chair, sobbing uncontrollably.

"And by that," Ben said, "you don't mean that she killed your husband, because she didn't, and you know it. You mean she stole his love. She alienated his affections."

Andrea's head was bowed. Her voice was broken, her face shattered. "Whenever I think about the two of them, being together, doing all those disgusting things, I—I—just can't stand it."

Ben spoke quietly but insistently. "And so you decided to get back at her, the best way you knew how. By making sure she was Suspect Number One. By making sure the law-enforcement community hounded her relentlessly, never giving up until she had paid the final price for what she did to you. That's what you wanted, wasn't it, Andrea?"

Andrea's face was wet and streaked. She looked broken and pathetic. "Was that so much?" she asked. "She took everything from me. Everything."

Ben nodded, then looked up at the bench. "That's all, your honor. I have no more questions for this witness. I think she's been through enough." He glanced back at the defendant's table. "I think we all have."

* 47 *

After the furious excitement of the last two witnesses, closing arguments were almost an anticlimax. LaBelle predictably rehashed all the incriminating evidence, focusing for obvious reasons on the forensic exhibits rather than the testimony of Andrea McNaughton. He reminded everyone on the jury panel that it was uncontested that the murder weapon had come from Keri Dalcanton's kitchen, that the chains had come from her bedroom, that her fingerprints were on both. And most compelling of all—that her skin was under Joe McNaughton's fingernails.

"The defense has been very clever," LaBelle cautioned them. "They've managed to come up with some explanation for almost every incriminating detail. Maybe the skin got under his nails during kinky sex. Maybe there was a fight when he told Keri he was breaking it off. On and on and on. But at some point you have to ask yourself—when do these stop being explanations, and start being excuses? Is it credible that there should be some outlandish, contrived explanation for every item in a mountain of evidence? Or is all of this simply proof of the obvious—that Keri Dalcanton killed Joe McNaughton in a fit of rage when he told her she would never see him again."

LaBelle left the podium and approached the jury, appealing to them with his calm, logical delivery. Ben could see why he had the reputation he did. He wasn't showy as such, but showy wasn't always good in a criminal trial. He was assured and sincere, and in the end run, Ben knew that was much more important to most juries.

"Bear in mind, too," LaBelle reminded them, "the psychiatrist who testified that Keri Dalcanton fantasized about killing Joe McNaughton long before she did—long before she ever had a reason. Even before his decision to end the relationship, murder was on her brain. Is that the dream of a normal, innocent lover? I should think not. That's the dream of a twisted, dangerous mind. All she needed was a motive. And when Joe McNaughton finally gave it to her, she made her sick dream a reality.

"When Mr. Kincaid speaks to you, he will no doubt talk at great length about reasonable doubt. For the most part, I'll leave that to him. But I will suggest to you, that the most important word in that phrase is not 'doubt,' but 'reasonable.' It is not enough for the defense to create doubts with wild speculations or crazy explanations. It is not enough to provide alternative explanations or—in a particularly crude effort—to pin the blame on the recently deceased who cannot defend themselves. There must be *reasonable* doubt. If there is no *reasonable* doubt that Keri Dalcanton killed Joe McNaughton, then you must deliver a guilty verdict. Indeed, you have a duty to do so. A duty you owe not just to me, or this court, but to everyone."

Ben made a conscious decision not to protract his closing. He had a real sense that the trial was over, at least in the jury's mind. In some cases, he felt the jury looked forward to closing; they wanted to hear the attorneys sort out the evidence and try to make sense of it all. But not this time. This time he felt the decision had been made—one way or the other. All he could do was remind them of everything he thought was important—and do them the courtesy of being brief.

Point by point, he identified the refutations made to all of the prosecution's so-called evidence. "The prosecution wants to make much of the fact that the knife came from Keri's kitchen—but she admitted that, just as she admitted that the chains came from her bedroom. What's important is not where they came from—but who used them. Similarly, the prosecution wants to make a fuss about her fingerprints being on the knife and the chains. But why shouldn't they be? They were hers! Of course she's held the knife, and she's admitted she used the chains. This so-called proof tells you nothing."

Ben leaned against the counsel table. "I want to take an extra moment to discuss the DNA evidence. DNA has been much in the news lately. Possibly too much. It has acquired a veneer of infallibility—because most people don't really understand it. They assume that DNA evidence equals guilt. But it doesn't. Not always. All DNA evidence can do is give you a likelihood, that is, the odds that the specimen came from the accused. But as anyone who's ever been to Vegas knows, odds don't always play out the way you expect them to. And you have to consider—even if her skin was under his fingernails, does that prove she killed him? Or does that just prove they spent a lot of time together, some of it in close contact, something which has never been in dispute? Keri explained that she and Joe fought briefly when he announced that he was leaving her—an understandable reaction. Is it so hard to believe that the skin got under his fingernails during that struggle? The prosecutor talks about our 'crazy explanations,' but isn't that explanation easier to believe than that this petite young woman killed him? I think it is. And if you'll look into your hearts, I think you'll find that it is, too.

"Finally, there is the testimony of Andrea McNaughton. Make no mistake about this—Mrs. McNaughton is a victim in this case, just as Keri is, just as Joe McNaughton was. I don't condone what she did—but I understand it. I think we all can. Still, the fact remains—she lied about what happened when she saw Keri Dalcanton. She lied consciously and intentionally, for the sole purpose of seeing Keri wrongfully convicted of murdering her husband. Worse, she enlisted the help of police officers, her late husband's devoted friends, in her single-minded effort to convict Keri Dalcanton. What she did brings everything she said—and everything presented by the prosecutor who knowingly put her on the stand—into question. When you eliminate Andrea McNaughton from the equation, what does the prosecution have left? A lot of evidence linking Keri to Joe McNaughton or proving that devices used in the murder came from her apartment. So what? What do they have that links Keri to the murder itself? What do they have that proves she committed the crime? Nothing, that's what. Absolutely nothing."

Ben carefully positioned himself directly before the jury. He looked each of them squarely in the eyes, one by one, then continued. "This case is unlike any other I have ever tried, in more ways than you can imagine. But chief among them is this: In most cases, I have to try to convince the jury my client did not commit the crime, without having the slightest idea who did. Not this time. This time I know with absolute certainty who the murderer was. Keri told you why and how it happened, in great detail. And no one has given you any reason to disbelieve what she said. To the contrary, it makes perfect sense and fits all the evidence presented by the prosecution.

"Kirk Dalcanton was unstable and unbalanced, and had been for some time. He had a criminal record. He was unemployed, unhappy. He was living below the poverty level. He had low self-esteem. He was ashamed of himself. He was psychologically tormented about his sexual identity. In short, he was exactly the type of person who might commit a violent murder. What's more, he—unlike his sister—had the necessary body strength and the motivation to do it. All of the most gruesome aspects of the crime—the mutilation of the body, the public display of the corpse, the word 'faithless' written in blood—all point to a male killer. Contrast that with what the prosecution has been telling you—that this hideous crime was committed by a nineteen-year-old girl. Which is more likely? you must ask yourself. Or to put it in the terms the judge will soon discuss with you: Is there any room for reasonable doubt?"

He paused, once again looking each of them in the eye. "I think there is. And I think you do, too."

After the closings were complete, the judge gave the jury its instructions, a long series of guidelines couched in dense legal language. Ben knew from experience that the instructions rarely made much difference to a jury's determination of guilt, although they sometimes helped determine which charge would be applied. In this case, except for the instruction reminding them of the importance of *reasonable doubt*, they were worse than useless. Everything would be decided when the jury resolved whether Keri was innocent or guilty. If she was innocent, she would go free. But if they found her guilty of this macabre crime, they couldn't help but give her the maximum penalty.

Finally, the jury was dismissed, and Ben, Christina, and Keri began the long wait. Ben still sensed that most of the jurors had reached a conclusion, whatever that might be, which would indicate a relatively short deliberation. But you could never be sure. One hour passed, while they sat in the courtroom. After two hours, Christina sent out for sandwiches. After three, the courtroom closed, but the judge let the jury continue to deliberate. Apparently he too held out hope that the case would be decided quickly.

After four hours of waiting, it was dark outside the courtroom, and Ben was beginning to consider the possibility of going home. "If the jury does reach a verdict," he explained to Keri, "they'll call. Nothing will happen till we're back in the courtroom."

Keri nodded. She was bearing up well, all things considered, but the tension was evident in her face. And who wouldn't be nervous—when her very life was being decided in the room next door. "You go on if you want, Ben. I think I'll stay a bit longer."

"Are you sure?" he asked. He glanced at his watch. "You'll miss *Xena*."

She smiled a little. "Life is full of little sacrifices."

Ben decided to remain. He sensed that Keri wanted someone with her. And there was more than that, actually. He sensed that she wanted *him* to stay with her. And he wanted to stay with her.

It was hard to chitchat with someone who knew that twelve persons were in the next room deciding whether she should be executed. Compared with that, everything else seemed trivial. Because it was.

"Any idea what you're going to do once you get out of here?" Ben asked optimistically.

"Well," Keri said, "I'm definitely not going back to stripping. That's over forever. Problem is, I'm not sure what that leaves. I'm not qualified for anything."

"Why don't you get a job at a gym?"

"As what? A barbell?"

"As an aerobics instructor. I'm pretty sure it doesn't require a college degree, and who would be better at it than you? You work out every day, you're in great shape. Shoot, you'd have people lining up to get in your class, just on the hope that if they exercise with you, they might end up looking like you."

She smiled, in spite of everything. "You're sweet, Ben. You know that? Really sweet." She turned to Christina. "Isn't he sweet?"

Christina nodded. "That's why I've stayed with him all these years."

"Really?" An inquisitive, almost mischievous expression played on Keri's face. "I thought you were in love with him."

"Excuse me?"

Keri held up her hands. "Sorry. I didn't think I was betraying any state secrets here."

Christina's eyes went skyward. "Kids. They think everyone's hormones are raging."

Keri gave her a sly look. "Methinks you doth protest too much."

"Put your mind to rest, Keri. He's all yours. I'm going for some coffee." Christina stood up and moved rather quickly out of the courtroom.

"Sorry," Keri said to Ben. "Didn't mean to chase her away."

"You didn't. She gets antsy during these long waits."

"So tell me, Mr. Trial Lawyer. What's the jury thinking?"

Ben shook his head. "I've tried cases long enough to know that, when all is said and done, juries are unpredictable. It's like betting at the craps table. You know what should happen. But that doesn't always mean it will."

A moment later, without warning, Keri's hand shot out and clutched at Ben's. "Ben . . . do you think they believed me?"

Ben peered into her lovely blue eyes. There were words he wanted to say, that he knew she wanted to hear. But he couldn't tell her something he wasn't certain of himself. She'd see the dishonesty in his eyes, and it would be worse than if he'd never spoken.

"I hope so," he said, finally, simply. "I hope so."

Hours later, the door of the jury deliberation room cracked open. A word was whispered to the bailiff, who immediately went to the judge. It was well past eleven, but that didn't stop Cable from reconvening the court. It seemed he wanted this to be over as much as everyone else.

"Bailiff," the judge said, as he walked back to the bench, "reassemble the court and contact the attorneys. We have a verdict."

* 48 *

LaBelle must've had a sense that the jury would return soon also, because it didn't take him and his staff ten minutes to return to the courtroom. Many of the reporters who had been covering the case managed to make it back, too. With astonishing swiftness, the players were reassembled to hear the jury's final word.

Ben watched the jurors as they filed back into the room. They all had solemn, sober expressions on their faces. They looked tired, no great surprise. But he also noticed that none of them were looking at Keri. Not so much as a glance across the table. Why didn't they want to make eye contact?

Despite the fact that everyone on earth desperately wanted to know what was written on the scrap of paper clutched in the foreman's hand, the judge led them through all the solemn formalities. "Madame Foreman, have you reached a verdict?"

A middle-aged woman on the front row, Juror Number Three (the one Ben almost removed but didn't), spoke out in a clear if somewhat nervous voice. "We have, your honor."

"Bailiff." At the judge's instruction, Brent crossed the courtroom and carried the all-important piece of paper to the judge. He glanced at it briefly. Years of experience had given Judge Cable a practiced stoic expression; there were no clues forthcoming there. He passed the paper back to the bailiff.

"I can't stand this," Keri whispered. After being through so much, this final interminable rigmarole was almost more than she could bear.

"We're almost there," Ben said.

She thrust her hand into his. "Hold me," she said quietly. She squeezed so tightly it practically cut off the flow of blood to Ben's fingers.

"The defendant will rise to receive the verdict."

Keri did so. Ben and Christina stood beside her.

"Madame Foreman," the judge intoned, "will you please read the verdict?"

The foreman flipped open the tiny sheet of paper which, at that moment in time, seemed more important than anything else in the world.

"On the first charge, for the willful and intentional murder of Joseph P. McNaughton in the first degree, we find the defendant, Keri Louise Dalcanton . . ."

Why did they always pause there? Ben asked himself. Did they think they were on television? Get on with it!

". . . not guilty."

Ben felt a tugging on his arm that nearly wrenched it out of his shoulder. "Did she say not guilty?" Keri asked. "I thought she said not guilty."

"She did," Ben said, squeezing back almost as tightly. "She did."

"On the second charge," the foreman continued, "for the wrongful murder of Joseph P. McNaughton in the second degree, we find the defendant, Keri Louise Dalcanton, not guilty."

There was no holding back the excitement now. Christina whooped; Ben shouted. Some of the reporters in the gallery actually applauded. And Keri leapt, literally leapt, into Ben's arms.

"Thank you," she cried, pressing her head against his shoulder. "Thank you so much."

"Thank the jury," Ben said, nodding toward the twelve people in the box, all of whom were now making eye contact. "They did it."

Keri looked across the courtroom and mouthed a heartfelt thank you. But she hugged Ben's neck all the harder. "You're the one who made it happen," she said. "You believed in me. You were the only one."

Judge Cable pounded his gavel. "We're not quite done yet, ladies and gentlemen. If you could please put the party on hold a few more moments." Judge Cable rattled through the final cautions and instructions to the parties and the jurors. He thanked the jury for their time and effort with a sincerity that surprised Ben, since he suspected Cable almost certainly disagreed with the verdict. "Ms. Dalcanton, the State apologizes for the ordeal you have been put through. You are now free to go." He slammed down his gavel, and at long last, it was over.

Keri stood beside Ben, poised like an anaconda ready to spring. "All right, Christina," she said. "I need your permission."

"My permission?"

Keri nodded. "Can I kiss him now?"

"Be my guest."

Keri sprang. Her lips pressed against Ben's with an intensity that took both of them by surprise. The kiss did not last long, but the passion behind it was strongly felt, just the same.

"And that's just a preview, big boy. Let's get out of here." She tugged his collar, urging him toward the back door.

"Wait a minute. We've got all these documents to transport. There's paperwork to be filed . . ."

"I'll do it," Christina said, with an expression not unlike a disapproving mother on prom night. "You two go . . . smooch. Or whatever."

"Thanks, Christina. I'll call you in—"

That was all he got out before the insistent tugging lifted him off his feet and halfway toward the door. And he was out of there.

THREE

*   *

Never Simple

* 49 *

His eyes closed, Father Danney sprinkled a fine layer of dirt into the gravesite.

"We need not grieve for this man, for we know that God cares."

Ben watched as the assembled mourners filed past the grave. Keri was holding up well. He had been concerned; after all the stress she'd been through of late, the last thing he wanted her to have to endure was a funeral. But tragic though it was, her tormented brother was dead. What she needed now was closure, and Ben knew that would never come until the funeral was finished and Kirk was laid to rest for eternity.

The priest said a few more words, then concluded the ceremony. The time to pay last respects had come. There were only ten people present, and some of them, Ben knew, worked for the church. Still, there was a tangible sense of tragedy in the air—tragedy and relief, as if this was acknowledged to be horrible, but was simultaneously perceived as the final chapter in a mercifully ended episode.

Keri paused by the open grave. She laid her hand gently in the dirt surrounding the opening. Tears sprang to her eyes, but for once, it seemed to Ben, they were not tears of terror, not the horrified reflex of a young woman overwhelmed by circumstances outside her control. This time, they were simply the tears of a sister who much loved and now much missed her only brother.

After a long moment, Keri scooped up a handful of dirt and poured it into the grave. A short beat later, she walked away.

Ben met her at the perimeter of the site. "How are you holding up?"

Keri leaned close to him, bracing her cheek against his shoulder for support. "I'm fine. Really." She hesitated. "But oh God I'll miss him."

Ben pressed her head against him. He felt her warmth stirring his blood into hyperdrive. He felt more than a little guilty, feeling such emotions at a funeral, but it was beyond his control. "The pain will fade. In time."

"I know," she said. He could feel her moist cheek through his shirt. "That's what bothers me."

"What do you mean?"

"Kirk loved me so much. He deserved better than he got."

"Keri." He pulled her away and looked at her levelly. "I know Kirk was your brother, and you'll miss him. But in many respects—this is for the best. What kind of life did he have to look forward to? Kirk killed someone."

"Yes, Kirk killed someone—but he did it out of love. Because of me."

"Keri, it's not your fault. You're not to blame."

"I know that. I didn't say I was. But I still wish that somehow, some way, we could go back in time. I could do everything differently."

"Don't torture yourself, Keri. What you need to focus on now is the future."

Her eyes closed briefly, as if in prayer. "You're right." She graced him with a tiny smile. "Can I see you later?"

"Of course. I have a couple of chores to attend to. Life as a landlord, you know. But maybe later . . ."

"Just give me a call when you're ready to come over."

"It's a date."

She pressed her firm body against him and gave him a long sweet kiss. "I'll be waiting for you."

Ben watched as her black-clad figure moved away. It seemed as though the further she went, the sharper and more intensely her taste lingered on his lips.

"So, kemo sabe. Hitting on women at funerals now?"

Ben pivoted around. "Mike!" He reached out and clapped his friend's arms. "When did you get back in town?"

Major Mike Morelli grinned, then shoved his fists deep into the pockets of his unseasonable trenchcoat. "Just last night, as it happens."

"Was your mission a success? Did you catch the bad guy?"

"Don't I always?"

"Yeah. You and Dudley Do-Right."

"But enough about me. Let's talk about you. Couldn't stay out of trouble while I was gone, huh? Not even for a few weeks."

"So you've heard? Those clowns you work with at Tulsa P.D. actually arrested me."

"I've heard. Penelope gave me the full scoop last night when I got in." He paused. "I'm sorry you had to endure that."

"You and me both. If I go my whole life without again experiencing delousing, that'll be just fine."

"I'm sorry I wasn't around to help."

"I don't think it was a coincidence. I think Matthews and his cronies waited until you went undercover to make their move."

"No doubt. I guess you've heard—Matthews has been suspended. I don't know if he'll ever work as a police officer again. Frank Bailey is being investigated by IA. They'll come up with some kind of punishment for him, but the general feeling is that he was more a follower than a leader. And he did come clean at trial, more or less. That counts in his favor."

"I agree. I don't want to see any more people hurt by this. They were all basically pawns in Andrea McNaughton's revenge game. Like I was just telling Keri, I think we should put this behind us. Move on."

"Noble sentiments. And speaking of your client Keri . . ." He leaned in a little closer and winked. "I gather the relationship has moved somewhat beyond attorney-client."

"What gave you that idea?"

"Oh, mainly that twenty-second smooch I just observed." He jabbed Ben in the ribs. "You old chick magnet, you."

Ben pushed him away. "I want to make it clear that we didn't let this thing develop until after the case was completed."

"Uh-huh."

"Well, maybe there were one or two slips. Three, actually. But still—"

Mike held up his hands. "Relax, Ben. I'm certain that whatever you did, you did it in a morally responsible, hand-wringingly ethical manner."

"And what is that supposed to mean?"

"It means chill out. I'm your friend. And I'm glad to see you finally connecting with someone."

Ben tilted his head to one side. "I have to admit, I'm feeling a little guilty about the whole situation."

"What, because of the attorney-client thing?"

"No. Because of her age. Which is roughly half mine."

"You're exaggerating. Besides, she's an adult and she can make choices for herself. You're not breaking any laws."

"No, not quite."

"You're probably the best thing that ever happened to that poor girl."

"Maybe, but still—"

"My God, Ben. Are you totally incapable of being happy? You've got a good thing here. Don't spoil it haranguing yourself because she's younger than you."

"I suppose you're right." Ben glanced up at the cloudless sky. It was fairly warm out, especially for this time of year in Oklahoma. "So when are we going to get together so I can hear about this archcriminal you tracked down? There's a game on tonight."

"Sounds good. We can drink beer, swap stories, and you can pretend to understand football. Say, my place at eight?"

"I'll look forward to it." Ben glanced at his watch. "What are you doing now?"

"Oh, work, what else? Now that I'm back, they've dragged me into the cleanup of this Joe McNaughton disaster. Well, triumph for you. Disaster for us."

"What's left to do?"

"For LaBelle, major damage control. When that verdict came down, he saw his reelection bid flittering away right before his eyes. He hasn't decided whom to blame yet—the judge, the jury, you—but I can guarantee he'll be on the evening news soon ranting about this miscarriage of justice."

"And for you?"

"Well, we finally found the dive where Kirk Dalcanton lived after he moved away from his sister. Man, you thought the place where she lived was grim—you should see this hellhole. I didn't think dives like this still existed in Tulsa."

"What do you have to do?"

"Oh, everything. Look for any additional proof that he was the murderer. Catalog his belongings, which I guess are now his sister's belongings, since she's his only living relative. In fact, there's some stuff you could take over to her. And judging by that last kiss, you're going to be seeing her soon."

"Let me think. Do I want to deliver to Keri her dead brother's belongings? I think that's a no."

"Come on, kemo sabe. It would save me a lot of time."

Ben frowned. "I'm entirely too soft. But I missed you, you big lug."

Mike fluttered his eyelashes. "I love it when you sweet-talk me."

Half an hour later, Mike parked his TransAm in front of a dilapidated flophouse just a few blocks from central downtown. Some parts of Tulsa's downtown area had been refurbished in recent years, giving people more and more reason to venture northward, even during nonwork hours: Greenwood, the Brady, OSU-Tulsa, Gilcrease Museum. Almost every time Ben came downtown it seemed he discovered something new and charming. But there were also isolated pockets of the past, places where it seemed nothing had changed for decades—except maybe for the worse.

Kirk's apartment—his room, to be more accurate, was barely habitable. The two-story house was a faded grayish color, so ill-maintained and uncared for that as he looked at it, Ben wondered that it could even remain standing. This place could be a poster house for landlords everywhere: DON'T LET THIS HAPPEN TO YOU!

Kirk had the room at the top, a converted attic, which Mike informed Ben he had rented for a whopping twenty dollars a week. As Ben stepped through the creaking door, he was almost knocked over by the putrid odor that assaulted him.

"How could anyone live here?"

The tiny room was so cluttered with stuff the two men could barely get from one end of it to the other. Despite the haste of his move, Kirk seemed to have taken with him everything that was of the remotest importance to him.

"Anyway," Mike said, "you can see that most of this clutter is just personal junk. Not going to help us understand anything about the murder. Not worth anything to anyone, except maybe his sister. And in most cases, probably not her. But someone has to take it."

Ben pushed his way through the room. "Funny, isn't it? Or not funny at all. Depressing. Some of this stuff must've been special to him. He may have used it, or looked at it, every day. But now he's gone and—pow. One week later, it'll all be on the scrap heap."

Ben saw some books, a few CDs. Kirk seemed to favor country-western, not exactly surprising for a boy from Stroud. Several Bibles, also not a gigantic surprise. Ben picked one up and found numerous passages underlined in red. In some cases, messages were scrawled in the margins, in what had to be Kirk's handwriting.

"Kirk was seriously into the Good Book," Ben murmured.

"No surprise there," Mike replied. "Don't get me wrong. The

Bible's a great read, especially the King James Version. But it's also a standard volume in the library of virtually every psycho you'll ever meet in this neck of the woods."

Ben kept sorting. He found a couple of magazines on tattooing and other means of "bodily enhancement." "There are magazines about tattooing? Three different ones?"

"Ben, there are magazines about everything. We live in the era of the niche audience."

"I guess so." He was surprised that he found only one photograph, of Kirk's sister, Keri. It had to be several years old; Keri looked thirteen at best. But it was lovingly framed, even cleaned, unlike everything else in the room.

"He loved his sister so much," Ben commented. "I can't even conceive of devotion of that magnitude."

"Just as well you can't," Mike said. "Given what it led him to."

Ben continued looking. He realized this was not much different from sorting through a dead man's pockets, but it was fascinating, all the same. After pushing aside some decorative brass doodads, he found a large cardboard box. "What on earth could this be?"

He opened it up—and gasped.

"What?" Mike said, whipping his head around. "What is it?"

Ben stared into the box, his mouth open, his eyes wide. "I don't believe it. I don't believe it."

"What?" Mike repeated. He stumbled toward his friend, knocking over items right and left. He peered into the box. "Okay, so what? I don't get it."

"No, you couldn't. But I do." Ben's eyes seemed glassy and fixed. "Oh, my God. I do."

Mike grabbed his shoulders. "Would you stop that? Tell me what's going on!"

"I can't." He pressed his fingers against his forehead. "My God, how could I be so stupid? How could I be so blind?"

Mike was getting angry. "Would you please tell me what you're talking about?"

Ben ignored him. He pulled away, grabbed his coat, and headed toward the door. "I'm sorry, Mike. I have to go. There's someone I have to talk to." He rushed out the front door and started down the decaying staircase. "Now."

* 50 *

It was taking her an inordinate amount of time to answer the door, Ben thought, as he paced back and forth in the narrow hallway. He knew she was home; he could hear noises inside. So why wasn't she answering? The delay was only increasing his tension level. Because, of course, deep down, he didn't really want that door to open. He dreaded the conversation he knew would follow. But there was no avoiding it.

At last the apartment door opened, and a patch of disheveled platinum blond hair became visible through the opening. "Ben?"

Ben peered through the chained gap, not sure what to say first. "I need to talk with you, Keri."

Keri licked her lips, then forced a smile. "Sure, honey. I want to see you, too. It's just—I told you to call first. I want to look my best for you. Could you come back—"

"We need to talk now."

"Couldn't it wait until I've had a chance—"

"No. Now."

With obvious reluctance, Keri slid the chain out of the lock and opened the door. Ben stepped inside. She was barely dressed, wearing only a T-shirt and panties, and the shirt was on backwards. Her near perfect figure was on display and impossible not to notice, but Ben tried to put it out of his mind.

Ben glanced around the apartment, which was a mess. Books were off shelves, tables were cleared. Large cardboard boxes cluttered the room. "You're moving."

The rise and fall of her chest did magnificent things to her near-transparent white T-shirt. "Yes, Ben, I am. You know this place is a dump. Now that the trial is over, I wanted someplace a little nicer—"

"You're leaving town, aren't you?"

She sighed. "Yes, Ben. For a while, anyway. I need to make a fresh start. Someplace where everyone doesn't think of me as a former murder defendant."

"Were you planning to tell me?"

"How can you say that? Of course I was. You know how . . . how I feel about you." She reached out and twined her fingers around his. "Actually, I was hoping you might come with me."

Ben slapped her hand away. "Stop that."

Keri recoiled, staring deep into his eyes. "Ben, what's wrong? Has something happened?"

"You could say that."

"Something about the case?" Deep creases crossed her brow. "They're not going to try me again, are they?"

"No, you're off once and for all this time. Never in a million years could the D.A. get the appeals court to set aside an acquittal twice. Especially not after the case has gone to the jury."

"Then what?"

Ben turned away. This was hard enough to do without having to stare at that magnificent figure, beautiful hair, deep blue eyes. "The police found the place where your brother was holed up. After he left here."

"I know." She paused. "And?"

"And I've been there."

"Ben . . . is there more to this? 'Cause I'm not really getting it . . ."

"I had a lovely opportunity to sort through all his personal belongings. Everything he left behind." He stopped and, unable to resist, he turned to face her. "Including his exercise equipment."

Keri's eyebrows rose. "His . . . ?"

"You heard me. What is that, a Stairmaster or something? Whatever. The point is, Kirk had it. But you know what I think? I think it used to be in your apartment. You said in court you didn't own anything like that and it was probably true— because it was Kirk's. And he took it with him when he left. But it used to be in your apartment. It was there when you had the knock-down-drag-out with Andrea McNaughton. She fell back and hurt herself on it. Just like she said in court. Right?"

Keri did not immediately answer.

Ben's teeth clenched tighter together. "Am I right?"

She still did not reply.

"I thought so. But what I don't get is, why did Andrea 'confess' that she had invented that detail when I called her back to the stand? That was a critical moment in her testimony. After I showed she had lied once, it was all a downward spiral. The jury never believed her again. But it was true! You really did have exercise equipment in your apartment."

Keri's eyes slowly rose to meet his. "It's true, Ben. My parents bought that thing for Kirk, back when they were still in our hair. I think they saw it on some infomercial and thought it would be good for him."

"So why did Andrea lie about it?"

Keri hesitated.

Another voice shattered the silence. "I can explain that."

Ben whirled around. His lips parted, stunned.

Andrea McNaughton was standing in the rear of the apartment.

"So," Andrea said, "Encyclopedia Brown finally figured a thing or two out, huh?" She crossed the room, passing Ben nonchalantly, and positioned herself on the lumpy couch. "Very impressive."

Keri glared at her. "Shut up, Andrea."

"Don't talk to me that way."

"I said, shut up!"

"Keri—"

"Listen to me!" Veins became visible on Keri's porcelain white neck. "I'm still his client. Anything I say to him is protected by that privilege deal. He can't repeat it, and even if he did, the cops couldn't use it. But you're not his client. Anything you say he can repeat all over town. So keep your lip zipped."

Ben stared at them both, his face transfixed by the dawning horror. "You did it together." He backed away from them. "You were both in on it together."

Keri rolled her eyes. "Took you long enough, didn't it?"

"I—I should've seen—"

"Yeah, you should've. But you didn't. Like most men, your mind was somewhere else whenever I was around." Keri laughed, shrill and brittle. "You probably said a million times, one petite nineteen-year-old girl wouldn't have enough strength to pull off this crime. And you were right. But two women working together—that's another thing altogether."

"But you two hate each other."

"Do we?" Keri smiled and then, touching her fingers to her lips, blew Andrea a kiss. "Men are so easily deceived."

"But, all those fights—I saw them—"

"Staged. That time Andrea came to your office because she supposedly wanted to tell Christina something? Wrong. She came to stage a fight. For your benefit."

"That can't be." Ben struggled to make sense of it all. "I saw the way you two went at each other. That was real."

"Sure it was, Ben. Just like professional wrestling." She laughed, then leaned toward Andrea. "The truth of the matter is, we're very close, aren't we, dear?" Andrea pressed close to her, and the two women locked lips for a deep and passionate kiss.

Ben braced himself against the wall. The room seemed to be moving, revolving around him. "But—*why?*"

Keri broke off the kiss and started to answer, but Andrea threw a sofa pillow at her. "Keep those pert little lips closed."

"He can't do anything about it, Andrea. He's sworn to secrecy. Besides the case is over. I can't be retried, and the cops will never admit they made a mistake and go after someone else. Right, Ben?" She grinned. "It's over."

"I asked you a question," Ben said, his voice hollow. "Why?"

"I'm afraid the answer to that question is all too pedestrian. Money. Joe had a lot of it, remember?"

"But Andrea was already married to him."

"He wasn't sharing."

"She could divorce him. By law, the money would be half hers."

"Actually, no. The money was in a trust fund from his grandparents, remember? And Joe was the beneficiary. So the money went to him and him alone. In the event of a divorce, she would get nothing. There was a time when Joe shared the loot with his beloved, but after things got frosty between them, he stopped. So what could she do? Divorce wouldn't help her get her hands on the goodies. But if Joe died, and Andrea was the beneficiary of his will, which she was, the proceeds of the trust fund would go to her. So he had to die."

"And you helped?"

"Strange world, isn't it? Who would've ever thought the two of us would get together? When Andrea came to my apartment that night, she was ready to tear my eyes out, just like she said. We had a bit of a tussle. Not quite as violent as she described it, but it was still a major league turn-on. Rolling around on the floor, our bodies pressed together. I thought she was hot, and I guess she felt the same way about me. Ten minutes after she arrived, we were making out like nobody's business. And when that was finished, we talked. To make a long story short, we realized we had a lot in common. Like for instance, that we'd both be better off if Joe McNaughton was dead."

"But—you weren't a beneficiary."

"No. But since Joe was going to break it off with me, I was out in the cold. Until Andrea offered me a slice of the pie for my assistance. Which I gladly gave."

"You helped her murder her husband?"

"Hey, I was the mastermind. I came up with the ideas. When Joe returned to my apartment on that fateful night, we were both waiting for him. I did most of the knife work. But Andrea was a big help with the chains and moving the body and such, weren't you, dear?" She quickly pointed a finger. "Don't answer that."

"Joe was a strong man—"

"Yes, a strong man with a strong taste for sadomasochistic sex. You may have noticed in those photos, he's always the one on his knees in the dog collar, and I'm always the one wielding the whip. That was the way he liked it. Actually, that was the way I liked it, too. And on that fateful night, when he came home, stripped off his clothes, got down on his knees, and asked Mommy to punish him—I did, with Andrea's assistance. Big time."

"Even if you had to kill him, why hang his body out in such a hideously public way?"

"To confuse and distract, of course. That was the plan, anyway. If he just turned up dead, Andrea knew she'd be the top suspect. But if he turned up chained in Bartlett Square, well, a whole new world of possibilities opened up."

"But why the mutilation?"

"Are you really surprised? Hell, Ben, you heard my shrink rattle on for more than an hour about my violent tendencies. How I fantasized about killing Joe. When the time finally came, I made the most of it."

Ben felt a choking in his throat.

"Andrea wasn't very happy about that part. Then she got this brilliant idea. She knew about Joe's investigation of Antonio Catrona. She thought that if we made it look like a mob rubout, that would confuse matters even further. And she was right. You used that red herring like a pro at trial, Ben."

"You—you planned out the whole thing!"

A light shone behind Keri's eyes, transforming those vivid blue eyes into something fiery and sinister. "What can I say, Ben? You take what the gene pool gives you. My mom was cruel and crazy, as I told you, and Kirk was seriously whacked, which you also knew. Is it a big surprise that my blood runs the same way? We Dalcantons, we're nothing if not consistent. Sexual flexibility and a serious taste for violence, that's like the family motto. Hell, even Matthews tried to tell you how violent I was when he came to my apartment. But would you listen? No—you were too busy sneaking peeks at my Wonderbra." She laughed. "I'd be lying if I didn't admit I enjoyed it, Ben. I snuck up behind Joe and clubbed him on the head so he couldn't resist—I guess that's when he got the concussion. I ripped his clothes off. Must've scattered his wallet and badge in the process. And then I took my little knife and tore his guts out." She licked her lips hungrily. "I savored each and every stroke of the knife. And I especially liked labeling the creep for what he was. *Faithless*."

Andrea couldn't contain herself. "You shouldn't have done that!"

"I told you to be quiet!" Keri shouted. The harshness of her voice sent chills down Ben's spine. "Andrea didn't like that touch," she explained, her voice suddenly eerily calm. "Didn't really fit with the mob-hit motif. And true enough, after that touch, it was inevitable that the cops would come sniffing around my panties. But I couldn't resist. He *was* faithless. He deserved it."

"My God—Matthews was right. He was right all along. He really was working to find some semblance of justice. And I—I—"

"Truth sucks, don't it?" Keri giggled. "The truly amazing thing is, we put it all together that one night. Granted, we made some mistakes. We shouldn't have used my knife, and we shouldn't have used my chains. But time was short; Joe was here before we had a chance to run out for supplies. We had to use what we had at hand." She paused reflectively. "Those two errors in judgment came back to haunt me, though. Although we successfully distracted the police from Andrea, we attracted them to me. But Andrea is nothing if not loyal. When the police came after me, she promised she'd find a way to get me off. And she did, too."

"How?"

"Well, first of all, by sending me to you. She knew you were a whiz in the courtroom, that you had a soft heart that would naturally go out to me when I told you about my boo-hoo childhood and hard-knock life. She also suggested that if there was a little romance in the air, you would become particularly attached and unlikely to be suspicious. And boy was she right about that."

Ben's face twisted, a mixture of shock and humiliation. "Then . . . all we did—you were just pretending. Just putting on another show."

"Sad to say, I was. I'm not proud of it. But it was necessary. Not that I minded or anything," she added hastily. "You're a regular guy, Ben. But a little too straight for me." A large belly laugh erupted from the base of her throat. "Way too straight for me, actually."

"You incriminated your brother. You made him your fall guy."

"Well, he deserved it, wouldn't you say, dear?"

Andrea nodded mutely.

"He's the one who screwed up our plan in the first place," Keri explained, and for the first time, a trace of bitterness crept into her voice. "He came in just after we polished off Joe. And he freaked. Totally out-of-his-head freaked. See, everything I said in court about Kirk was basically true. He

had serious emotional problems. He had low self-esteem, sexual confusion, a violent temper. Religious obsessions. And he was fond of his sister. Quite fond of his sister." She paused, running her fingers slowly through the strands of her silky hair. "We were very close. If you know what I mean."

Ben felt the gorge rising in his stomach. It took all his strength to suppress his urge to be ill.

"So anyway, he comes in at just the wrong moment and sees me and Andrea on top of Joe, both of us drenched in blood. It sent his already fragile mind into a frenzy. He didn't know what to do. Talked about calling the police."

"But you stopped him."

Keri grinned. "He'd been lusting after me all his life, since we were kids. Remember when I told you my daddy and I were close? It was true." She winked. "Another clue you missed, Sherlock. Anyway, I think Kirk had always been jealous of what Daddy and I had. So when the time came that I needed his help, needed him to do some horrible things he otherwise would never think about doing, I gave him what he'd wanted all those years. His dream come true."

Ben was unable to speak.

"Mind you, I made it worth Kirk's while. I gave him a good piece of action, I really did. I mean I could've just done it quick and dirty, but I knew he'd been waiting for this a long time, so I tried to make it memorable. And I think I succeeded. I hadn't been a stripper all that time without learning a few things. After all the bumping and grinding was done, I told him to stop crying and help. And it worked. Kirk kept his mouth shut—even helped us move the body around. It was great. Sent poor Kirk over the edge, though. Kirk had me on some kind of exalted plateau, in his twisted little mind. Some kind of madonna-whore thing, I guess. I don't know." She saw Ben's reaction and smiled. "You're surprised I know about things like that. You might be amazed at what I know. I'm a bright young babe. Well read. Matthews tried to tell you I was smart, remember? But of course, you didn't listen to him. I

may be from Stroud, Ben, but I'm nobody's fool. Anyway, after we were done, Kirk bailed. Took all his stuff and ran out of the room. He was totally out of his mind." She paused. "He's the one who slashed that woman in your office, you know."

"What!"

"Oh, yeah. I kept an eye on him, even after he flew the coop. I had to—he was a security risk, right? That's why I was out so often, late at night. He was doing all kinds of bizarro stuff—mutilating his body, sleeping with prostitutes. He was trying to expiate his guilt, trying to come to terms with what he'd done, to Joe and to me. When he went to your office, sadly enough, I think he was looking for me. The super at my apartment told me he'd been by asking after me; they suggested he try your office, which he did. He'd finally decided to strike back. He thought by killing me, by venting his anger on the source of his pain, he could rid himself of all that guilt. But alas, I wasn't there and your librarian buddy was. So she took the fall. Later, he realized he'd made a terrible mistake. Which only intensified his despair."

"Why didn't you tell me?"

"Use some brains, Kincaid. If you'd gotten your hands on Kirk, he would've spilled everything. No, after that business with the librarian, I realized he was too dangerous to live."

"But—but he killed himself. I saw it!"

"Yeah, he killed himself. With my help. I made a late night visit to his hellhole of an apartment. Happily, he'd just been with a prostitute, so he was feeling particularly guilt-ridden. I said exactly the words I knew would push him over the brink. And sure enough, he went down. Fifty stories down."

"But I saw you! You were torn apart with grief!"

"Quite the little actress, aren't I?" She laughed. " 'Oh, Ben, I love you so. Please hold me.' " She laughed again, loud and bitter. "Do you remember exactly when Kirk jumped? It was when Matthews told him I was coming to get him. I was the guilt he could never escape." She shook her head. "What a fool Kirk was."

"Your brother loved you!"

"My brother was a headcase ever since my parents died. Before, actually. He was such a simp. He was much better off after they were out of the picture; he just couldn't see it. Mother's perverted pranks weren't even the worst of it. They were always riding us, trying to control us. Butting into my private life. Telling me I was dirty and sinful. So I remedied the situation."

"You—you said they were killed in a traffic accident."

"They were. It's bad news when a truck comes at you in an intersection. Particularly if someone has drained most of your brake fluid."

"I can't believe it. I—can't believe it." Ben knew he was babbling, but he couldn't think of anything else to say. It was as if his brain was frozen and nonfunctional.

"Oh hell, honey, you haven't heard the worst of it." She turned toward Andrea. "Should I tell him?"

Andrea shook her head.

"Aw, come on. I want to."

Andrea continued shaking.

"Spoilsport."

"Tell me what?" Ben bellowed.

"I'm sorry, Andrea, but I just can't hold this back any longer." She leaned forward eagerly on the sofa, providing an ample display of cleavage. "I'm the one who planted the knife in your office."

"What!"

"You heard me."

Ben grabbed the edge of the kitchen counter, trying to steady himself. It was all too much, too impossible. "I could've been convicted of murder! I could've been disbarred! Why in God's name would you do that?"

"To throw the dogs off my scent, dearie. I knew you'd

never be convicted of anything. And I also knew that if they found the murder weapon in your office, you—and maybe others as well—would be convinced someone was trying to frame me. See, I knew about the Blue Squeeze. Contrary to what you proved in court"—she giggled a bit at that one— "Andrea wasn't behind the police harassment. Why should she want to hassle me? It was all that bozo Matthews's idea, trying to prove his manhood by deifying his former partner. But once we knew about it, Andrea figured we could use it to muddy the waters. To create more reasonable doubt. And to make you more certain than ever that I was innocent."

"So you put the knife in my file cabinet?"

"Of course. And I phoned the anonymous tip to Matthews. Think about it, Ben. Who else would have that thing? It was my knife, after all. Happily, I didn't leave it in my apartment, so the cops didn't find it. I had that much sense. But I knew where it was. I retrieved it and planted it on you. Brilliant, huh?"

Ben found himself barely able to speak. "And—and you don't have any . . . regret?"

"I'm proud to say that I do not. Now, Andrea, here, is another story."

Andrea gave her a silent, cold glare.

"Andrea has a bit of a whiny streak. She says she wanted to punish Joe, not to kill him. She didn't approve of mutilating his body. *Wah, wah, wah.* She says I seduced her husband, then I seduced her. Made them both do horrible things they should never have done. She says I ruined her life." She scooted closer to Andrea on the couch. "But you still love me, don't you, Andrea? That's what you hate most. You despise yourself for it afterward, but you just can't resist me." She pressed her body against her collaborator. Andrea hesitated, but soon her lips were locked with Keri's for a protracted kiss.

Ben pushed himself away like a man recoiling from a monster. Which he was. "You lied to me. You lied to everyone."

"I'm afraid that is correct."

He moved toward the door. "If you think I'm going to keep quiet about this, you're wrong."

"You have no choice. You can't say anything."

"Watch me."

"Settle down and think for a minute, Mr. Crusader. What are you going to accomplish here? No one can touch me. As you said yourself, I cannot be retried for the same crime. Never again."

"They could go after your accomplice, then."

"Andrea? Based on what? The hearsay ravings of a defense attorney? Which they can't use in court? I don't think so. Besides, you know as well as I do that after the D.A. loses a case, they never bring charges against a different defendant. Because to do so would be to admit they were wrong the first time. That they were trying to convict an innocent person. No D.A. is going to do that—certainly not Mr. Politico LaBelle." She leaned back into the soft sofa. "Face it, Ben—it's over. If you go flapping your mouth, the only thing you'll accomplish is getting yourself disbarred."

Ben's jaw was clenched so tightly he could barely speak. "I can't let you get away with this."

"Uh-huh," Keri said, bored to tears. "Honey, you don't have any choice. Tell you what. When you figure out how to get back at me, be sure to give me a ringy-dingy. I'll be somewhere in the Bahamas, improving my tan." She laughed, then waved her hand in the air. "Oh, stop quivering in your boots like some outraged moron. You screwed up and there's not a damn thing you can do about it. So pack up your moral outrage and leave already." She turned back toward Andrea, her lips parted, her eyes wide and hungry, running her fingers through Andrea's lustrous black hair. "And close the door behind you."

* 51 *

Ben sat in his car, staring at the open window on the third floor of the apartment building. His brain was a blur. All the thoughts, revelations, surprises, kept whirling through his head, spinning around him, making him dizzy with disappointment, and worst of all, the inescapable knowledge that he had made a total fool of himself. How could he possibly be so stupid?

Every so often, he would see one or the other of them float past the window. He couldn't tell what they were doing. Packing, maybe. Having dinner. Having wild and passionate sex. The possibilities were endless.

At one point, he saw Keri's barely clad figure come to the window, stop for a moment, grin, then move on. Did she know he was there, watching? Was Keri intentionally taunting him, flaunting the fact that there was nothing he could do to stop her? Probably not, but it was making him crazy, just thinking about it.

He pressed his fingers against his temples. He couldn't keep this bottled up any longer. He had to tell someone. But who? What Keri had said was right: the attorney-client privilege protected everything she'd said, not only the parts that incriminated her, but the parts that incriminated Andrea as well. He couldn't tell anyone—

Except someone who was inside the privilege. He had a partner now, by God. A member of the firm. She couldn't tell anyone else, but he could tell her everything.

But how? He didn't want to stop watching the apartment. He had to make sure Keri didn't blow town, had to follow her if she did. If she left that apartment, chances were she'd be gone forever.

Slowly, carefully, he considered all the possible options, weighing the ramifications of each.

And then he remembered his mother's Christmas present.

He popped open his briefcase and pulled out the small metallic gray Palm Pilot. He typed out a message to Christina on the little keyboard. Then he transmitted it to myFax.

After he was done, he turned off the electronic gizmo and put it back in the briefcase. It must be true that confession is good for the soul, he mused. By no stretch of the imagination did he feel good. But he did sense the tiniest alleviation of the awful aching in his gut. The disquietude that ravaged his brain was easing—only a little, but enough that he could almost think clearly.

His eyes, however, remained focused on that third-floor window. He settled back into the seat and waited for his message to be received.

"Ben?"

Mike stepped through the glass doors that led to the main lobby of the office. The doors were locked but fortunately, Ben had given him a key some time ago, when they were working together on an Internal Affairs case.

"Ben? Are you in here?" Probably not. But he had missed their eight o'clock get-together and he hadn't been at home and he wasn't answering his phone. It was probably stupid to worry, but Ben had raced out of Kirk Dalcanton's apartment with a stricken expression on his face, and he did have a profound talent for getting himself into trouble. Look what happened when Mike went out of town for a few weeks. He just felt better when he knew what his friend was doing.

"Ben? Are you here?"

He heard an abrupt beeping sound. A sign of life? He

walked to the front desk, the post normally occupied by Jones. So what was the—?

Ah. The fax machine. Someone was sending a late-night message. Probably an advertisement for a 1-900 sex number or something equally important. Or was Ben expecting it? Did this mean he would be here soon?

He glanced at the page spit out by the printer. No, it was for Christina. So it couldn't possibly—

Wait a minute. He scooped the fax up. He didn't normally read other people's messages, but before he'd even realized it was for someone else he'd read more of it than he could disregard.

His eyes quickly scanned the short message. Jesus God— could this possibly be true?

He saw the name at the bottom of the page. This message was from Ben. So it had to be correct.

His buddy was going to be pissed that Mike had read his message. Tough. Mike couldn't overlook this. He snatched the nearest phone receiver and began dialing.

"Maurice? I need three patrol cars immediately. Here's the address . . ."

"Police!"

Mike didn't give them a second chance. He shouted "Police" again, then knocked down the door.

It was an old door, well worn and probably cheap to begin with. It didn't take much effort. He swarmed into the apartment, Sig Sauer at the ready. Six uniformed police officers closed in behind him.

"I have a warrant," Mike shouted, as he glided through the apartment. "A warrant to search, and a warrant to arrest." He motioned to the officers. "Spread out," he told them. "Cover the whole place. Fast."

Mike was the lucky one who burst into the bedroom. He recognized the persons inside immediately. Keri Dalcanton was on one side of an unmade bed, throwing on a white T-shirt. Nearly naked, Andrea McNaughton was on the other side.

The bedspread was thrown off and the sheets were dangling crossways. This bed had obviously seen some spirited action. Clothes were strewn about all over the floor. The room was stripped almost bare; everything was in the packing boxes that littered the apartment.

But those weren't the details that ranked most prominently in Mike's mind. There was one other.

Andrea McNaughton was holding a gun.

"Please lower your weapon, Mrs. McNaughton," Mike said, in a voice that sounded a lot calmer than he really was.

She looked back at him with eyes as cold as frost. "No."

"I don't want to hurt you," Mike continued. He could hear the other officers gathering behind him. But the doorway created a bottleneck; they couldn't get in. And at the moment, he couldn't move without quite possibly getting himself shot. "I have a warrant for your arrest. Please lower your weapon."

"Don't do it," Keri snarled. "Aim for his head."

Andrea did not lower the gun.

"I have a warrant for your arrest, too, Ms. Dalcanton."

She laughed at him. "The hell you do. I've been acquitted, asshole."

"I'm arresting you for perjury," Mike explained. "You lied on the stand. And given more time, I'll bet I can think up a few more charges to nail you with."

"Son of a bitch." Keri turned toward Andrea. "Kill him, Andrea. It's our only chance."

"There are six other officers standing behind me," Mike said quickly. Keeping his voice calm seemed to get harder the longer that gun was pointed at his forehead. "You have no chance. Give it up."

He watched Keri's eyes flash all around her. Like a trapped rat in a cage, she was desperately looking for a way out. And not finding any.

"She's the one who did it," Keri said suddenly, pointing at

Andrea. "I knew about it, but she was the one who killed Joe."

Andrea kept her eyes trained on Mike. "Keri, shut up!"

"She's the one you want," Keri continued. "She's the killer. She did all the sick stuff, with the knives. She's a psycho, totally."

"Keri!" Andrea shouted. "Shut your goddamn mouth!"

She didn't. "I'll turn state's evidence. You're going to need a witness, right? Give me immunity and I'll give you a killer."

Andrea's face trembled with rage. "Keri, close your fucking *mouth*!"

"I'm offering to talk. Please. You have to protect me from her. She might hurt me!"

"Me hurt you? You ruined my *life*!" Spittle flew out of Andrea's mouth. "You stole my husband. You butchered him."

"See?" Keri said. "See how crazy she is? Give me immunity, and I'll tell you everything that—"

"You traitorous bitch!" In the blink of an eye, Andrea whipped her gun around and fired. The bullet struck Keri in the neck. She fell backward onto the carpet. A second later, Mike fired. He hit Andrea in the arm, knocking the gun out of her hand.

"Call for an ambulance!" Mike shouted. He rushed inside. Keri was already unconscious. He ran to Andrea. Her arm was gushing blood and her eyelids were fluttering, but she was still awake.

"I don't know what . . . happened to me," Andrea said. Her voice was too soft to even be considered a whisper. "All my life, I've never done anything wrong. I was a good girl. And then . . . then . . . all at once . . . I blew it."

"You're going to live," Mike reassured her. "I'm going to get you to the hospital."

Her eyelids slowly closed. "Please . . . don't bother."

"Your honor, this is an outrage!"

In all the years she had worked with him, Christina had

never seen Ben so angry. His face was red, he was breathing too fast, and every word came out as a shout.

"That was confidential information, your honor! The police department had no business reading my confidential communications!"

Judge Hart's lips were firm and set. She tapped her reading glasses against the bench as she spoke. "Major Morelli has already explained how he obtained the information, Mr. Kincaid. Do you dispute his story?"

"No, I don't dispute it. But it's no excuse. That information was absolutely privileged."

"Maybe it was, but he got it, just the same. And Keri Dalcanton was not his client. He had no duty to her. To the contrary, he had a duty to see that any information pertaining to a murder was turned over to the law-enforcement community. As far as I can see, he acted entirely properly."

"He had no business being in my office in the first place!"

Judge Hart turned her attention to Mike, who was standing next to Assistant D.A. Dexter, both of them pointedly not making eye contact with Ben. "How did you get into the office, Major?"

Mike cleared his throat. "I have a key. Ben—er, Mr. Kincaid gave it to me on a previous occasion."

"And why were you there?"

"I was looking for Mr. Kincaid. We'd made an appointment, and he didn't show up. I didn't mean to read the message intended for his associate, Ms. McCall, but before I even realized to whom it was addressed, I'd read more of it than I could ignore."

Judge Hart shrugged her shoulders. "He's committed no crime. I suppose if you want to sue him for invasion of privacy you could, although I don't think I'd recommend it."

"Your honor," Ben said, "I strongly urge you to invalidate this improper, unconstitutional search and to suppress all information obtained as a result."

"Wait just a minute, Mr. Kincaid." The judge looked at him

sternly. "I gave you what you wanted before, when the police were using photocopied search warrants. That was a violation of fourth amendment rights. But there's no constitutional violation here. And there is no way on God's green earth I'm going to exclude critical evidence in this case again. Your motion is denied."

"Your honor," Ben shouted, "you can't condone this egregious conduct when—"

"Mr. Kincaid, I've ruled. Now give it a rest or I'll hold you in contempt." She rapped her gavel and strode out of the courtroom.

"It doesn't matter anyway, Ben." This came from Mike, who slowly crossed the courtroom to Ben's table. "We just got a message from the hospital. Keri Dalcanton is dead. Died from the gunshot wound."

Ben's lips parted wordlessly.

"Andrea McNaughton is going to be okay. She'll stand trial for her crimes."

Ben glared at him coldly. "You had no business reading Christina's fax."

"I know that," Mike said flatly. "I told you—I didn't mean to. But after I did, there was no way I could pretend I hadn't. Not after I knew that those two had conspired together, and that they were preparing to leave town and might never be seen again."

Ben's expression did not change.

"Ben, I'm a cop, not a defense attorney. I can't let the bad guys get away. Not if I can help it." He looked at Ben earnestly a few more seconds, then frowned and left the courtroom.

* 52 *

As soon as he got the call on his cell phone, Ben blitzed through rush hour traffic to St. John's. Barely half a minute later, he was racing down corridors, up stairwells, across hallways, until he finally arrived, breathless, outside Room 522.

"How long?" he asked, barely catching his breath.

The whole office staff was crowded into the small hospital room—Christina, Loving, Jones. Jones was seated beside the bed, Paula's hand clasped in his.

And Paula's eyes were open.

"She came around about half an hour ago," Christina explained. Ben pressed forward, trying to maneuver his way closer. "She's still groggy. But she seems to understand what we're saying."

"Has she spoken?" he said in hushed tones.

"A little bit. Not very informative."

"Does she remember—?"

Christina shook her head. "She remembers being stabbed. But she never knew who it was. You know what she was so anxious to tell us that night? She'd found a memo in a file indicating that the Stroud police suspected Keri was involved in her parents' death. But they could never prove anything." She looked down at Paula. "She was way ahead of us."

Ben didn't comment.

Jones was speaking in hushed soothing tones, stroking Paula's hands. "I was so worried, Paula. I can't tell you how I felt. It was like—like—I can't even explain. It was horrible."

Paula's lips were chapped and dry, but she still managed a small smile. "Didn't . . . feel so hot on this end . . . either."

Jones squeezed both her hands between his. "I don't want to ever be separated from you again, Paula. Never."

Her tired eyelids fluttered. "Quite a . . . commitment . . . from a modern guy like you."

"I mean it. I really do. I—"

They were interrupted by the sound of the pneumatic door swooshing open. Ben saw a nurse with brown hair and brown eyes enter the room carrying a clipboard. Billie Barnett, R.N., according to her nametag.

"How's my patient?" she asked.

Jones wiped his eyes. "She's still awake. And still talking."

"Wonderful. Any trouble communicating?"

"No. She seems . . . just like she always did."

"Except duller," Paula added.

Barnett smiled. "You'll get your strength back in time. It's going to take a while, though, before you're really up to snuff." She pressed her hand against Paula's forehead, then quickly took her pulse. "How do you feel?"

"Tired." Her eyes wandered over to Jones. "But happy."

"After all you've been through," Nurse Barnett said, "that's pretty darn good."

"So what's the prognosis?" Ben asked.

"The prognosis is terrific," Barnett answered, slapping a pencil against her clipboard. "Mind you, her body has been through a terrible shock, and her brain has been struggling to deal with that. But she's on the mend. The doctors see no indications of any permanent damage, not to her body or mind. Another week or so and she can probably get out of here. And in two months, maybe three, she should be just like new. Except for the scars."

"Will they hurt?" Paula asked.

"Hurt? No, no. But you'll probably want to get rid of your string bikinis."

Jones grabbed the nurse by her arms. "Do you mean it? She's gonna be just like new?"

"Yes, of course. That's what I—"

Jones whirled around like a top. He crouched down and clasped Paula's hand in his. "Marry me."

Paula blinked. "What?"

"You heard. Marry me."

Christina's eyes went bug-wide. "No!"

"I didn't ask *you*, Christina." Jones leaned close to Paula, his face open and imploring. "Please, Paula. I know there's nothing special about me. But it would mean so much to me."

Christina bounced up and down. "I can't believe it!"

Jones looked at her harshly. "Then step outside." He turned back to Paula. "Since I met you, everything about my life has changed for the better. I know I don't have much to offer you. I know I'm difficult and complicated and—and—"

"Quirky," Christina suggested.

"Obnoxious," Loving offered.

"Reserved," Jones said, pointedly ignoring them. "I know I don't always express my feelings like I should."

Paula smiled faintly. "*As* I should, puddin'."

Jones persevered. "I know sometimes I don't tell you how important you are to me. I know I'm not your dream man. I'm just a crummy office manager in a crummy law firm—"

"Hey!" Ben said. "Watch that."

Jones's head twisted around. "Who invited you clowns to this proposal, anyway?"

Chastised, they all took a step back. But didn't leave.

"Anyway," Jones said, returning his attention to the matter at hand, "I know there's no reason on earth why you should want to be married to me. But you're the most special woman I've ever known." He pressed her hand against his cheek. "So would you please do me the very great honor of becoming my bride?"

Paula's head trembled. "You are so wrong," she said tremulously.

His face fell. "I am?"

She nodded. "There's something very special about you."

He inched forward. "Does that mean—?"

"Of course I'll marry you, you big galoot. C'mere." She wrapped her arms around his neck and hugged him as tightly as she could.

Ben nudged Christina. "Maybe we should leave these two—" He stopped short. "You're crying!"

Christina dabbed her eyes. "That's the sweetest thing I've seen in my whole life."

Ben led her outside to give the newly engaged some privacy. Loving and the nurse followed their lead. When Ben and Christina got to the waiting area, she was still dabbing her eyes.

"Don't you just love it," Christina said, composing herself, "when everything has a happy ending?"

"Yeah," Ben said, voice flat. "Very happy."

"You're still thinking about Keri, aren't you? Ben, I'm sorry about the way that turned out."

Ben shook his head. "I should've listened to you. Your instincts are always better than mine. You understand people. And you never liked Keri. That should've told me something. But instead of being smart, I just assumed you didn't like her because—well, I should've paid better attention, that's all." He turned slightly. "I won't make that mistake again."

"Keri was sociopathic, Ben. Deeply. The more I think about, I think she wanted people to know she was a killer. She may not have been conscious of it but, bottom line, I think that's why she wrote 'faithless' on McNaughton's chest, and used her own chains, and so on. She wanted the police to know she had killed him. And that there was absolutely nothing they could do about it."

"She was counting on me to save her. That was her one mistake. Because in the end, I was the one who betrayed her."

Christina led Ben to a sofa and sat beside him. "Ben, you've got to stop beating yourself up about what happened. I know you think Mike shouldn't've read that fax. But let's be honest here. Keri was a murderer. Several times over. It's hard to get too choked up about it."

"Those were confidential communications, Christina. If we allow the cops to invade that once, it could erode the whole privilege."

"I don't think that's likely. But at any rate, I don't want you to blame Mike. He's a true friend, and you shouldn't treat him otherwise. What happened was not his fault. You were careless, making it possible for Mike to get that information. If Keri'd lived, she could've sued us for malpractice."

"She was a multiple murderer, Christina. No jury would ever award her damages."

"Still, you should be more careful. You knew Mike had that key. You knew you were late for that football date. And it was only logical that when Mike couldn't find you at home, he'd try your office. He just lives a block away. You should have known that he would—"

All at once, Christina froze. Her hand flew to her mouth. "Oh, my God. Oh, my God."

Ben's forehead crinkled. "What's your problem?"

"You *did* know! You knew all along! That's why you sent that fax. You *wanted* him to find it!"

Ben looked away. "Don't be ridiculous."

"I'm right, aren't I? You did it on purpose."

"Christina, just leave it alone."

"You did. I know you did."

"Christina, if the bar committee thought I'd intentionally revealed a client confidence, I could be disbarred. Let it be."

"Okay." She tried, but it was impossible. "But I'm right, aren't I?"

"I don't know what you're talking about." His eyes drifted to the bay window. The sun was setting, giving the rolling hills of Tulsa a crimson patina. "Believe it or not, I've been thinking about Sergeant Matthews."

"That blowhard?"

"That blowhard was right. So tell Loving not to punch his lights out, okay? Wouldn't seem right, somehow, given the circumstances."

"True."

"You remember what he said? When he arrested me?"

"I remember a lot of nasty things he said. What did you have in mind?"

"What he said when he snapped the cuffs on me, back at the office." Ben continued looking toward the window, but his gaze seemed to turn inward. "Justice is never simple."

Acknowledgments

First, I want to thank my friend and editor Joe Blades. My life and work have been enriched by his editing genius and continuous support.

Also at Ballantine, I thank Gina Centrello, Kim Hovey, and Cindy Murray, as well as Tamu Aljuwani and the rest of the trade show and library folks—and Brenda Conway and everyone else in Ballantine's fabulous sales force.

My appreciation also goes out to my agents, Robert Gottlieb and Matt Bialer, for their guidance and their enthusiastic efforts on my behalf—and to all the booksellers who have been so generous to me: Scott Perry, Dee Hausam, Steve and Joanie Stephenson, Cynthia Jackson, Kristin Ferguson, Ann Thrasher, and many others at bookstores all across the country.

Special thanks should go to my criminal law expert, Arlene Joplin, for reviewing the manuscript, advising me on many issues, and making me aware of several real-life instances of "end-runs" around the Constitution's double jeopardy protection not unlike the one portrayed in this book. I also thank my friend Dave Johnson for keeping me up-to-date on the latest developments and techniques at the police department. And I must thank my wife, Kirsten, who also read the manuscript and advised me to take out all the boring parts.

Readers are invited to e-mail me at: wb@william bernhardt.com. You can also visit my Web site and learn more about me than you ever wanted to know: www.william bernardt.com.

Please turn the page for a sneak peek of the newest thriller by William Bernhardt:

FINAL ROUND

Coming in hardcover in April 2002 from the
Ballantine Publishing Group

Prologue
Tuesday Night

Death came so suddenly he didn't even have a chance to scream. All at once, the lights were out—as if someone had thrown a switch inside his brain. Blood and bits of flesh burst from the side of his head. He was dead before he hit the ground.

The man standing over him swung his golf club in the darkness, smiling with satisfaction. Dead in one stroke—not bad at all. Almost like a hole in one, in a perverse sort of way.

Why hadn't the man listened to him? he wondered. He swung the club angrily back and forth, chopping at the air. A boiling rage consumed him. Why, why, *why?* He hadn't wanted it to happen this way. But what choice had the man left him? None, that's what. None at all. He had tried to be reasonable. He had offered to be accommodating. But in the end, it had made no difference. In the end, he simply had no alternative.

Now there was the question of what to do with the corpse. It would have to be disposed of in some way or another. He peered down at the motionless body. Blood still poured out of the huge gash on the side of his head, seeping into the white sand, creating a sticky sanguine pool. Dark and . . . disturbing.

A thought occurred. Why do anything at all? He'd had no time to plan for body disposal, and anything he did now would create a risk that he would be seen. Why not just . . . leave it where it was? Sure, the body would be found in time, but that was inevitable in any case. The key was not whether it would be found—but when. And who would be around when it happened.

Yes, that was the solution. All he had to do was scrape the sand around until nothing was visible . . .

That worked perfectly. And how could anyone complain? They were called *hazards*, after all. His victim probably didn't realize that meant it could be hazardous . . . to his health.

The man smiled, laughing to himself at his little joke. And there was a certain pride in having once again taken care of himself, once again protected himself from those who would bring him down. Those who fought him. Those who tried to deprive him of what was rightly his. Who wouldn't take pride in that? He was a self-made man, after all. In every possible sense of the word . . .

Somewhere behind him, back on the fairway, he heard something. He froze. What was it? Was anyone out there? Was someone listening? Could someone see what he had done?

He whirled around, trying to look every direction at once. He didn't spot a soul. Perhaps it was a bird, perhaps just the rustling of the branches on that huge maple tree. Or nothing at all. But he couldn't be sure. There could have been a witness.

He hoped not, though. Because if someone had seen, if someone had the slightest hint of what he had done . . .

Then he'd have to do what was necessary. Again. And again and again, if it came to that. Whatever it took.

If you enjoyed
William Bernhardt's *Murder One*,
don't miss his other thrilling
novels of justice:

PRIMARY JUSTICE
BLIND JUSTICE
DEADLY JUSTICE
PERFECT JUSTICE
CRUEL JUSTICE
NAKED JUSTICE
EXTREME JUSTICE
DARK JUSTICE
SILENT JUSTICE

Published by Ballantine Books.
Available at bookstores everywhere.

**Ballantine Books
proudly presents**

NATURAL SUSPECT

**A collaborative suspense novel, devised by
William Bernhardt, and with contributions
from these bestselling authors:**

**Leslie Glass
Gini Hartzmark
John Katzenbach
John Lescroart
Bonnie MacDougal
Phillip Margolin
Brad Meltzer
Michael Palmer
Lisa Scottoline
Laurence Shames**
and
William Bernhardt

**Now available in hardcover
wherever books are sold.**